WHO THE FUCK IS ROCKY PHANTASMIC?!

DANIEL AEGAN

Copyright 2024 Daniel Aegan
Published by Freedom Lane Publishing
This book is not to be copied or distributed, electronically or otherwise, without the express permission of its author.

Cover model: Heather Jarvis. Photography by CortneyOH Photography

Cover by Daniel Aegan using copyright-free imagery & fonts. No part of this book has been aided or generated by the addition of artificial intelligence either in the writing of the text or in the design of the cover and internal graphics.

This is a work of fiction. All names, locales, businesses, and events are products of the author's imagination. Any resemblance to actual persons—living or dead—or events is purely coincidental.

****

Also by Daniel Aegan:

Blood Drive
Lost Women of the Admiral Inn
Kai the Swordsman: The Imprisoned King
Excalibur Nights
Double Zero: An Anthology
The New Council: Blood Drive 2
I'm in Sci-Fi Hell
The Unholy Mother of the Demonic Child
Reign of the Unfortunate
The Adventures of Trash Rat
The King of America: Blood Drive 3
Bad News
Infinite Zero: An Anthology
In Search of Channel Void
Humans Are Trash
My Good Friend Dr. Debaucherous

Read more at DanielAegan.com

For Bree.

DANIEL AEGAN

O, IT'S GOOD TO BE THE MANAGER

"I don't know, nor do I care what you think you know about me. If I did, we wouldn't be having this conversation right now, would we?"

In the not-so-distant past, one watching a man like Hugh Buster wouldn't have been able to decide whether he berated himself in a fit of public insanity or not. In the present, however, it has become all too common for people to have personal conversations like these during their normal human tasks. Hugh knew of this phenomenon, but he didn't care. Besides, he relished the times he could be by himself, despite talking through his Bluetooth earpiece.

Hugh's breath came from his mouth in little clouds in the frigid Maine morning. Winter's bite had come early this year. It always made him laugh. All those bozo scientists who used to cry over global warming needed to visit Maine in autumn. They'd be sure to change their tunes about it in a cold-ass heartbeat.

Dark gray clouds blotted out the vision of the sky above, but that wouldn't have mattered much anyway since the sun hadn't deemed it necessary to rise for Hugh's march across the parking lot as his boots crunched the chunks of salt strewn all over the place. The big red rectangle with white letters spelling out 'Pastime Plaza' loomed above all like a golden calf for retail savages. The store's slogan, 'America's Creation Destination', called those blessed or cursed with creative mindsets toward it like a beacon.

And the kingdom of arts and crafts awaited its master's arrival.

Well, a kingdom fit for a retail manager if not a master.

WHO THE FUCK IS ROCKY PHANTASMIC?!

Hugh's hair was neat and clean, and his clothing complemented his height. Hugh was *The Manager* and a picturesque one at that. Not a single hair stood out of place, and you'd never find loose threads sticking out of his clothes. You'd be hard-pressed to find anyone who embodied the title of *The Manager* quite like Hugh Buster.

"I told you already, Sheila," Hugh said into the Bluetooth device on his ear as he unlocked the front door. "I don't know if the CEO is guilty or if it's all fake news. Either way, he's stepped down, but I'm hearing it's a temporary change until the whole thing with the stolen artifacts is sorted. The store isn't going to be closed, so don't worry about me losing my job. I don't know why the liberal media is painting Mr. Jennings as an evil version of Indiana Jones. It's what they do now, I guess."

Hugh closed the door behind him, relocked it, and punched in the code to disable the alarm. "Look, honey, I gotta go. My receiving manager texted me about something urgent but refused to go into any detail. I don't know. A truck probably crashed into the bay again. These drivers are a bunch of drunks. I'll text you after my wife goes to bed tonight. Maybe we can get together in a couple of days. I'll tell her I have to work a closing shift again. Get some sleep. It's almost four in the morning for Christ's sake. Love you too."

Hugh ended the call with his sidepiece and sighed. She loved putting a bratty toe or two over the line just to see how he'd react. As annoying as the act proved to be, trashing her back for it had become somewhat of an amusing game. It usually ended in a fit of sweat-covered passion, and that suited them both.

I don't know, Hugh thought as he walked through the dark store. *Maybe I'm sending mixed messages.*

Hugh passed the Halloween decorations. The aisles were a mess. Some of the unpainted ceramic pumpkins were cracked, broken, and left on the shelf. Some straw-filled witches had been leaned against the shelves as well with their fake faces staring at him as he passed. They might've been scarier had they not been white with their features outlined in black, waiting for some old lady to buy them to have her grandkids paint them while she sipped cooking sherry and watched her offspring's offspring with a mixture of pride and boredom.

"I can't wait to chuck all this shit into the dumpster," Hugh said aloud to the displays of all their décor for sale. "Halloween is a holiday for heathens and hooligans."

DANIEL AEGAN

Even though Pastime Plaza branded itself as a Christian establishment, it still stocked products with imagery of ghosts and witches, despite the unholy intentions of those beings. Soon the whole place would be full of paint-your-own nativity scenes, First Christmas coloring books, and all sorts of goodies that uplifted good people's souls instead of condemning them to sin.

Hugh ignored the mess. The employees on first shift would have to make cleaning it up a priority since his closers did not. He'd have to have a chat with his closing supervisors about making straightening the holiday section a priority. Otherwise, they'll have to start staying after their shifts without pay to do it. Maybe the staff will threaten to unionize again. Oh, wouldn't that be a festive treat for everyone involved? He could get himself a brand new staff for Christmas!

Hugh passed the framed artwork on the shelves right outside the large double doors that led to receiving with a yellow and black 'EMPLOYEES ONLY BEYOND THIS POINT' sign that sometimes went ignored by some of the braver customers who wanted to see for themselves if certain items were stocked in the back. The photo closest to Hugh's eye level had 'Jesus cries for you' written under a painted crucifix. Someone had taken a black marker and wrote 'HE WATCHES YOU JERK OFF' under it on the glass.

"Damn kids," Hugh muttered as he grabbed the photo to take to the back. "You won't find this shit so funny when you're burning in Hell for it." He dropped the picture off by the Damages department counter and walked to the receiving dock.

A huge, wooden crate had been placed on the floor, taking up a lot of space in the receiving area. It looked to be twenty feet square and five feet tall. Whoever had sent it had nailed it shut and covered the wood in stickers in some language Hugh had never seen before. Nothing Pastime Plaza carried was so big it needed to be shipped in a box like this.

"Don!" Hugh called. "Where you at?"

"Right here," Don, the robust receiving manager, replied, lumbering out of his office as if Hugh had just woke him up. Don wasn't a quick-witted man, but he had turned out to be a perfect addition to the Pastime Plaza team. It's not like anyone could do the job, even if Hugh didn't find it too difficult. Their home office managed most of the deliveries and logistics, but Don had that certain something that caused blue-collared truck drivers to eat out of the palm of his hand. Hugh had never been the jealous type, but he couldn't talk to the everyman quite like Don the receiving manager.

"Is that what you called me for?" Hugh said, turning back toward the monstrosity of a wooden box. "What is it?"

Don walked next to Hugh and stared at the box with his meaty fists on his hips. "I don't rightfully know. We weren't due for any deliveries, and I wasn't here to let this one in."

Hugh turned toward Don. "You didn't? I thought that's not supposed to happen."

"It's not."

"Then who dropped this off, and who let them in?"

Don shrugged. "Someone with keys and the alarm codes. It would have had to have been a few guys at least to haul something this big and heavy unless they had some machinery to move it. Other than that, your guess is as good as mine. I figured maybe you could check the security cam footage and find out. Oh, it also had a note attached to it addressed to you."

"You should have said so from the start." Hugh sighed. "Can I read it? Maybe it'll shed a little light on what we're supposed to do with this thing."

Don went to his metal desk and brought back a manilla envelope with Hugh Buster's name written across the top in black letters. No address or any information had been printed on it.

"That's weird," Hugh said. "I expected it to be heavier with such a big envelope."

"I think it's a letter, or maybe it's instructions on what to do with this. It might be a new holiday display, though it would take up a lot of space on the sales floor."

"That would be nice." Hugh opened the envelope. "I always wanted to have a life-sized nativity display out front, but Home Office always said it would take up too much merchandise space."

Don's first guess proved to be correct. The envelope contained a letter handwritten on a single sheet of paper. Hugh held it in his hands, and his eyes widened as he did. He whistled as his eyes washed over the black letters, ending with the signature on the bottom. It might've ended up framed in his office if it hadn't been for the nature of what it said.

"Well?" Don asked. "What does it say?"

"It's from Jeffery Jennings, the CEO of Pastime Plaza," Hugh replied. "He's asking us to keep this box safe for him."

"Oh? Does it say what's inside?"

Hugh stared at the letter. "No, but he does say we shouldn't open it under any circumstances." He lowered his hands with the letter and looked at the box. "This is going to be a nightmare to keep back here. Why me?! This is a national chain, and he sends this huge box to my store to sit on it! And here I am, thinking hearing from Jeffery Jennings would've been an honor."

"What do you think's inside it?"

"Don, I have no idea."

"Have you seen the stuff in the news about Jennings? They say he's been buying and hoarding religious artifacts from halfway 'round the world. He's gotten in legal trouble for it."

"So what? The news says a lot of stuff."

"Do you think this is something Jennings wants hidden? The reason he sent this box all the way up here and snuck it inside in the middle of the night means it's important to him, right? He doesn't want it to be found by anyone else."

Hugh stared at the box. "No. It can't be that. That would be...that's crazy talk, Don."

Don shrugged. "I don't know, Hugh. If it is, can we get in trouble for having this? Possession is nine-tenths of the law or whatever."

"That's an old cliché. I don't think that holds up."

"Still, I don't want to hold this if I know it's illegal. I don't know what this is or who Jennings stole it from, but I don't want to be the idiot holding onto it when the feds show up lookin' for it. Know that I'm sayin', boss?"

A tension headache threatened to upend Hugh's entire morning. The store didn't open for another three hours either. It wasn't a good time to be battling against these little annoyances that would eventually contribute to a full-blown migraine.

"What do you want me to do?" Don asked, breaking the silence. "The way I see it, you'd be in more trouble than me, bein' in charge and all. Maybe we can bring it out to the woods, leave it there, and act like we don't know nothin' about it."

"We can't do that." Hugh placed his hand on the wood. Something big dwelled inside. If Don was right, then whatever Jeffery Jennings wanted hidden had some religious significance. What if it's connected to Jesus Christ himself? What if it legitimized Christianity for all the atheists and non-believers? The whole world could be saved by what's in that box, and Jeffery Jennings wanted to hoard it in the backroom of one of his stores because some idiotic law said he couldn't own it. What a man did with his fortune was up to him and God, and the long arm of the American justice system shouldn't have any say in it.

"Hand me a crowbar," Hugh said.

"What?" Don asked. "You're going to open it?!"

"If I'm going to hide this for him, I need to know what I'm hiding. I'm not going to stay ignorant about this in case you're right about what it might be. I'll open it, seal the box back up, and we can find a place to leave it till Jennings comes asking for it."

"I don't think that's a good idea."

"I don't care whether or not you think it is. If you want to plead ignorance later, don't look when I open it. I have to know what's inside, though. Please hand me a crowbar, Don."

Don hesitated for a moment, but he relented with a sigh. He grabbed his crowbar from its spot hanging on the wall near his tools and handed it to Hugh.

"I hope you know what you're doing."

Hugh took the crowbar and went to work as Don backed away. He found a space to hook the crowbar's claw onto the wood and pulled.

"That's not how you use it," Don said. "You need to use the chisel edge on the other end to pry the wood apart. The claw is for pulling up nails."

Hugh swore under his breath as he turned the crowbar around and jammed the end between the pieces of wood. He put his weight on it, prying the top open with the sound of nails squealing as they were forced out of the wood. With the same action performed on each of the top's four sides, it loosened enough to be pushed off with a little effort and clattered to the ground. Hugh leaned over the box and peered inside.

"Oh my."

Don inched forward. "What is it?"

"It's…it's…so…"

Smoke and red light burst from the box and flooded the storeroom, covering the whole area in a black and crimson aura. Through all the chaotic energy, the screaming of the two men caught in the storm could be heard alongside inhuman laughter.

DANIEL AEGAN

THE WRITER
&
THE SUPERHERO

"Imagine gut-wrenching explosions, bloody terror, superheroes, horror, firefights, action, dark comedy, cannibalism, drama, and an all-you-can-eat helping of raw, unadulterated sex. What do you think about that?"

Dave sat back in his chair, watching the look on his best friend's face. Albert had always been his sounding board for all his writing projects, and this newest one would surely blow him away.

"That's it?" Al asked in return. "That's your elevator pitch for this thing?"

Dave sighed. "That's not exactly an elevator pitch. Are you saying you find none of what's in this project appealing?"

They were having lunch in a quiet restaurant in New Haven called Canner's, and the two had used this place as their meeting spot for the last ten years, stopping by before or after many of their misadventures. Dim lighting illuminated the restaurant, and the sound of soft music completed the ambiance of the dining experience. If they'd come at night instead of the middle of the afternoon, the music and ambiance would have been dialed up a bit more for the sake of evening eating and dating.

"It's not that it's unappealing," Albert, the taller of the pair, replied. "All you did was list a bunch of genres and buzzwords. Sure, I like explosions and raw sex as much as the next guy, but what makes that different from everything else they're putting in movies and TV shows? And superheroes? Haven't they been done to death and beyond at this point? You're going to need a better hook if all you've got is a list of bullshit like that. If you're trying to make the leap from books to movies, then you're going to have to up your game a hundredfold."

Albert's criticism had always been harsh, but he was rarely wrong. Dave had always gone to him with his ideas for a reason. Sometimes his projects needed a hard kick in the ass to make a mediocre idea into a worthwhile project.

Dave had always admired Albert. He had that classic good-looking aesthetic, and he came off as charming. Sometimes that could be a little infuriating, but it worked for him. Dave didn't put in as much time at the gym, but working full time along with balancing family life and his writing made him have to choose how to best bide his time. He could choose walking around the block rather than finishing a pesky chapter or two, but the latter seemed like a better option after working a full eight-hour day.

"What are you thinking now?" Albert asked. "I can almost see the gears in your head churning through the gray matter."

"I don't know," Dave replied. "I feel like if I can get this deal going it will give me so much more room to breathe. Forget the money that comes with landing a gig like this. I can write it, let it go through the production channels, and sit back while it works itself out. Self-publishing my stuff is great, don't get me wrong, but it's a lot of fucking work. Most of the time it feels like I'm busting my ass at a glorified hobby."

"There's nothing wrong with that if you enjoy it as much as you claim to."

"I know. I mean, I do love it. I never did it with the express goal of finding a needle in a haystack and winning the writer lottery, but I'm not going to ignore an opportunity like this when it presents itself out of nowhere. Besides, Heather would kill me if I let this pass me by."

Albert laughed. "How is she doing? It's been a while since I've seen her."

"She's good. Her mother is watching Kayla this weekend, so she's spending some time away with her boyfriend so I can work on this project."

"Oh yeah? She's got sexy guys taking her on vacation now?"

"They're not far, and I'd barely call it a vacation. They booked a hotel by the beach in Milford, and they're probably going to spend most of the weekend there anyway. I'm not complaining. I need the time to work, and maybe I'll hit an app and find a date for myself if I can make some forward momentum by Saturday night."

"I still don't get how you and Heather do the whole open-slash-platonic marriage thing. She's allowed to have boyfriends and go on sex dates by the beach. I would never let my wife do that shit."

"Why not? Everyone cheats in one form or another, and it's not like I don't get mine. She's the one who married a queer guy. This is the best way for our marriage to work."

"I know, I know. I'm not in the same situation, so I'm not going to judge your open marriage or your queerness or anything. I'm also not having this same old debate with you, and Deborah isn't cheating on me in any form as far as I know. I'd hope she'd tell me. Maybe you should add some polyamory to your write-up or whatever you're calling your pitch."

"It's crossed my mind once or twice." Dave chuckled and took a sip of his iced tea.

"Do you two ever get some crossover action going and share boyfriends?" Albert asked with a smirk. "Must be nice if you're both dating men."

Dave laughed and shook his head. "You're thinking of swinging, and we don't swing. We do our own thing. It works for us." He added a short shrug for effect.

"Putting all that aside," Albert said, "expand on what you're doing with this brave new writing project of yours. All I know so far is that it's an action comedy mashed with horror full of superheroes and explosions. It sounds like a hot mess, but I'm sure there's a common thread somewhere."

"Oh, and I've thrown in some mob stuff, too! But I'm still kind of debating how involved I want it to be in the plot. It's sort of an homage to the late-night garbage horror movies they used to play on TV till they went off the air at three in the morning. They owned their craziness rather than pretending to be something they weren't, and that's what I want to embrace."

"You're not helping the '*this project is a hot mess*' argument. You can't jam everything you want into a single story."

"It's possible. This wouldn't work as a standalone movie, but it would work as a ten-episode series, especially with the prospect of multiple seasons if it does well enough. The trick is to know when to focus on which story arc and how to transition back and forth between all the elements at play."

"Will you have any drawn-out conversations in the mix like Quentin Tarantino?"

Dave laughed. "I hope to avoid anything like that. I don't need to pace it with forty-five minutes of people talking leading to three minutes of action. I don't know how he gets away with it."

"Good writing." Albert offered a wide smile.

"That's debatable, isn't it?"

Albert shrugged.

Dave laughed as something caught his eye. A huge fly flew past his face, making him flinch. When he opened his eyes again, he saw that the left side of Albert's head was covered in them. They bit into his flesh, drawing trickles of blood that came down his face in small rivers. Albert said something Dave couldn't understand, but he didn't scream or flail about the restaurant for help. It looked as if he didn't even notice the insects swarming and biting him.

"Albert," Dave said, feeling his breath hitching in his lungs. "Are you…are you alright?" He wished he hadn't said something so asinine, but Albert either didn't notice or didn't mind being eaten one tiny bite at a time.

Flies swarmed around the restaurant, covering the patrons and waitstaff in clouds of black. Dave couldn't hear anything other than buzzing. He watched a woman at the table next to them speaking to her friend. As she spoke, maggots fell from her mouth onto the salad in front of her. Dave moved to grab the waitress, but when she turned he saw the flies had eaten half her face, chewing a hole through her cheek, exposing the inside of her mouth. The crawling masses of black crawled between her exposed teeth as blood stained her chin.

Dave turned back to face Albert, ready to suggest they make a run for it, but in the short time he'd observed the others, the flies had bore a hole through Albert's eye socket, and maggots wriggled from the empty hole, waving as if to catch Dave's attention.

"What the hell is this?" Dave asked, barely able to hear himself over the buzzing of the insects. He looked at his arms and hands as his stomach tumbled over itself. He wanted to vomit, but a disgusting thought came into his mind, and he couldn't stop picturing the insects seizing on the opportunity to dine on his vomit before deciding to shoot down his throat in a torrent of black buzzing to consume him from the inside out. They'd turn him into a puddle of ooze, enjoying a fly orgy on his corpse so that their maggots could be born from him.

"Tell me about your not-so-silent partner," Albert said.

Dave blinked, and his private horror show had ended. The flies were gone, and the half of Albert's face and head they'd eaten had returned. The waitress passed, and Dave noticed he could no longer see through the festering hole in her cheek. His head felt dizzy form the sudden change in reality, and he grasped the table, taking in a deep breath. He closed his eyes, keeping them shut tight.

"Dave," Albert said with his voice full of concern. "Are you OK? What's wrong?"

"Nothing," Dave replied, opening his eyes again. "You ever smoke some strong bud that hits you the next day out of nowhere?"

Albert chuckled. "Weed flashback? That hasn't happened to me since high school. What the hell have you been smoking?"

"Just the regular stuff, but a bit more lately since I haven't been sleeping." Dave left out the part that he'd needed to start smoking a little more at night to help ease him into sleep because of some vivid nightmares that made no sense when he didn't. He'd see the type of stuff like he'd just seen with his waking eyes, but he figured it came with the territory of writing intense horror scenes.

"Can I get you anything else?" the waitress asked, causing Dave to jump. He didn't even hear her sidling up to the table since he couldn't get his mind off what he'd seen.

Dave nodded. "Coffee, please. Thank you."

"Right away."

"Are you sure you're OK?" Albert asked. "You're looking a little pale, bud."

"I'm fine. Like I said, I haven't been sleeping. This project gets stressful sometimes. What were you asking me before I zoned out on you?"

"I wanted to hear more about this partner of yours you've been bragging about. You've dropped enough hints about this celebrity backer for your project, and I figured you could finally stop being such a tease and tell me who you're seeing already."

Dave forced a laugh, and he found it helped his mind return to reality. "I'm not *seeing* anyone. It started as a thread on Buzzer, and we started talking. Before you suggest it again, it was nothing sexual. He's

WHO THE FUCK IS ROCKY PHANTASMIC?!

looking for something of a comeback project, and I want to write something similar to what he's looking for."

The waitress dropped Dave's coffee at the table, and he thanked her with a nod. He took a sip, ignoring the burn on his tongue. He needed to wake up and keep sharp. The last thing he wanted was to fall prey to his grogginess and have another waking nightmare in the middle of his conversation.

"Oh?" Albert asked, smirking. "And he wants to run away from horrific explosions while snapping witty dialogue?"

"Isn't that what everyone wants?"

Albert popped a fry into his mouth. "So, who is it? Tom Cruise? John Travolta? Antonio Banderas?"

Dave sighed. "Do you remember Cliff Quentin, the comedian?"

"No. Wait… Not the guy who got canceled for that racist joke about his black girlfriend?"

"The joke was more offensive to coal miners if you ask me," Dave muttered, taking another sip from his coffee mug. Talking about all this quelled his busy mind, and he felt grateful for it.

"Still! Don't tell me you're getting into bed with him. Your project is going to wind up doomed before it even gets off the ground. No, Dave. Come on. The guy's been canceled for fuck's sake!"

"No he isn't. No one is ever *canceled*, though there are people I wish were. His standup specials are still all over WebFlix, and he's been podcasting like crazy since the whole incident."

Albert scoffed. "Everyone podcasts, Dave. My teenage nephew has a weekly podcast where all he does is take deep dives into new swear words he learns on the school bus. He has like a thousand listeners."

"Wow. Send me a link to that when you get the chance."

"You'd be better off getting Cody to do a show with you. His podcast might be immature compared to what's out there, but he's not going through what Cliff Quentin is."

"And what's that? Cliff made his big apology for the joke, and he's been out of the public's eye since then. People can't hold a grudge forever if he's improving himself, right? Besides, it's not as if cancel culture is a tangible thing. As long as we're all moving forward, there's no reason he can't come back into the public spotlight at some point."

"Not as if anyone who's not canceled is trying to be in your project either," Albert added with a playful smirk.

"The joke in question was something between Cliff and his girlfriend. Was it offensive? Yes. Should he have said it on stage? No. Either way, people should see it as water under the bridge at this point."

Albert sat back and crossed his arms. "You didn't find it offensive?"

Dave shrugged. "Doesn't matter what I think. I'm a white guy, so I'm not the target of a joke about black women. I'm not saying it wasn't wrong, only that I wasn't the one offended by it."

"You're only making excuses because you're going to work with him on this project, which I get. You're going to have to be ready for people to come after you for working with him is all I'm trying to tell you."

"By the time this is all said and done, that joke will be long gone. Cliff is going back on tour starting tonight. He's going to be at the Deuce's Wild Club right here in New Haven, and he and I are going to go over the details of our show before he pitches it."

"So much for rewarding yourself with some anonymous gay sex for getting your writing done today. Sounds like you have other plans tonight."

"Shit. I forgot about that. And we just call it 'sex' by the way. We don't need to say it's *gay sex*. The two guys being there without women is what makes it gay, so you're being redundant. I might have time between writing and meeting up with Cliff to hook up, though."

The waitress came by and stood by the table. "Can I get you gentleman anything else, or are you all set?"

"Just the check," Albert replied. "Thank you."

"No problem." The waitress dropped the check on the table. "You can take care of that whenever you're ready." She walked off to check on her other tables.

"Alright," Albert said, picking up the check and glancing at it. "This one's on me, but I expect you to get the next one after your show or whatever is a hit." He put his credit card inside and pushed it near the edge of the table.

Dave laughed. "If this hits, I'll buy you dinner every night for a whole year."

"Sounds like a plan. If I can get free later, maybe I'll go to this comedy gig and show some support for your new business partner."

"I'll be there either way. Don't mention the project, though. It's still hush-hush until we can get a script he can pass along to his production connections."

WHO THE FUCK IS ROCKY PHANTASMIC?!

"Assuming he has any."

Dave sighed as the waitress grabbed the check and trotted off to process it. "That's crossed my mind. He says he's still got people in the production end of WebFlix, and they'd love to work with him again." He scratched his nose as he contemplated what he'd just said. "I hope he's not wasting my time. Hell, if he is, at least I'll have the story. I can always flip it into a book and self-publish it."

"There you go. For what it's worth, I hope he's not bullshitting you. Sounds like a major story you've got there. Can't wait to see what you do with all those blood-soaked explosions and raw sex."

"And superheroes. Don't forget them."

Albert shook his head. "Fucking superheroes. Can't you do this thing without them? Doesn't seem like they'd mesh well with the rest of what you're trying to put together."

Dave laughed again. "I don't see how I can at this point. The story may only be in my head, but it's already taken on a life of its own. Once that happens, there's no containing it."

"Alright, Stephen King. You do you, and I'll be sure to watch it the moment it hits wherever it's ultimately going."

"Thanks. That's all I ask."

The waitress returned with the leatherbound booklet containing the check and thanked them. Albert scribbled his signature, added some cash for a tip, and told Dave, "Get some sleep at some point. I know this is all exciting for you, but you're no good to anyone dozing off in the middle of conversations."

Dave huffed. "Now you sound like Heather."

"She's not wrong."

"I'm good, really." Dave stood and pushed his chair under the table. "Tonight will be a late night, but after I meet with Cliff I can get some rest. I mean, I will get some rest. Promise."

As Dave turned to leave, a fat fly buzzed past his ear. He followed it with his eyes as it hovered over the table for a moment before landing on the edge of Dave's coffee cup. As it sporadically buzzed, a trickle of blood ran down the mug from where it sat.

"That's so gross," Albert remarked, spotting it as he pulled on his coat. "I hope that thing didn't come out of the kitchen."

***

DANIEL AEGAN

"One more page. Come on, Dave!"

Dave sat in his home office, and he couldn't remember the last time it had been so quiet. Kayla, his daughter, was off playing with her cousins, and she had even brought the dog with her. Heather had her own playdate with her boyfriend to enjoy some quality time. It was the perfect time for Dave to get some writing done.

As it turned out, writing scripts was a whole new beast Dave hadn't planned on wrestling. He had given up after a page and had written what he wanted as a short story instead, planning on turning it into a script as the next stage in this new drafting process.

I need this to be simple enough for Cliff to follow, Dave told himself. *He's not dumb, but he doesn't seem like the type who reads much of anything without a sexy woman showing some skin on the cover.*

Dave took off his glasses and rubbed his weary eyes. He had been at his desk since leaving lunch with Albert to get something solid written he could use when he met Cliff in person. It hadn't all been in vain. He had mapped out some of the twisting story arcs and polished the characters' personalities. All in all, he had the puzzle of the plot almost put together. He only hoped it all stayed together once Cliff added his input and comedic twist into the mix.

Too much time had passed for a quick date or a hookup. Cliff's show started at nine, and dinner time had come and gone as well. To make matters direr, Dave hadn't even paused to eat anything since his lunch at Canner's hours ago. With a snap of his laptop closing for the night, he decided that a quick meal would have to suffice before heading back into New Haven to catch Cliff's routine and go over the plans for their show.

I should've napped or something, Dave thought as he splashed cold water on his face to get ready to head out. Before he started writing, he put a lot of thought into the flies at Canner's and what he'd seen, but he'd come to find it all silly. The last thing he wanted at that point was for Heather to find out he'd fallen asleep in the middle of a conversation in a restaurant. The nightmare wouldn't worry her much, but the sudden bout of narcolepsy would for sure. She'd already been on him for his bad sleeping habits since he started working on his secret project with Cliff on top of working full-time and keeping up with Kayla. He'd not only been burning the candle at both ends, but he'd created a whole third end and began burning that too.

I'm going to be up until at least one or two in the morning tonight, Dave reminded himself as he left the house, locking the door behind him.

WHO THE FUCK IS ROCKY PHANTASMIC?!

Nothing worth doing is ever easy, right? Heather will see that when I'm all done. Everyone will.

The chill in the night bore through Dave's jacket, but this kind of weather was common in New England in mid-November. The sky looked like it wanted to dump a cold rain, but it held off. Maybe it needed the right moment to make the night drearier. He could've picked a weekend off back in August when the weather was more pleasant. His thoughts drifted to his darling wife Heather, who was no doubt enjoying a view of an empty beach from a hotel bed she shared with her lover. At least she had some companionship.

"Don't get jealous now," Dave chided himself as he pulled out of his driveway. "You could've planned something, too, but you chose to work on this deal instead. Keep your eyes on the prize."

Dave laughed at his cliché and pulled into a burger place to get something to eat. He had attempted many times over the years to give up eating like this, but he couldn't pass up the prospect of a quick and greasy dinner before heading to a comedy club. He didn't want to be sitting at the bar and nursing a drink while trying to figure out which bar food would give him the worst shits in the morning. At least he knew what came along with a fast-food burger. A place called Deuce's Wild might end up doing a number on Dave's lower intestines.

A fast food meal in the driver's seat suited Dave anyway. He'd done it plenty of times at work, and it never bothered him. He ate while parked next to a dog park, keeping his eye on anyone coming near his car. It wasn't too late, but it was still dark enough for someone to sneak up on him. People sometimes get mugged or worse in New Haven, but this area felt safer. Homeless people liked to come by and ask for money, but that's the worst that's ever happened to Dave in this area. One time someone tried to talk him into buying them a pair of boots.

But this particular Saturday night in New Haven was quiet. There didn't seem to be too many people milling around the streets. It might've been too cold for it. Even the hipsters weren't walking from one coffee shop to another. Then again, Dave had ventured off the beaten trail to eat his quick dinner without being watched or judged for the sin against his own body.

Dave grabbed his phone, found the last text he'd gotten from Albert, and clicked the link, eating while the podcast started.

"Hi, this is Cody, and you're listening to Cody from the Bus."

"Good name," Dave muttered through a mouthful of burger.

"I've got a new word to talk about today," Cody continued from his prerecorded podcast studio, which was likely a laptop sitting on his bed. At least he had a decent microphone. "I heard this one yesterday, and it's been stuck in my head ever since. This kid Julian kept saying it, and I didn't even think it was a real word at first. Well, without further ado, today's swear word is…"

Dave's eyes grew wide as he choked. He took a sip from his soda as he killed the podcast, glad no one else had been with him to hear the vileness that had come from Cody's innocent mouth. Dave expected to hear something obscene, but he had no idea kids knew words like that. He didn't even know people still used that particular curse word, and he wouldn't even have put it in any of his books, not even the raunchiest of them.

"Holy shit, kid," Dave said, shaking his head. "You're going to wind up getting yourself canceled for sure."

Someone rapped their knuckles on the window, startling Dave. Had some passerby heard what Cody had said? Were they there to kick Dave's ass because of what they'd overheard?

"Step out of the car," a commanding voice said.

Dave swore under his breath, using a word Cody might've covered on an earlier episode before he'd brought out the big guns. He didn't realize he parked somewhere illegal, and he hadn't even noticed any red and blue flashing lights behind him. He looked in his rearview mirror to confirm, but he saw a Cadillac, not a police cruiser.

Oh fuck, he thought. After everything, he'd get robbed or carjacked after all. Or maybe not.

"Is everything OK?" Dave asked, opening the window a crack.

"Are you David Bryant?" the man standing outside asked. Well, the fact that they knew his name ruled out a random mugging or a carjacking, but hearing his name made things so much scarier.

Two other men made themselves apparent. One stood near the passenger door in case Dave decided to escape that way, and another loomed behind his car. A fourth watcher sat in the driver's seat of their Cadillac, ready to chase after him if he sped away.

"What is this?" Dave asked, frantically thinking of who he could've pissed off. He didn't deal with loan sharks or anything like it, and anything controversial he had written had been under a pseudonym. His job as a desk jockey wouldn't lead him down any road where men would be knocking on his car window in the middle of the night. If it wasn't Dave's fault these guys were looking for him, who could it...

Cliff Quentin.

Shit, Dave thought. *What if he owed these guys money or something, and he told him about their show venture? They may be looking for their piece of the payday before it even comes for anyone.*

"Are you going to come out?" the man standing next to his window asked, knocking again. "If I have to ask again, I'm going to get upset. When I get upset, sometimes I break windows and pull motherfuckers out of their cars by their hair. But I don't want to do that. Boss doesn't want you hurt."

"Who's your boss?"

"Come out, and we'll talk, David. That's all. Leave your phone on the dashboard with the screen up. Don't make this get ugly."

It's pretty ugly already from my point of view.

Dave took his phone from the cupholder and placed it on the dashboard as requested. He took a breath. He had no idea what would happen to him when he stepped out of the car. It could be an elaborate prank or imminent murder. In Dave's dark mind, he couldn't find an in-between.

"Alright," Dave relented. "I'm coming out."

At least this is happening here, Dave thought as he opened the car door and stepped out into the cold night air. *If Kayla or Heather had to see this, it would be a whole lot worse.*

Dave's mind's eye showed him his young daughter standing next to a closed coffin. Whatever these men were about to do to him was so bad, it would end the prospects of an open-casket wake.

Stop it. For all you know, these thugs are from the IRS and are looking for some back taxes or something.

"What's up?" Dave asked. It was all he could get out. Forcing casual greetings might end up being what saves his life.

"Are you David Bryant?" the man asked. He was tall with stylish stubble on his face. His dark hair was greased back as well, and he wore one of those puffy jackets and jeans. He didn't look ready to dole out an ass-kicking, but his stern face said he wouldn't be against it if it came down to it.

"Yeah..." Dave replied, taking a step back. "What's going on? Did I do something I'm not aware of doing?"

"I'm a friend of the family, only not yours. Get in the back of our car. We're going for a little ride."

"Why? Where are you taking me?"

"We're going to ask you some questions is all. Get in the car, and we'll take you to see the boss. He'll answer whatever you have to ask if he feels like it. I'm just here to pick you up and make sure you take the ride, so stop asking so many friggin' questions and get in the car before I drag you in there by your friggin' hair."

"Don't look like he's cooperatin'," another, bigger guy said, approaching from the other side. "Grab his arm. I'm not standin' in the cold all night while this asshole pisses himself."

Maybe I'll get a decent story out of this if I can manage to live long enough to tell it. Dave's inner voice remained calm, even though his body had other plans on how to deal with his predicament.

"Get away from me!" Dave exclaimed, walking backward as his cowardice took over his body. "I'm not the one you want!"

"Grab him already, Johnny!"

Hands grasped his arms, and Dave felt like he was back in the schoolyard in the fourth grade being dragged under the jungle gym to get a pink belly or have some bully try to spit in his mouth for fun. One set of hands grabbed his arm and pulled so hard he felt like his shoulder would pop out of its socket at any moment. Another arm wrapped around his neck and pulled him upward.

"This little shit is squirmy!" the thug named Johnny snapped. "How about we knock his lights out and put him in the trunk?"

That prospect did nothing to calm Dave's panic, and his thrashing against his assailants doubled.

"Vincenzo wants him alive and conscious," the other thug replied. "He'll calm down in the car."

"Shit. He better not bite me, Leo! If he does, I'm bitin' you!"

"Get him in the damn car!" the third shouted, standing near the Cadillac. "Keep shoutin' and some mook's gonna come by and take a fuckin' video of us workin' over here."

Dave caught a break when the bigger of the pair, Johnny, slipped on some wet leaves in the street, allowing him to get out of the choke hold and run a couple of steps. It worked until someone slammed the back of his leg with a club.

"We're gonna have to break his legs or something," the man with the club said. He had gotten out of the driver's seat and had joined the party happening on the street. "You said we need him alive and conscious, but you didn't say squat about him keepin' his ability to walk."

"No!" Dave pleaded, sitting on the street, holding a hand in front of him. He knew he'd beat himself up later for acting like a coward, but his heart started pumping way too much blood to his brain and the rest of him to do anything but beg and try to get away. It was one of those fight or flight situations, and Dave had chosen flight without consulting with whatever part of him would opt to fight instead.

Of all the characters I've ever written, none of them acted like this when faced with a challenge.

"It's too late to do this the easy way," the man with the club said as he approached. "You were given that option, and you spit it back in our faces. We tried to be as polite as possible about this. Now we're gonna make sure you don't run away when we tell you to get into the fuckin' car. I won't break your legs, but I am going to have to bruise your knees a bit to keep you in one place. Capeesh?"

Dave tried to scoot away, but a set of legs blocked him while a pair of arms dragged him to his feet and put him back in a chokehold.

"Do it! Bash his knees real quick so we can get the fuck outta here." A set of rough lips came so close to Dave's ear he could feel them. "If you scream when he hits you, I'm going to shove a pile of leaves in your mouth like you're a friggin' scarecrow, ya dig?"

"Leave him alone!"

The four men looked around to find the source of the voice. Dave tried as well, but it wasn't easy with his windpipe pressed against a hairy forearm. A figure walked toward them in the center of the street. Their features were obscured by shadows, but he could see their strides were full of confidence.

"Mind your own damn business!" the man with the club snapped, turning around. "Let's not involve the good people at Yale Hospital tonight. They have enough to deal with without having to put your face back together!"

The figure stepped into the light, and Dave's eyes widened at what he saw. A man who stood a hair over five feet tall and only a few years out of manhood stepped toward him and his assailants. He wore a green hoodie with the initials RP sewn to the front with a yellow cape trailing behind him. A pair of torn, black denim pants completed the ensemble.

Even in the dark, Dave could see the unmistakable tinge of budding facial hair on his tan face.

"Let him go," the figure said. "I don't want to hurt you."

Dave fell to the ground. Pain shot up his legs from his knees when he hit the pavement. It felt like these guys weren't going to need to use the club on him after all.

"You're going to stop us?" Johnny asked, laughing. He took a gun from the back of his pants. "Who the fuck are you to do anything, kid?"

The figure lifted his chin and placed his hands on his hips. "I'm Rocky Phantasmic, and you're going to live to regret learning my name."

Silence followed as Rocky Phantasmic's proclamation settled into everyone's heads. After almost a full minute, uproarious laughter erupted from the four men. If the coming of promised violence wouldn't attract anyone, Dave thought the sounds of someone tickling a pack of hyenas might do the trick.

"What a name!" one of the men exclaimed. "Did you realize your last name is a friggin' adjective?! Get the fuck outta here before you get yourself hurt, kid! This don't concern you!"

"Wait a second!" one of the others said. "I know you. You're Richie Pimento, that stinkin' rat's kid."

The two men closest to the interloping hero laughed, but the one named Leo shrank back to the other who had been throttling Dave with his forearm.

"That can't be Richie Pimento, Johnny," he whispered.

"It's him," Johnny whispered in return. "I'm sure it's that little rat bastard."

"No. We killed Richie Pimento."

"We didn't go a good enough job if he's standin' right in front of us, actin' like he's got balls of kryptonite."

Leo scoffed. "Ain't like we've never seen a dead man walkin' before. Let's kill him twice and make sure he stays dead this time." He aimed his gun at his green-clad target. "Hey, Richie!"

Dave flinched as the gunshot rang out in the night and the flash from the gun illuminated them all for a fraction of a second. The bullet hit Rocky square in the chest, but he stood there with a hole in his green hoodie, staring at his would-be assassin. The ringing in Dave's ear subsided enough to hear the bulletproof young man address the gunman in a firm voice.

WHO THE FUCK IS ROCKY PHANTASMIC?!

"I already told you my name is Rocky Phantasmic. If you're an evildoer, I will take you down."

"Kid's got some heavy-duty body armor," Leo said, stashing the gun back in the waistband of his pants. "It ain't gonna do him no good if we bash his head against the street a bit. What say, you guys? Care to help this mook clean out his skull before we take him for a ride to the harbor?"

The other three chuckled. The man with the club went first, smashing it against Rocky's face. The cracking sound made Dave think his rescuer's jaw had broken, but the attacker pulled back a broken club, staring at it with widening eyes.

"The fuck?" the man said, looking from the broken club in his hands back to the kid. "What the hell are you?"

Rocky leaned a little closer. "I'm a superhero."

The man flew into the air a millisecond later, coming to rest on top of his Cadillac. The windshield smashed outward, and he let out a groan. The other man attacked, and Rocky landed a punch, hitting him in the chest. He sailed backward, over Leo and Johnny's heads, landing in the street with a thud and a scream.

"What the hell, kid?!" Leo exclaimed. "Are you on friggin' meth or something?!"

"You're going to leave now." Rocky stepped toward them. "This man is under my protection, and you won't be taking him or hurting him anymore."

"Come on, you little shit! My orders come from Vincenzo Scaletta himself. I know you weren't close to the family business, but you know I can't return empty-handed. Let me do my job. I promise I won't hurt the guy. Cross my heart and all that jazz."

Johnny put his meaty hand on Dave's shoulder, squeezing hard enough to prevent him from attempting another escape. "Yeah, we'll take good care of him. We promise."

"I think you guys should listen to him," Dave said. "I don't know this dude from Adam, but it looks to me like Rocky's got your number."

The back of a hand connected with the side of Dave's head. He couldn't argue that it hadn't been earned, but that thought didn't do him much good as the world spun the wrong way on its axis. His skull thumped on the hard street as he fell from the blow.

Once the world came back into focus, Dave propped himself up enough to see Rocky lash out at Leo and Johnny. The backhand must have set him off. The fight didn't last long, thankfully, and it ended with Rocky standing above the two men as they sat in the street, groaning.

"You can tell Vincenzo Scaletta anything you want about what happened here tonight," Rocky said, stepping past them as the world faded as if his vision slowly lost power. "I already told you this man is under my protection, and he'll stay that way."

Dave let out a short huff of a laugh before unconsciousness took him and thought, *Cliff isn't going to believe this is why I missed our meeting.*

2.

THE CANCELED COMEDIAN

"This is not a fucking comeback show," Cliff said, staring at his hard face in the mirror. "It's not an apology tour, either. Make sure those motherfuckers in the audience know that before they insist you've turned into a woke-ass pussy."

Cliff obsessed over his hair and face as his big New Haven show became imminent. He couldn't remember the last time he had gotten in front of a stage and performed a solid set of standup comedy. Living a life of writing for sitcoms and podcasting was good and all, but sometimes you need to get back to your roots.

"That's right. It's time to get back to my roots and show everyone that I'm not going anywhere. You can't cancel me!"

The backroom of Deuce's Wild was a place he remembered well, though he'd never been in this particular club before in his life. The backrooms of all the comedy clubs more or less looked the same. He had a loveseat on which he assumed worse comedians than him had gotten head while waiting to go on stage, and the table in front of it probably had tens of thousands of lines of cocaine snorted off it.

It had all come down to this night. Deuce's Wild was far removed from the big time. Hell, Cliff didn't even know why it had an apostrophe in its name. Did some cheap New Haven mobster named 'Deuce' own it at some point in the club's history? Did New Haven even have a seedy mafia underbelly?

None of that mattered in the end. All Cliff could do at that point was pray to the comedy gods that he'd get noticed by someone who'd give enough of a shit to grant him a shot at something bigger. Maybe he would get back to writing or punching up sitcom scripts. He'd lived that life before, and he fantasized about getting in front of the camera for more than a cameo of a pizza delivery guy. If he hadn't stumbled into the dregs of cancel culture, he could've been there already.

Even with Cliff's checkered recent past, he still planned on getting up, over and over again if that's what he had to do.

"Five minutes!" one of the stagehands said, sticking his head into the room. It reminded Cliff of the yellow guy with red hair from the Muppets that worked for Kermit as the unsung hero of the Muppet Show. One would have to have thick balls of felt to run around and be Kermit's intern with the number of problems they had on that show.

What the fuck was that Muppet's name?

Cliff lit a cigarette and dragged the ashtray closer. He let out a stream of smoke, watching it dissipate around his serious face.

"You're going to have to smile, big man," he told his reflection. "If you look miserable, the audience is going to be miserable. You can't pull off that Steven Wright shit. No one does that deadpan schtick any more. It's as dead as disco, motherfucker."

Cliff fixed his black tee shirt, pulling it downward. It fit tight against his pecs. He'd get shit for looking like a gym rat, but the tight black shirt and jeans was his look. Even if he didn't get any laughs, at least the women in the audience will have something to look at.

Unless they're still pissed at you for the coal miner joke.

Cliff took another drag and snuffed out his cigarette. It felt like a waste, especially with the cost of cigarettes skyrocketing, but his nerves weren't going to let him smoke any more than that. Maybe after the show he'd be in the mood to have another. He could do it onstage, but then people would think he'd be copying Andrew Dice Clay, and that's the last thing anyone would want. Clay's material didn't age well, not in this climate of accountability.

"You ready?" the stagehand asked, returning.

"Scooter!" Cliff replied.

"Excuse me?"

"Scooter. It was the name of Kermit's assistant on the old Muppet Show. That's who you remind me of. It was driving me nuts for the last couple of minutes."

WHO THE FUCK IS ROCKY PHANTASMIC?!

"They're going to announce you soon," the-stagehand-not-named-Scooter said. "Follow me."

At least the stage wasn't too far from the dressing room, which had little room to get dressed. Cliff stood to the side as Deuce's Wild's MC—a sickly-looking comedian named Jamie Dox—joked to the small audience of a few dozen people. Some had scattered to the bar area to have hushed conversations despite the MC's warmup set. It wasn't a huge turnout, but Deuce's Wild wasn't a huge venue.

"Are you guys ready for tonight's headliner?" Dox asked. The crowd cheered and clapped.

Cliff took the crowd's exuberance as a good sign, though why would they pay money to see him if they planned on being silent and miserable? He had to remind himself that sometimes These small venues got filled with people who came expecting not to laugh like it was a challenge to leave the house just to be dicks like a gaggle of comedy club Karens.

"You know him from dozens of guest spots on various sitcoms and his standup specials on WebFlix. You've seen his appearances on Celebrity House Sitters and Slut Island. He's done all the late-night shows and once shoved Jimmy Fallon in a New York deli. Hailing from Boston, Massachusetts"—he paused for effect—"Cliff Quentin!"

Cliff took to the stage, waving to the crowd as they halfheartedly cheered. "Thank you for that... Well, it was an introduction, at least, but I've seen more enthusiasm when the guy at Burger Queen tells me my number three with extra pickles is ready."

The joke got some laughs, but it was mixed in with some boos and a couple of hisses.

"I'm kidding with the guy! I'm sure he's great the moment his shift at Burger Queen starts."

Again, his joke was met with a mixed reaction, though this one felt like it had been met with less laughter.

Fuck it. Give them what they came here for then.

"So, are there any coal miners in the audience tonight?"

That one hit, and Cliff smiled as the crowd went nuts for it. Most of the cheering came from the men in the audience, but he expected that. Most women didn't *get* him.

"I had planned on starting this set with some observational shit about religion, but I figured we can talk about the elephant in the room before we get started, and I'm not talking about the bouncer at the door.

"Yes, I was a victim of what they've been calling *cancel culture*. For what it's worth, I didn't think it was real either until they came for me in the middle of the night with torches and pitchforks for telling a joke. It wasn't even a good joke. It was something I used to say to my ex-girlfriend in private. She thought it was funny, so I didn't think anything in particular was wrong with it. Sure, it might've been a tad racist, but I'm not a racist guy. I was dating a black chick for God's sake!

"And before you ask, no, I will not repeat the joke.

"That brings us to the other elephant in the room we're not supposed to talk about. It's the pussification of America in real-time. Shit, you can't even get decent blow from middle school students anymore. Everything is being painted in pastels and earth tones, and the thought police are telling you what you can and can't think in case some oddball who now has a digital voice with a handful of mindless drone followers might find it offensive.

"Look, I'm not saying I should have told the joke onstage. Getting dumped for doing it is proof enough I shouldn't have. I didn't commit any crime or anything heinous. I made a joke. So what? If this generation heard the standup my father let me listen to when I was a kid in the eighties, their heads would implode!"

Cliff paused. At least half the crowd nodded in approval. They ate up the shit he dropped, and they wanted seconds. Some murmured, making it hard to tell if he had their approval. Not that it mattered. He couldn't turn back now.

"Anyway, I'm not condoning hate speech, and I'm not going to stand up here and pretend every cancellation wasn't justified in one way or another. We're only human, and we never stop growing as people and as a people. Know what I'm sayin'? All I ask in the future from everyone, impossible as it sounds, is that you give someone a chance to explain themselves if they've somehow offended you. Nine times out of ten, it was a misunderstanding and an opportunity to grow. The other one out of ten, though, is probably a secret Nazi."

The audience cheered, giving him the best reaction he'd gotten so far. If the crowd had come for the sole purpose of getting offended, they wouldn't have bought tickets in the first place. That had been Cliff's going theory, and he was glad he could get through his little speech with this crowd. Others would have claimed he'd just doubled down on his bullshit, but luckily they weren't at Deuce's Wild.

"If there is a God," Cliff started as the cheers died a bit, "and he is loving and merciful, then why did he think it would be a funny idea to give guys like me tiny dicks?"

***

"My grandfather had a saying," Cliff said, ending his hour of comedy. "He would always tell us, 'You either end up in the back of a hearse or the back of a garbage truck'. What he meant was whichever corpse conveyance we wind up in the back of is up to us. To help his analogy, he wound up in the foundation of a strip mall outside of Boston. Thank you, everyone, and goodnight!"

The crowd clapped, cheered, and some even whistled as Cliff gave them a wave while leaving the stage. It hadn't turned out as bad as he had feared, even though it was his first time on stage since the unpleasantness of the attempted cancellation. Maybe people were ready to come around to embrace him once again.

With the evening a success, Cliff wiped the sweat off his face and sat down in the small dressing room with a long sigh. He laughed at nothing in particular. The fear he'd felt in the weeks leading up to the night left his body, and he'd gotten one step closer to getting back to his roots and starting anew. The second step would be meeting with that damn writer and working on that show idea of his.

Cliff picked up his phone and saw there was no missed text from Dave. "Maybe he's here," he said, getting back up with a grunt. He went to go get a drink and greet his adoring public. He had no idea what the writer guy looked like, but he'd recognize his would-be celebrity partner for sure.

I'm the key to the money shot after all.

Time flew by as he enjoyed a rum and coke, talked with the audience who had enjoyed his show, signed some autographs, and posed for some pictures. In the pre-cancelation times, a woman or two would find him to sign their breasts, but that didn't happen now. A cold breeze entered through the front door, so they might not have wanted to expose their bare skin to it.

Once the clock zipped past one in the morning, Cliff gave up hope of meeting with the writer. He downed the rest of the drink and sent him a text message, busting his balls for blowing him off.

"I'm only in Connecticut till the end of the day tomorrow," he texted. "Hit me up in the morning. Otherwise we'll have to do this shit over the phone or something unless you want to drive up to Massachusetts. Your call, dude."

Cliff reread the message and hit send, muttering a few obscenities. Part of him always believed the writer would get cold feet and blow him off. It happened too many times to count on anyone coming through. With another huff, Cliff stuffed his phone in his jacket pocket and got ready to leave.

"Hey!" Jake, the owner of Deuce's Wild called. He wore a tight tee shirt like Cliff's, only his had the club's logo of the two of diamonds on top of his right pec. "You OK to drive, man?"

Cliff shook his head. "I'm good. I took an uber here from my hotel, but I can walk back. It's not that far, and I enjoy the brisk night air."

"Alright. Thanks for coming by tonight. It was a good show. Good luck with the rest of the tour."

"Thanks." Cliff shook his hand and went out into the misty early morning. He didn't want to admit it to Jake or anyone else, but there was no tour. What he hoped to accomplish was an exercise in getting back to his roots. There were no set dates or club lineup. He'd go where his agent could book him last minute, and he'd drive to each location as they came along. It would be an adventure to remember.

Nothing worth doing was easy, and Cliff had wanted to do this his entire career, corny as it sounded.

You either end up in the back of a hearse or the back of a garbage truck.

His grandfather's motto. He had said it all the time, but Cliff had never asked what it meant. As far as he knew, none of his grandfather's friends' bodies had been carted away in a garbage truck after they died, even if the rest of the family claimed Cedric Quentin's murder ended with his body being buried under several tons of concrete somewhere for snitching on a crime he'd witnessed. The story of Cedric's end had never been confirmed, and the family never spoke about his disappearance. Still, it made for a decent enough anecdote to end his set, even if it wasn't exactly a joke, and the dose of quasi-wisdom included with it made it pop. It almost felt like he'd never been canceled.

And that was the funny thing about the bullshit they'd dubbed 'Cancel Culture'. Until it happened to him, Cliff dismissed it as something that only existed in the heads of the easily offended teacup poodles and social justice warriors of social media. He still wrestled with it as a tangible thing that existed in his fucked up version of reality, but the only way to get out of a cancelation was to own it, admit where you were wrong, and keep pushing so those internet snipers and keyboard warriors know you're not going to take their shit like everyone else—at least that's how he saw it. He could always double down more than he already had, but that tact never worked for anyone.

Cliff lit a cigarette and glanced down the street, spotting a garbage truck, idling, waiting. It sat partway out of an alley with the driver visible through the filthy window. His face couldn't be made out, but the eyes were vivid though the grime.

That's not ominous at all, Cliff thought. He snorted a quick laugh that turned into a cough. The golden hour for garbagemen had already begun in New Haven. It did seem a little weird, however, that there they'd be working this late on a Saturday night—or this early on a Sunday morning depending on one's disposition.

"Cliff Quentin!"

Cliff turned to the source of the voice. His first thought turned to Dave Bryant. Perhaps the writer had come super late after all. The man jogging toward him wore a thick coat and had a wool hat over his head. He held his cellphone, already filming the experience.

Even Connecticut has fucking paparazzi.

"What's up?" Cliff asked.

"How was the show, Cliff?" the paparazzo asked in return.

"It went well. The crowd was great, and I got a lot of good laughs. It was a lot of fun. New Haven is great."

"Is this the first stop on your comeback tour?"

Here we go.

"It's not a comeback tour. I did have a little hiccup in my career, so I'm trying to get back to my roots to straighten it all up. All in all, I think it's a good start. So, if that's all you wanted to know about, I'm heading—"

"It must've sucked getting canceled. I mean, you lost all those gigs, your girlfriend dumped you, and now you're walking the streets at one in the morning. How did it feel to spiral back down to our level?"

"Your level?" Cliff offered a snort of a laugh. "I see what you're trying to do here, you bitter troll. You want a reaction from me, so you can post it on your internet channels. I don't see anyone on any levels or tiers. We're all human, bro, so you can fuck off with that bullshit."

Cliff turned to walk away, leaving the conversation where it was. He took two steps before another comment came from behind him. Cowards always attack when all they can see is your back.

"Did you tell any of your signature racist jokes in there? Have you hooked up with any other black women to smear them on stage like the last one?"

"I wish you hadn't said that."

The paparazzo chuckled. "Why? Is it true?"

Cliff reached out and grabbed the cellphone before the paparazzi could step away. He hadn't been counting on a comedian having reflexes that fast, but a lot of them grew up on the streets and knew how to handle themselves in a fight since having a quick wit and a smart mouth made you a target.

"Hey!" the paparazzo snapped. "Give that back!"

"One second." Cliff ended the video and made sure not to save it. The short conversation was gone, so he chucked the phone as hard as he could into the air. It landed on the roof of a duplex.

"What the fuck, dude?! Not cool!"

Cliff shrugged. "Go climb the side of the building and get it back. Next time try being nicer and you won't lose your fuckin' phone, asshole." He turned and walked down the street.

"You fuckin' dick!" the paparazzo shouted. His dull voice echoed in the cold night. "Once I get back online, I'm going to tell everyone what you did to me! I'm trashing your ass! You can't treat people like you're above them all!"

"Fuck off, you little creep," Cliff grunted without bothering to turn his head or raise his voice. That's all he had to say. Nothing more, nothing less.

You'll be one of the corpses in the garbage truck.

Cliff looked up from the street, noticing the idling garbage truck had disappeared. He hadn't even heard it pull away.

***

Life's all about savoring the little victories. It's like that since so few of us experience anything more than that. Even though Cliff hadn't exactly overthrown a tyrannical dictator, he smirked with satisfaction at trouncing the troll who'd tried to capture him in an irritating *gotcha* moment.

WHO THE FUCK IS ROCKY PHANTASMIC?!

That'll make a great bit for my set.

Cliff laughed at the jokes life tossed his way. If you couldn't laugh at the bullshit this world spewed all over you, then what *could* you laugh at these days?

"Beware sinners!" a man wearing what appeared to be five coats shouted from the steps of the church on the corner. "He Who Walks Above has returned from his hellish dimension, and he's come to claim our souls as his own!"

Don't these assholes take a day off?

"You there!" the lice-ridden prophet exclaimed, coming down the steps toward Cliff with a filthy finger pointed toward him. "Have you been marked by He Who Walks Above? Does he watch you sin and sleep?"

"I'm not interested, pal," Cliff replied, quickening his pace. The last thing he needed was to get involved in a religious debate with an insane hobo. "Go sell it somewhere else."

"There is virtue in sin to those who use it as currency in the world of the undead." The hobo pulled a flyer from the stack he carried and shoved it into Cliff's hands. It happened so fast he couldn't stop it. "You should beware of the plot against you. He Who Walks Above watches and waits. He's a patient demon, so ancient he has no ancestors! He Who Walks Above already lived when time began its labored flow!"

Labored flow? What the fuck is he on about now?

"Thanks." Cliff accepted the flyer without looking at it in an effort to get away. "I'll keep that in mind the next time sinning crosses my mind."

"You can't joke your way out of your ultimate fate, comedian," the hobo whispered.

Cliff's breath froze in his lungs, and his feet felt as if they'd been glued to the sidewalk. "What did you say?"

"Beware of your sins!" the hobo shouted, mounting the church steps once more, spreading his arms. "This city will burn! It will be cleansed with righteous fire from the sky!"

"Right." Cliff sighed. "You're insane. I get it."

With that, he put the church steps to his back and walked in the direction of his hotel. Walking back from Deuce's Wild had seemed like such a good idea at the time. He thought even New Haven needed to sleep, but it seemed the nutjobs inhabiting the city stayed up all damn night.

Cliff realized he still had the prophetic hobo's flyer in his left hand. He walked under a streetlight and realized it wasn't a flyer for a fringe church based on whatever wacky deity he shouted into the night, but one for discount laptops. The phrase 'HE WHO WALKS ABOVE' had been written in big block letters by what Cliff could only assume was a crap crayon. The streetlight flickered and went out, leaving him in the shadows of the trees and duplexes that neighbored the church.

Cliff swore under his breath and dropped the flyer on the ground. He didn't care whether or not he left it in the street. He didn't want to catch any disease or whatever from handling something covered in human shit.

"Hey, man. Don't be litterin' in our neighborhood!"

A group of four boys watched from their darkened stoop. The one in the front wore a purple hoodie. He looked like the oldest of the quartet, but he couldn't have been any older than fourteen.

"That guy handed me a paper covered in shit," Cliff said. "What was I supposed to do with it?"

"You can fuckin' eat it." The others laughed behind him.

"Yeah. Funny."

"Nah." The kid got up and walked toward Cliff. "I mean it. Pick up that paper you dropped on the ground in front of my house and eat it."

Cliff stared back, not knowing if they were pranking him or if they were for real. It occurred to him that it wasn't the first time that night he felt that way, and he wondered if the universe itself had decided to prank him for shits and giggles.

"I'm good. Sorry about the flyer. If you want, I'll find a garbage pail and throw it away for you."

"I told you to eat it!" The kid lunged forward with his fist raised. If he had known that Cliff worked out with boxers, he might not have attempted to throw an obvious punch. Cliff's reflexes worked before his tired and slightly inebriated mind could work out the flaws in punching a teenager, and the kid fell on his ass after a fast jab to the nose.

"Shit," Cliff said, leaning down to offer the kid a hand to get back on his feet. "Sorry about that. You shouldn't attack adults you don't know." As an afterthought he added, "Unless they're trying to drag you into a windowless van. Those fuckers you can attack as much as you want."

The kid slapped Cliff's hand away. "Fuck you, motherfucker." His trio of friends got off their stoop, helping up their fallen fellow before attacking as one. The last thing Cliff wanted to do was beat the shit out of a bunch of kids who looked like the ne'er-do-wells from an old Disney movie, but they left him no choice but to defend himself. He felt his right fist connect with the front of one of their faces, and his other socked a kid on the side of their jaw. The fight didn't remain in Cliff's favor once the first kid he'd socked had gotten back into the fray. It was four against one, and the size of his opponents didn't matter when they attacked while surrounding him in a square of teenage fists and boots. Cliff covered his head and face with his arms as the assault continued since he couldn't do anything else. Maybe one had a knife or a gun, or maybe they'd get bored with pummeling him and give up. Either way, the wind had been knocked out of Cliff's chest, and escaping wouldn't be an option unless he could find an opening to haul ass and pray they didn't feel like chasing him.

Then, with a huge shove, one of them knocked Cliff onto the street.

"Get that fuckin' paper!" the lead kid ordered. "I'ma make him eat that thing!"

Eating the shit-covered flyer would be the worst of two evils, and Cliff tried to get away. He had his legs under him again, but a quick boot to his ribs sent him back to the ground, and he was once again guarding his face and head with his arms as the quartet stomped and punched him like the ending of an out-of-control wrestling match.

At least this night can't get worse from here.

The sound of clattering metal and voice-cracking screams came next. The punching and kicks had subsided, though, and that made the surrealness of the whole beatdown all the odder. Cliff stayed on the ground, keeping his arms over his head, feeling like a coward who'd been bitten by a radioactive armadillo and had taken over its traits.

That would work well in my set.

The night became silent a fraction of a second after a boot connected with his temple, save for the hobo prophet's sermon around the corner. Cliff gathered his wits and forced himself to get back to his feet even though his body protested the movement. The kids hadn't been that strong, but he'd wake up covered in bruises and scrapes anyway.

Did they knock me out and leave? Cliff thought, looking around the empty street to see if his attackers were somewhere lying in wait. *How much time has passed since that last kick to the head?*

Something else felt off. There were four metal garbage cans placed by the curb, and Cliff didn't remember if they'd been there or not. He remembered tossing the paper to the ground. If the cans had been the whole time, he would have used that instead of littering and igniting the teenage street fight.

The computer flyer with 'HE WHO WALKS ABOVE' drawn on it blew to Cliff's feet with a cold breeze. With a sigh, Cliff bent over and picked it up. It was best to put litter in its place, after all. Some goofy-ass mascot had said that during a childhood cartoon.

Guess they were right. I sure learned my lesson about littering.

Cliff chuckled at the thought, wishing it didn't hurt his ribs to laugh. He lifted the lid of the trashcan closest to him and fell back when he saw the slack face of one of the kids who had attacked him staring back at him.

"FUCK!"

The swear echoed in the night, and Cliff stepped forward. He couldn't have seen what he thought he saw. It was impossible. With a shaking hand, he opened the lid again, slower this time, as if that would make what waited inside any less horrifying.

The head looked up at him as it had before, and the rest of the kid's body had been chopped up and shoved into the trashcan with it. If Cliff opened the other three trashcans, he knew he'd find the rest of the kids who'd kicked his ass.

Someone must have dropped some acid or something in my drink back at the club.

Cliff placed the flyer in front of the kid's dead face and placed the lid back on top, obscuring it from view. He looked down the road and saw the red lights of the back of a garbage truck glaring at him as it drove into the misty night.

"There's no trash pickup on Sunday morning," he said, eliciting a chill up his spine.

With his statement hanging in the air, Cliff turned and hurried back on his route to his hotel to sleep off whatever else this horrid night could throw at him.

Maybe someone somewhere was having a much better night.

WHO THE FUCK IS ROCKY PHANTASMIC?!

3. THE POLYAMOROUS WIFE & THE BROKEN PRIEST

The view would have been spectacular had the night sky not been obscured by dark clouds blotting out the moon and stars. The ocean crashed against the beach, sending a cold and salty mist into the air. It would have chilled one to the bones, but the beach was empty. No one ventured near the water when the temperature dipped toward the thirties. Even if it wasn't quite freezing, it was still too cold to dip one's toes into the Long Island Sound.

Then again, it was warm enough in Heather Bryant's hotel room.

A moan escaped her lips as she ran her hand down her stomach toward her panties. "Come to bed, baby. If I have to wait any longer, I'll do it myself."

Lee chuckled. He stood wearing nothing but a white towel around his fuzzy stomach and chest. He had a thick, burly body, and that's how Heather liked her men. She didn't want a featherweight on top of her. She wanted to feel her lover's girth in every way like a supervillain threatened to crush her for interrupting their schemes.

"I'm OK with that as long as I can watch," he said.

"Shut the fuck up and get over here. I didn't pay for this hotel room to fuck myself."

Lee nodded once and let his towel drop to the floor. His body wasn't the only thing girthy about him. He'd already grown hard when he climbed onto the bed and over Heather's smooth body. His rough hands explored her, moving to her bare breasts.

Heather let a long, sweet moan escape her mouth. She felt Lee's breath on her neck as he ran his lips and bearded face against her. This was right where she wanted to be at this moment, trapped between the sheets and a man's flesh. She moved her leg, rubbing it against Lee's side, making him squirm. His rock-hardness moved against her panties. If it could talk, it would be begging for her to rip them off, but that wasn't her job.

Lee obeyed the silent command, moving his hands down her body. He moved off her, letting the cool air come between them. Heather liked keeping the air conditioner on high, even though it was so cold outside. If they were supposed to keep warm, they had each other's bodies and hot showers for when they got too dirty.

Heather shifted her legs, helping her panties find their way around her ankles. Lee tossed them to the floor, and came back down, pushing his face between her thighs. They were both nude now. Heather wore nothing but her wedding rings, but her husband was far from her mind as Lee kissed and teased her thighs with his lips and tongue.

"Do it already," Heather ordered in a whisper, grabbing Lee's hair, forcing his head forward. "Stop messing around down there!"

Lee obliged, putting his tongue to work against her clit. He acted like a ravenous animal, and Heather was the only thing that could sate his bestial hunger. She smiled, wondering if a bite would turn her into a werewolf. But that nonsense could be saved for one of her husband's fantasy books.

"Don't stop," Heather groaned, pulling a pillow over her face to stifle a coming scream. She could hear her muffled voice as its pitch rose along with her pulse. The walls of these hotels were too thin to let out a long, screaming orgasm, though some of the other customers might enjoy a little late-night show.

Heather pulled the pillow away from her face and said, "Get over here and fuck me, Lee."

Lee pulled his face away from Heather's crotch and crawled back on top of her. This time, however, he slid inside her. She moaned, and her nails found his back and dug into his flesh.

"Not too hard," he whispered.

Heather nodded and let up. As much as she wanted to leave trails of scratches all over him, Lee's wife wouldn't appreciate it if she found them later. Not all spouses were as OK with extramarital affairs.

WHO THE FUCK IS ROCKY PHANTASMIC?!

Lee thrust, pushing himself deep inside her. She reached behind her and grabbed at another pillow, her body rocking with Lee's motion. Her mouth opened in ecstasy, and she felt close to climaxing a second time within minutes of her last orgasm.

"Cum with me," she moaned.

"Yeah?" Lee asked.

"Yeah."

Lee buried his head next to Heather's, and she could feel his weight on top of her again. His pelvis quickened, and so did her libido. She fed on the energy, letting it surge through her entire being. She had her hands on Lee's back again as the climax took her, and she convulsed, matching her lover's gait. Lee groaned as he finished, letting his body stiffen for half a minute before it came to a rest.

Lee let out a long, satisfied breath and fell to the bed next to Heather. "Wow."

Heather nodded. "I agree."

The couple lay in the king-sized hotel bed, resting in each other's arms once their act of lovemaking ended. Heather could feel weariness taking over her body, and she knew she'd sleep soon for at least four or five hours. The only question in her mind was whether or not she'd do it alone.

"Why do you wear these when we meet like this?" Lee asked, fiddling with Heather's wedding and engagement rings.

"Because I'm happily married," Heather replied with a small smile. "Why don't you wear yours when you're together?"

Lee sighed. "That's out of respect for my wife. She wouldn't like what we're doing. She wouldn't take to an open marriage like you and your husband."

And it had been a good marriage so far. Like all relationships, it had its ups and downs over the last fifteen years, but everything remained stable. Dave had itches his wife couldn't scratch for him, and he had acknowledged the same for her. Heather didn't know the extent of her husband's queerness when she married him. Hell, Dave didn't know himself until after he'd done a lot of soul-searching during a particularly rough patch in the marriage.

"Opening up the marriage let my husband explore his sexuality," Heather said aloud. "And it allowed me to do the same. Do you know what we found out?"

"What?"

"We found that two people can be in love, raise a child, make a house into a home, and have relationships outside of each other. It's not cheating when you can be in sync with your partner while maintaining that sexual openness and awareness. Does that make any sense?"

"A little. It still sounds like cheating to me."

Heather chuckled. "Dave has a saying for that. *You call it cheating when you treat your marriage like a fucking game*. His words, not mine."

"I get that."

"Shut up and let me get a little sleep. Wake me when you have to leave, though. I don't want to wake up to wonder how long ago you left me in bed by myself."

Lee yawned. "I have a few more hours. Lisa thinks I'm pulling an overnight shift, so I can't get home too early. I can get up around five, shower quick, and head home."

Heather nodded as sleep covered her mind in dull static. "I thought we'd have all weekend together."

"I wish I could have all that time with you and more, babe."

"I'm your supervisor. I can always forge a fake email to get you off the hook if you need it."

"Don't worry about it. She won't even miss me."

"Her loss."

"Your gain?"

Heather smiled and let out a long breath. They were both asleep a minute later.

***

Am I dreaming?
Of course, you are. The sky isn't black.

Sometimes it is, but the weather forecast hadn't called for any epic storms. If they had, the lovers' retreat in the hotel by the beach would have been canceled for sure. Dave wouldn't have made an appointment to hang out with that comedian friend he'd made online, and their daughter would be with them. They'd be fleeing the storm or riding it out in the cellar as a family.

But Heather found herself all alone.

The storm gained momentum as it pounded the shore. Heather stood on the beach, letting the frigid water wash over her feet and shins. They had become buried in the sand, gluing her to the spot. Even if she had wanted to run, she'd waited too long. The clouds formed into a funnel and came down to skim atop the water, sending seawater into the air in a fine spray as it made its way toward her.

Everything felt so surreal, and Heather knew she'd fallen asleep and dreamed of the beach and the storm.

"This isn't a dream," she said in a low voice as lightning arced from the clouds around the tornado. "This is a fucking nightmare!"

A thunderclap boomed. Another flash came, and a bolt hit the beach next to her, sending sand and smoke into the air. Two more claps followed, and Heather screamed into the storm. She tried to run, but her feet were stuck. The seawater rushed toward her, covering her up to her stomach. She tried like a woman possessed to free her feet, but it was useless. Escaping the swelling sea would be impossible now, and the funnel of clouds and chaotic winds came for her with its unrelenting energy and naturalistic power. It felt more like an unstoppable beast than a storm.

Heather prayed, but she didn't ask for a miracle. All she asked of whatever deity that might've heard her was for her death to be quick and painless. She didn't want to die being twisted through the air, only to have her bones smashed as her body hit the water, drowning her after her broken body couldn't do a simple doggy paddle to save herself from succumbing to the dark water.

Two more bangs came, but not from the sky.

"What?!"

Heather sat up in bed, realizing she'd soaked the sheets with cold sweat. She thought she might've screamed in the real world while the images of the storm assaulted her in the nightmare, but her lover slept regardless. The banging returned, and she realized it hadn't been a storm's thundering at all. Someone pounded at their door.

"Lee," Heather whispered, pushing his meaty shoulder. "Wake up."

"Shit," Lee groaned. "Did I oversleep? I set a damn alarm on my phone to go off at—"

The pounding returned, and Lee sat up as well. "Who's that?" he asked.

"I don't know," Heather replied. "I paid with a good credit card, so we shouldn't be getting kicked out. Do you have your gun with you?"

"Shit, it's in my car in the lockbox. I didn't think I'd need it tonight."

Three more pounds came. "Bryant!" a rough voice shouted from the other side. "I know you're in there! Open the damn door!"

"Is that your husband?" Lee asked, pulling up his shorts. "I thought you said he was cool about us doing this!"

"That's not Dave. He wouldn't call me by my last name, and he sure as hell wouldn't be screaming like a goddam psychopath."

Lee looked toward Heather. "Get dressed. I'm going to deal with this asshole one way or another."

Another thud came, and then five or six more in quick succession. Whoever had come gave up on their first and started kicking the door instead.

"Be careful."

Lee nodded. "I'll be as careful as I can be." He moved toward the door in nothing but his shorts. "I'm coming, but no one by that name is here! My name's Lee McCormack, and I'm here with my wife."

"Liar!" the voice called in return. The door blew open with the sound of what sounded like a blast of thunder. She had to remind herself that the nightmare had ended. This was the real world, and someone screaming her last name had blasted a hole through her hotel room's door with a shotgun or a rifle.

"Fuck." Lee stumbled back, holding his gut. Blood poured from his abdomen where the shot and shrapnel from the door had struck him, and he wound up on the floor with his back against the bed, gasping for breath. One more kick had the door open, and his assailant stepped into the room, brandishing his shotgun.

"Did I get you with that shot?" the man asked. "Good. That makes things much easier for all of us."

In another life, the interloper could have been Lee's brother, only he didn't have a gut, and he wore a full beard of brown and red around his face instead of the salt-and-pepper stubble Lee sported. He'd dressed in a black shirt, black pants, and the white collar of a priest, making the situation seem as weird as Heather's vivid dream of the beach, only she knew she'd returned to the waking world for an all-too-real nightmare.

Heather shrunk back on the bed, covering he nude body with the comforter. *Is this how I die*, she thought, *naked in a hotel room with someone else's husband, gunned down by some psychopathic priest with my name on their lips?*

"You have the wrong room," Heather pleaded. "Please, let me call an ambulance for him, and you can leave."

"Shut up," the priest grunted. He lowered himself to his haunches, looked into Lee's face, and narrowed his eyes. "You're not David Bryant. Who are you?"

"I already told you," Lee replied through his gasping. "My name's Lee McCormack. I'm not the guy you're looking for."

"Maybe not." The priest stood, smacking the butt of his shotgun against the side of Lee's face, knocking him unconscious. His body lay still on the floor, bleeding into the carpet.

"Please," Heather said. "Let me help him. He's not who you're looking for, and he'll die if I don't!"

And let me warn my husband that someone's trying to kill him!

The priest rested his shotgun on the top of the dresser, lying it under the television screen. Heather saw her reflection in the black surface, wondering if anyone had called the police or at least the front desk after the amount of noise the priest had made pounding, kicking, and blasting at their door. He had made enough of a ruckus to wake the entire hotel by her estimation, yet no one came to help them.

If they're smart, they'd be on the highway by now, driving as far away from here as possible.

"Let me help him," Heather repeated.

"Wait one moment, missy." The priest had her purse, rummaging through its contents. Did he want money? He found her wallet and flipped it open, reading her driver's license. "Heather Bryant," he mused, nodding. "That must make you David's wife after all. But that's not David bleeding out onto the floor, is it? Who is this man who'd lie with another man's wife?"

"He's who he said he was," Heather replied. "Lee McCormack. I know him from work. Please, let me help him."

"I'm not letting you do anything, adulteress. I've been looking for your husband since dusk, and the demon's voice led me here. Your husband's scent is still on you. I guess you'd like that for your sinner's tryst. Adulteress whores always revel in that reek, I suppose."

"I'm not an adulteress, and I'm not a whore," Heather said. "I'm a woman, a wife, a mother, and that's all. Now will you please let me help the man you shot before he dies on a cheap hotel rug!"

The priest looked her in the eyes, and said, "No." He picked the shotgun up once more and aimed it at her chest. "Put on your clothes. You're coming with me."

"Why?"

"You're going to help me find your husband."

Heather stared into the priest's face, waiting for him to waver to show some kind of tell. He narrowed his eyes at her, not even showing a slight tic. She knew he wouldn't be convinced to let her make a call, so she did her best to redress herself in the clothes Lee had thrown to the floor after stripping her of them, wondering if the priest would keep to his vow of celibacy—assuming he'd taken one and wasn't traipsing in a Halloween costume. He'd already broken the *thou shall not kill* commandment after all.

Heather looked at her lover's body and the shallow rise and fall of his breathing as she completed the task and left the comfortable hotel room by the beach with the crazed priest's shotgun against he small of her back, leaving behind everything except the clothes on her back.

***

Neither Heather, nor anyone except the hopelessly curious, ever wondered what priests drive. Maybe they'd have something with a sunroof to keep you within sight of God's holy light. That wasn't the case for Heather's kidnapping priest. He drove a rusty Oldsmobile station wagon. You didn't see many of them on the road. The engine protested and groaned, likely held together by prayers answered by the Almighty himself.

"Lee might be dying," Heather said, breaking the silence in the front passenger's seat of the Oldsmobile. She had a chain around her waist, secured with a padlock that sat on the space where her thighs met. The priest had locked the other end to a metal harness on the back of the station wagon. If she wanted to escape, she'd have to crawl in the back and unlock it. She couldn't get out of the door inches from her without the keys, which hung inside the priest's vestments on a smaller chain of their own.

"He's not dying," the priest grunted. "The shot went through the door before it hit him. He's probably got a gut full of splinters from the door from when it blew off. If his stomach had been a bit harder, it might've only been a minor flesh wound. Gluttons are always *soft*."

"If you hadn't come with the gun, you could've found out how hard he could be."

The priest chuckled at that. "Oh yeah? I guess you'd know better than me, adulteress. When he wakes up from his little nap, he could crawl to the hospital and get a couple of stitches for his trouble."

Silence reigned once more. How could there be any civil conversation between a kidnapper and their victim? The priest didn't seem like the type who liked to talk either way. Still, Heather's curiosity couldn't be satisfied, not when so much went unsaid or unanswered.

"What do you want with Dave?" Heather asked. "He's never hurt anyone. If this is a religious thing… Look, I know we don't follow your catholic roots by any stretch of the imagination, but what you're doing is insane!"

"This has nothing to do with your roots or how you've sinned to the brink of blackening your souls to the point of no return."

"Then why are you coming for my husband?"

The priest didn't answer. The only response Heather got was him hardening his face and staring at the road ahead of him.

"At least tell me who you are and where we're going. I think you owe me that much."

"My name is Father Stephen MacDougal. As for our destination…" He pulled Heather's license from the visor and held it with two fingers. "We're going to see if your husband's home. I had scented him, but it led me to you first. The Lord works in mysterious ways, but demons are more thorough than He."

A shiver rose along Heather's spine, and her mouth went dry. "Demons? What…What's that supposed to mean? Why would anything lead you to kidnap me and shoot my boyfriend in the gut?"

"It's not my fault he was there lying with a woman who isn't his wife. I went to kill David, but harming a sinner is never an accident, adulteress."

"I asked you to stop calling me that. How would you like it if I started calling you 'psychopath' after every other sentence?"

"The label you give me has no bearing on the one I give you. My judgment comes from the Lord, and yours comes from your want to tear others down to your level."

Heather huffed and watched the road as Father Stephen made a left turn toward her house. If any words could help her make heads or tails out of the situation, the priest would find a way to twist them in his favor. All men who put themselves on a level with God and Jesus made excuses as to why they were better than everyone else. The irony of their own sins was lost to the void of oblivion.

"This is your house," Father Stephen said. It wasn't posed as a question, nor did he seek confirmation. The statement hung in the air as he pulled into the driveway.

Heather glanced at the clock and saw it was a little after three in the morning. There were no cars in the driveway. Heather's was still in the hotel parking lot, and Dave had a meeting with that comedian he'd befriended online. Still, he hadn't planned on being out all night. He wasn't the kind of guy who stayed up past midnight, but his latest project was important to him. The worst-case scenario would be that he took a taxi home after having too much to drink at the comedy club.

With a silent prayer, Heather sent her intention into the infinitely silent universe that her husband's meeting, or anything else in the world, had kept him away from their home.

"Let's go," Father Stephen said as he put the car into park, shut it off, and opened his door. He climbed out with a grunt, and Heather sat, thinking she'd be forced to wait in the cold car while the priest broke into her home to search for her husband.

Father Stephen went to the back of the station wagon, and Heather assumed he would get whatever tools he needed to break into the house or his trusty shotgun. Instead, he unlocked the chain and came around to the passenger side door. He stood outside it holding a hunting knife.

"If you run, I'll get you and gut you like a wild animal. Nod if you understand."

Heather nodded.

"Good." Father Stephen finagled the chain toward the front of the station wagon and held the end, backing up so Heather could get out. She was aware she could yank it from his hand and make a run for it, but she'd be dragging ten feet of chain behind her. Father Stephen would stomp on it, trip her up, and cut her open from her crotch up to her neck. She'd probably make it as far as the sidewalk before he caught her, spilling her guts onto the driveway for an early morning jogger to find.

"Open your front door and let yourself inside your home," Father Stephen said, speaking in slow, deliberate words.

Heather approached the door. The unknowing of what the murderous priest had planned swam around her mind. Would he force her to call out to Dave and shoot him when he appeared or did he have a slower means of torture and eventual death in mind?

WHO THE FUCK IS ROCKY PHANTASMIC?!

The door stood open a crack, and Heather's heart dropped. She pushed it open with a shaking hand. The inside of her home had been trashed. Someone else had been there and had ransacked the place. A tear rolled down her cheek, and she changed her prayer to ask that this wasn't why he husband wasn't at home.

"We're too late," Father Stephen said, walking past Heather, dragging the chain on the ground to look over the mess of their home. "He's either been taken or tipped off that he's being hunted. Whoever did this wanted it to look like a burglary. This is sloppy."

"Who else is hunting my husband?" Heather asked. "Why is any of this happening?!"

Father Stephen rummaged in his pocket and brought out Heather's cellphone. He must've taken it back at the hotel. He held it between himself and Heather and said, "Call him."

"And tell him what?"

"Find out where he is."

"Why should I do that if you're going to kill him when you find him?"

The priest sighed, lowered his head, and shook it. "There are stronger forces at play than your noble want to see David safe, despite your blatant disregard for your wedding vows. I need to kill him to save the world, and I'll make it as quick and as painless as possible. The others who want him, however, aren't as neat and nice as I am. They'll torture him, peel his flesh from his bones, and feed it to rabid dogs while he hangs from the ceiling, watching as the beasts consume him a bite at a time."

"Why, though? Why is he in the middle of all this?"

Father Stephen took a long breath and stepped closer to Heather. "He's been marked by an evil spirit who should not exist in our universe. There is a prophecy not written by human hands, and your husband is one of the people who can help see this prophecy to fruition. David Bryant can help bring about the Demonic Apocalypse, and he is the one they've chosen for their dark ritual."

He's crazier than I thought.

One more thought circled in Heather's mind. *Dave always said relying on prophecies is lazy writing.*

Heather took the phone from Father Stephen's hand. Her body tremored, knowing her betrayal would set him off in a rage that would end with her bleeding on the floor. She'd die in her own home. There was some comfort in that at least.

The moment Dave answers, Heather thought, *tell him to go somewhere to hide and call the police. They'll come here based on the call, find my body, trace my night back to the hotel where Lee is hopefully not dead, and put together what's happened. They'll find the priest, put him away, and Dave will be safe and raise Kayla. At least she'll have one of her parents.*

Still, this is a lot of faith to put in the police to do their job right.

Heather pushed the last thought from her mind and unlocked her phone. She found Dave's number and called it.

"Put it on the speaker," Father Stephen ordered.

Heather nodded and did as he asked. The phone rang for what felt like an eternity. Finally, the monotone voice of a woman picked up, giving them instructions on how to leave a voicemail.

"Try it again."

Heather ended the call and redialed the number. Again, it went to Dave's voicemail. Wherever he was, he didn't have his phone on him. It hadn't gone straight to voicemail, so it wasn't dead or destroyed.

"Find him."

"What?" Heather looked into the priest's face as tears threatened to pour from her eyes. All Dave had to do was answer, and she would shout her warning as quickly as possible. If there was any way to take control of the situation, she failed to figure out how to do it.

"I might be a priest, but my brain's not from the Middle Ages. You're a family, and all families have these things. You can track his whereabouts by his phone, right?"

"No."

"Are you saying you can't or won't?"

"What does it matter?" Heather asked in return. "Either way, you don't find him."

The back of Father Stephen's hand connected with the side of her face, and her body rocked from the blow. Heather wasn't a pushover in any sense, but tears flooded her vision and her knees buckled. If he hit her again, she'd be on the floor unconscious.

Like Lee...

Father Stephen snatched the phone from her hand. She hadn't locked it after the call, and the priest had free reign to go through it at his leisure. He found the family phone tracker app that allowed Heather, Dave, and Kayla to know one another's location. He smiled at the screen and tossed the phone to the floor amid the rest of the mess.

"I know that neighborhood. Let's go see your husband."

***

Father Stephen brought them to New Haven, near the comedy club to which Heather knew Dave had planned to go. She didn't tell the priest about it. She didn't want him to go there and happen upon him, even though Deuce's Wild had to have been closed since two in the morning. Dave hadn't made it all the way there either way. They came across his car parked next to a small dog park a few blocks away.

"That's his car," Heather said, more to herself. The blood in her veins had turned to ice, and she thought his body would be in the backseat or the trunk. Whoever else had been *hunting* him had gotten him to him first, and he didn't have fair warning about any of this madness coming for him.

"Wait here," Father Stephen muttered, putting the Oldsmobile into park.

"What?" Heather asked, whipping her head toward him. "No! If my husband's there, even if he's dead, I need to see him. I need to know!"

"You'll know, but not before I do."

Father Stephen left the station wagon. Heather watched, her vision threatening to blur with whatever tears were left in her system. The whole ordeal since her nap with Lee had been interrupted had taken no more than two hours, but it felt like she'd been bound and dragged for days.

So, she watched, helpless to do anything but pull on the restraining chain around her waist. Father Stephen looked inside Dave's car and shook his head. He opened the unlocked door and peered around the interior for a minute before popping the trunk. Heather leaned forward to get a better look, and she could see that Dave's body hadn't been stashed inside it. She breathed a sigh of relief. That meant he could still be alive and safe somewhere, though she still didn't know who else wanted her husband dead.

Father Stephen looked around the outside of the car and the ground under it. Heather could see shining specks of broken glass in the road from her vantage, but they didn't look like they'd come from Dave's car. They could've already been on the road from some break-in or just some city kids smashing bottles in the street for fun.

Something else lay on the ground near the curb. Father Stephen bent, picked up what looked like a broken billy club, and examined it, tossing it away into the dog park. He took one last look around the ground and returned to the car.

"Your husband's gone," Father Stephen said once he returned to the driver's seat. "He left his phone on the dashboard, and the passenger's seat had trash from a fast-food restaurant. I don't know what happened. He either abandoned the car, or he's been taken by the Enemy."

Dave's eating burgers in his car again, Heather thought. *At least I know why he was here. A quick dinner before the show. That means he wasn't home when it got trashed. God, I hope that's true.*

"What are you thinking?" Father Stephen asked, staring at her with his dark eyes. "Do you know where he is?"

"No, and I'm glad I don't. He could still be safe as long as he's not within your crosshairs."

Father Stephen tsked and put the car into drive, leaving Dave's car unlocked next to the dog park. "Your husband is far from safe, adulteress, and I have *other* ways to track him, even though I don't like using them."

"What do you mean?"

"I'm going to find your husband, kill those who want him alive, and kill him myself. Now that I have you, I can scent him better. All I need is a bit of rest to regain my focus. It's not too late. I can still find him and stop what's to come."

Heather watched out the window as the priest drove. *This isn't all that bad. Dave's still alive somewhere. If we do find him, the priest will kill his captors, and then I can do whatever it takes to kill the priest and get Dave far away from these goddam demonic cultists or whoever wants him. That's the only option. I only hope he's somewhere safe right now.*

4. THE ORIGIN OF ROCKY PHANTASMIC

"I am safe."

Dave didn't know why he had said it as he awoke. He also realized he had never put much thought into ceilings and how they can become familiar or unfamiliar. It was an odd thought to have upon waking, but the ceiling above him with large patches of missing paint felt as unfamiliar as they come.

"Where the…"

The smell of his new surroundings hit Dave the moment he sat up. Wherever he'd been taken hadn't been cleaned in forever, and the reek in the air had the aroma of body odor, a sink full of moldy dishes, and dust. His nose burned, and he stifled a sneeze. The apartment looked as bad as it smelled. Clothes were piled in front of a dresser, a single table had been buried under mounds of comic books, and the walls looked like they needed a good, hard scrubbing.

He knew the morning had come, but the exact time would remain a mystery since there were no clocks in the vicinity. Dave searched his pocket for his cellphone, but he had been ordered to leave it on the dashboard of his car. He wanted to text Heather and let her know he was alright in case she got home early. She'd be surprised to find him missing, and she'd worry for sure when she couldn't find or get in touch with him. She couldn't know he had to get out of dodge before the bad guys who wanted to kidnap him found her to use as bait.

That's how bad guys operated in the movies anyway.

The sun cut through a grimy window above the kitchen sink, and Dave realized he'd been brought to a one-bedroom apartment. From the height of the window, he surmised it was in the basement of some building. He climbed off the couch where he had been laid to sleep and looked out the window, standing on his toes to get a good look. He saw a strip of grass that led to a parking lot. The only car visible was missing a wheel and had been propped up by a stack of cinder blocks.

"I guess I wasn't taken somewhere with a five-star rating."

"Are you awake?"

Dave turned toward the sound of the voice. There stood his savior from the night before, and the memory of being attacked and rescued came flooding back all at once.

"Holy shit, you're the guy!" Dave said, pointing. "You were decked out like a superhero with a hoodie and cape. You beat up those guys who attacked me. It was… Holy shit!"

"I guess that means you're awake."

"Your name," Dave continued, watching his rescuer walk past him toward the minifridge that sat where a regular-sized refrigerator should have been. "What was it? Rocky… Rocky something. Rocky Fantastic!"

"Phantasmic," Rocky corrected. He turned from the fridge holding a silver and red can of Demon Energy. "The name's Rocky Phantasmic." With a flick of his finger, he opened the can and took a long drink from it.

"Rocky Phantasmic," Dave repeated. "Those guys said you had another name. Rick or Rich… Right?"

"Richie Pimento. He's dead."

"Oh. I'm sorry. Was he your twin brother? Was that why they mistook you for him?"

"No. I was Richie Pimento, but that was another life."

Dave stood in the kitchen and stared as Rocky pulled the old blanket and pillow off his couch and sat down, holding his energy drink in his left hand. He seemed smaller than he had the night before, but Dave's perspective had been a bit different when the shit hit the fan.

"How old are you?" Dave asked.

"I was twenty-three."

Dave laughed. "Funny. I was twenty-three too, but that was almost fifteen years ago."

WHO THE FUCK IS ROCKY PHANTASMIC?!

Rocky didn't offer any other information or indication that he had gotten the joke. Dave assumed Rocky hadn't yet left his teenage years, but he might've been a late bloomer or something.

Rocky took another long sip from his energy drink, staring off toward the blank screen of the television.

"Aren't you going to turn it on?" Dave asked.

"Power's been shut off," Rocky replied.

"Then how does the fridge work?"

"I put ice packs in there. If you want a Demon, help yourself."

"This..." Dave looked around the small apartment. Nothing added up or made any semblance of sense. He still didn't know why he'd been attacked, and his savior—this perpetual man-boy who had named himself Rocky Phantasmic—didn't seem like the type to offer anything but short, uninformative responses.

"Look," Dave said, standing between Rocky and the unworking television. "I need some answers. Anything you can tell me would be useful. Who were those guys who tried to attack me last night and why? Who's their boss, Vincent Whatever? They said he wanted me alive. Why? Who are you, and why did they think they killed you?"

"The only thing I can't answer is why they're after you. I can answer the rest if you'd like, but it's not a fun story."

"I don't care if it's fun or not. I need to know what I'm up against."

Rocky stood and went to the kitchen table. He rummaged for a moment and returned with an obituary page. The grease stain that covered half the page made the paper almost see-through, but it was still readable.

"*Vincenzo Scaletta died in his home surrounded by family and friends*," Dave read aloud. He looked up from the obituary. "Wait a minute... He's dead?! How the hell is this guy sending his goon squad after me if he's dead?"

"I don't know. I didn't know he was still around till I heard my cousin use his name last night."

"Cousin? Those thugs are your cousins?"

Rocky nodded. "Not by blood. I don't think so anyway. It's all muddled up. It's a family, but not a traditional *family* if you get what I'm saying."

"I do. I've seen The Sopranos, and those cousins of yours were giving off low-level mafia vibes. I still don't get how I'm involved in all this." Dave looked at Rocky, who seemed to have lost interest. He stared off again, this time looking toward the apartment's lone window.

"OK," Dave said. "Tell me your story, and I'll do my best to fill in the blanks."

Rocky nodded, and the dazed look in his eyes subsided. "Alright. Get comfortable. This is the origin story of how mild-mannered Richie Pimento became the superhero known as Rocky Phantasmic."

***

The reason the power is off in the apartment is because dead men can't pay their electric bill. But that's getting ahead of the story. This isn't the tale of the superhero called Rocky Phantasmic. This tale is about the man who had to die to be reborn and rebranded with gifts beyond his wildest fits of imagination.

This is the tale of Richie Pimento.

Richie sat at a table in a restaurant with a comic book open in front of him. His eyes scanned the images of Cricket-Man as he trounced his archnemesis Dr. Everything after an epic battle. The genius supervillain had built a small army of androids with metal tendrils for arms to take over the city, forcing the black-clad Cricket-Man to go to war to save Pristine City from being overrun and utterly destroyed.

"The deadline's at five Richie! What the hell do you think you're doing sitting there reading those stupid comic books again? You're on the clock, kid. If you don't deliver, they'll bash in my kneecaps. You know how Gino loves whacking people around with that damn club of his!"

The voice and the ire behind it belonged to Butch Barone, brother-in-law to Vincenzo Scaletta. He spoke with a meaty voice that matched his thick and robust body. His relation to the Scaletta family wasn't too important to the young man sitting at a table at Butch's Pizzeria reading the latest issue of Cricket-Man instead of making the ever-important delivery. Everyone had a name, and some people used theirs like weapons. The Pimento name, however, could have been a dollar store water gun when you needed to fight a guy with a bazooka under his trench coat.

"What do you got?" Richie asked, keeping his eyes on his comic book so he would see how Cricket-Man saved the day, which he always did. "I'll get it anywhere before five. Guaranteed."

WHO THE FUCK IS ROCKY PHANTASMIC?!

Butch looked toward the ceiling and let out a groan to end all groans. "Come on then! It's after four already, and you're still on your ass." He snatched Richie's comic book, rolled it up, stuffed it in the pocket of his filthy apron, and dropped a thick manilla envelope on the table. "That's for Vinny Scaletta. Head down to his club on East Street and give it to his man at the door. Make sure he knows it's from me."

"Alright, boss." Richie stuffed the envelope into a pocket under his jacket and left, whistling a tune he'd made up for the occasion.

"Tone-deaf little shit got his head screwed on all wrong," Butch muttered, heading back toward his kitchen. "He's gonna get me friggin' killed someday."

Richie unlocked his bike, mounted it, and pedaled down State Street. He'd make the delivery to the Red Curtain with time to spare. It would have been better to bring some subs or a pizza with him, but a mysterious envelope would have to be good enough. Besides, he'd lost count of how many times he'd been mugged for food. It had gotten so bad at one point that assailants waited in a parking lot around the corner to pounce on him the moment he passed. They'd taken his cellphone last week, and he still hadn't gotten around to figuring out how to scrounge enough money to replace it. Butch had to call in a favor to get a couple of the family's nephews to take care of the mini-thugs for Richie. It's one of those things one didn't bring up unless they wanted to get a hard slap in the face as a reminder of what happens to those who talk too much.

Butch called it 'the family business', but Richie had heard it called by other names. They weren't an actual family like you'd see on some primetime sitcom, bonding and learning life lessons from their seasoned parental units. If one could draw a family tree, however, there'd be branches connected to branches of everyone marrying into everyone else's family. Richie's father had married Butch's cousin, which was the roundabout way he'd ended up a delivery boy for his pizzeria.

Richie never asked about the family business. He knew better. His father refused to admit it existed, and Butch's aforementioned slap could hit hard enough to rattle one's teeth. It worked out better to pretend it didn't exist. That's what all the uncles and grandfathers wanted. Silence.

Staying silent had been especially hard after Richie's father disappeared and stayed that way.

But that doesn't have much sway on this story.

Richie arrived at Scaletta's club in record time. Well, he assumed he had. He didn't have a phone anymore, so there was no way to tell how fast he had gotten there since he didn't wear a watch. People only wear watches nowadays as fashion statements, and no Pimento in New Haven or possibly the world knew anything about what is or isn't fashionable.

Richie locked up his bike around the utility pole a hundred feet or so from the Red Curtain's door. He walked to the front door and froze. The bouncer wasn't there. Now, Richie hadn't ever been inside the Red Curtain. It felt like a forbidden temple. The guy had been there every time in the past to take whatever delivery to the bosses, whether he happened to bring grinders, pizza, or mysterious envelopes of the utmost importance.

Butch had stressed the importance of this delivery and what would happen if it were to be delivered late, so Richie took a calculated risk and entered the club.

The Red Curtain had a reputation among young men. Richie could have gone any time he liked, but he'd been forbidden since the day he became old enough to do so. His mother didn't want him there, and Butch slapped him every time he asked why he couldn't go. Richie once took the slap, looked Butch in the eyes, and asked again why he wasn't allowed.

"*Because I said so*," Butch had replied in a gruff and stern voice. That was Butch's answer to a lot of Richie's problems.

There were no accidents. There were only opportunities. Also, Richie didn't want to get slapped for missing his delivery. With the threat of Butch's thick hand whacking him in the face, he entered the Red Curtain. He had always imagined it full of people with women dancing on the stages to hair metal music. Afternoons must've been slow because the stages were all empty. The only thing reflecting on the mirror-lined walls was a geeky kid wearing second-hand clothes with an envelope in his pocket, and the only sounds were the soft footfalls of his worn-down sneakers.

"Hello?" Richie called. "Is anyone here? It's Richie Pimento! I got something from Butch Barone!"

Silence. Someone had to be there, though. They wouldn't have left the door unlocked otherwise. Maybe the guy at the door had to use the bathroom. No one could stand in one place all day, not even if Vincenzo Scaletta himself had ordered you to do it. It was doubtful he'd be the type of man who'd run a place that allowed the bouncer to pee outside the front door of a suave club like the Red Curtain.

WHO THE FUCK IS ROCKY PHANTASMIC?!

The train of thought plowed forward in Richie's mind as he walked toward the men's room. He heard voices coming from the other side of the swinging door. He pushed it open and peered inside, taking a sharp breath when he saw the figures on the other side.

The bouncer, the guy who usually worked the door, pressed some other guy's head against the sink, allowing a freshly emptied eye socket to bleed. Someone else turned toward Richie—a guy he had called his cousin when he was younger. Johnny Longo let out a breath, tossed his hammer onto the sink, and took a step toward Richie.

"Dammit, Richie," he groaned, walking toward the only way in or out of the men's room. "I really wish you hadn't seen any of this."

Richie turned to run back into the afternoon sun, but his body hit something solid. It would have sent him sprawling on his ass, but a hand gripped the hair on the back of his head to keep him from falling. The face of Vincenzo Scaletta stared into Richie's face with a scowl that would have turned fresh milk sour in a nanosecond.

Most of what Richie knew of the man who gripped him by a handful of his hair had been from stories and pictures, even though he had heard the man referred to as his uncle numerous times when he was a kid. Vincenzo had been a handsome man, but the looks were long gone. The old man holding a young man of twenty-three was still strong, but he looked like a bell pepper left out in the sun.

"I thought I heard a rat squealing in my club," Vincenzo said through his gritted teeth.

Johnny burst from the men's room a fraction of a second later. "Oh." He looked at his boss holding the kid by the back of his head. "Thanks. You saved me from having to chase that damn kid."

"Why the hell isn't Tony at the door?!"

"I needed a hand for a minute," Johnny replied, "and Leo had some pressing matters to take care of."

"The two of you, I swear." Vincenzo let out a long, exasperated sigh. "Guess this friggin' bullshit can't be helped now, and I'll deal with it later. Who is this kid, and what did he see?"

"That's Richie, the Pimento kid. He saw our wayward mule friend with his eyeball punctured. He saw it all."

"I won't say anything!" Richie blurted. "I swear!"

"Sure, you won't," Vincenzo said with a sour breath. "You know, kid, I trusted your father once when he said the same thing. And you know what? I wish I hadn't." He let go of Richie and shoved him, sending him into Johnny's waiting hands.

"Find your cousin Leo and get rid of the kid," Vincenzo ordered. "Dump him in the harbor along with the mule's body, and lock the fucking door if no one can watch it. Lucky it was Pimento's kid and not anyone who'd put up a struggle."

"NO!" Richie exclaimed. "I swear I won't talk! Don't put me in the harbor! Please, Mister Scaletta! I won't even tell Dutch or my mother!"

Vincenzo scoffed. "As I said, your dad said the same thing. Give him my warmest regards when you meet him at the bottom of New Haven Harbor." He nodded toward Johnny and turned away.

Something hit the back of Richie's head, and he dropped to the floor like a sack of rotten tomatoes.

***

"You sure have a way with a story, kid," Dave said. "Has anyone ever told you that?"

Rocky shrugged. "I guess. This is the first time I've told anyone this story."

Dave nodded. "So, they tried to kill you, right? But you came out of the harbor and…got superpowers?"

"That's not exactly how it happened."

"I'm still fuzzy on all that. Are you an actual superhero, or was what I saw that night a fluke brought on by trauma stress?"

"I don't know."

Dave looked into Rocky's earnest face. The kid hero had a way of weaving a tale that made it seem like he somehow knew nothing yet understood everything. He'd left a lot of blank spaces in his convoluted origin story.

"That old boss guy," Dave continued. "What's his name again, Vincenzo Scaletta?"

"What about him?" Rocky asked in return.

"He's dead, right? He can't hurt you anymore."

Rocky gave a single, dry laugh. "Yeah? You'd think so, right?"

"What's that supposed to mean?"

"The night this all happened was also the same night he died. Well, the night he supposedly died anyway."

Dave hesitated before speaking again. After a brief pause, he said, "I'm starting to get the feeling you're leaving plot holes on purpose. It's as if you want me to stumble and fall into one."

"No! I don't even know what that means. I wasn't even done with my story yet. You interrupted and summed up the ending in a single sentence. There's a lot more to it than that."

"Oh? I was trying to spare you from having to tell the part with the attempted murder."

"It wasn't attempted."

"OK. Well, if you want to tell it, I want to hear it. You've sucked me in with this narrative, and now it's time to finish me off with its climax."

Rocky tilted his head as he observed Dave's face.

"Sorry," Dave said. "I'm a writer. Some of us talk like this sometimes. Please continue with your origin story."

"Alright. You've met my cousins already. Leo and Johnny."

Dave nodded. "It wasn't too pleasant, but I know who you're talking about. The two ring leaders of that circus in the street."

"The smaller one is Leo. He's smart. Johnny is stronger and tougher, but he's not as bright. Together, though, they're the brains and the brawn. Perfect villain material. They're not quite on a supervillain level, but they're much worse to deal with than a handful of henchpersons. Everyone calls them the Unmade Men."

"Why? Like they aren't *made men* material like you said they aren't on the level of supervillains."

Rocky shrugged.

"OK," Dave said. "I guess that tracks with what I know of them so far. Go on."

"So, I'm in the pitch blackness of…"

***

…the trunk of Leo's car. Richie squirmed on the plastic tarp that separated his body from the upholstery. It was tight, even though the Cadillac had a spacious trunk. Guess it might've been more comfortable with only one person there.

Richie never learned the name of the man the others had called a mule, and it would remain a mystery to him forever. Whatever the case, he had died sometime between the time his bleeding face got smashed against the bathroom counter and when they hurled his lifeless body into the plastic-lined trunk.

"I gotta get out of here," Richie told himself. It was a good idea, but he could only shimmy and squirm. Leo had tied Richie's hands behind his back and his ankles for good measure. He didn't have much of a chance of escaping, now.

But the car never moved, and Richie heard no voices. He didn't know why they'd left him alive. Maybe Leo and Johnny wanted to torture him for a while. It made him wonder if everything could be an elaborate joke like they'd let him out after a few hours and have a good laugh at little Richie Pimento who pissed himself while trapped in a trunk with the mule.

But he knew deep in his diminishing soul that it wasn't a joke.

Superheroes never get thrown into trunks, Richie thought. *They'd be strong enough to pull their way out and fight their way to freedom. If I had that kind of superpower, I'd be dragging Vincenzo and his Unmade Men to prison by now.*

Richie's dire situation finally forced him to understand the hierarchy of the villainy that had eroded New Haven right under his nose. The subtlety of it all acted as camouflage. They could have dressed it up any way they wanted, but you could see it if you trained yourself and honed your skills. He didn't need to be a delivery boy right now. He needed to be a superhero.

The realization hadn't done much for him, and the hours stretched onward unchecked. After what could've been days, the voices of Leo and Johnny swam through the air, bringing Richie out of a nightmarish sleep. He couldn't understand what they said, but he could hear their talk turn into laughter as they drove to where their prisoner would meet his ultimate fate.

The car stopped, and Richie lurched forward, hitting his head on something solid and metal. The flashes of light in his vision were all he'd seen in the last handful of hours. The trunk opened a few minutes later, and Leo and Johnny's faces appeared between the trunk and the stars.

"Time for school, kid," Leo said with a sickening smile. "Did you do all your homework last night?"

"Don't fuck with him like that," Johnny argued. "It's bad enough we gotta seal him in a bucket and dump him in the ocean. There's no point in making fun of him before he dies."

"Stop it, or you'll make me cry." Leo rolled his eyes and let out an annoyed groan. "You need to learn to relax, you lug nut, and find the little things in life to make you smile. Otherwise, what's the point in living?"

"Come on, Richie." Johnny dragged him out of the trunk. Two rusty metallic barrels had been set near the Cadillac, and a small fishing boat waded in the water off the dock. "This won't be as bad as some of this shit we've done to people. Trust me, you're getting off light here."

"I didn't do anything," Richie whined. Talking made his throat burn, but he powered through it. "This isn't fair."

"Nothing in life or death is, kid." Leo pried the top from one of the barrels with a crowbar. He jumped back a couple of steps. "Whoa! What the hell was in these friggin' drums?"

"I dunno," Johnny replied. "Industrial runoff or some shit."

"Be careful breathin' near that thing. The last thing you need is to suck in a lungful of cancer." Leo looked over at Richie. "Hey, you don't need to worry. Wipe that look of horror off your face. You won't be breathin' it long enough to get cancer."

Richie's feet left the ground as Johnny hefted him into the air and dropped him feet-first into the drum.

"Sorry about this," Johnny said. "I really am."

"Will you stop it with that sad sack shit already?" Leo asked. "I'm startin' to get a hard-on listening to you."

Johnny pushed Richie's head down, and Leo replaced the top, hammering it back in place with a mallet. The reverberation of the blows shook Richie's body, and it took every ounce of willpower to not vomit with the chemical stench around him. Darkness blinded him again as he crouched inside the drum that would soon be his impromptu coffin. The only comfort he had was that it wouldn't last much longer.

Richie couldn't help but listen as Leo and Johnny did the same to the mule's body. They moved him to the boat next, jostling him as they heaved it aboard. He must've been close to the engine since its humming was all he could hear as they took their ride into New Haven harbor.

"Alright," Leo said, getting closer to the drums after the engine noise died down. "We're far enough out. Let's dump these two assholes and get back home. I'm freezin' my tits off out here."

Richie heard the splash as they pushed the mule's drum overboard. If he'd been able to move, he would have been frozen in fear. His body tremored, and his teeth were clenched. This was it. There would be no coming back from the bottom of the harbor.

The pitch-black world tumbled and rocked as the drum hit the water. Richie hit his head on the cold metal, and he thought he'd lose consciousness from the blow. It would have been much easier if he could sleep through his drowning.

Richie thought he heard the sound of the boat leaving him to sink, but that would be impossible, and he assumed his mind had conjured the sound. The drum filled with cold saltwater from tiny rust holes near his feet. His body shook harder and more violently than it had before.

"Save me," Richie said, listening to his echoing voice in his death chamber as his palms hit the lid over his head. "Let me out of this thing!"

But no one would hear his screams. It's not like fish even had ears, and they probably didn't care about human bodies in metal drums sinking to the bottom of their watery dominion.

The water rose to Richie's chin when he heard the alien voice in the darkness. It said, "*Life for life.*"

"What?" Richie asked, spitting out the saltwater that had made it into his mouth. "Who said that? Am I..." The water had risen too high, and he couldn't continue the conversation. After another ten seconds, the water rose high enough to stop him from breathing altogether.

This is it. This is the end.

Water made it into Richie's lungs, and he choked, letting out the last of the air that he'd been saving in there for the final precious seconds of life. His head swam in a sea of fire as his body convulsed in the drum. His body forced his mouth and nose to suck in the water, fighting against every fiber of Richie's being when saltwater rushed into his body instead of lifesaving air. Richie twitched once or twice, and then stopped, floating in chemical-laced seawater in a metal drum at the bottom of New Haven Harbor.

As it turned out, dying is as bad as they say it is. But for Richie, it wasn't quite over with death.

"*Life for life. If these terms are acceptable, release yourself from your prison and walk amongst the living once more, Richard Pimento.*"

Richie opened his eyes. He hadn't died, after all. Not yet. He pushed out with all his might, getting his hands over his head and his feet on the bottom of the drum as it hit the harbor floor with a dull thud. Fresh air replaced the water and chemicals in his lungs, and his muscles burned with renewed intensity. He screamed, sending a stream of bubbles out of his mouth, and with one, final push, the top of the drum came free, and Richie beat his feet, sending his body upward like a missile.

***

"When I burst out of the water," Richie said, "I was reborn. I never learned how to swim, but I could do it well enough to get back to the shore by Lighthouse Point. I don't know how I did it at the time, but my life had been saved.

"I haven't put all the pieces together, and I doubt I ever will. Whatever chemical was in that drum must have altered my DNA, giving me superpowers. I'm super strong and pretty much invulnerable. I can't fly, but I can jump really high and far. I don't shoot lasers from my eyes though, but I'm OK without that power."

"Yeah," Dave remarked. "That one might've been a little too cliché to add to everything else you got. Who was the voice, by the way?"

Rocky raised his left eyebrow. "What voice?"

"The one that said, 'a life for a life' and told you to free yourself from your watery bonds or whatever. Did you ever find out who that was?"

Rocky shrugged. "Maybe I did it. Or it might've been God."

"Maybe." Dave sighed. "You did almost die, after all."

Rocky's face turned into a mask of confusion. "No. I didn't *almost die*. I did die. I thought I made that clear. Do you want me to describe how I drowned in the drum again?"

"No!" Dave held out his hands. "I mean, I got it the first time. I thought you were being colorful and pushed your way out at the last second."

Rocky shook his head. "I died down there, and I was brought back to life by fate and DNA-altering chemicals." He looked at his clenched fists as he drew it upward. "This gift is mine to wield as I see fit, but destiny has given me the purity to use this power to defeat evil whenever I see it." He rose to his feet next, standing in front of Dave with his fists on his hips. "As long as evil dwells in the hearts of man, I will put right the wrongs they do. I am Rocky Phantasmic, and I am a superhero."

Dave sighed. "Great, superhero. Can I assume fighting evil means following your cousins around and stopping them from kidnapping people who are eating fast food in their cars by dog parks?"

Rocky sat down again. "That was a coincidence. I'm not ready to take down the family, but they've already seen my face and know I'm alive again. I knew I should've made a mask to go with the rest of the costume!"

"How long ago was this?"

"It happened just last night. You were there."

"I mean the whole 'getting tossed into New Haven Harbor and being reborn as a superhero' thing."

"I dunno. A few weeks ago. A month maybe."

"You had said that Scaletta died the same night you were tossed in the harbor. So, he's been dead for at least a few weeks by your estimation, right?"

Rocky nodded. "Right."

"And your cousin, Leo I think, said he's giving them orders to kill me. That's the part that's got me scratching my head."

"It could be his son, but they call him Vinny. I don't think he liked sharing the long version of the name with his father." Rocky finished the last of his Demon Energy and tossed the can into the sink from the couch. "I don't think he ever ran any business. He might not have even been in New Haven at all, but I wasn't keeping track of him. When Leo said 'Vincenzo Scaletta', he meant the old man. None of them, the Unmade Men included, don't respect the son much."

None of this makes any sense, Dave thought. *The one he mentioned would've had to have been the son, and Richie couldn't have died and still be walking and talking now. This shit with people after me is weird, but not on this level of weirdness.*

Dave looked into Rocky's serious face.

The superpowers did look impressive against that mob muscle, though. Didn't he take a bullet to the chest without any body armor? He took the club to the face and didn't even flinch, too. Did that happen, or am I imagining details now or dreaming them like the killer flies at the restaurant? Shit. I can't believe I'm buying into this kid and his story.

"Now that you know my origin," Rocky continued, "you see why I brought you here." He stood and looked up to the window. "I know these men, and I can't stand idly by while they put you in a drum of your own. I don't know if you'll be lucky enough to gain superpowers to escape from a cold, watery doom."

"No," Dave agreed. "There's only a slim chance of those exact scenarios playing out the same way twice in one universe."

Rocky turned back to face him. "You will fall under my protection till I deem it's safe for you to be without my aid. If that means I have to defeat my former family and put them behind bars, then so be it. It's time I use my superpowers to face the enemies of my past to make the world safer for those they'd harm in the present…and also the future."

"They saw you, though, and they named you." Dave stood and paced around the tiny basement apartment. "I mean, if this was your home at some point, they'll come looking for you here, right?"

Rocky nodded. "That makes sense."

"Then we have to leave. I have a wife and daughter, and I don't need them knocking on my door and finding them."

Heather and Kayla won't be home for a bit, and I don't have my phone to call them to warn them about any of this. Once I'm a safe distance away, I can figure out how to get in touch and have her take Kayla to her mother's place in Pennsylvania until this nonsense is all sorted.

"I'm going to have to draw them away," Dave continued. He looked at Rocky. "My Uncle Benji has a place up in Maine. He's not using it this time of year, but I know the keycode to get inside. I need to make sure your cousins or whoever is after me knows I'm leaving, though, but I can't let them know where. What I need is time to figure this all out."

"Then I'm going with you," Rocky said, a look of heroic stoicism on his face. "If anyone from my former family is coming, then I'll be there to fight them off."

At least he can tell the authorities all about them.

"OK. That sounds like a halfway decent plan. First things first, though. Where the hell do we start?"

Rocky shrugged.

DANIEL AEGAN

5. THE UNMADE MEN & THE UNDEAD BOSS

"Start again, from the beginning."

Leo rolled his eyes. "As I already told you, he slipped on some wet leaves or some shit. I wasn't paying much attention when he fell on his ass, but that's what happened."

The nurse had exercised patience, but it wouldn't be infinite. He let out a long, drawn-out, overly dramatic sigh and pushed his thick glasses up to massage the bridge of his nose. When he was done, he pushed his black bangs away from his eyes and gave Leo a gaze that said, *It's been a long night, asshole.*

"What else do you want me to say?" Leo asked. "The clumsy gagootz slipped on some friggin' leaves and fell over. Shit happens. The city will be lucky if he doesn't sue."

"Your friend will be lucky if he can walk right again without a cane for the rest of his life," the nurse said. "What about your other friend with the cracked ribs and the dislocated shoulder?"

Leo shrugged. "Mikey tripped tryin' to help get Gino off the ground. The whole thing looked like some circus clown shit."

"And you're sure there's nothing more to these injuries? They're pretty severe for people who *just slipped*."

"What else do you want me to say? Some people are more fragile than others."

WHO THE FUCK IS ROCKY PHANTASMIC?!

The nurse wrote down the information, offering another annoyed sigh while he jotted down the story of how Mikey and Gino wound up in the hospital. Hell, it was way more believable than what really happened. How was Leo supposed to tell a nurse that a son of a snitch you dropped in New Haven Harbor had returned from the dead with superpowers to beat up two of the toughest guys he knew like it was nothing?

"Are you going to wait for them here?" the nurse asked.

Leo shook his head. "Nah. I don't got the time to babysit those two. They're grown men. They can call whoever they want when they're all patched up and ready to go home."

"You seem like a good friend."

You got a shitty fuckin' mouth for a kid makin' insinuations about how Mikey and Gino got hurt, Leo thought. Aloud, he said, "Thanks. I appreciate your candor." He forced a toothy smile, got up, and followed the signs to the exit.

"Friggin' asshole nurse," he muttered, shoving open the exit door, letting the cold morning wind hit him in the face. It felt good having some air around him not surrounded by germs. He spotted Johnny, parked next to the curb shoving a donut in his mouth.

"How'd it go?" Johnny asked through a mouthful of jelly and pastry as Leo got into the sedan and settled into the passenger's seat. "They OK?"

"No, they aren't OK, you idiot. Gino's gonna need a cane to get around, and Mikey's gonna be laid up with a busted shoulder and cracked ribs. Richie did a number on them both. What do you got here? I'm starvin'." Leo grabbed the white box of donuts from the dashboard and pulled out an éclair, shoving half of it into his mouth.

"I got you a coffee too," Johnny said. "Light and sweet. Should still be hot."

"Thanks." Leo took off the top and took a swig. "How's the caddy?"

"Caddy's fucked. My guy can fix it, but he said parts are hard to come by. Either way, he's got it locked up for now in case anyone wants to know what happened to it."

"Friggin' Richie Pimento." Leo ate the other half of his éclair without bothering to savor it. "What the hell is he doing alive, let alone acting like friggin' Superman."

Johnny didn't have an answer, which wasn't at all surprising. Instead of anything constructive, he stated the obvious by saying, "We need to tell Vincenzo about this."

Leo glowered. "Yeah, I know we do. I'm not looking forward to that particular conversation, though. Vincenzo ain't one for bad news. Shit. Start drivin'. The sooner we get this over with, the better."

Johnny put the car into drive and headed for the Red Curtain Club. Leo watched New Haven in the early morning from the window. He knew Vincenzo would already know they fucked up. They should have been back with the writer hours ago, yet here they were, annoyed and empty-handed with two fewer men on top of it all. If they were lucky, the big boss man wouldn't be in a 'shoot the messenger' kind of mood. Besides, there was still one tiny saving grace, and Johnny decided to vocalize it for both of them.

"What's he gonna think about Rocky... I mean Richie bein' alive?"

Leo scoffed. "Doesn't matter what he thinks about it, Johnny. He wants the writer, and we didn't get him. The reasoning as to why isn't going to impress him much."

"But...we killed him, right? There's no way he could've gotten out of that drum and survived. I saw him get shot, too. Damn kid took a bullet to the chest and walked away like it was a mosquito bite or something."

"Shut up and drive. I don't want to think about it right now."

Johnny nodded and turned down East Street. Leo wished for a longer drive to sort the thoughts swirling in his mind, but the red bricks of their clubhouse came into view before he could even figure out where to start. Everything had gotten so fucked up ever since he and Johnny kicked a metal drum containing a kid from the neighborhood into the harbor. Maybe if they hadn't done it, things would've gone differently now.

Leo almost laughed at his thoughts. Richie Pimento returning as a thrift shop superhero named Rocky Phantasmic might not have been the weirdest shit that's ever happened. At least it would be in the top five.

Johnny parked the car in their usual spot. He turned and looked toward Leo. Even with all his muscles, he'd always been a follower. He wasn't quite spineless, but he might've been born with only one ball. It was one of several reasons the pair of them had never been considered *made men*.

Although, things could change in the right light.

"Come on, Johnny," Leo said, opening the door and stepping into the parking lot. "We don't want to leave the big man waiting."

Leo fixed his jacket as he made his way to the back entrance of the Red Curtain, where Vincenzo waited for them to return with the writer.

WHO THE FUCK IS ROCKY PHANTASMIC?!

He used his key and unlocked the door, hesitating for only a moment. He closed his eyes and pushed it open, walking the back halls of the club.

Johnny hit the light switch as he entered behind Leo, illuminating the hall with flickering fluorescent light. It led to the main stage area, which remained dark during the daytime hours. The stages were devoid of *talent*, but that would all change when The Red Curtain opened for business later that evening. The smell of spilled booze and old sweat from the night before lingered in the air, and an old Dean Martin tune played instead of the music the girls and their patrons enjoyed while the action happened. Only one man sat in the darkened room, smoking a cigar, nodding to the crooning of The King of Cool.

"You're late, boys," Vincenzo said without bothering to turn to look at them. "Where's the writer?"

"That's the problem, boss," Leo replied, lowering his head. "He got away from us."

Vincenzo groaned as he got up from his seat. "Where are Mikey and Gino? Did they stop for espresso on the way?"

"They're in the hospital. Gino got his back busted up pretty bad, and Mikey dislocated his shoulder."

Vincenzo glared. "What aren't you telling me?" His eyes darted to the left, landing on Johnny. "What happened?"

"We got jumped trying to get the writer," Johnny replied.

"Who the hell had the balls to jump the four of you?"

"It was Rocky Phantasmic."

Vincenzo stared with his eyes narrowed. "Rocky Phantasmic? Who the fuck is that?"

"It's Richie Pimento," Leo replied.

Vincenzo's gaze landed on Leo once more. "Richie Pimento? I thought the two of you offed that son of a rat-fuck."

"We did! We dropped him in the harbor the night…the night…"

Vincenzo took a step forward. He was so close Leo could smell the cigar smoke and decay on his breath.

"The night of what?" he asked. "Say it."

"The night you died, boss. We dumped him in the drink the same night you died, and now he's running around as strong as an ox, saying he's a friggin' superhero named Rocky Phantasmic."

Vincenzo took a long breath, and Leo thought for sure he was about to fly off the handle and berate them as usual. To his surprise, though, he laughed.

DANIEL AEGAN

***

The drum splashed into the harbor and sunk beneath the waves. Johnny watched the water as the rusted metal disappeared.

"We don't know if that kid would've talked," he said, watching the bubbles break the water's surface.

"What?" Leo asked looking at Johnny. "You still blabbin' about that? The kid's pop was a snitch. That type of shit runs in the blood. It was the boss's call, and I'm not about to question the boss."

"Me neither." Johnny looked away from the water and made his way back to the front of the boat. "I'm just sayin' is all."

Leo followed. "It's business, and this is the business we've chosen. Don't forget that."

"I won't." Johnny brought the boat back to life and steered it back toward its dock. He didn't say anything else on the subject of Richie Pimento. It wouldn't matter either way. It didn't help matters to speak about the dead, especially when you were the one of the pair who pushed his drum into the harbor to join all the others down there. Some things were meant to be left unspoken, and that went double for things that could later become incriminating.

They got back into the car and drove past the security guard's kiosk. Johnny slowed down when he waved to them.

"You two doing some stargazing?" the security guard asked.

"Yeah," Johnny replied. "We saw all the dippers tonight." He passed over a hundred-dollar bill. "Here. Get the wife something nice to make up for all these overnight shifts."

"Thanks." The money disappeared into his pocket a second later. "It's not a bad job. Funny thing, though. Damn security system is busted, and it don't record everything right. Anyway, have a good night, fellas."

Johnny nodded and drove away.

"He's good people," Leo said, "and good people know how to look the other way and keep their damn mouths shut."

"Right," Johnny agreed. He drove, pulling into the parking lot of Red Curtain where Leo's car waited for him. "You headin' home for the night?"

Leo wasn't paying attention. "It's too late for this many cars to be here. Something's goin' down."

WHO THE FUCK IS ROCKY PHANTASMIC?!

Johnny looked around the lot as he pulled closer. The club should have closed an hour and a half ago, but the lot was still full. The cars didn't belong to random patrons, though. They belonged to other members of Vincenzo Scaletta's family and associates.

"We should go inside and find out what's what," Leo said, climbing out of the car. Johnny followed. He hoped they'd missed a private function for one of the guys, but the weight in his gut told him otherwise. It knew as well as Johnny's brain that Leo's first instinct had been right. Something bad had gone down.

The Red Curtain Club was quiet. The older members of the family sat around the bar, speaking in hushed tones. A bottle of aged scotch sat between them.

"Hey," Leo said, approaching the group of his elders. "what's going on? Everything OK?"

"No," Tony Bianchi replied. He was a heavy man with a head of gray hair. He looked like he had been dragged out of bed to be out of the house. "Vincenzo's gone."

"Gone?" Johnny asked, stepping next to Leo. "Where'd he go?"

"He died, numb-nuts!" Tony snapped. "You don't think he up and went to Hawaii, do you?"

"Please excuse my cousin," Leo interjected. "This is just a little shocking. We were with Vincenzo earlier, and he seemed fine then. It's a little unbelievable that he's passed is all."

Johnny should've let Leo do all the talking. He'd always been better at putting words together for the both of them.

Tony nodded in Leo's direction.

"How'd it happen?" Leo asked.

"He had a heart attack right here in the club," Tony explained. "One minute he's walkin' around with a drink and a cigar, and the next he's on the ground. The only blessing of the whole thing is that he didn't suffer." He picked up his glass and held it up. "To Vincenzo!"

"To Vincenzo!" the others echoed, downing their drinks.

***

The days following the death of Vincenzo Scaletta came like a whirlwind, leaving nothing good in its wake. Vinny, the son, returned to New Haven to oversee his father's funeral arrangements along with his stepmother, Vincenzo's widow.

"This is a damn shame," Leo remarked in the funeral home with his fellow enforcers standing around in a circle. "I heard from Rocco that he left no instructions on how we should carry on without him in charge, and Vinny sure as shit ain't pickin' up that torch."

Johnny nodded. He didn't have the brain to figure out the politics of *the thing* they all had in common. He didn't know how bosses were chosen, and he didn't have the faintest notion of how they were supposed to choose.

"He liked you two guys," Gino said, giving Leo and Johnny a nod. "He always said you were dependable. It's a pity he never put you guys forward to become made men."

Leo scoffed and looked away. "Is that a joke? Made men for what, this empire of rat turds we've built in New Haven? Watch what happens now that Vincenzo's gone. All his buddies are going to try to claw their way to the top and tear through everything they've built like bloody snot through a wet tissue."

"Jesus, Leo!" Gino groaned. "Do me a favor and never write poetry."

"Look at us though!" Leo continued, turning to look around the room. "Most of Vincenzo's closest associates were as old as he was. Which one is gonna drop next, and who's going to have their hands in their pockets when the body drops? That's why he never named anyone he'd want to be his successor. He knew without him this all goes to shit."

"That's not true," Johnny argued.

Leo looked at him and tsked. "Yeah? How so? Can you explain to me how we keep this shit going without anyone with the balls to take over a leadership role?"

"Give him a break!" Mikey snapped. "This thing of ours ain't over. Someone will take the reins and keep it going. They have to."

"Right." Leo turned to leave, but he returned a few seconds later. "Not for nothin', but maybe these golden oldies need to let us with young blood still in our veins have a shot at runnin' shit. Most of these guys can't even send a text message without askin' their grandkids how to do it. We'll take care of them like we always have, but the future don't belong to them. It belongs to us."

"That's dangerous shit you're sayin'," Gino said, shaking his head. "Be careful who hears that."

Leo waved a hand. "What am I sayin'? I'm in mournin' over here. It's one of the five stages of friggin' grief, I'm sure. Fuck it. I'm goin' out for a smoke."

Johnny watched Leo leave, fighting the urge to follow him. They'd spent so much time together at Vincenzo's behest that he couldn't watch him walk away without following. They'd been paired together for so long that it felt like a marriage of sorts—not that Johnny would ever say that aloud, even if he could speak as eloquently as the others. Speaking like that would start rumors that ended in dark parking lots.

"Look out," Gino said, motioning toward the other side of the funeral hall. "Here comes trouble in an ugly fuckin' suit."

Vinny the younger came toward the small group, flashing a handsome smile on his chiseled face. Even in the throes of being middle-aged, he kept that boyish charm that could remain unspoken and still make a statement. Johnny didn't find his black and navy suit ugly, but he'd never been one for fashion. His mother had even picked out his suit for the funeral.

"Good evening, boys," Vinny said, joining the circle. "I'm glad to see you still like to stand in these little cliques during funerals."

"We were just talkin'," Gino replied. "Ain't nothin' wrong with it."

Vinny laughed. "I'm not saying there is. I haven't seen you guys in so long, and here you are. It's like you've never changed."

"I'm sorry for your loss, Vin," Johnny said, extending a hand. "Your father was a great man. We're all at a loss without him."

"Thanks, Johnny. I'm sure he'd appreciate the turmoil the business will fall into without him to shove it along."

"Oh," Leo said, rejoining the group. "He was expressing his grief for your father's death. We're all feeling it, Vinny. There's no need to get all uppity about it."

Vinny turned toward Leo. "Who's getting uppity?"

Leo met Vinny's gaze. After a moment of sucking air through his teeth, he said, "I'm sorry too. It's a hard loss when someone who meant so much to us passes."

"That's a good line. Did you get it from a Hallmark card, or was it something you saw in a cartoon?"

"This is your pop's funeral. I know you never wanted to be part of this thing he helped build here in New Haven, but that's no reason to extend your disrespect for those of us who stayed and helped him keep it running all these years."

"Walk away," Gino urged, putting a hand on Leo's shoulder.

Leo swatted Gino's hand away. "Fuck it. My own pop was a piece of shit who wouldn't give me or my ma the time of day. Vincenzo, on the other hand, helped us out when my old man skipped town for good. Vincenzo was more a father to me than the man who claimed to sire me had ever been. We're family, Vinny. All of us here owe a lot to that man, despite what you think of him and this business of ours. You have my respect as the son of a great man and a role model, but that's as far as it goes."

With that, Leo left again. This time, he didn't return.

"Great," Vinny said. "I can't believe I came all the way back here for this bullshit." With that, he left as well, mingling with the old men his father counted as friends.

"Did all that happen?" Mikey whispered. "I mean with Leo and the old man?"

"Nah," Gino replied. "His father's down in Boca Raton enjoyin' his retirement. I'd say seventy percent of that story of his was made up on the spot to make Vinny feel like a shit. Leo's good at layin' it on thick like that. It's why the boss liked him so much."

***

"Shit's fallin' apart faster than we can glue it back together," Leo said as he walked toward The Red Curtain's entrance at nine in the morning two weeks after Vincenzo Scaletta's funeral. "I've been able to keep my own ventures runnin', but so many guys are lookin' for guidance right now."

"And the old guys are letting it all fall around them," Johnny finished. "I heard the business is going to wind up getting split among four of five guys. No boss anymore. *Bosses*."

Leo scoffed at that notion. "Might as well shut it down. The moment there's a squabblin'—like these ancient motherfuckers do more than they shit—there's going to be a battle on the streets while they kick back and watch it unravel. The only one able to keep it all together was…"

"Vincenzo!"

Johnny had stopped in his tracks before the name escaped his lips. Leo followed his gaze and saw what he had. Vincenzo Scaletta stood in front of them wearing the suit he'd worn in his casket, though now it looked to be caked with dirt and mud. He stared back at them like they were the ones out of place.

"Well?" Vincenzo asked. "They didn't bury me with my keys, so one of you is going to have to let me into my club."

"Right away boss," Johnny replied, rushing forward. He unlocked the door and held it open, letting Vincenzo pass. Leo followed, breathing in the mingling scents of dirt and decay.

"Thanks," Vincenzo muttered, walking through the empty club. "I need to use the little boy's room. Don't go anywhere."

Leo waited by the bar, watching as their deceased boss walked into the men's room like he needed to take a normal morning dump. "What the fuck is he doin' here?!"

Johnny shrugged. "Takin' a shit?"

"He's dead, Johnny! I saw him in his casket! He's dead, and he was buried. If this is some sick fuckin' joke, I'm going to strangle whoever's behind it!"

Johnny didn't reply. All he did was grab a bottle of Sambuca, take a swig, and slide it across the bar toward Leo.

"It's nine in the morning."

"Yeah?" Johnny asked. "And Vincenzo Scaletta's supposed to be dead. I think we need it to deal with this shit."

Johnny didn't use this kind of critical thinking often, so Leo decided to give him the benefit of the doubt. He grabbed the bottle, took a swig, and winced at the burning in his throat.

"What do we do now?" Leo asked, seeking advice from Johnny for the first time ever.

"Wait for him to finish in the bathroom," Johnny replied with another shrug. "We can find out how he's not dead after."

Leo nodded. "Right. We wait and find out how our dead boss became our undead boss. Sounds like a reasonable thing to do."

They waited in silence. After a half hour, Leo began to believe he'd hallucinated the whole thing. He looked toward Johnny, who watched the men's room door, confirming at least that they'd shared the vision.

"Dead men don't walk to their old clubs," Leo said, breaking the silence. "They don't."

Johnny nodded. "Vincenzo isn't dead. You said it yourself. He's undead."

Leo took another swig of sambuca. "*Undead*. I think you've stayed up watching too many old horror movies. They've fried your friggin' brain, Johnny."

Vincenzo didn't emerge for another forty-five minutes. He had cleaned his face and hair in the sink, but his clothes were still filthy. He walked up to the bar and grabbed the bottle between his two enforcers, taking a swig of his own.

"Sorry about the wait, gentlemen," he said, putting the bottle back on the bar. "I know you haven't had to shit out a couple of gallons of embalming fluid, but I'll spare you the details. All I'll say is that it is not a pleasant experience."

"Is it really you?" Johnny asked.

"Of course, it's me!" Vincenzo snapped. "Who the hell else would it be?"

"But you died," Leo said. "I mean, it looked like you did anyway.

"Yeah, well…" Vincenzo let out a sigh and sat on one of the barstools. "You know there's a lot of weird shit that happens in this world of ours. It happens all the time, but we choose to ignore it and carry on with our lives like it doesn't happen."

Johnny watched with a blank expression on his face. "I don't understand."

Vincenzo looked toward him, but another scolding didn't come. He sighed and said, "I woke up in blackness, and I thought I'd gone blind. It took me a few minutes to realize that I was in a wooden box buried under six feet of dirt. Whoever bought that damn coffin hadn't skimped on it, either. I punched and clawed and ripped at it till it busted. Then I climbed my way through six feet of busted casket and dirt. Once I was breathing the free air again, I walked back here with the filth of the earth all over me."

Leo and Johnny were both silent as Vincenzo finished his short tale. He looked at them each in turn and let out a sigh.

"You two have to do something for me," he said, "no questions asked. Capeesh? Actually, it might turn out a few somethings."

"Anything," Leo said. "You know we'd do anything for you, boss."

"There's this writer mook who hangs out in New Haven named David Bryant. I need you to find him and bring him to me alive. Grab Gino and Mikey if they're around, but don't tell them I'm back. You can tell them it's my order, but let them assume I gave it to you when I was still alive." Vincenzo looked at Leo and then at Johnny and let out a long sigh. "I'm glad it was you two here today who found me. I don't know if any of the others are ready for something like this. Not yet."

Leo nodded. "Alright. David Bryant, the writer. We should be able to get him back here no problem."

"Good," Vincenzo looked toward the back room. "I should have a clean suit here unless someone's ransacked my shit since I've been gone."

"No one's touched anything," Johnny confirmed.

"OK then. I'll be here haunting the club till I can figure out how to get back into the world of the living. It might be fun to scare a few years of life off a few of my old pals if they come back there to do business. Try to get me a car at night. I want to visit my mistress and see if this zombie pecker of mine is still good for something. After that, I'll see to getting back into the swing of things."

Vincenzo cackled and stood. He turned to look at Leo and Johnny once more, giving them a nod of approval.

"You're both good boys. Get that friggin' writer, bring him back here alive and as unharmed as possible, and let me know if you run into any hiccups."

"Alright, boss," Leo said. "We'll let you know if we run into any problems."

***

Leo waited for Vincenzo to stop laughing at the problem they had encountered when attempting to kidnap the writer.

"Richie Pimento is calling himself Rocky Phantasmic now," Vincenzo mused, putting his cigar back in his mouth and taking another pull of thick smoke. "*Life for life*. Guess I know what that means now."

"Listen, boss," Leo said. "I don't know how to ask this since you didn't want us asking questions about this job you gave us, but what the hell is up with you and Richie not bein' dead? Is it the end of days or something?"

Vincenzo sighed. "I didn't want to tell you everything. I thought the less you knew the better, but I see now that I'll need to come clean if I expect you to help, especially after this latest development."

"Did you get superpowers too?" Johnny asked.

Vincenzo gave Johnny one of his old stink eyes before answering. "Nothing like that. I was able to crawl my way out of my own grave plot, but I can't do what you described that damn kid doin'. If I could, I wouldn't have had to ask the two of you to do my dirty work."

"That's what I'd like to know about," Leo said. "What's so important about this writer, and why is Richie back from the dead defending him?"

"The night I died I experienced more pain than I'd ever felt in my entire life, and it was all focused on a single, solitary second. My heart burst. At least it felt like it did. That wasn't the end, though. There's darkness after death. Darkness and suffering. I heard others crying out for help, and I knew I'd be one of them soon, but I never made it to Hell. I was offered an alternative.

"A voice came to me, offering me a return to the land of the living as an undying vessel of theirs. I'd have the freedom to do as I choose, but I'd have to comply with whatever was asked of me. I found the deal fair enough, as I didn't feel ready to die in the first place. Then again, who ever feels that way? So, I accepted the deal, with the fine print that there'd be a life for a life. I didn't know what that last part meant till you mentioned the Pimento kid had come back as well."

"I don't get it," Johnny said.

Leo rolled his eyes. "There's a big surprise."

"It's the cosmic deal working itself out," Vincenzo explained. "The one who allowed me to come back couldn't bring only me back. He had to bring back my opposite as well. Richie Pimento returned as this Rocky Phantasmic character. Maybe it's that, or maybe it's that he was the last guy I had put to death. That's the best I can figure it, anyway."

"At least that stupid 'Phantasmic' name makes sense," Leo added. "What about this David Bryant character? Where does he fit into all this magical nonsense?"

Vincenzo shrugged. "I didn't ask. All I know is that He Who Walks Above wants him."

"He who what?"

"Oh, that's who brought me back. He's some demon on a level with the literal devil if I had to guess. Whatever he is, he wants the writer, and he wants him alive. If I want to remain walking among the living, He Who Walks Above needs David Bryant."

Leo nodded. "OK, boss. I don't know what to make of all that, but I didn't know what I'd expected by asking my undead boss how he came to return from the dead."

"Undead boss?" Vincenzo asked. He mused on it for a moment and laughed again. "I kind of like that title. Oh, I almost forgot. I called in a favor from a friend in the old country. Pick him up from the airport at one before you go looking. I wasn't sure he'd come in handy, but it's a good thing I had the wherewithal to make the call."

"Who'd you call?" Johnny asked.

"They call him Duro Assassino," Vincenzo replied. "It means the hard assassin."

"Why do they call him that?" Johnny asked.

"Because he gets a rock-hard erection when he kills. I thought the stories about him were fake when I heard them, but I began to think otherwise after my ordeal with life, death, and rebirth. If Rocky Phantasmic wants to be a superhero, then we can give him a friggin' supervillain for his troubles."

"I'm lost again," Johnny said.

"For once, I'm there with you," Leo added. "I don't even know how we're supposed to find the damn writer and that little wannabe superhero rat-fuck. We don't know where they went, and we have zero leads."

Vincenzo laughed. "Don't worry, fellas. All will be made clear soon enough, and I have a way for you to find where you need to go. Get Duro, kill Rocky Phantasmic, and bring the writer to me. I'll keep my ears sharp and to the ground. With luck, we won't have to deal with any more of these fucking wild cards getting in our way."

6. THE COMEDIAN'S TALE: A HANGOVER, SOME PIZZA, & A PSYCHIC

Cliff opened his eyes and sat up in his hotel room bed. He had slept through all of the morning and a chunk of the afternoon, but it didn't surprise him. He often slept like an unemployed teenager while working on the road. There wasn't much daytime work for a comedian on his level. But that's not what was on Cliff's mind.

His sleep had been plagued with nightmares, but he had suffered through them without waking. Reality bled with them, and he couldn't figure out what had happened the night before and what hadn't. Of course, the hangover didn't help.

"Those kids," Cliff said, sitting atop the sweat-covered sheets. He had left the heater on high all night, and the room felt like a rainforest prison cell. "They're…"

The image of the metal trashcans and the mutilated bodies inside came back to him. If it were a dream, it didn't feel like one. The dead eyes staring back at him didn't feel like something his mind would create to torment him in his sleep.

"Someone drugged me at the club, slipped me a mickey or whatever. That's it. It has to be."

That had been his theory last night after his eventful walk after his show. That would account for the nightmares, but…

Why can't I remember them now?

As bad as the dreams had been, Cliff tried to focus on them. He couldn't conjure up the images that had played out in his mind's eye while he slept. It was probably a godsend, but he still remembered the hobo priest, the garbagemen, and the badass kids who ended up in the trashcans.

There was no helping it. Cliff would believe what he believed until he could put it out of his mind and he pissed whatever drugs he'd been slipped out of his system. Time healed all wounds or some shit like that.

Cliff got to his feet and made his way to the shower. He had slept in nothing but his socks, and he peeled them off on the carpet so he wouldn't have to bend over and turn the lingering hangover into a fit of vertigo that would knock him on his ass. He turned the shower on cold, ignoring his body's fight or flight response when the icy water hit his skin.

As the frigid water shocked Cliff's system into doing whatever it was that he hoped it would do, he thought of who was to blame for everything that had happened the night before.

Dave Bryant.

The damn writer hadn't shown up at the show, causing Cliff to stay there long enough to get a little too tipsy. He might not have ingested whatever drug had fucked with his brain either if the meeting about the new show idea had gone off without a hitch. He considered sending a nice 'fuck you' text after his shower, but he needed the show regardless. He also needed something to keep his 'getting back to my roots' tour from turning into a permanent thing, but he'd have to do it without Dave Bryant's big idea.

Cliff's days of being a twenty-something upstart in the world of standup comedy were long gone. He had operated under the assumption that the writing and acting gigs would keep him employed until he had a big enough nut to retire. But shit only pans out that way for a select few lucky enough to receive that grace, and there was no such thing as cancel culture back when Cliff Quentin entered the comedy world like a dynamo laced with cocaine.

Cliff finished showering and brushed his teeth even though doing it made him feel like puking. He grabbed his phone, which only had five percent battery left since he'd forgotten to charge it before passing out. He'd received zero messages. Dave didn't even think it fitting to offer an apology or an excuse for missing the show and blowing off their meeting.

"Someone better have died," he said, putting the phone in his pocket. He made a mental note to charge it again after he got some lunch. He had to call his agent to see where he'd be heading next. The next show the following week would be in Boston, but he needed to get some smaller ones in the area to fill the time between them. If he didn't work, then he wouldn't make any money. That's how comedy and capitalism work.

One thing that would help, however, would be a greasy lunch and lots of caffeine. Cliff followed that train of thought down State Street to a restaurant called Butch's Pizzeria. They didn't have any customers, adding to the growing list of miracles. He walked up to the counter and eyed a picture in a frame of a young man with a mess of dark hair, chubby cheeks, and a wide grin. A piece of cardboard had been taped under it that read 'RICHIE WORKED HERE'.

"Goddam tragedy," a gruff man in a white tee shirt and an apron that hadn't had a good day in a long time. "Kid left here on a delivery one day and never returned."

Cliff nodded and looked at Richie's somber face. "I hope he comes back someday."

The man scoffed. "What do you need?"

"Give me a small pizza with the works and a bottle of Coke."

"Alright. I'll get the pie right out. You can get your Coke from the cooler over yonder."

"Thanks." Cliff got his bottle and found an empty table. He brought his soon-to-be-dead phone back out of his pocket and fired off a text to Dave that read, "Where the hell were you last night?" He stared at this phone for a minute before adding, "I'm still in New Haven for the day. Get back to me ASAP, and maybe we can still meet up."

"Unless you also wound up on a delivery you'll never return from," Cliff added, muttering aloud to himself. "Goddam tragedy." He looked over his shoulder to make sure the pizzeria's proprietor didn't hear his off-color comment.

Cliff grabbed his charger from his pocket and plugged it into the wall outlet under his table, thanking whatever deity had offered yet another miracle to aid him through his hungover afternoon. He placed it on the edge of the table and let it charge while he waited for Dave to return the text. The phone didn't buzz at all.

"Fuckin' nerd ghosted me," Cliff muttered, shaking his head. It figured. The moment a new opportunity arose, the universe saw fit to take it away. No, not the universe. Dave Fucking Bryant.

I need to get the fuck out of New Haven.

The pizza came ten minutes later, and the need to remove himself from New Haven abated for a little while. Everything else might've sucked at that moment in time, but the pizza tasted pretty fucking fantastic. Cliff ate the entire small pie while his greedy stomach gurgled through the meal.

Once it had been devoured, Cliff's phone finally buzzed. He tilted his head, expecting to see that it was Dave ready to apologize for his absence the night before. It wasn't the writer, though.

"Hey, Randy," Cliff said after accepting the call.

"Cliff, my man!" Randy exclaimed. "Glad I could catch you. How are you doing today?"

"Can't complain aside from a hangover from last night's show and that writer asshole ditching me. What's up?"

"Have you been on social media at all today?"

Cliff swore under his breath. "No. I haven't charged my phone, so I've been trying to not use it. What have I missed?"

"Did you ask about coal miners and mocked everyone who canceled you over a racist and misogynistic joke?"

Cliff looked up at the ceiling and let out a loud groan. "That's not what happened. You didn't see these people, Randy. They were staring at me with this look in their eyes. I wasn't going to get away without addressing it, so I asked if there were any coal miners in the audience and did a little tirade about cancel culture. So what? It was way tamer than the shit on my podcast, and I delivered it well enough to appease them. When I was done, they applauded me."

"Well, that's not what they're reporting."

"Everyone's a fucking paparazzo now. The sentient dildos bitching about what I said at the show probably weren't even there for fuck's sake."

"Speaking of the paparazzi, did you smash someone's phone for taking a picture of you? You're supposed to be on an apology tour, and this isn't how you apologize. This is how you cement your guilt in the court of public opinion!"

"I didn't smash anyone's phone! I threw it on a roof. Huge difference."

"Not from where I'm sitting."

"Where's that, Randy, the toilet?"

A wry chuckled came from the other end of the call. "You know me so well, Quentin."

"I gotta go. I can't deal with this shit right now."

"Wait! There's another reason I'm calling. You got another gig in the area."

"What? Between here and Boston during the week?"

That figured. As much as Cliff had wanted to book as many shows as possible, he'd been looking forward to staying with his family and meeting up with some friends in his old stomping grounds outside Boston. On the other hand, he couldn't turn down the work. Despite the anti-buzz he'd gotten on social media, the show at Deuce's Wild had gone as well as he could've hoped to get his tour moving. People were talking about him again, and that had to be worth something to someone.

"There's a bar in Easthampton, Mass looking for an MC for an open mic night on Wednesday," Randy explained. "I already told them you'd do it."

"An open mic night? Really, Randy? Jesus."

"Hey, you're the one who said you need to get back to your roots to make everything right again! I'm trusting you here. I don't make money unless you make money, and now you're telling me that writer with the big-ass show idea is blowing you off. Not good, my dude."

"Alright, you goddam drama queen. What do I have to do for this open mic thing?"

"Show up, do a short set of your material, and add some jokes between the bombing local morons who think all they have to do is tell jokes on stage to be a standup. That's all. I'd steer clear of the cancel culture rants this time around."

"Gee, thanks. I'll try that tactic. Anything else?"

"Nothing else on the radar for now, but I'll keep looking. I'll text you the information for the open mic night. In the meantime, I'll try to find some posts about last night's show that aren't negative and amplify them from our account. Keep chopping away at those roots."

"That's not what I'm supposed to be doing with my roots, but thanks. I'll see you, Randy."

The sound of a toilet flushing preceded Randy's, "See you, pal."

Cliff ended the call with a groan and put his phone down. The temptation to call Dave to yell at him returned since the shitty open mic night felt like his fault as well, but he stopped himself. What good would come of any of it anyway? He had to stop burning bridges if he wanted to get his career back on the right track.

"Fine," Cliff muttered, shoving his phone in his pocket, coiling up the charger wire to go with it, and getting up from his seat. "Guess I'm on my own as usual."

WHO THE FUCK IS ROCKY PHANTASMIC?!

***

The time to move on had arrived. There's no helping it when it comes. Cliff could've waited all day and stayed an extra night if he had wanted, but it wasn't meant to be. The only thing that could've kept him there was a text or call from Dave with a good excuse as to why he blew off their meeting, but he knew better than to expect one. Cold feet had won out over the chance to do something great as it did with cowards, and now Dave's big opportunity to be something more than a simple indie writer was leaving New Haven and heading north to Massachusetts.

But not quite yet.

Cliff hadn't realized it when he parked his car a couple of blocks from his hotel, but he had done so right outside a psychic's place of business. He felt like a moth with a neon fetish as the sign blinked and buzzed advertising, "WALK-INS WELCOME" in glowing red letters. He blinked a few times as he considered it. It had been a while since he'd done anything like it. The last time had been with his ex-girlfriend who believed in all that occult shit. They'd been in Salem right before Halloween the year before, and the reading seemed accurate enough. If only the psychic could have predicted how badly the coal miner joke would go over…

"What the fuck," Cliff said to himself, relocking his car and walking toward the psychic's porch. The psychic had made their business out of the first floor of a multifamily home. A wooden sign nailed to the wall instructed him to ring the doorbell for service, so he did so, standing at the door like he was about to ask if a friend could come out and play.

Cliff expected an old woman with a headscarf and a huge wart on her nose to answer the door, so seeing the younger psychic surprised him. Their hair had been cut short and dark red, and they wore an orange and brown sweater. They didn't have much makeup on, only some black eyeliner that put Cliff's mind at some Cleopatra cosplay.

"Oh," Cliff said, rubbing the back of his neck. "Hi."

"What's wrong?" the psychic asked. "You seemed surprised someone came to the door after you rang the bell."

"I thought…never mind."

The psychic cocked an eyebrow. "Are you here for a reading, or is there something else you need? I'm all set on religion if that's why you've come."

Cliff laughed. "You're the psychic. Shouldn't you already know why I'm here?"

"If I had a dollar for every time I heard that one, I wouldn't have to do any actual readings. Come inside and we can get started with whatever it is that's bothering you."

"Now you know something's bothering me," Cliff said, entering the home and taking off his jacket. He hung it on a hook by the door. "I guess you've proven your point."

The psychic sat at a round table, lit a candle, and placed it at the center. "If you've come with a closed mind, you're going to leave disappointed. I don't do parlor tricks, and this isn't open mic night. If you've come to ridicule, I suggest you do it elsewhere."

"I'm actually a comedian." Cliff pulled out the chair and sat across from the psychic. "My road agent scheduled me for an open mic night in a few days. Weird, right?"

The psychic smirked. "Now you've witnessed my power, comedian. We can start by you telling me what you expected when you rang my doorbell since you didn't make an appointment."

"I happened to be in front of your place. To be honest, I expected an old lady to come to the door, not a young one."

The psychic cleared their throat and tapped a round button on their shirt with black letters on a solid, yellow background that read, 'THEY/THEM'.

"Oh. Sorry."

The psychic shrugged. "No biggie. Now you know. My name is Toni, by the way, with an 'i'."

"Nice to meet you. I'm Cliff, spelled the regular way."

"You said you happened by my place by chance?"

"Yes."

"And, as luck would have it, I was entertaining walk-ins at the moment your interest became piqued."

"Yeah, I guess you could say that." Cliff said as he thought, *Your blinking sign stating as much lured me here as well.*

Toni leaned on the table, looking into Cliff's face. "I don't believe in coincidences, Cliff. I never have. It goes against my profession." They picked up the deck of cards, shuffling them between their dexterous fingers like a poker dealer. "I feel like you were compelled to see me today. Something is bothering you, but I don't need to be a psychic to know that. It's written all over your face. What I want to know is what's causing this aura of anxiety and chaos I sense around you?"

Cliff chuckled. "I mean, you can Google me and find a thousand or so people calling me an asshole online."

"That's not what I mean. That's *their* issue with you. I'm looking at the issue *you* have with you."

Cliff sighed and looked away. "I don't know. I keep getting in my own way maybe. Actually, some really weird shit went down last night after my show, and I can't make heads or tails of it in my head."

"Good." Toni stopped shuffling and placed the deck on the table next to the candle. "That feels like a good place to start. Cut the deck."

Cliff reached forward and separated the deck, leaving two neat stacks of cards. "Don't you want to hear about the weird shit? Some of it might be up your alley."

"I want to see if we can find out why the weird shit manifested itself to you in the first place." Toni moved the candle aside, picked up the cards, put the two stacks together, and pulled the first one from the top, sliding it to the middle of the table.

Cliff leaned to look at the card. It was the Tower, showing a building rocked and cracked by lighting. It burned, and a woman stood on the ground, also on fire.

"It's upside-down," Cliff said.

Toni nodded. "The Tower is reversed. Guess that confirms what you told me. You've begun a personal transformation, but you're resisting it yourself. You're not changing because you want to change. You're changing because you feel you need to."

Cliff huffed. "Sounds about…somewhat right."

"Your resistance has been noted by the ether, and that could be what's making you feel like all this weirdness is happening around you."

"Wait. You don't understand. What happened was—"

Toni held up a finger and produced the next card. It showed a man on the front hammering a chisel into what looked like big yellow coins with stars carved on them.

"The Eight of Pentacles," Toni said, "also reversed. You believe you're working hard, but the results you've gained aren't the ones you thought you'd receive. This can cause frustration and confusion, bringing forth that negative energy I feel oozing from your pores."

"Negative energy? Come on now!"

"You want everything to be perfect, and you want it now. You don't want to put in the hard work. You want what you believe is coming to you, whether it's earned or not. The fact that both these cards showed up in this reading reversed tells me you're an impatient man, and the one you're most impatient with is yourself."

No shit.

"This is your livelihood we're talking about, too," Toni continued. "When upright, this card would show you honing your craft and mastering your skills. In your case, it's your comedy and whatever you want to come of it. You're stopping yourself from your ultimate goal."

"Does it say anything about a damn writer ghosting me and screwing me out of my ultimate goal?"

"Let's see." Toni flipped the next card. The image was of a man at a desk, scribbling on a scroll with a quill. On the bottom of the card, the phrase 'The Scribe' had been written.

"There he is!" Cliff exclaimed, pointing at the card. "A scribe is a writer! I fuckin' knew he'd show up! I told you!"

Toni inhaled a long breath. Cliff looked from the card to their face, and he could tell something wasn't kosher.

"What's wrong?"

"This isn't a card."

"What? You shuffled, and I cut the deck like you asked. That's him. That's the writer I told you about. He blew me off last night, and I saw some crazy shit on the streets!"

"That's not what I mean." Toni looked into Cliff's eyes, unblinking. "There is no card in the tarot called 'The Scribe'. I've never seen that card in my life, and I've used this particular deck exclusively for years." They drew back their lips in a sneer. "What did you do?"

"I didn't do anything."

"Is this some kind of hidden camera thing? Is this part of your comedy act? Am I going to be on the internet later, claiming you trolled a local psychic with some sleight-of-hand wannabe David Copperfield bullshit? What's your endgame here, Cliff?"

Cliff moved away from the table. "I have no idea what you're talking about. I don't do that kind of schtick."

The room darkened, and Cliff looked out the window. Some dark clouds passed by overhead, obscuring the sunlight over the neighborhood. It wasn't only that, though. The flame of the candle burned black now, and the wax melted off it like an icicle lying on the sidewalk in August.

The face of the tarot card had changed as well. It no longer showed The Scribe scribbling his story on his parchment. It showed a lanky demon with long legs and a city of block-shaped buildings on the ground under its crotch. A gigantic, uncircumcised, demonic penis hung over the buildings with a menacing presence. Its eyes were red and yellow as it stared back at Cliff from the card.

The caption on the bottom of the card read, "He Who Walks Above".

"Is that one real?" Cliff asked, breaking his gaze from the card, looking toward Toni. They didn't answer, though. They stared back with tears of blood running down their cheeks.

"You either end up in the back of a hearse or the back of a garbage truck," they said in a voice that didn't belong to them. It had grown deeper, harsher. The candle burnt out with a wisp of gray smoke, and Toni rolled their head back and laughed in the demonic voice.

"You've been marked, comedian," Toni continued, tilting their head in a quick, whiplash-like motion. Their eyes had turned red and yellow like the image of He Who Walks Above from the tarot card that may or may not be real.

"Leave me alone! I don't want this! I don't want any of this!"

"It doesn't matter what you want! This is bigger than you and your paltry career! Wherever you go, I'll be there, watching, waiting. You cannot escape your fate."

"Fuck fate and fuck you!" Cliff flipped the table over, sending the cards and everything on it clattering to the floor. Toni, or whatever the fuck had been using them as a puppet, stared with a look of utter fascination plastered on their face. "I don't need this shit, so leave me alone!" He turned to leave, stumbling on the chair he forgot he pushed behind him. He kicked out at it, sending it rolling to the far wall, where it knocked a potted aloe plant off a wire shelf to the ground.

With all obstacles now out of his way, Cliff pushed the door, almost sending it off his hinges, leaving the house for the late afternoon sunshine.

Cliff was halfway to his car when he realized the sky was no longer black. He looked up, but there were only a few fluffy puffs of clouds against light blue. Ignoring all the weirdness, he got into his car and turned the ignition. It roared to life.

Toni stood on their porch, watching with their arms crossed. They glared, but they did it with their own eyes. Whatever had happened, they looked pissed, and they were aiming it at Cliff and not the demonic presence that had interrupted his tarot reading.

It wasn't real, Cliff told himself, looking ahead instead of at Toni's accusatory face. *It's whatever they slipped me last night. It's still in my system, hitting me like an acid flashback.*

Cliff didn't want to stay long enough for Toni to come down and tell him everything he had done from their perspective. He was sure their story wouldn't match his anyway. Instead, he put the car into drive and put his foot on the gas. The car lurched forward as he hit something.

"Fuck!"

Cliff got out of the car again, taking a brief look at Toni, who now leaned on their railing, watching. Sweat beaded on Cliff's forehead, and he wiped it away before it could sting his eyes. He looked at the front of the car and saw that he had hit an overturned metal trashcan. The contents had spilled onto the curb and into the street, but Cliff couldn't look at it. He didn't want to know what he'd see when he did. The memory of the dead eyes of the punk kid from the night before flashed in his mind's eye, and it took all his willpower to push it away long enough to get himself under control.

"You need help!" Toni shouted, shaking their head as Cliff got back into the car. "You need to pay me fifty bucks for the reading, too. You can tack on another hundred for all the shit you broke, you fuckin' asshole!"

"I'll mail you a check!" Cliff shouted. He backed up a couple of feet, bumping into the car that was parked behind him.

"I'm going to find whoever slipped me those drugs," Cliff said, putting the car into drive again. "When I do, they're going to be the one in the back of a fucking garbage truck!"

Cliff hit the gas again, swerving to miss the trashcan. He looked in his rearview mirror to catch a brief glimpse of Toni and some of their neighbors watching as he drove away.

"Fuck all of you," he said, glaring in the mirror. He put his eyes back on the road and focused on not rear-ending any of the other cars on the road. He had an hour or so drive to Easthampton, and the only stop he planned on making would be to get the strongest cup of coffee on God's green earth.

WHO THE FUCK IS ROCKY PHANTASMIC?!

7. THE WRITER & THE GARBAGE PSYCHIATRIST

Dave looked over his shoulder as he walked toward the street where his life had been turned upside-down by a quartet of thugs who wanted nothing more than to kidnap him. He still didn't know the reason why, and Rocky's superhero origin story hadn't shed any light whatsoever on the situation. It had made things even more confusing than they already were. Where did Dave—an engineer by day and a writer by night—fit into the world of organized crime?

Rocky Phantasmic made everything odder. Low-level thugs and mobster shit were one thing, but a self-proclaimed superhero created in the depths of New Haven Harbor made everything more surreal than it needed to be. Still, Dave owed his life to the young man who'd named himself his protector.

"Don't get twitchy now," Dave said, seeing how tightly Rocky held his backpack in his hands. "I'm the one who should be looking behind us to make sure we're not being followed."

Rocky had wanted to wear his costume in case something happened, and it had taken a while to convince him how bad of an idea that would be. A green hoodie with a yellow cape sewn to the back would be way too noticeable. Even in a city full of oddballs, it would draw too much attention. It had taken a lot of effort, but Dave convinced him to keep the superhero getup in his backpack for the time being.

Rocky looked back to ensure they hadn't been followed. "I can't help it. I know the costume doesn't give me my superpowers, but I should be wearing it in case I need it."

"You seem like you've read a lot of comic books. Didn't you catch the parts where they keep their identity secret? No one's going to head out in broad daylight wearing their costume when there are no heroics to be done. Besides, you don't even wear a mask, and you're supposed to be dead."

"I was going to make a mask," Rocky admitted, "but I didn't want it to block my sight in a fight."

"Touché."

They turned the corner, and Dave felt a wave of relief to find his car where he had left it. The walk from Rocky's basement apartment to the dog park took almost forty minutes.

"It was amazing you were even here when I needed you," Dave mused. "Why were you over here?"

"I was making my rounds around the city," Rocky replied. "All the street-level superheroes do it. I was on the lookout for muggers or whatever when I heard the commotion."

"And how'd you get me back to your place without anyone taking notice of you carrying a grown man?"

"I ran. I jumped over a house or two on the way to make better time."

"I think I'm glad I was out cold for that. I would've puked for sure."

Dave walked to the driver's side door, looking around one last time to make sure the guys Rocky had called the Unmade Men or their goonish friends weren't staking it out in case they returned, not that it mattered much. They'd have already been spotted if they were lying in wait.

"Shit," he said. "My phone's gone. I wanted to call my wife and give her a heads-up. You don't have a phone, do you?"

Rocky shook his head. "Nope. It got stolen before I died."

"Right. I forgot about that minor detail in your story. I'll have to find a phone somewhere once we're far enough away from here." Dave looked around the car, spotting his keys on the floor. "Score! I'd hoped I dropped them somewhere around here. Looks like my luck isn't all bad."

Dave looked at Rocky, who stood near the back of the car. "Look, Rocky, you don't have to do this. I know you swore an oath to protect me or whatever, but you don't owe me a thing. If anything, I owe you my life, not the other way around. You've been through hell already, and I can't ask you to get sucked into whatever nonsense I'm about to go through."

Rocky shook his head. "You already know I'm coming with you. Even if I don't owe you anything, the men who are after you now are the same ones who killed me. I go where you go till this is all over."

Dave smiled. "OK. I knew you'd say that, but I'd feel like a shitty person if I didn't give you one last out." He looked at Rocky, who stared at him even though he'd finished talking. "Get in. We've got a lot of road to cover."

***

Dave drove north on the highway. He knew he should've left more of a breadcrumb trail for the Unmade Men to follow before disappearing off the map, but he didn't have a tangible solution for that problem. Maybe they'd see his car gone and assume he came back for it to take on the road. Maybe he should have had Rocky put on his green and yellow costume and scream from the window in an obscene spectacle as they left the city. Either way, it didn't feel like he'd done enough on his way out to get their attention and keep it away from his family.

"I need to reach out to Heather," Dave said as they sat in Hartford traffic. "I fucked up. They're going to go to the house, I know it. I should have stayed. I shouldn't be on the road like a coward while these assholes take out whatever anger they have against me on her. Should I go back?"

Rocky shrugged. He'd sat in near silence with his backpack on his lap since they left New Haven to go on their little adventure.

Dave shook his head. "She's got to be home by now, and she's going to see that I'm not there. She'll try my phone, and I won't be the one who answers it. She'd call the police, right?"

Again, Rocky shrugged.

Dave slammed his hand on the wheel. "FUCK!"

"Worrying isn't going to help," Rocky told him. "We'll be at your uncle's cabin in no time, and we can reach out to the authorities from there. You said yourself it's not that long of a drive."

Dave gave a single, joyless laugh. "Yeah. It would be even quicker if this fucking traffic would let up."

"Hey," Rocky said, putting a hand on Dave's arm. "It'll be OK. You're doing the right thing."

"That advice is subjective at best."

Red lights blazed as the sun dipped below the horizon, making way for the evening. Horns sounded as traffic dragged forward, making each minute excruciating. Dave did his best to keep his composure.

After an hour and a half, they drove past what had caused all the traffic in the first place. Three of the four highway lanes had been shut down due to a horrific collision, and the one lane that moved did so at a snail's pace thanks to a combination of people waiting until the last minute to merge and their incessant need to rubberneck. Dave didn't like staring at highway brutality, but he couldn't help himself as he passed he wrecked cars. Four of them were pulled off to the side, and the highway was littered with metal debris and glass. Four bodies were laid on the ground as well covered, and a dead buck lay on the hood of the car in front of the others. Its head was upside-down, and it appeared to be staring at Dave with its mouth agape and its tongue hanging out.

"Oh my God," Rocky said in a low voice as they passed.

"God wasn't watching when that shit happened." Dave took his eyes off the violent upheaval so he wouldn't wind up rear-ending the driver in front of him at four miles per hour. He focused on the road and put his foot down on the gas once all four lanes opened back up to an empty highway. The image of the bodies and the buck stayed in his mind's eye no matter how hard he'd tried to think of something else.

Once Hartford and a handful of towns were behind them, Dave found a rest stop and pulled into it, bringing the car to a shaky halt. "I don't know about you," he said, "but I have to take a wicked piss ."

"Me too." Rocky undid his seatbelt and got out of the car, stretching in the cool autumn air. "It's colder up north," he remarked as Dave also exited the car.

"We're not that far north. We're still in Connecticut, not Canada, but it is getting pretty cold for this time of year. I wouldn't be surprised to see snow before Thanksgiving this year."

"OK."

Dave walked toward the building that housed restrooms and a counter full of brochures and pamphlets of all the boring stuff one could do in Connecticut. "Let's get this piss break done and get back on the road. I want to get somewhere safe and call my wife."

They entered the men's room, and Dave made his way to the urinal to do his business. He turned his head to see Rocky enter one of the stalls, and he figured their stop was going to be a little longer than anticipated.

All those Demon Energy drinks could've been good for his stomach, superpowers be damned.

"I'll be outside," Dave called. "Don't rush it on my part. I don't want you to rupture something."

"OK," Rocky replied.

Dave washed his hands and left, breathing in the crisp air. The cold felt good after sitting in the car for so long.

"David."

His name spoken by a masculine voice came to him on the breeze from the forest behind the rest stop. Dave turned, but there was nothing but dying grass ahead of the trees. He had heard that rest stops were a notorious meeting place for queer men, but hadn't that been decades ago? Either way, there shouldn't be anyone up this way who knew his name, let alone a former flame spending time waiting around a place like this. Once he put a little more thought into it, the whole thing felt worrisome.

I'm hearing things. No one said my name.

Still, Dave ventured toward it, unable to deter himself from following what he could only describe in his head as the most curious of siren songs. There wasn't even a tune. He'd only heard his name, but he felt compelled to find out who had spoken it.

"This is crazy," he said aloud.

Trash littered the ground, despite there being trash cans placed every ten feet or so. It rolled around in the breeze, condensing where the grass hadn't been trampled. The absence of wind strong enough to do something like that struck Dave the moment he found himself caught in the middle of a whirlwind of garbage and debris. He turned to leave, but the sights and sounds of the highway were gone, replaced with a wall of what looked like a well-decorated office.

"I'm so glad we can have this time together."

Dave turned to face what should have been the forest behind the broken fence. The scenery had been snapped away along with everything else. The worn ground and trash had been replaced by carpet, and the window behind the desk to his left didn't show the side of the rest stop in which Rocky made a roadside bowel movement. It showed a suburb that could have been one of the nicer areas of New Haven, complete with elm trees basking in the sun. The weirdest thing by far was the man sitting in the middle of it all. He waited, allowing Dave to absorb his new surroundings with a patient smile. His hand moved past his brunette beard and pushed his glasses up his nose. He wore a casual brown suit with no tie and khakis. The cuffs were high, showing plaid socks.

"Welcome, David. I apologize if I startled you, but I didn't know how else to get your attention."

"You apologize?!" Dave snapped with a short huff. "Jesus, man! What the hell is this?"

The strange man smirked. "You're taking this as well as I'd hoped. Although, we have to talk about your snap decision to berate me."

"Listen, whoever you are, I saw some strange shit yesterday, and this whole ordeal is just the icing on the cake. Are you going to tell me who you are or why you know my name at least?"

The man in the suit shifted in his seat and jotted down a note or two in a leather-bound journal that sat on his lap. With a sigh, he said, "We can dispense with the hostility if it's all the same, David. I'm not here to intimidate or harass you. To the contrary, I'm here to help."

"You can start helping by telling me who the hell you are."

"Oh, I've forgotten my manners. This whole thing is new to me as well. My name is Dr. Frederick Nielsen, undead psychiatrist."

Dave sighed. "I think I preferred those mobster wannabes to being forced to see a phantom shrink. No offense, but is there a point to this supernatural therapy session?"

Dr. Nielsen jotted another note, put the pen on the journal, and fixed his glasses before eying Dave. "Would you care to take a seat?"

Dave would've rather turned to run as far away from his impromptu undead therapy session, but something compelled him to walk around the coffee table and sit on the brown leather couch across from Dr. Nielsen. He figured it would be his best bet since whatever force had brought the psychiatrist's office into being wouldn't allow him to leave it until that preternatural force was satisfied. Still, Dave refused to lie down and spill his guts regardless of the circumstances.

"Alright, Frasier Crane. What's this all about then?"

Dr. Nielsen intertwined his fingers and observed Dave from above them. "What can you tell me about your ancestry?"

"My ancestry? Not much. A bunch of white people kept having sex till eventually I came out of it. That's all I know."

"I see. Your parents never told you anything about your lineage or where you came from?"

Dave shrugged. "We weren't that talkative of a family."

"Do you want to elaborate on that?"

"What's there to tell? I was an only child, and my parents weren't the type of parents they based sitcoms on. They didn't even talk to their parents much because of past drama with both of their families, so I didn't have much of a relationship with my grandparents either because of it. My father thought it was a great idea to jump in front of a moving train to get revenge on my mother for some stupid fight they were having. I was thirteen when he did that. Despite it all, my mother still loved him and mourned him to a fault."

"And you feel he didn't deserve to be mourned?"

Dave shook his head. "Nope."

"What happened to your mother?"

"As I said, she mourned my father hard, and nothing else mattered much after that. Breast cancer wound up bringing them back together. She didn't even fight it. She just let herself die like a fart on the wind."

Dr. Nielsen nodded, watching Dave, urging him to continue with his subtle mannerisms.

"Wait," Dave said. "What am I doing? I didn't sign up for a therapy session. Why do my parents matter now? Am I supposed to posthumously forgive them for being shitty parents to stop this group of assholes from terrorizing me in the street? I don't get it."

"I'm not here to urge you to forgive your parents or accept that they were mentally ill. Even if you knew little about their lineage, you still share it, and that's what's important."

"It doesn't feel that way." Dave let out a long sigh. He hadn't meant to speak so much, but he wound up spilling more of his guts than he wanted. "You're not suggesting I'm somehow part of that fucked up mafia wannabe family Rocky told me about, are you? That would be totally fucked."

Dr. Nielsen shook his head. "I'm afraid it goes beyond that. Your line may be broken, but your blood is still the blood of all who came before you. The men who are after you aren't after you for anything you've done. They're after you for something your ancestors did centuries ago."

"What is that exactly?"

"That, David, is a question to which I wish I had the answer."

"Let me get this straight: you've interrupted my quest to feed me some bullshit about my parents and my unknown lineage, but you don't know what I'm supposed to know? I don't have any relatives to call to find out whatever it could be, either. I wouldn't know where to start aside from searching my last name, which is way too common to do anything but send me down a rabbit hole of people with the last name 'Bryant' throughout history."

"You can look at it that way." Dr. Nielsen removed his glasses and held them with both hands on his lap.

"What the fuck are you even doing here then?"

Dr. Nielsen sighed. "I was sent here as a shade to aid you as a penance for what I did in life."

"Penance? Penance for what?"

"I died in the eighties, and I was a registered Republican. So…you know." He spread his hands and offered a light shrug. "I've done some stuff, and let's leave it at that."

"How'd you die?"

"Autoerotic… Never mind. That's not important right now."

"You're a real piece of work, doc."

"Look, David. I was a man of science in life like most of those in my profession. I didn't pay much mind to the spiritual until after I died and was surprised to find out an afterlife existed. By the way, none of the religions I studied even came close to what happens after we die."

"Yeah? So what?"

"So, you're going to have to contend with your ancestor's errors. It's not fair in life, but whatever they did marked everyone born of their seed. This *tainting*, for lack of a better word, will be carried by anyone of your lineage until it's severed."

Dave thought of his daughter and hoped she'd never have to go through anything like this. "And I'm the only one? I know I was an only child, but I'm sure there were brothers and cousins while this line of ancestry was being built. Why does this come down to me?"

"It's passed from first-born son to first-born son, etcetera."

"Do mothers and daughters not count then?"

"I know it's *cool* to hate the patriarchy nowadays, but this was written in another time. I'm not making this up as I go. This is how it is, and it's why it falls on your shoulders now to deal with it."

Dave nodded. "You mean to end it."

"No." Dr. Nielsen shook his head. "I mean you'll have to *deal with it*. A better way to put it would be that you must endure it to whatever end. I'm not here to spout an ancient prophecy or give you some grandiose mission and tell you that you're the chosen one to destroy evil in the world and bring about a thousand years of peace. I'm here to warn you that whatever wants you for whatever happened in your ancestry wants to fuck you up beyond all recognition. Whatever you do with that information is up to you."

Dave stared into Dr. Nielsen's serious face. "Couldn't you have said that from the start?"

"No. Psychiatry doesn't work with absolute values. To understand your plight, you must first understand why the plight exists in the first place. Throughout all this, what is that you've wanted?"

"What do you mean?"

"Is there anything on your mind or in your heart that you want more than anything else during your unexpected duress?"

Dave thought for a moment, but the answer should've been apparent. "I want to make sure my wife and daughter are OK and none of this shit comes to haunt Kayla like it's haunting me."

"Interesting." Dr. Nielsen jotted a note on his pad.

"What?"

"You have a bit of a hero complex, yet you're running away to avoid confrontation."

Dave huffed. "I'm avoiding confrontation? I don't know if you know this, but I'm not equipped to deal with this bullshit, let alone confront it. Maybe try not talking out of your ass."

Dr. Nielsen aimed a knowing glare at Dave's face.

"What the hell," Dave continued, shaking his head. "I have a superhero riding with me now. Fuck it, right?"

"Ah, now we come to the relationship with the young man who has joined you in your hero's journey. Do you feel any homosexual tendencies developing toward him?"

"What? He's like fifteen years younger than me, and he's the one who insisted on coming. He's already saved my life once. Why am I even discussing this? It seems like the worst possible use of my time."

"Your defenses are back up, David. You've developed them in your youth to deal with your parents, and they still haunt your decisions in your present life."

"Oh, fuck you."

A scratching sound came from outside of Dr. Nielsen's office, and Dave had to remind himself that he wasn't sitting on a couch talking to an actual person. He was still on a grassy field adjacent to a highway rest stop having an imaginary therapy session with the ghost of a shitty shrink who'd been anything but sage-like.

"It's an unfortunate truth," Dr. Nielsen continued, "that the burden of our parentage, or ancestors in your case, falls upon our shoulders. I can't say I envy you, but I believe you can overcome this and any obstacle you face."

Something squealed from the other side of the wall. It sounded like someone had crossbred a pig and a rat and branded it with a hot iron. The ceiling cracked and began to fall inward. Old napkins and plastic waste fell to the floor. Dr. Nielsen seemed unfazed by his tiny world falling apart around him.

"You see, David, our ancestors' burdens become ours to bear, and we must bear them with as much tenacity as we can muster. Otherwise, history will repeat itself, and we will become our ancestors and embody them and their sins."

The wall behind Dave cracked, and he got up from the couch. He turned, facing a degree from Harvard School of Psychiatry, which he wasn't sure was real. Dr. Nielsen could have gotten his degree from the back of a cereal box for all he knew, but that wasn't the most pertinent thing at the moment.

"Dr. Nielsen, do you have a rat problem?"

"A what problem? I don't think you understand. This is precisely what I've been trying to—"

The wall caved inward, but it wasn't drywall or plaster that fell to the ground. Newspapers, plastic cups, and fast food bags fell around the little area. Dave kicked a condom off his foot, and it landed on the creature that had been making the noise.

It wasn't a crossbred pig-rat chimera after all. If an animal like it existed on earth, Dave had never seen one. The creature was the size of a possum, covered in brown and black fur that looked more like a porcupine's quills. It opened its mouth, showing three rows of pointed teeth, and its yellow and black eyes focused on its prey.

"WHAT THE HOLY FUCK IS THAT THING?!"

Whatever the holy fuck it was, it hadn't come alone. More of them clawed at the walls from the outside, turning Dr. Nielsen's office and all its décor back into the trash from which it had been created by whatever psychiatric magic the shade of the shrink had used to make his makeshift office.

A creature fell through the ceiling and latched onto Dr. Nielsen's shoulder with its jaw. "Fuck!" Dr. Nielsen snapped. "I'm already dead, you little bastard!"

The creature bit down, taking a chunk of Dr. Nielson's flesh and bone, chomping at it as others clawed all over the psychiatrist, pulling him down to the ground. The creature shook the chunk of Dr. Nielsen, shaking it like a dog that caught a squirrel. The rest of Dr. Nielsen's body unformed, turning into the same trash that made up his office.

"Why are you staring at me?!" he exclaimed, turning his gaze to Dave. "Get the fuck out of here!"

***

Dave didn't have to be told twice. Whatever ghost magic that held the psychiatrist's office together failed, and it reverted into trash like the end of the second act in a version of Cinderella no one in their right mind would ever want to see. With a hard push, the wall fell apart, and Dave found himself back in the cold night air of the rest stop surrounded by litter.

Dr. Nielsen's office might've been gone, but the little monsters that had taken the illusion apart were still present in reality. Dave had hoped they had come for the sole purpose of taking the shrink back to Hell, but luck wasn't on his side—not anymore.

Dave ran, but the creatures were hot on his trail, hissing and nipping. He tripped on some of the trash blowing in the wind, which had picked up since before his psychiatric session. He scrambled as one of the little monsters crawled up his back with sharp talons that bore puncture wounds wherever it stepped, huffing and snorting as it climbed.

Panic set into Dave's body, and he tried to find a weapon among the garbage, but nothing within reach would help him. Defending himself with a burger wrapper was out of the question. The only thing he could grasp was a stick that was barely a foot long, so he grabbed it, flipping the creature over so it landed on the ground in front of him. Dave jabbed the stick forward, poking the creature in its eye.

It didn't do much of anything, but the creature threw its head back and let out a wail. Even though no bodily harm had been done, it bought Dave precious seconds, allowing him to get his feet on the ground and move. The other creatures didn't waste any time, and they chased him, screeching and chattering as they hunted their prey.

Dave climbed into the bed of a pickup truck, ignoring the pain shooting up his leg as he banged his shin doing so. He aimed a kick with his left foot, nailing one of the creatures in the face as it tried to get to him. It was a desperate move, and Dave found himself trapped as his attackers surrounded the truck, clawing at the metal with their talons to get a taste of human flesh.

"Leave me alone, you little fuckers! Go find someone else to eat!"

Their pursuit had slowed. Now that the creatures saw they'd trapped their meal, they savored the hunt. The sound of their high-pitched chattering drove screws through Dave's brain. He kicked out again, but the creature dodged it, opening its mouth and shrieking. One climbed up with one eye closed, drooling at the prospect of getting some revenge against the eye-poker. At least ten of them walked on or around the truck. One gnawed on the tire breaking it and wobbling the truck in what could've been an attempt to knock their prey down, not that they needed it at this point.

"I don't know what you want," Dave said, "but it looks like you're hoping it's dinnertime. I've got some bad news for you though." He looked around, licking his lips. If he ever hoped for a miracle, now would be the time. "I probably taste awful!"

A creature blinked and lurched forward. A long, black tongue flicked out of its mouth. Its jaws moved, making a clicking sound.

Is that little fucker laughing?

"Rocky! Where the fuck are you?!

"LEAVE HIM ALONE!"

Rocky fell from the sky in his green and yellow costume, landing in a crouch next to the truck. One of the creatures lunged for his face with its teeth bared, and it met a hurtling fist, sending it back a few hundred feet. All of the creatures left Dave alone for their new foe. One of them tried to eat Rocky's fist as he tried for another hard punch, but it found that the young superhero's skin was impenetrable, even to their alligator-like jaws. Rocky had to rip the thing in half to get it off of him, and it had taken the end of his sleeve with it, leaving tendrils of green fabric blowing in the breeze.

Another creature went for Rocky's feet, but its skull got crushed against the pavement with a stomp of a strong right foot. Blood and brains oozed from between Rocky's boot treads. Rocky kicked out at another, sending it toward the highway where a passing eighteen-wheeler nailed it while blaring its horn at the audacity of its plight. One flew at Rocky's face, but it wound up killed by a set of superpowered palms in a forceful clap that echoed in the distance.

| WHO THE FUCK IS ROCKY PHANTASMIC?!

With a few more stomps, a couple of punches, and one last creature being torn in half, the creatures had all been dispatched. Rocky Phantasmic's job was finished.

"Looks like you've saved my life twice now," Dave said. "I don't know if I'll be able to pay you back for even one."

Rocky turned toward Dave. His eyes were wide, and his chest rose and fell with short breaths. He looked at his arm where he had lost part of his sleeve.

"What were those things?!"

Dave laughed. He couldn't help it. Even after everything Rocky had been through, a pack of wild land demons could still shake him.

"They were little monsters from Hell if I had to guess," he replied. "You didn't think a superhero gig would be easy, did you?"

Rocky watched him. After almost a full minute, he laughed too. It died after a while, though, as he looked at the missing part of his superhero outfit.

"Aw, man. I really liked this hoodie."

"We'll find you another one at a Star-Mart or something." Dave climbed down from the back of the truck. "I don't think we'll find another hoodie with a cape, though."

"That's alright. I have my sewing kit in my backpack. I can fix something if we get the right material."

"Hey!" a large man shouted, running from the rest stop. "What the fuck did you assholes do to my truck?!"

8. THE DEMONIC HOUNDS OF THE UNDEAD

Heather's eyes sprang open as a door slammed shut, jarring her out of a broken and worrisome sleep. She sat up, rubbing her head. Night had come again, but she hadn't left the small, brick apartment in which Father Stephen had left her. The chain that bound her around her waist kept her from escaping, and Father Stephen had locked the other end to a cinderblock in the center of the room.

The psychopathic priest hadn't returned from wherever he'd gone, and he trusted his captive to stay in her room. All he'd taken with him were the keys to Heather's chain. She could escape any time she wanted, but she'd have to do it while carrying the cinderblock and dragging the chain behind her. It would be a slow and noisy escape, and she'd be recaptured the moment Father Stephen found her. Then again, if the police or some good Samaritan found her first, she might find herself rescued.

I didn't work out with those damn kettlebells every other morning for nothing!

But Heather knew escaping would do more harm than good. She had a plan in her head, and it hinged on her getting closer to Dave before she sprung her trap. She'd have to improvise and choose her moment. She imagined the scene in Return of the Jedi when Princess Leia choked out Jabba the Hutt with the very chain that bound her to him.

As fitting as an ending as that would be for the insane priest, she'd have to bide her time until the moment presented itself. For now, Heather left the camping cot and ventured around her temporary room just to do something.

Exposed brick jutted from the walls. The apartment felt more like a room in an old factory made to look like a shitty living quarter. Father Stephen could've been squatting, and that wouldn't be surprising in the least. Heather couldn't imagine a church that would house a priest whose hobbies included shooting through doors with a shotgun, hunting men, and taking women hostage. Some priests were up to their elbows in scandalous nonsense, but Father Stephen didn't seem like your run-of-the-mill sex pervert. No, his sins of choice were assault, murder, and kidnapping.

Heather made her way to the bathroom dragging the chain across the wooden floor. The warmth left her through her bare feet as she walked. She reached the bathroom and did her business after moving her chain to aid herself. The bruising and irritation around her waist had grown to be more than a nuisance. It made sleeping difficult, and she needed more than a few short waves of broken sleep to keep her sharp and alert. Her circadian rhythm had become unhinged, and she found her body longing for the morning only to find the beginning of night instead.

The chains weren't tight, but they weren't loose enough for her to attempt to squeeze out of them. Maybe if she could dislocate her hip she could free herself, but what would that accomplish? Also, she didn't know if such a feat were even possible without crippling herself or dying, not that she'd be able to deal with the pain.

Heather shook her head in an attempt to push the dark thoughts out of it. She washed her hands and walked toward the windows that overlooked whatever city or town Father Stephen had brought them. She had fallen asleep for a while in the car, and she couldn't tell how long it had been. From her vantage, it looked like the outskirts of a city, somewhere with a few factories and warehouses. The building was adjacent to a scrapyard full of cars and other vehicles that looked well past their warranties. It looked more like a vehicular graveyard than a car lot. It felt like a forgotten patch of land from a bygone era of American industry. A dark church in desperate need of repair stood half a block down the road on top of a hill.

"That's where he is now," Heather said aloud, pressing a hand against the frigid glass. "You won't want them to see what you've done, so you've left me to rot in this rat-infested shithole while you rub elbows with the other priests."

Then, something popped into her head. "Could they all want Dave dead? Did he commit some crime against the Church?"

Heather had read a lot of her husband's stories, but nothing should've caused something like this. Dave wasn't a fan of organized religion, and some of what he wrote did have some not-so-thinly veiled commentary about it. Then there were the ultra-conservative trolls he often fought on social media through his author account. Some of them might've been the types to throw on some priestly vestments, grab some guns, and go hunting for a writer with a different political view while complaining about demons and whatever else crawled up Father Stephen's ass to bury itself in his supple brain. This, however, felt different than those imagined scenarios.

It was all ridiculous, of course, but why else would any of this be happening? Heather had a handful of broken pieces, and the picture of the puzzle she'd been trying to put together in her mind hadn't made itself any clearer than it had been the night Father Stephen burst into her hotel room and knocked her entire world onto its ass.

My parents have to be worried sick right now. No one came to pick up Kayla today, and they're going to find the house in disarray. Dave and I are both missing, and they're going to call the police to find us if they haven't already.

Heather sat on the bed and pulled on her socks, followed by her boots. She should have considered herself lucky Father Stephen had given her the option to wear them along with some actual clothes, but she knew better. The last thing he needed was to someone spot her looking like a kidnapping victim instead of someone taking a joyride with a priest in a piece of shit Oldsmobile station wagon.

There has to be a phone around here somewhere. Maybe this place has an old landline I can use to call my parents and the police.

The room had no phone, of course. Father Stephen hadn't given her many amenities aside from a bathroom and a pile of gas station snack foods that would've been better suited for a stoner watching a horror movie marathon. Heather didn't think her stomach could handle much of it, but she risked a couple of Slim Jims for the protein along with a bottle of water. She followed her meager meal with a Twinkie since her options were so limited.

Heather lifted the cinderblock, grunting as she carried it an inch or two off the floor. She explored the building and found there wasn't much to it other than the small area Father Stephen had left her. She'd hoped to find somewhere a pack of squatters would've lived to see if any had left a cellphone or anything else she could use, but the whole place looked empty. Maybe the priest's friends from the church kept it that way to bring their holy victims of whatever crusade they believed they fought. The thought of them using the building as one huge murder room sent a shudder through her body.

The search for a landline phone turned out to be in vain, and Heather gave up with a sinking heart. The plan to wait out Father Stephen and eventually overtake him before he could kill Dave returned to her mind, but she wished she could get a warning into the world instead. Revenge would be sweet, and getting close to Dave would be better, but what if the difference between life and death for her family meant messaging someone for help?

Heather's hopes turned to her new plan. If she could get out of the warehouse and walk down the street with the cinderblock and chain, she might find someone who'd help her. Then again, Father Stephen, one of his pious cohorts, or some random pervert with a rapist's fantasies might find her first. This plan had a lot of flaws in it, but any options would dissipate into the stale air the more she thought about them. With time against her, she had to do something, anything.

A set of two metal double doors separated Heather from the outside. She didn't know how well Father Stephen had locked or barricaded it, but she threw caution to the wind along with cinderblock. With a crash, the doors flew open. When the cinderblock hit the ground, it broke into five or six pieces, leaving Heather with one less burden.

I should have thought of doing that from the start.

Heather gathered up as much of the chain as she could carry and ventured outside the warehouse into its neighboring scrapyard. The nights had already begun growing colder. It wasn't uncommon for November in New England, but something about the icy chill she felt through her clothes felt off, unnatural. In any case, the frigid air was the least of her worries. A priest with a penchant for shooting people still hunted her husband, and he might not think twice to put some buckshot into the woman he refused to call anything but an adulteress or a whore.

Something moved to Heather's left and she turned toward the sound, freezing in her tracks. She had made a lot of commotion when she broke free of the warehouse, and anyone lurking around the building would have heard it for sure. Maybe Father Stephen had returned to find the doors busted open and his captive walking free, carrying the chains that should've kept her bound to her makeshift prison cell.

He'd have no reason to hide and sneak.

"Who's there?!"

No answer came aside from something scurrying along the ground. That something sounded big, and it hid between the cars. Heather guessed the warehouse had a population of raccoons or other vermin, even though whatever ran around the old cars sounded a lot bigger. A snarl and a deep bark came, and Heather knew they were a lot meaner too.

A dog lifted its head, observing Heather with its beady, unblinking, black eyes; six of them. Its lips curled in a sneer, showing blunt, yellow teeth and black gums. The dog monster towered over her at seven feet tall, and it had quill-like spears along its back instead of fur. Heather backed away, wondering what kind of disgusting dog breeder would set out to create such a horrid creature.

Two more skulked around the scrapyard, emerging from the shadows, coming to see what their brother had found. One padded toward her from the other side of the building, sniffing the air as its face came into view. The third walked from the street, jumping over the fence in a single, fluid leap. Heather looked around herself to find a way out. When she realized there wasn't one, she forced a smile and said, "Good doggies."

***

"How close are you to finding David Bryant?"

Father Barnabas watched his former fellow with a stern look after his question. He'd always been one of the Vatican's best interrogators in this area of the country, but this particular query didn't call for torture, and the one sitting across the small, circular table in his church's rectory wouldn't flinch with some harsh prayer or a spritz of holy water as some of his charges might.

Father Stephen—the younger of the pair of holy men—sighed while rubbing his beard with his left hand. "That's not a fair question to ask, and you know it."

Father Barnabas shook his head and ran a hand through his fine, brown hair. He hadn't shaved, and a coating of shadow had grown on his exasperated face. Waiting for something to happen didn't suit him much, and it showed. Even the look in his dark brown eyes didn't convey much pity or anything resembling sorrow for Father Stephen's plight.

Father Stephen had left the adulteress in the abandoned hobo hotel and went to the church without having to drag her there for the other priest and God to bear witness. The Vatican wanted an update on his mission, and Father Barnabas found himself relocated to a church near David Bryant where he could supervise and work as a messenger for his superiors.

"It doesn't matter if my questions are fair or not," Father Barnabas said. "I need answers, and you know I answer to a higher authority who will ask me a lot harder than I'm asking you right now. How close are you to finding David Bryant?"

Father Barnabas might've been the one in the field working, but he'd retired to the management side of things after a leg injury. Chasing unholy creatures and boogeymen that went *bump* during any given night was hard work, and there weren't many working in this program of The Vatican's agent program that lasted more than a decade or so before they became unable to continue. Some took paltry jobs like Father Barnabas and others... Well, they're awarded posthumous plaques to hang in the last church that housed them. Then there are those who venture too far into the mouth of evil, leaving The Vatican no choice but to cut them loose. Some of those men remain useful, even in exile.

They called them 'exorcists' if they had to call them anything at all. It made for a good cover since most people dismissed exorcisms as Hollywood nonsense or stories of people who've dipped more than a toe into a hot pool of insanity. The Pope himself denied the agents' existence when pressed, and no one admitted outside the church that the program existed in the first place since they'd gotten good at cleaning up their messes and keeping them private while doing it. As long as evil roamed freely, however, The Vatican vowed to keep it under their thumb, and that went double for super demons who wanted to cover all reality in its veil of darkness. For that purpose, men like Father Stephen and Father Barnabas became men of the cloth along with vows to eradicate evil in any form it takes. It was a commitment none of them had ever taken lightly, not that they'd make that choice without full knowledge of where their paths might lead.

"I was following his scent," Father Stephen replied after a long pause, "but it led me to his wife first. It might've been the pheromones from her adulterous affair that threw off the demon's senses and led me away from my true target. I can use her, though. Her want to see her husband alive and keep him safe will drive me right to him."

Father Barnabas let out a long sigh. "You're leaving a mess in your wake, and I'm growing tired of cleaning it up. I heard about the man you shot in the stomach."

"Did he survive?"

"He did, and the local police are asking about an unhinged man dressed up like a priest. Once you leave here, you're on your own. You can't bring this kind of violence onto the church's doorstep. If you're caught and arrested, the Vatican and all agents, myself included, will disavow you. This ends here and now."

Father Stephen looked away, but he turned his gaze back to his superior's scowling face. "I know that. This was always my burden to carry, and I read the Demonic Testament knowing it would be my final mission. I knew The Vatican would turn its back on me, and I'd be on my own to prevent the unthinkable from happening. I don't regret my choice. The demon is gorging itself on my mind and soul from the inside like a gluttonous entity, but it's the only way to stop the Enemy. The Pope himself said so. *The Enemy would see in a second if we sent a whole army, but they may overlook a single man*. It doesn't matter what you think or how many doors the church slams in my face. I'll find solace for the sins I've committed on my path when I arrive in Hell, knowing I sacrificed my life and my soul to do what needed to be done."

It was Father Barnabas's turn to look away. "It's a burden none would take lightly. What you learned from your reading was invaluable to our cause, and casting one's immortal soul into the pits of Hell for the greater good is the grandest sacrifice one of our station can make. For what it's worth, I am sorry my orders prevent me from doing more. I've taken a huge risk even letting you into this church with the demon riding inside you. I couldn't do what you've done, even before my injury. The sacrifice you've made is bigger than anything I've done or ever will do."

"Thank you. I appreciate you saying that, and I understand your hands are tied by more than red tape. The demon inside me makes men like you uneasy. It's not that you are soft, but it knows you oppose it and its kind."

Father Barnabas nodded. "How much longer do you think you have before the demon takes you completely?"

Father Stephen shrugged. "I don't know. It's caused me to do some heinous things already, but the predator's instinct it's given me will help me hunt down David Bryant and give me the gall to kill him without a moment's hesitation. In the meantime, it's grasping onto the darkest parts of my soul and magnifying my urges to cause pain and suffering to those I believe deserve it. It's quieted since I entered the church, but it'll be back in full force once I'm outside."

"At least your acts of violence aren't random."

"Not yet anyway."

"And you still have the Demonic Testament in your possession?"

Father Stephen nodded. "It's in a lockbox in my station wagon wrapped in a blessed cloth. I need to keep it near. Once this mission is over, make sure whoever takes me out gets it back to the Vatican without reading it."

"That's already in motion, Father."

"Good."

Silence filled the rectory kitchen aside from the ticking of the clock on the wall. This night—as with all the nights Father Stephen had left to live—will lead him closer to his goal and his prey. He didn't know how long he had to stop the plots of the evil entity against whom they moved, but he had long since resolved to see it destroyed. What happened to him in this life and the next didn't matter in comparison.

"I should go," Father Stephen said, pushing his chair back and standing. "I don't know how much further I have to go, and I don't know who the Enemy will send after me once they pick up my scent."

Father Barnabas rose as well. "May God guide you on your quest, Father."

Father Stephen smirked. "He may yet, but He'd find himself in competition with the demon in my mind."

A resounding bark filled the night, shaking the windows of the rectory. Father Stephen turned to the window and saw the warehouse down the road where he'd left the adulteress. He squinted, making out a couple of large, black animals skulking through the scrapyard.

"My dear Lord, what are those?" Father Barnabas asked, making the sign of the cross as he looked in the same direction as his elder.

Father Stephen swore under his breath. "Demonic hounds," he muttered. "Looks like the Enemy's gotten my scent." With that, he strode out of the church into the cold evening.

***

DANIEL AEGAN

Heather moved between the cars while keeping as low to the ground as possible. It felt stupid since the dog monsters had already seen and scented her. An aching settled in her lower back from walking crouched while holding the chain locked around her midsection.

She could hear them pacing and walking around her in a circle. Were they here for her, or did they come to stop the priest from killing David? If the latter were true, then she might be better off leading them to him to do the dirty, murderous deed.

Or maybe the priest summoned them as guard dogs, Heather thought. She wondered how badly she might've miscalculated her attempted escape. It occurred to her that she shouldn't have been so flippant while she jumped between her plan to stay with Father Stephen until he found David or to escape and go about it on her own. Her family still needed to be warned, but would they believe any of this in the first place? Did she?

The sound of metal twisting into a deformity of its original design as it crunched against the ground filled the air, and Heather turned to see one of the dog monsters pushing a car with no tires till it flipped upside-down as it moved toward her. It snarled with a guttural rumbling. A thick stream of saliva dripped from its mouth, making it appear rabid. She turned to flee the other way, but she stopped short when she realized she had somehow wandered into an office decorated by the blandest person to have ever existed.

"Hello," a bearded man in a chair said. "My name is Dr. Frederick Nielsen, and I'm—"

One of the dog monsters burst through the ceiling, showering the office in pieces of scrap metal. The dog monster bit down on Dr. Nielsen with its massive jaws, dragging him upward as the rest of the office fell around Heather in piles of scrap metal.

"NOT AGAIN!" he shouted.

The dog monster swung its head, hurling Dr. Nielsen into the side of the brick building. He shattered, sending more metallic debris to the ground. The dog monster looked back toward Heather as if it was measuring her with its mouth agape. A torrent of steaming drool fell from it and splattered as it hit the ground.

Heather backed away. Her feet clattered through the metal. She almost tripped on an old washing machine door, but she kept her footing. The dog monster moved as well, eying her as if it had always been her fate to die a human chew toy.

WHO THE FUCK IS ROCKY PHANTASMIC?!

Heather ran. She had to hold her chain close to her body so she wouldn't drop it and trip. The dog monster behind her barked and jumped, landing on the ground in front of her. Heather turned in an attempt to give it the slip, but one of the others blocked her way with its head lowered. The third waited by the entrance to see what its brothers would do.

Heather had nowhere to run. She couldn't climb the fence and barbed wire with her chains, and the dog monsters would never allow her to get that far if she tried. Her only hope would be to get back into the building, use the lack of open spaces to confound and elude the trio of predators, and hide till they gave up on searching—assuming they would.

"Fuck it," Heather said in a low, harsh breath. "Come on, pups! Want to come in from the cold?"

Heather made it a few steps before a bang split the quiet evening. The dog monster closest to the fence jumped and turned toward the street as it got back to its feet. Father Stephen walked from his station wagon with his shotgun in his hands.

"Back away, demon spawn!" he exclaimed before firing another round that hit the hound in the side of its face.

The dog monster winced and pulled its head back. It backed away from the priest and snorted through its nose. Heather smelled something in the air and knew the priest wasn't playing fair.

He's using sulfur rounds!

Heather turned away after Father Stephen fired another shot, this time nailing the dog monster in the chest. She ran toward the warehouse to get away from all the madness in the scrapyard. She didn't make it far, though. The dog monster that had been stalking her hadn't given up, and it got between her and the building, sliding to a stop with its head lowered and its teeth bared as it growled.

"You gotta be kidding me! Go after the damn priest, Cujo!"

The other two dog monsters had scrambled to get away from Father Stephen's attack. One of them caught its paw in the barbed wire and fell to the street. Father Stephen took advantage and blasted it through its eye. It twitched once and stopped moving.

The hound that had been blocking Heather leapt into the air. It landed and ran toward the street to avenge its fallen sibling, breaking through the fence. The other dog monster was there already, but Father Stephen held it at bay with a wooden crucifix on a short pole. Even though the holy talisman worked, the charging dog monster had the chance to even the score.

Father Stephen noticed the new dog monster coming as it burst through the fence and turned toward it. Its momentum stopped as it slid to a halt at the sight of the crucifix. The other circled the priest, ready to pounce from behind where the symbolic gesture of Christ's death wouldn't force it to hold back its malice. The priest held his ground, but it would be a matter of time before one of them tore his flesh to ribbons, splintered every bone in his body, and turned him into a pile of demonic dog shit.

"Shit," Heather muttered. She knew she should use the chance she had to escape, but she found that part of her didn't want to see the priest die a gruesome death, even if he did have it coming. Besides, she still needed Father Stephen to lead her to Dave if she had any chance of recusing him from all this craziness.

I need a fucking weapon.

Anything would do. In Heather's mind, she only had to distract one or both of the dog monsters long enough for Father Stephen to blast them with a killing shot of sulfuric buckshot. Heather may not have liked it, but it was her only hope to get out of there without getting torn to shreds. She opened the door to a beat-up van, hoping to find something she could hurl as a distraction, but she found nothing except a dozen or so old carpets rolled up in the back. She was ready to give up when she noticed a set of keys sticking out of the visor.

"Hell yes," Heather grunted as she took the keys and put them in the ignition. It whirred, struggling to come to life. "Come on!" She watched Father Stephen as the engine fought to come alive, but it refused to turn over. The priest did his best to keep the dog monsters from destroying him while he formulated a plan, but they wouldn't let him think too long. He couldn't get a shotgun blast off while holding his crucifix to keep the beast at bay.

Heather turned the key again, gritting her teeth as she gripped the wheel with her left hand, shoving her foot on the gas and pumping it as if her grit would be enough to start the stubborn van. "START, YOU FUCKIN' PIECE OF SHIT!"

The van roared to life at Heather's obscene command, and she wasted no more time. She put it in drive and slammed her foot on the gas without knowing if it would crap out again. She cut the wheel, and the van's bald tires squealed against the parking lot. It burst through the opening the dog monster had made in the fence, slamming into its side as it turned toward the sound of the van.

Heather lurched forward as the airbag deployed, catching her before her body could slam against the wheel or fly through the windshield. The moldy carpets behind her surged forward as well, slamming into the back of her seat. She might not have been going fast enough to kill herself, but it had smashed into the dog monster hard enough to knock it into a roll.

Steam and smoke poured from the van's engine as it died for good. Heather had sacrificed it to save her kidnapper. She wondered if the mighty van had died in vain when she saw the dog monster get back up and limp toward her, but it collapsed in the street before letting out a long, steaming breath.

The van lurched again from the side, rolling, sending Heather in a heap at the roof, which had become adjacent to the ground under it. Pain rang out in her back, and she felt lucky she didn't break her neck or get broken to hell by the carpets when they fell on and around her. She'd ache in the morning, especially where the carpets hit her, but at least she'd live to ache—if she ever made it to the morning.

The remaining dog monster's toothy maw ripped the passenger-side door from the van and threw it into the air with a jerk of its head. It barked as it ripped at the metal to get at Heather. She screamed and scooted herself toward the back of the van over the rolls of carpets to escape its sharp teeth and probing tongue. The growling that filled her head and vibrated her body would follow her into whatever afterlife she'd face after it consumed her. A shot rang out from the other side, and the dog monster yelped. One last bang came, followed by the slap of the dog monster's body hitting the street.

Heather panted for breath as she lay on the van's ceiling, unable to bring herself to move. The musty smell made her want to gag, but she fought the reflex since breathing had become her biggest priority. She didn't know if the ordeal had ended or if another attack would come, but she felt as if she'd run out of gas. For all she knew, a fourth dog monster had been lying in wait. Maybe a fifth and sixth would come to join the party with the rest of their evil litter.

"Are you alive in there?" Father Stephen asked from outside the busted back door of the van.

Heather groaned and pulled herself into a sitting position amid the mess of carpets. "I survived," she admitted. "Are there any more of those nasty things out there?"

"Not yet." Father Stephen crouched to peer inside the van to find Heather prone and still chained. "We need to get moving before the forces that move against us send something else." He reached a hand into the van, but he pulled it back the moment Heather tried to use it to pull herself out. "No. Hand me the other end of your chain."

Heather huffed and looked away from her captor. She pulled the chain from around the rolls of carpet and gathered it up before tossing it toward Father Stephen. It clattered as it fell on the ground, and he bent over to pick it up, holding it while Heather crawled over the carpets and out of the van. It might've been a sexy scene if it were in an eighties hair metal music video and she hadn't gotten so bruised up from her vehicular attack on the evil dog monsters from Hell and the chaos that ensued afterward.

"We're still doing it like this, then?" she asked. "You realize I just saved your life when I could have driven away and left you for dead, right?"

"You've escaped your bonds once already," Father Stephen replied as he walked her toward his station wagon like a pet. "My mission is too risky not to take the precaution of keeping your chain locked. I gave you a bit of freedom, and you smashed the cinderblock to attempt to escape. I won't make the same mistake again."

Heather sighed. She should've assumed she'd come to regret saving the priest's life. Then again, a time would present itself soon enough when the chain wouldn't be enough to stop her.

"OK then, Father. Chain me to your shit-mobile again, and let's get out of here. As much as it sucks, I don't want to stick around and find out if whatever sent these dogs after us has any more pets."

Father Stephen nodded and opened the door to let her into the passenger's seat of his station wagon. Once she'd settled into it, he went to work locking her chain to the back again. He returned, sitting in front of the steering wheel with a grunt.

"For what it's worth," he said as he brought the engine to life, "you have my thanks for saving me. Those demonic hounds were formidable opponents, but you fought well."

Heather scoffed. "That's putting it mildly. I almost killed myself saving your ass from becoming kibble n' bits."

Father Stephen let out a grunt as he swerved around the dog monster corpse Heather had created as he drove away from the scene of their unholy skirmish. "I'm sure the Enemy will take us more seriously now that we've not only survived his attack but slayed three of his darkest creations.

He sped up the highway onramp. Traffic was light, and he pulled into the left lane, pushing the engine to its limit. If Heather had to guess—and that's all she'd been able to do since her life had been interrupted—she'd assume he wanted as much space between the dog monster corpses and them.

She didn't blame him.

"Where are you taking me now?" Heather asked.

"North." Father Stephen replied.

Heather watched the road. Her body wanted a good, long, healing sleep. Her bumps and bruises from the ordeal with the dog monsters throbbed with a dull pain, but there'd be no helping that for the time being.

"I know you have this whole masochistic mindset," she said, "but I want you to be straight with me."

Father Stephen kept his focus on the road. "About what?"

"Are you serious? About everything! You've got me chained up like a dog, and you're dragging me God-knows-where in the middle of the night. I assumed you were some kind of psychopath at first, but now… Now I don't know what to think. Those…dog monsters or demon hounds or whatever they're called… I need to know what all this means and why you believe my husband needs to die."

Father Stephen let out a long breath. "I've always worked alone, but your involvement can't be helped at this point. I'll tell you what I can if you'd like, but knowing isn't going to help you or save your husband."

"I know. Still, I need to know."

"Next time we stop, I'll tell you what I can. It's a lot of information, and I need to think about where to start and how to best present it."

You mean you want to figure out which parts to leave out, Heather thought. Aloud, however, she said, "Thank you."

Father Stephen nodded. "Rest while you can. I have a feeling you won't find any restful sleep once I've explained the world within our world that imprisons the Enemy and his demonic forces. I don't expect you to have a restful night's sleep again after learning what I have to tell you."

He went silent after that, and Heather didn't press him again. She'd have to be smart while playing the role of the curious kidnapping victim to learn all she could before springing her trap. Father Stephen could think he was the one in control all he wanted, but he had no idea what a woman was capable of doing when you put her in a corner and threatened her family.

Father Stephen was going to find out soon enough. Heather planned on making damn sure he wouldn't ever forget it.

WHO THE FUCK IS ROCKY PHANTASMIC?!

9. THE UNMADE MEN & THE SUPERVILLAIN

Johnny pulled into the diner's parking lot. He hadn't driven far off the highway to find somewhere to eat and maybe take a dump, but it still somehow felt like they'd veered too far off their route, even if they weren't sure where the route was supposed to lead them in the first place.

"Hey," Leo said from the passenger seat, looking in the rearview mirror. "Do you eat?"

Of course, Leo hadn't asked Johnny that. The man he addressed sat in the backseat, right in the middle to watch the road ahead of them. Vincenzo said his name was Duro Assassino, and he'd been with Johnny and Leo since they picked him up from the airport earlier that day.

Duro wore a tight white shirt, one that showcased his abdominal and pectoral muscles. He had black tattoos going up his arms and under his sleeves of barbed wire and blood. Some more of the tattoo was visible through the shirt, and it looked as if his whole torso had been inked. It ended around his neck, where it looked like a choker made of black wire.

"He ain't gonna say nothin'," Johnny said as he put the car into park. "He hasn't said a word since we picked him up. I don't think he knows English. Or maybe he's one of them mutes."

Leo turned and looked Duro in the face. "Nod if you want something to eat."

Duro stared back with his cloudy, gray eyes. A small smirk spread on his face, but he didn't acknowledge the question in any way.

"Forget it," Leo said, unbuckling his seatbelt. "We'll be inside getting a bite to eat. If you want to join us, we'll be there. Maybe they got pictures on the menu. You can point at what you want for the waitress."

Again, Duro declined to take part in the conversation.

"I give up!" Leo got out of the car and slammed the door shut, storming away toward the diner.

"He's a hothead, but he's not too bad," Johnny said in lieu of an apology. "You don't have to wait in the car while we eat. Even if you don't want anything, you can still sit inside with us."

Duro didn't move or respond. He stared at Johnny with the same smirk on his face as if playing the silent assassin with his two American hosts amused him.

"OK. Suit yourself. We'll be in the diner if you need us."

Johnny left the car. He almost turned on the alarm, but he didn't want it blasting if Duro decided to get out and join them. They had stored all their weapons and tools in the trunk, and they didn't need any lawmen poking around.

"He looks suspicious as hell sitting in there by himself," Leo muttered as Johnny joined him. "The whole quiet-man thing he's trying to play is gonna get real old real quick. You know what I'm sayin', Johnny?"

Johnny nodded. "Yeah, I get'chu, Leo. I don't know what the boss wants us to do with this guy. We can escort him all over the place, but he's creepin' me out. Even if he tells me to fuck myself, it would be better than the silent act he's pullin'." He looked away from the figure sitting in his car and back to Leo. "Are we still goin' the right way?"

Leo sighed and reached into his jacket pocket. He pulled out a black box and flipped the top open, revealing a compass with no writing or directions on it. A red and white needle pointed northward.

"So far, so good," Leo replied. "I don't know how this friggin' thing is supposed to work, but the boss says it'll lead us right to where we need to go. It's some more of that demonic magic or whatever the fuck is causin' all this horror movie bullshit. I don't know where Vincenzo got this thing, and I don't know how he found out about that silent mook in the car."

Johnny looked over his shoulder as Leo entered the diner. Duro hadn't moved an inch. As far as he could tell, he remained as still as stone, watching from his place in the backseat like he needed some purpose to find him instead of the other way around.

With a jingling of bells above the door, Johnny went into the diner and jogged to catch up to Leo. "Why is he with us anyway?" he asked.

"Because the boss wanted us to take him."

"I know that, but why did he want us to take him?"

"I thought that was made clear." Leo huffed. "If we need to take out a friggin' superhero to get the writer—dumb as that bullshit sounds—then we were always going to need a supervillain on our side. We can't take out the kid on our own. You saw how he juggled Gino and Mikey like ragdolls and put them both in the hospital with no effort whatsoever. You're tough, Johnny, but not tough enough to take out a powerhouse like Rocky Friggin' Phantasmic."

"You mean Richie."

Leo shrugged. "Richie's dead as far as I'm concerned." He walked to a waitress and had a short conversation about where they should sit and if they could get quick service since they couldn't stay long. The waitress agreed and said they could sit wherever they wanted.

Johnny looked back out toward his car with Duro. *Is he really a supervillain?* he thought, scratching the stubble on his chin. *I wonder what his superpowers are.*

"Oi!" Leo exclaimed. "Snap out of it, Johnny. We can get a seat where you can watch the car if you're worried about it. If Duro is going to do anything, at least we'd see him doing it."

"Right," Johnny agreed. He went with Leo and took the side of the booth facing the parking lot. He wished he hadn't. Even through the foggy glass diner window, he could still see the storm brewing in Duro's eyes, and he couldn't stop thinking about what could happen if he unleashed it.

***

Back at the Red Curtain Club in New Haven, Johnny and Leo's undead boss walked through a crowd of people. He smiled as he greeted and welcomed all who had come in honor of his resurrection. Word had spread fast through the family. How could it not? Guys didn't claw their way out of their own burial plots every day, and the return of Vincenzo Scaletta was cause for celebration!

"There he is!" Dom Maturo exclaimed, holding his arms out, his gut protruding like he'd smuggled a boulder into the place. He wore a dark brown suit with clashing a mustard-yellow tie. Dom had never been a fashionable guy, but he'd always been a decent cousin to have in a fight or in the family business.

"Here comes the Raging Buck!" Vincenzo shouted in return, accepting the hug from Dom's meaty arms.

Dom planted a wet kiss on the side of Vincenzo's head and pulled back. "Still with that Raging Buck nonsense! Couldn't you have left that sense of humor of yours back in the afterlife?"

Vincenzo laughed. "It takes a lot more than a life-ending heart attack to make me forget you blasting that buck in the face with your pistol when it jumped out from between the trees. I don't know which of you was more afraid!"

Dom leaned in close. "Burying bodies in the woods is a young man's game, Vin. Don't send me back out there."

"Wouldn't dream of it, bud. You'd keel over and drop dead the moment your shovel hits the earth. Trust me, I know what that's like now. It ain't a fun way to go out."

Vincenzo looked around the club while Dom laughed off the prospect of dying in the woods with a shovel in his hands. The place was packed with family and friends. They'd all been shocked to find out he'd been resurrected, but he assured them he hadn't returned a vampire or a zombie or anything else they'd seen on some late-night movie. He was himself and still head of the family. It was a good thing, too. Sounded like everything started falling apart the moment his body hit the floor.

"It's so good to have you back, chief," Dom said, slapping a large hand on Vincenzo's shoulder. "I don't know what this family was supposed to do without you."

"Me neither." All joy and glee had gone from Vincenzo's voice. What they'd built here was a house of cards. It had always been that way. That stack of flimsy, laminated cardboard had been built in the crisscrossing shadows of the New York families and the Irishmen in Boston. Theirs was a small and quiet operation in comparison, but that didn't make them illegitimate.

"Thanks for comin' down, Dom," Vincenzo said, patting his cousin on the shoulder. "Excuse me. I gotta take a piss."

"By all means." Dom excused his compatriot and went to the bar to order himself another drink. If history proved to be any indication, he'd order a handful more throughout the party and end the night puking in the parking lot while insisting he could drive himself home.

Vincenzo made his way to the bathroom, shaking hands with the people who had come to wish him well on his second life. He excused himself half a dozen times, apologizing that, resurrected or not, he couldn't ignore nature's call.

The girls on the stage danced for all of the party guests, shaking their chests and straddling their poles. They'd grown accustomed to the men who owned the place, but they didn't say a word about what they thought they knew about them. Vincenzo watched as he walked, glad he did so amongst the living once more. One of the girls would wind up in his office on all fours by the end of the night as a gift. Some of them recoiled at the sight of him since they also danced at his wake. They weren't as welcoming as Vincenzo's family and associates, but they'd come around. Women came and went at the Red Curtain Club, and sooner rather than later, the Undead Boss would be an urban legend with nothing to back it up but rumors. Only the family, blood and otherwise, would know the truth of his Jesus-like act.

But that's how it should be.

"How's it goin', boss?" Gino asked, hobbling near him with the use of his crutches. "Have you heard from Leo and Johnny?"

"I hope not to," Vincenzo replied. "If I hear from them, it means they screwed up. Silence is golden."

"Oh. That's cool."

"We'll talk later. If I have to wait to piss any longer, it's going to come out my friggin' ears."

Gino nodded. "Right. Of course, boss. I'll go mingle."

"Don't squish anyone's toes with those damn crutches."

Vincenzo finally made it to the bathroom. As he drained his lizard, he reflected on how his family had accepted his return with open arms, and he'd been grateful they had done so instead of chasing him down with pitchforks and torches like some old black and white horror movie his father—God rest his wretched soul—had made him watch as a kid. He'd been apprehensive about outing himself as undead, but things seemed to have worked out. Some members of the family were surprised, some thought he'd come to see them as a ghost, and more than a few dropped to their knees in prayer, thinking Vincenzo Scaletta had returned to drag them to hell for what they'd done with their lives. Those guys wound up with a slap to the side of their heads to bring them back to reality.

All in all, however, it felt nice to know his family came around so quickly to accept there's more to life, death, and what lies beyond the veil of everything.

Vincenzo did his best to push those thoughts out of his head while he stood in front of the toilet, giving it his business. Gino had brought up Leo and Johnny's mission. Their absence at Vincenzo's homecoming party had been noted, and he'd been tightlipped about where he'd sent them and why. He hadn't stopped thinking about those two and the writer, and he had hoped that the party in his honor would take his mind off all of it, allowing him a moment's rest from the anxiety that came along with not only being the boss but running errands for the entity that had brought him back from beyond the grave.

Leo and Johnny aren't alone anymore, Vincenzo thought as he finished emptying his bladder. *They've got Duro with them, and he's going to be the difference-maker if that Rocky Phantasmic brat is still hanging around the writer.*

Vincenzo had heard about Duro Assassino years ago. He'd kept in touch with his old family in Italy since his grandmother's death. She had come to America as a middle-aged immigrant and kept the memories of the old country close to her heart. She loved telling scary stories, and she insisted that they were real. When she got older and her mind started deteriorating, she told anyone who would listen about how many people she had killed, and it had been mostly children.

Most of her family dismissed this as dementia making itself comfortable in her brain. They said she had seen one too many television shows about murderers, and they seeped into her deteriorating mind. There was no way to find out either way. She would have done this long before anyone kept track of this kind of thing on the internet, and people sometimes live their whole lives without certificates that verify birth or death.

So, Vincenzo theorized that his sweet, old Nonna might've committed acts of murder in her youth. She might've even been a witch in the old country for all anyone in their large family knew. Vincenzo had traveled to Italy himself to inform them of her passing, and he celebrated her life with them, even though there weren't many left who remembered her. The whole family fascinated him, and they all had stories that were reminiscent of vampires, werewolves, witches, and zombies. He listened with intensity about the veil between the world of humans, demons, and what lay beyond death.

Vincenzo kept this connection to the old world after that trip, and it's how he knew the deal to come back to life was legit when the demon presented it to him. It was also why he believed Duro Assassino was exactly what they said. He trusted the stories and the lore completely, and he'd been rewarded for that trust.

In the present, Vincenzo finished his business in front of the Red Curtain Club's toilet and zipped up his fly. He walked to the sink and turned on the faucet, letting the warm water wash over his hands. He looked up in the mirror to check his hair when the image of himself and the rest of the bathroom behind him disappeared, replaced with a pulsating black cloud.

"What the fuck?!" Vincenzo snapped, stepping back from the mirror. The lights went out, and two yellow eyes appeared in the moving blackness, focusing on him with their red slits. They were a predator's eyes, and he'd seen them before, but never like this and never on this side of the veil.

"*VINCENZO SCALETTA,*" a voice spoke from within Vincenzo's head. It rumbled and burned at the same time. Sounds weren't something that generated heat, but the words spoken by the entity in the mirrored wall defied that kind of logic. When you made your own rules in any given reality, what use would you have for things like physics? "*WHY ARE YOU COMMISERATING WITH YOUR FRIENDS AND FAMILY WHEN YOU HAVE A TASK TO COMPLETE?*"

Vincenzo steadied himself despite his body shaking as if his blood sugar had plummeted straight to Hell. He felt his stomach loosening and tightening in a steady, unsettling rhythm, and his hands and arms felt like they wanted to tremble and shake. His knees threatened to turn to jelly as well, and he might've pissed his pants if he hadn't already taken care of that particular issue.

He also knew the owner of the eyes and the speaker of the demonic voice in his head. It was the one who called him back from death and allowed him to walk once more with the living. It was the embodiment of all those horror stories, the demon without a true name Vincenzo knew who called itself He Who Walks Above.

"*SPEAK!*"

"What do you want me to say?" Vincenzo asked, fighting to keep his voice steady. "I am doing what you've asked. I've sent two of my best men to pick up the guy you wanted, and I've sent them with some extra muscle in case they run into any problems."

"*YOUR MEN HAVE ALREADY FAILED YOU ONCE. THEIR FAILURE IS YOUR FAILURE, AND IT WILL NOT BE TOLERATED!*"

"You can't fault me for what happened! You never told me that some kid I had killed would also return from the dead with friggin' superpowers and stop my guys from collecting this Bryant character for you! That information would have been helpful, you know."

"*THE OTHER WHO RETURNED AS YOU HAD MATTERS NOT. I DID NOT ASK FOR AGGRESSION OR EXCUSES! YOU MADE A DEAL TO WALK ONCE MORE WITH YOUR BRETHREN, AND I MADE THAT HAPPEN. YOUR END OF OUR BARGAIN WAS TO BRING ME DAVID BRYANT, AND YOU HAVE YET TO DELIVER.*"

"Look, I know you're a demon from the netherworld or whatever you call your version of Hell, but I do things how I've always done them. I'm the boss here, alright? You had to have known that when you picked me to do this chore for you. I delegate the job, and it gets done. I wouldn't have sent my boys into the shit if I didn't have complete faith that they can do this. I sent them with the compass, and they were headed in your direction the last time they checked in with me."

The evil eyes narrowed. He Who Walks Above was either measuring Vincenzo in search of a lie or readying a flaming attack that would turn him to ashes where he stood.

"What?" Vincenzo asked. "This is my business. This is what I do. If you didn't trust me, you wouldn't have delegated this task to me. It'll get done, and you'll see that your trust was not misplaced."

The door to the men's room opened, and Dom walked inside. "You still in here, Vin? Why did you shut off the—"

He Who Walks Above turned its gaze toward the interloper, and the intensity behind the eyes glowed with hellfire. Dom froze when he saw what the mirrors showed, and his scream turned to an inhuman shriek as his skin stretched off his bones and his thick body turned inside-out with the sound of raw human meat being pulled apart and ripped as it rewrapped itself around Dom's skeleton.

A misshapen hunk of flesh, muscle, and loose intestines landed with a splattering thud, spreading blood and viscera onto the floor. Two lidless eyes watched in terror, unable to close or blink. Dom's lungs and heart twitched to a stop as their host died.

"THOSE WHO DISAPPOINT ME DO NOT DIE WELL. YOU WILL DO WELL TO REMEMBER."

Vincenzo looked away from what had once been his cousin and friend, turning back to He Who Walks Above's eyes. "No, I suppose they don't die well. I won't disappoint you. You'll have your prize. I guarantee it."

The mirror cracked, and blood seeped from the walls, oozing from between the tiles. More of it bubbled and poured from the toilets and urinals.

"I HAVE HAD ENOUGH EXCUSES. ENSURE DAVID BRYANT'S DELIVERY TO ME YOURSELF, OR I SHALL RETURN. NEXT TIME WE SPEAK, I WILL NOT BE AS POLITE."

The eyes and black cloud receded from the mirrors, leaving Vincenzo alone with Dom's disfigured body. He grasped the sink to steady his body. He felt like he'd collapse. It had taken every ounce of strength and energy he had to speak with the demon, and the whole ordeal left him feeling like he had gone ten rounds against a heavyweight boxer. He wondered what would have happened if He Who Walks Above had been serious.

Minutes passed as Vincenzo regained control over himself. He splashed some cold water onto his face and looked at himself in the cracked mirror, ignoring the sight of the bloody walls behind him. He looked paler than usual, almost ashen. His stomach still turned, but that might've been from the stench that emanated from the pile of meat that had once been Dom 'Raging Buck' Maturo.

I'm going to have to get out into the field myself this time, Vincenzo thought. *It's my undead ass on the line. I can't let Leo and Johnny fuck this one up on me.*

A group of people rushed into the men's room. They stopped dead in their tracks and looked at the scene. Cracked mirrors, blood all over the place, and the mangled, inside-out corpse on the floor.

Vincenzo shook the water off his hands and looked toward them. "What the fuck are you assholes staring at? Go get a fuckin' mop and clean this place up if you got time to stand there like a bunch of friggin' idiots."

***

"Should we check in with Vincenzo?" Johnny asked.

Leo looked up from his phone. "What for? We got nothin' to report. He already knows we got Duro with us. We'll call him when we get the writer. No point in annoyin' him for no reason. He's gotten pissier since he came back from the dead."

Johnny shifted in his seat.

"What?" Leo asked. "You got something to say about the boss?"

"I don't know." Johnny shrugged and fiddled with his fork, poking at what was left of the grayish meatloaf he had ordered. "What is he, though?"

"He's the boss. What else do you need to know?"

"I mean, is he a zombie now? A vampire? A Frankenstein?"

Leo sighed. "I've been thinkin' about that, too. See, he can't be a zombie if he ain't hobblin' around eatin' people's brains. He's not a vampire because he would've had to be bitten by one, and I don't think Vincenzo is out drinkin' blood and shit."

"But he can be a Frankenstein?"

"No, he can't be one of those either. If he were a Frankenstein, he would've had to been put together in a lab by a nutty scientist-type, ya dig?"

"So, what is he then?"

Leo shrugged. "He's the Undead Boss. He said he liked that one, so that's what we're gonna call him."

"Excuse me," a scrawny teenager said from across the aisle from them. He sat on a barstool with a plated hamburger in front of him, wore a red, long-sleeve shirt with a black vest, and had a face full of acne scars. "Frankenstein wasn't the monster. *Dr.* Frankenstein was the scientist who *created* the monster. Also, what are you guys talking about? Is that a show or a book with the Undead Boss? I haven't heard of anything like that, but it sounds cool."

Leo and Johnny looked at the kid as he fixed his glasses and waited for one of them to answer his question.

"Come on, kid!" Johnny said. "Leave us the fuck alone, and let us enjoy our meal in peace."

"Yeah!" Leo agreed. "Listen to little Pat Sajak over here with all the friggin' questions!"

"Pat Sajak didn't ask any questions," the teen said. "He's the Wheel of Fortune guy. You're thinking of Jeopardy."

WHO THE FUCK IS ROCKY PHANTASMIC?!

"Will you shut the fuck up!" Leo snapped. "My friend and I are trying to enjoy our meal, and we don't want to listen to you yappin' about whatever bullshit you think we give a shit about!"

"Mind your business," Johnny added, pointing toward the kid with his fork. "We don't want to have to mind yours, and you won't want that neither, kid."

"Hey!" a large man with a square haircut and a huge overbite exclaimed as he walked toward them from the restroom. "What did you just say?" His eyes narrowed at Johnny as he paced toward them. He rolled up the sleeves of his sweater as well in a menacing threat.

"This ain't none of your concern," Johnny retorted. "Walk away before you and I have a problem."

"Oh, I think I'm going to make it my problem." The man walked up to the teen. "You OK, bro."

The teen nodded. "Yeah. They're just being assholes."

"Oh!" Leo exclaimed. "We were mindin' our own business before you started in with us. Why don't you check that mouth of yours at the door next time you decide you wanna get in the middle of grown people's conversations."

"Do not talk to my little brother that way." The man approached the table. "Now, are you two greased-up idiots going to offer him an apology, or are *we* going to have a problem?"

"Don't copy me," Johnny said with a scoff. "I'm the one who said the thing about having a problem. Come up with something original, you truckstop loser."

The man went for Johnny, but Leo intervened first, punching the man in the gut from where he sat. It distracted him long enough for Johnny to grab the man by his hair and slam his face into the table. The resounding clamor of it echoed through the diner, and everyone turned to watch the action.

"We better get outta here," Leo muttered.

Johnny nodded. "Yeah."

Leo took some money out of his pocket and left a few twenties on the table. He stopped for a moment and dropped a few more on the unconscious figure lying next to the table. "Tell him to go buy some aspirin for the headache he's gonna have," he told the kid sitting at the bar, who watched with his mouth open. With that, Leo turned and walked toward the door, but the festivities weren't over yet.

"You two stop right there!"

Leo and Johnny both turned to see a quartet of men walking toward them. Each one looked meatier than the last, and none of them had decided to wear clean clothes out to dinner. Leo only counted one neck between the whole group.

"Guess this is *that* kind of diner. Think you can take the three mooks on the left, Johnny?"

Johnny cracked his knuckles. "Should be able to, Leo."

"Alright, bud. Let's go dancin'."

Leo took a single step when the glass crashed inward between them and the four men coming toward them. Duro stood there, brushing the broken glass from his hair. He unbuttoned his shirt, removed it, and tossed it to the floor. His bare torso was chiseled and covered with the barbed wire tattoos that Leo had seen on his arms and neck already.

His sudden appearance through the window had rattled Leo and Johnny's attackers. They sputtered out rushed apologies as they backed away, but Duro didn't seem like the type to be swayed by begging. All he did was smile and lunge forward.

Leo watched as Duro grabbed a man by the head and hurled him through another window. He kicked out at another, sending him into the wall with the crack of bone. Duro laughed, twisting the third's neck in a single, snapping motion. The last one tried to run away, but Duro grabbed him by the back of the neck and slammed his face into the floor with a crunch.

Duro straightened to observe the carnage he had dished out in a matter of seconds. He nodded and turned back to his escorts. The smile had gone back to his evil smirk, and he walked toward them. Leo learned then that Vincenzo hadn't been bullshitting them when he told them Duro sported a rock-hard erection when he killed. It was there, pitching the mother of all tents in Duro's pants, bigger and bolder than life itself.

Richie don't stand a chance against this motherfucker, Leo thought with a widening grin.

A shotgun blast sounded, and Duro flinched when the shot hit him in the side of the head. Instead of falling to the ground and dying as a normal human being would have done, he turned toward the source, glaring at the chef who had shot at him.

"Shit," the chef muttered. "That ain't right at all."

Duro made it over the counter in a single jump, picked up the chef by his neck, and slammed him back down onto the floor. Leo couldn't see what had happened, but from the cracking sound, he had to have shattered his spine along with breaking the rest of the bones in his body.

"Come on, Duro," Leo said, motioning toward the door. "Let's get the fuck outta here before some other moron with a death wish tries some shit on us. We've got a lot of road to cover."

With a slight nod, Duro agreed. He followed Leo and Johnny back to their car to continue their pursuit of David Bryant and the superhero who called himself Rocky Phantasmic.

Kid's not gonna know what hit him, Leo thought with a wry chuckle.

10. THE COMEDIAN GETS TAKEN OUT WITH THE TRASH

Cliff had never been big on napping. He'd always said only babies and old women took naps. After the weekend he had, however, he needed to get as much rest as possible. He didn't need his psyche cracking at the edges—not when the future of his career hung in the balance.

The Cliff Quentin Back to My Roots tour continued, and it had brought him from New Haven, Connecticut to Easthampton, Massachusetts. The drive hadn't been too long aside from a bunch of traffic because some dope had hit a deer, but he felt like he'd driven an entire world away. Still, he felt trapped in his hotel room due to his body acting like a little bitch.

This feels more like the Back to My Room *tour*, Cliff thought as he lay in bed. *I feel like I got grounded for jerking off at church and got sent to bed without any fucking dessert!*

Cliff sat up with a yawn. His newest stop was cozier than the last. No odors of former guests lingered in the air after permeating the carpets and drapes. Something about his temporary digs in Easthampton felt fresher than the New Haven hotel in which he'd slept the night before. It gave him the sense of a new beginning to his journey, even if he'd only had one other stop on his agenda so far.

After a quick piss, Cliff felt renewed. Whatever drugs had caused him to hallucinate all that crazy shit had finally flushed itself out of his system. He could put his New Haven misadventures behind him and get it out of his head for good.

WHO THE FUCK IS ROCKY PHANTASMIC?!

Maybe I'll get a decent bit out of the experience. I just hope getting drugged after my first show isn't the highlight of my trip.

Before anything else, though, Cliff needed dinner and maybe a trip to the local cannabis dispensary. California weed is amazing, but he still missed the shit in from his home state of Massachusetts.

He had gotten a few steps away from his hotel when his phone rang. He checked the phone and accepted the call since he wouldn't dare ignore it and send it to voicemail.

"Hi, Aunt Dorothea."

"Cliffy! I'm so happy you answered your phone!"

Cliff rolled his eyes. He almost always answered when his aunt called, but she couldn't help her tendency to be overdramatic about pretty much everything.

"You caught me," Cliff said with a polite laugh. "I literally just stepped out of my hotel to get some dinner."

"Oh? Where are you now? Still in Connecticut?"

Cliff's night and day in New Haven flashed in his memory unbidden, and he felt like he hadn't shaken it. Maybe whatever chemicals he'd been slipped hadn't gotten pissed out of his system yet.

"Hello?" Aunt Dorothea asked. "Cliff? Are you still there?"

"Yeah. Sorry. I zoned out for a second."

"You're not smoking weed again, are you?"

Cliff shook his head and sighed. "No, Aunt Dorothea. I am not smoking weed. I'm not in Connecticut anymore either. I'm in Massachusetts. I have a gig in Easthampton on Wednesday night."

"You're here in Massachusetts? Why aren't you coming to see me and your cousin for dinner? We'd love to have you!"

Cliff sighed again. Of course he'd love to see his aunt and his younger cousin Missy. He had planned on visiting all along while on this tour. Aunt Dorothea knew it would be around the weekend when he was closer and playing in Boston, but they'd never nailed down a date. They hadn't seen each other much over the last year or so, but it had been a turbulent one.

Aunt Dorothea acted as the matriarch of the Quentin family. She was Cliff's father's sister, and she had raised her nephew since his mother died and his father took off to Arizona or New Mexico or some fucking state with a desert climate. He'd complained endlessly that city life and the northeast didn't suit him at all. As it turned out, being a father didn't suit him much either, but dumping his kid on his only sister happened to be in his wheelhouse.

But Aunt Dorothea stepped up to the challenge without a second thought. She collected Cliff and raised him alongside her daughter as his legal guardian, even though she had her own struggles as a single mother. Her husband had left too, but he hadn't gone to venture into the desert for God knew what reason. He left to shack up with his secretary. The last Cliff had heard of his Uncle Sylvester was that he'd been arrested for insider trading or some other white-collar crime suited for conmen of a certain tax bracket.

"I'd love to come by," Cliff replied. "I'll be in Boston for a weekend gig. I'll let you know when I'm free."

"Nonsense!" Aunt Dorothea exclaimed. "You shouldn't even be in a hotel right now. You can stay with us in your old room. It looks nicer without all those posters of women in bikinis since your cousin and I converted it into a proper guest room, but I'm sure you can sleep well enough without being surrounded by wet cleavage."

"Did you throw the posters away?"

"Yeah. What else would I do with them?"

"Those were collectors' items! I had some rare playmates on the wall!"

"Well, I was tired of walking by the room and having them watch me with their sad, dead eyes. If you want to get them, you'll have to talk to the garbagemen to let you rummage through the dump since I threw them out months ago."

...you'll have to talk to the garbagemen...

Cliff shook his head, killing the echoing of his aunt's statement.

"Alright," he said aloud. "Look, it's almost two hours to get from here to your house. I'll make you a deal since that commute to go back and forth means I'd be driving the dystopian highways of this fucked-up state for four hours if I stayed with you. I'll do the show on Wednesday night and shoot over to your place on Thursday morning. Then you'll have me for a long weekend aside from when I have to do my Boston show on Saturday night. Deal?"

"Deal. Speaking of deals, how'd the meeting go with that writer you told me about? Are you moving forward with the show?"

Cliff groaned and pinched the bridge of his nose. "The little shit ghosted me and never even had the courtesy to send me a text with an excuse. Guess the pressure of going bigtime was too much for his cowardly ass."

"Oh well. The world needs cowards too, I guess. It takes all kinds. Maybe you'll come up with your own show idea to pitch. You don't need him. We'll see you soon, though."

"Yes, you will. Thursday night."

"Thursday afternoon. Don't stay out all night and sleep all day. You know I hate it when you do that."

Cliff smiled. "Alright, Aunt Dorothea. I'll see you Thursday afternoon then."

"Good. Love you, Cliffy."

"Love you too, auntie. Bye-bye."

Cliff ended the call and put his phone back into his pocket. He couldn't help the smile on his face. He felt good about something for the first time in a while. Aunt Dorothea always knew what to say, and visiting her and Missy would be a much-needed stop on his tour.

He'd been so focused on the phone call and the thoughts of stopping home for a spell that he hadn't noticed how far he'd walked from the hotel. He'd parked blocks away, and he now found himself in a suburban neighborhood surrounded by houses with big lawns and little ceramic gnomes peeking at him from between the bushes with creepy shit-eating grins.

"Shit," Cliff groaned, turning to go back in the direction of his hotel. "Fucking suburbia."

***

Cliff ate a quick dinner at a small chain restaurant while most of the patrons chattered their lips off about some breaking news about a diner that had been smashed up with some fresh corpses inside it. It sounded like just another day in America.

"Another shooting?" Cliff asked, looking up from his empty plate when the waitress came by to collect it.

She shook her head. "No, not this time. It sounds like a brawl that got way out of hand. The police are looking for clues about the men who started and ended the fight. I'm glad they didn't come in here. Is that bad?"

Cliff shook his head. "Not at all. That's survival guilt. Pray for those who died, but be thankful it wasn't you. That's how I get through the day whenever shit like this goes down."

The waitress nodded, took Cliff's plate, and walked it to the back. He wondered if he had offended her by his outlook, but he thought it was the best way to get through life when a dystopian state loomed right around the corner for all of them.

Cliff got up and dropped a tenner on the table for the waitress. He didn't feel like having any more conversation, so he figured it would be best to walk to the counter and pay his bill.

"This is awful," a woman said next to him.

Cliff got ready to roll his eyes and groan, but he stopped himself. His eyes wouldn't roll since they'd seemed to glue themselves to the tall, slender woman who stood near him watching the unfolding news story on the wall-mounted television. Her black hair shined in the fluorescent light, and Cliff had to remind his mouth to close before a line of drool fell from its corner. A small part of his soul had always longed for Asian women, and the specimen standing mere feet from him was breathtaking.

"Yeah," Cliff managed to get out, watching the woman and not the news story about those who had been killed in a diner not unlike the one in which he stood. "That shit is terrible."

The woman turned toward him, locking eyes for a moment before looking over his whole face. "You look familiar."

Cliff smirked. "I do, but I'm really modest about my familiarity."

"I know you! You're Cliff Quentin, right? The comedian."

Cliff's smirk grew into a beaming smile. "You caught me. I am Cliff Quentin the comedian. Don't tell anyone I'm here. I don't want anyone mobbing me to death in a restaurant."

"Too soon," the man behind the counter said, holding out a ticket for Cliff to sign while shaking his head. "After what happened at that diner? Come on, man."

"Sorry." Cliff grabbed the paper and put his autograph at the bottom. He turned back toward the woman and said, "Sorry. My jokes don't always go over that well, but that's how the business is right now with this cancel culture bullshit."

The woman smirked. "I like a man with a dark sense of humor. I'm June, by the way."

Cliff returned the smile. "I'm Cliff, but you know that already. Do you want to go out and grab a bite to eat or something?"

June laughed. "Didn't you just pay your bill from dinner?"

"Oh yeah. How about some drinks, then?"

"How about some weed at my place? Do you smoke?"

"Yeah, I do on occasions like today. I was about to hit the dispensary down the road."

Jane's smile grew. "Small world. Let's get some flower and see what happens."

Cliff nodded and walked out of the restaurant with June by his side. With everything he'd gone through over the last couple of days, he needed a win. If his luck could hold, he may even be able to start a long streak of it.

***

"When I smoked weed when I was younger, we called it trees," Cliff said, passing the bowl back to June after taking a hit. "It does look like little trees if you don't cut the stems off like they do at dispensaries."

"You can't smoke the stems anyway." June exhaled a small cloud of smoke. "It's too harsh on your throat." She passed the bowl back to Cliff, who accepted it for another hit.

"I shouldn't smoke too much of this." Cliff let a stream of smoke float from his mouth to the ceiling. "I had a drink spiked after my last gig on Saturday night, and I don't know if any of that shit is still floating around in my system."

"Oh no." June took her bowl back from him. "What happened?" She lit the flower and took a slow drag.

Cliff shrugged. "Normal acid trip shit, I guess, assuming that's what got put into my drink. Saw some freaky shit, almost got my ass kicked by a gang of middle schoolers, and pissed off this psychic."

June laughed, and it turned to coughing as smoke spewed from her mouth and nose. Once she got herself out of control she asked, "You pissed off a psychic while on acid?"

Cliff laughed with her. He hadn't found it funny at the time, but the weed in his system compounded over time helped him find the humor in the situation.

"I felt so bad about it afterward," he admitted. "I flipped over their table and stormed out because I thought the tarot cards were possessed by a demon or something. I didn't even pay for the reading."

"But why would you go do that if you were tripping? That sounds like a bad idea in the first place."

"I don't know. A lot of freaky shit had happened up to that point. I thought a bunch of shit had happened at least. Something happened, but not what I thought happened. Does that make sense to you, or am I rambling?"

"Maybe." June put the bowl on the table. "Hey, come here."

Cliff obliged and leaned closer. Their lips met, and they kissed on the couch while June's Lana del Rey record played in the background. She had a cozy home, and it felt cozier with them together. Cliff's hand ventured around June's body, and she didn't stop him. She moved her hands as well, exploring the inside of Cliff's tee-shirt to rub the hair on his chest.

"Is this a perk of working on the road?" June asked, separating from Cliff's lips.

"It's one of them," Cliff replied, "but it might be my favorite."

They kissed again, and Cliff squeezed June's thigh through her leggings. She gave a soft moan in return and moved her hands along Cliff's body once again. Cliff was ready to ask if she wanted to move the party to the bedroom when June stopped.

"Hold on," she said, backing away. She picked up her phone and read the screen. "My husband's home." She returned the text, clicking away at the screen like she hadn't just announced that the world would crash into the sun in a few seconds.

Cliff stood. "What?! You didn't tell me you're married, and you're not even wearing a ring!"

June shrugged. "Is that a problem?"

"Is it a… Why aren't you freaking out?! Your husband is about to bust us on the couch with your hands up my shirt!"

June rolled her eyes. "So? You're worried that I got to second base with you? Are you fourteen years old?" She giggled, and Cliff couldn't understand how she found the situation so funny, even if they were both high as kites. Cliff told jokes for a living, but he didn't find being murdered by a jealous husband particularly amusing.

The front door opened before Cliff could ask June if her husband kept guns in the house. He backed off the married woman and did his best to make it look like they were having a conversation on the couch—even though he was now standing—and not smoking weed and making out.

Alright, Cliff thought amid his paranoid panic. *There's only one way out of this situation. Pretend to be as gay as possible, and maybe he'll buy it and let you go.*

The husband walked around the corner, looking at his wife and the interloper near the couch. He was burly, but not too much so. He had a neat brunette beard that matched the hair on his head. He wore a suit with a loosened tie. To Cliff's surprise, he didn't even flinch at the sight of his wife being home alone with a strange man while smoking weed and listening to soft music.

"Wow," he said. "You weren't joking. You really scored with Cliff Quentin!"

"I haven't scored yet!" June retorted with a laugh. "I was about to, but then you came home and interrupted us." She turned to Cliff. "This is Jim, by the way. He's my husband."

"It's a pleasure." Jim held out a hand and shook Cliff's, grinning like a goon. He picked up the bowl from the table. "Well, since I'm home now, can I join you two?"

"I don't mind," June replied. To Cliff, she asked, "Is it OK with you if he joins us?"

"Sure." No other response had come into Cliff's mind. He was high, horny, and not sure how Jim would react if he declined. "I mean, it's your house and wife, right? Who am I to stop you?"

"Good man." Jim sat on the couch. "Come and sit with us." He put the bowl to his mouth and took a long hit from it. "I've been looking forward to blowing off a little steam all day. This day just would not end!"

"It's so cool you're into this," June said to Cliff as he took the place next to her opposite of Jim. She kissed him in a dumbfounding moment. When she moved to kiss his neck, Cliff risked a look toward Jim, who took another hit while watching. His erection had become more than apparent through his khakis.

What the fuck is happening here? he asked himself as if he didn't already know the answer.

"It's so cool that you're into this," June repeated. Did she want Cliff to confirm he was as cool as she assumed?

Cliff didn't ask what she meant. He didn't have the chance. She turned and moved toward her husband, kissing him next. Cliff didn't know what to do. Part of his brain told him to leave the house and pretend the tryst never took place, but he sat transfixed as the woman he'd been fixing to fuck made out with her husband instead of him.

Either way, this'll make a killer bit if I can think of a way to make it funny.

June reached for Cliff. When she realized he wasn't right next to her, she moved off her husband and back to him. Jim followed, kissing his wife's neck from behind while she clawed at Cliff's body and pressed her lips to his neck.

"Come on, baby," June said in a sultry voice, meeting Cliff's gaze. "You wanna join us upstairs where the three of us can all stretch out and get comfier?"

Cliff caught a look from Jim and got a wink. He didn't know if the married couple had planned this all along or if the whole thing played out the way it had by coincidence like a badly written porn plot. Still, he couldn't ignore the chemistry between the three of them, and it didn't matter if his mind told him that bad horror movies also started this way. Every inch of his body screamed at him to say yes and go *stretch out* with the swinging couple on their marital bed, and he'd always gone with his animalistic instincts.

"Sure."

June smiled. "Alright then." She got up and helped Cliff get back to his feet. She took his hand and led him upstairs. Jim followed. They made their way to the master bedroom, which lived up to its title. A king-sized bed stood against the far wall, and skylights showed the evening sky above the house. The whole thing was connected to a master bathroom complete with a shower and a jacuzzi tub.

"I need to take a quick shower," Jim said, standing near the bathroom door. "I don't want to climb into bed smelling like work. Feel free to start without me."

June hopped into the bed and lay in the center with a giggle. "Don't be too long, darling. Otherwise, Cliff and I will be finished before you can come join us."

Jim laughed. "I won't be too long." He stripped off his shirt as he went into the bathroom, and Cliff looked over his body. He noticed the muscles he could see bulging in Jim's back.

Shit. I guess this is happening.

June sat up and pulled her shirt over her head, revealing her stomach and red bra. She bit her lip and kicked Cliff's leg with a playful foot.

"What are you waiting for? Don't you want to have me to yourself for a bit before my husband comes to gobble us both up?"

Cliff did. He climbed on the bed, kissing June's body as he climbed over her smooth skin, pausing from it to pull her panties off in a single motion. Another giggle fit emanated from between her red lips. He pulled off his shirt next, and June pulled herself up to help him with his belt buckle and get his pants off. June's bra was the only piece of clothing between them now, and Cliff made it a thing of the past by unhooking it and tossing it off the bed like it was radioactive. His pants followed into the abyss over the side of the bed.

"This feels much better." June pulled Cliff toward her, kissed him, and hooked her legs around his. He could feel warmth radiating from her, begging for him through her body heat. The weed had his head buzzing, and June had other parts of him doing the same thing. He was ready to take the playful kissing and rolling around to another level when he saw Jim exit the bathroom with a towel tied around his waist.

"I'm glad to see I'm not the only one who's gotten naked." Jim dropped the towel to reveal his erect penis. Cliff watched as he sauntered toward the bed while June kissed his neck and rubbed his thigh.

"Have you ever been with a guy before?" Jim whispered, climbing onto the bed to put Cliff between him and his wife.

Cliff thought about lying as he would in any other situation when asked that, but he figured this particular situation was different. "Yes," he whispered in return. "A while back."

"Would you mind doing it again, or will we be taking turns with June?"

"I...well..." Cliff looked at June, who stared back at him with a smirk as she bit her lip again. He could tell she wanted them all to play together instead of her simply being the meat in a man sandwich. It wouldn't be so bad. The last time he'd been with a man didn't go too badly. It wasn't his go to fantasy, but it worked on occasion.

"Yeah," Cliff finally answered. "I mean, I don't mind it at all. Fuck it, I'm here, right?"

Jim smiled and kissed him. It felt different than kissing June's soft lips and smooth body. It was rougher but in a good way. He could feel Jim's beard against his face, but it didn't turn him off. To the contrary, Cliff's erection had morphed into a full-on rager now that their devil's three-way had officially leveled up.

June didn't want to be left out, and she moved to get between them, sucking and pulling each of the men in her bed in turn while they made out. Cliff pulled away from Jim long enough to enter June next, fucking her while Jim kissed his neck from behind and rubbed his body.

Cliff and Jim took turns on June, and she loved every second of it based on the moaning coming from her mouth. Everything culminated with Jim fucking his wife doggy style while she sucked Cliff. All the two men had to do was high-five and complete the perfect Eifel Tower moment as they climaxed in both of June's ends.

"You good?" Jim asked, quickening the pace of his thrusts.

"Yeah," Cliff replied. "I'm good."

"You're going to wind up in the back of a garbage truck for this shit, Cliffy-poo."

Cliff backed up, and his penis came out of June's mouth with a popping sound. "What the fuck did you just say?"

"I asked if you're good. I'm about to…" Jim's eyes rolled back, and he looked at the ceiling as his moans intensified.

"Come here," June said, grabbing at Cliff. "I want you two to finish at the same time."

"No," Cliff backed up further, stumbling off the side of the bed. "Why did you say that to me about the garbage truck? Did you hear that from my act?"

If Jim heard what Cliff had asked, he didn't feel like acknowledging while he came inside his wife. He let out a guttural groan while grasping June's hips. June bared down on the sheets with her red fingernails, letting out a squeal of her own. Jim collapsed a few seconds later, lying in the bed.

"Holy shit." He looked toward Cliff, who was still staring at him. "Did you finish too?"

"He didn't," June answered. "What's wrong, Cliff? Did you want to add to this cream pie instead of making me swallow it?"

"Why did you say that to me?" Cliff asked again, staring into Jim's eyes. He knew he looked crazy, and the accusation sounded crazier. "Why did you bring up the garbage truck?"

"Garbage truck?" Jim asked in return. "What the hell are you talking about?"

"Are you calling me a fucking garbage truck?" June asked. "What the fuck, Cliff?! I'm not into that degradation shit!"

"That's not…" Cliff let out a long sigh. He closed his eyes tight and shook his head. "I'm not saying you're a garbage truck. Jim said… He said…"

"Are you OK?" Jim asked. "You're not looking so hot, man."

"He said someone slipped something in his drink last night," June said. "It might still be messing with his system."

"Shit." He climbed off the bed, walking around to get closer to Cliff. "No worries if that's what's up. You want a Powerade or something?"

"I have to go." Cliff grabbed his shorts off the ground and slipped them over his legs. He was still hard, but he ignored the want to finish what he'd started. He should have been climbing back into bed and finishing with whichever of the happy couple wanted it the most, but the chill that climbed up his spine had spread. He had to leave before something bad happened.

Cliff ignored June and Jim's concerns about his well-being as he picked up the rest of his clothes from the floor. He didn't blame them for worrying about him. If Jim was fucking with him with that garbage truck line, there would be hell to pay, and Cliff didn't want to punch a man in the face after what they'd just done and almost finished together. That wouldn't help him to get his career back on track at all.

I should've left the moment the husband came home. These swinging motherfuckers have been playing with me from the start!

"Cliff!" June called as he left the bedroom to descend the stairs and leave. "Wait! I drove you here!"

Cliff ignored her as he headed into the night, carrying his clothes in his arms.

***

The night was cold, and it felt colder as the frigid breeze hit the sweat coating Cliff's skin. He paused to pull on his left sock, followed by the right. He hobbled into his pants next and got his shoes on his feet. With the tee shirt, he'd gotten completely dressed and avoided getting stopped by a cop for his indecent exposure.

Cliff walked to a corner and looked for a street sign to help him get back to the main road. He didn't think he'd find himself wandering the streets at night, but it was the second time in the last three days. At least Easthampton was a suburb and not full of hobo prophets and middle-school hooligans attempting to drive him insane.

But then there was Jim, the bisexual, enthusiastic swinger husband. Why did he say what he said, and did he know that it would set Cliff off the way it had? Why bother getting to the point of climaxing if he had planned on fucking with Cliff's mind from the start? Maybe Jim had gotten jealous that Cliff's dick was bigger than his.

Guess that's why they call it a devil's three-way.

Cliff pulled his phone out of his pocket to check his GPS program for the best walking route back to his hotel. He had no signal, though, so the app refused to even give him his current location.

"Fucking suburbia," Cliff muttered, shoving his phone back into his pocket. He looked for anything that could help him, but he stood by an intersection that made way for houses, trees, more houses, some more trees, and a whole bunch of garbage cans.

Must be trash night.

Cliff assumed he was going north. He had no idea if it would lead him to a main road, but he felt like he should wind up somewhere he could at least get a halfway-decent cell signal. Maybe there'd be someone he could ask for directions. But people don't walk the streets at night in neighborhoods like this—not unless they were up to something nefarious.

"Or lost."

Cliff stopped and let out a sigh. He felt stupid, and he considered going back to June's house to ask one of them for a ride. He'd have to apologize for leaving the way he did, and he figured he'd have to swallow his pride to do it.

But when he turned around, Cliff realized he had no idea which house was June and Jim's. He couldn't even remember what her car looked like.

Am I still stoned? Shit. I can't even tell.

He felt it, even if his adrenaline tried its hardest to compensate for what the THC had done in his brain. He continued his random walking, checking his phone every block or so to see if the signal had returned. He became more lost, and none of the streets seemed to be labeled—not that knowing whether he was on Oak Street, Maple Avenue, or Sycamore Lane would help him in the slightest. He could've tried knocking on one of the doors that had their lights on like a trick-or-treater, but they might think he was crazy and call the police. That might help in the long run, but it would lead to even more problems if they recognized him and floated the story of him getting high before getting lost in a suburban neighborhood.

It'll still make a good bit, though.

"Not without a fucking punchline it won't."

Cliff heard the sound of machinery rumbling and turned toward it. A truck pulled down the other side of the street at a snail's pace. The red lights blared as it slowed, and a stench on the light breeze hit Cliff's face. He squinted through the glare of the headlights and saw a black and gray garbage truck coming toward him.

"They don't collect trash at night," Cliff said aloud. "The old boomers in the neighborhood would pitch a fit about the noise."

The truck stopped, and the passenger side door opened. One of the garbagemen dropped from their seat and landed on the street with the smack of their boots against the pavement. Cliff stepped back, lost his footing for a moment when he left the sidewalk, and stumbled onto a damp lawn. A cloud of flies followed the garbageman out of the truck, swarming around him like a living, insectile aura. Buzzing filled the quiet night as they approached Cliff.

"What do you want from me?!" Cliff shouted as he regained his footing.

The garbageman stopped in the middle of the street and tilted its head. They stood in the glow of the streetlight, and Cliff could see that it wore thick, blue coveralls, a dingy reflective vest that had gotten way too dirty to be effective, and a pair of protective gloves. They also had milky-white eyes and a slack face that made it look like a zombie from a bad late-night B-movie.

"This isn't real," Cliff told himself. "The weed triggered another acid flashback. That's all. Garbagemen aren't after you. This isn't happening."

You've been marked, comedian!

The psychic had said that, and so had the hobo prophet, only the latter had mentioned some deity with a four-word long name. Could it be true? Could he have been marked by some weird-ass entity, or did the drinking and drugs cause this latest round of outlandish hallucinations?

The driver of the garbage truck got out next, followed by another cloud of flies. This garbageman was beefier and had a paler face. They dragged a can off the curb and slid it into the street. The top fell with a clatter, and the trash inside spilled out. The garbageman placed it in the middle of the road and pointed a gloved finger in Cliff's direction. They opened their mouth, and more flies escaped along with some cockroaches. If they meant to speak, they failed.

They want you to get in the can, numb nuts.
"Hell no!" Cliff shouted. "Leave me alone!"

Cliff turned and ran. He didn't check to see if the garbagemen followed. He knew they would. He only had to outrun them long enough to find somewhere safe to hide or for the drugs in his system to wear off.

Weed doesn't make you see shit like this, a voice in Cliff's head told him. *And nobody slipped anything into your drink—nothing that would have lasted this long, if at all. You know this is real. You've been marked by He Who Walks Above, and he wants you riding in the back of that garbage truck like you've always been meant to do.*

"Fuck you!"

Cliff crashed through a fence, tripping before rolling on the ground. He checked himself for any debris or holes in his skin before getting up and running through the property toward a parallel street. He got there, huffing from his run. If he knew he'd be running for his life through suburbia, he would have focused more on cardio rather than weight training at the gym.

He was lost even more than before, but a grateful feeling spread throughout his body when he saw he hadn't been followed. It didn't last long, though. The garbage truck—or maybe a new one—drove around the corner, blinding him with its high beams.

This must be how a deer feels before it's smashed to shit by an eighteen-wheeler.

The truck's tires squealed as it turned toward him and picked up speed. It smashed into a set of metal cans, sending them flying along with the trash as it spilled from the tops. Cliff jumped out of the way as it passed, knocking a mailbox off its wooden post in its wake. He came back up after rolling to see the truck screech to another stop. The whole truck exuded flies and other vermin now, and it had left a trail of red slime on the road that looked like a mixture of clotted blood and mucus.

The two garbagemen emerged again and walked toward Cliff. They watched him with their lifeless eyes and unanimated faces. The beefier one—the driver—pulled down on a lever near the back of the truck, and the compactor lifted, revealing an inside full of garbage and human bones with strips of rancid meat still stuck to them.

I don't think this is what Grampa meant when he said that shit about riding in the back of a garbage truck. He was never this literal. It was a damn metaphor for Christ's sake!

"It was meant to be a life lesson, you fuckin' idiots! Live your life well, and you can end your life in the hearse. Live like a trash human, and you wind up in the back of the garbage truck."

The garbagemen didn't care about Cliff's explanation. Their ears might've been too full of literal shit to even hear what Cliff shouted at them. They weren't going to wait all night. They moved forward, this time doing it faster than a zombie. The clouds of flies followed them, and the buzzing intensified.

Cliff tried his best to dodge the coming attackers, but his left foot caught the edge of the curb, causing him to falter. He lost precious milliseconds, and the garbagemen pounced on him. They each took one of his arms and dragged him to the back of their truck. Cliff struggled and tried to break free, but his feet slipped in the slime on the road.

"Stop it! Let me go, you assholes!"

The flies surrounded him now and began crawling on his flesh. They made their way under his shirt and continued all over his body, sticking to the sweat. Some of them bit into him with their tiny insect mouths, and his body cried out in pain. He couldn't even hope it would be over quickly since he didn't know what the demonic garbagemen wanted with him, and he didn't feel lucky enough to receive a quick and painless death. He Who Walks Above had marked him, and Cliff would never find out who that was or why he'd marked him in the first place.

"What do you want from me?!" Cliff cried as his body inched toward the back of the garbage truck. The reek was strong enough to choke him, but he forced himself not to vomit so he could plead for his life. "Tell me what you want me to say! Don't put me in the back of that truck!"

"You either end up in the back of a hearse or the back of a garbage truck," Cliff's grandfather's voice said from the menagerie of trash and human remains waiting for him on the other side of the truck's gaping asshole. *"I tried to warn you, son. Now you'll have to take that ride and see for yourself."*

"No, Grampa!" Cliff exclaimed. "I don't want to! I don't know what I did to piss off that demon! I don't deserve this! I don't!"

The garbagemen tossed Cliff into the back of the truck, and his body slid down the slimy metal ramp before splashing in a vat of a concoction that might've been a combination of blood, shit, and bile. The flies and roaches under his clothes thrummed and jittered in enthusiasm as he soaked in the putrid juices. Cliff splashed in it, trying to climb back out despite the two garbagemen waiting outside of it. His escape would be in vain, and he knew it the moment the meatier garbageman pulled the lever down, closing the hatch ahead of him. The compactor came down, blotting out the dim glow of the streetlights. Cliff screamed, but no one would hear him. Cold metal pressed against his body, forcing him into the shit and blood stew, pushing his body against the floor. The air escaped his lungs, and he felt the pressure building on his chest. He'd pop at any moment, adding his juices to the mixture, feeding the demon living inside the garbage truck.

I should have finished in June's mouth, Cliff thought as the darkness overtook him. *If only I'd done that, I wouldn't have...*

11. THE HAUNTED CATACOMBS BENEATH THE STAR-MART

"I don't get why your costume has to be green and yellow," Dave said. "Do those colors signify anything?"

"Nope," Rocky replied. He pushed the hoodies on the rack aside. He hadn't yet found one he liked.

"Then you can use any hoodie, right? Why not a red one with a black cape or a blue one with a red cape?"

"It has to be green with a yellow cape. I haven't been on the superhero scene long enough for a costume change. It wouldn't make any sense."

Dave sighed. "Nothing's made sense over the last few days, so I don't think you have anything to worry about there, bud." He leaned on the blue shopping cart, which they'd filled with provisions for their stay at Dave's uncle's cabin in Maine. He had grabbed plenty of canned soup, a couple of loaves of bread, peanut butter, jelly, and two five-gallon jugs of water. He didn't know how long they'd need to stay, but it's always best to be prepared. Judging by the clouds that had been creeping over them, a storm would make an appearance soon. If it turned into a blizzard, it would keep them inside the cabin for an extended stay.

Their luck had changed for the better, but only by a bit. They had found an all-night Star-Mart off the highway in New Hampshire, and it had everything they needed and then some.

"Once you find some new clothes, we can grab some board games or a deck of cards," Dave said. "I don't know what my uncle has there aside from a thousand books."

"Aha!" Rocky exclaimed, reaching into the rack and pulling out a New York Jets hoodie. "Green!"

"That works. You can put your RP logo over the insignia. You don't want people around here thinking you're a Jets fan. I'm surprised they even have Jets merchandise this deep into New England."

Rocky dropped the hoodie into their cart. "Let's head over to the fabric department. I can find some good material for a new cape."

Dave smiled as Rocky jogged toward the fabric area in the far corner of the store. The young superhero had an innocent mind. Despite beating a few men in New Haven and eviscerating the little critters at the highway rest stop, he hadn't displayed any motivation toward wanton and unnecessary violence. Everything he did, he did for his moral code. It was all nonsense he'd gotten from comic books, but he made it work in the real world. Anyone else with that kind of power would use it for financial gain or to get revenge on their perceived enemies. Rocky Phantasmic, however, lived the good guy lifestyle and didn't waver from it. Dave found it admirable and endearing to behold someone like Rocky in the real world instead of fiction.

When Dave got to the fabric department, he found Rocky looking through the merchandise in search of something that would be good enough for a new cape for his superhero costume. Dave watched, and some of the nonsense he had heard from Dr. Nielsen in the phantom psychiatrist's office popped into his head, and it wasn't just the part about Dave's latent attraction toward his younger travel companion.

"Are you OK?" Rocky asked.

Dave shook the daze out of his head. "Yeah, I'm good. I can't get what happened at that rest stop out of my head is all."

Rocky nodded. "Me too. Those little monsters were messed up like land piranha."

"Not that part. Before that when I spoke to the creepy ghost-shrink."

"Oh? Why is that bothering you?"

Dave shrugged. If he could give Rocky an honest answer he could understand, he'd tell him everything. From the sins of his ancestors becoming his problem, to the attraction he may or may not be feeling for Rocky, and back to him having to deal with all the insanity he'd endured since the night some c-lister mob goons knocked on his car window.

However, one thing had floated to the surface above everything else, and Dave thought Rocky might have a nugget of wisdom about it.

"Do you think I'm a coward, Rocky?"

Rocky turned toward him with a roll of bright yellow fabric in his hands. "No. Why would I think that?"

"I'm running away from my problems instead of facing them head-on. All I've done since the shit hit the fan was run and hide behind a literal superhero's cape. I might've left Heather to deal with some of this, and I can't even get in touch with her to find out if anything's happened to her. I'm worried about Kayla, too. I know leaving her with her grandparents while I sort this out is the right thing to do, but what if the people after me go after her?"

Dave had been able to talk someone into letting him make a call on their cellphone, but Heather hadn't picked up. The call went straight to voicemail, which meant Heather's phone had died or she'd left it off. It freaked him out when it happened, but Rocky mentioned that his cousins, the pair of goons dubbed the Unmade Men, would have answered it if they had taken her to demand he come to them to get her back. His wisdom helped a little, but the guilt still hadn't left his mind.

"I mean, what's staying at a cabin in the middle of fuckin' nowhere going to do to help anyone?" Dave continued. "I'm hiding like a hermit and hoping all this bullshit works itself out, but I'm kidding myself. If Dr. Nielsen was telling the truth, then I'm not escaping anything."

"For what it's worth," Rocky replied, "I don't think you're a coward. And I should know. I spent most of my life a coward. Actually, it was all my life since it took dying to turn me into a hero. You're doing the only thing you can. Besides, when they come for you, as you know they will, I'll be there to fight them off. Part of this was drawing them away from your family, remember?"

"Yeah, I remember. That was before, though, back when I thought the only thing after me were your cousins and not monsters and demons or whatever."

"That doesn't matter. You haven't wavered off your course, and that's admirable." Rocky rubbed the spool of yellow fabric on the side of his face. "This is it. This is the one. I'm going to ask the lady at the counter to cut a few feet of this for me."

Dave smiled again. Rocky was as far from being a sage as one could be, but he turned out to be wise. Dave pushed the shopping cart closer when the lights in the store went out.

"Shit. Of all the times to have a blackout. The storm hasn't even started yet."

"This isn't a blackout," Rocky said, looking upward. "The lights are still on. I can feel them."

Dave cocked an eyebrow at him. "You can?"

Rocky nodded. "The fluorescents are still buzzing above us." He turned to look down the aisles. "We're alone. Everyone who was in the store with us is gone."

"We are." Dave confirmed it with his own eyes. "Maybe the ghost-shrink is going to come back and discuss the bully that gave me a pink belly on the bathroom floor and how that might have contributed to me developing a queer lifestyle later in life."

Rocky turned toward him. "What?"

"I was being facetious. Not all bullied kids wind up gay. Well, a bully did teabag me when I was a freshman in high school, but I didn't like it much then. Unless he knew I'd turn out queer before I did, there isn't any correlation between that and me eventually coming to terms with my queerness."

Rocky blinked a few times. "You've lost me."

"Don't worry about it." Dave took a couple of steps forward. "I'm rambling as a defense mechanism probably. Dr. Nilsen would be sure to point that—"

Dave couldn't finish his statement. The ground under his feet crumbled and dumped Rocky and him into the void underneath the Star-Mart fabric department.

***

Rocky moved like lightning. He kicked off the circular stone wall surrounding them and aimed himself to catch Dave before turning in the air and kicking at the other far wall to slow the descent. When he hit the ground, he did it holding Dave like a literal damsel in distress—not that he could've been anything else in that scenario.

"Thanks," Dave said as Rocky let him on the ground. "That was… Thanks. I couldn't have done that myself."

"Don't mention it." Rocky looked upward to the pale gray circle at the top of the chasm. "I can jump up there if I can launch off the wall a few times."

Dave nodded. "I've done that in some Super Mario games, so I understand the physics of what you're suggesting."

"What is this place? Did we fall down a sink hole or something?"

"I wish it were that simple." Dave walked forward. He didn't have a better answer. It was dark, but he could see they'd been dropped into an underground tunnel. The aroma reminded him of the mouse or the rat that had died in the kitchen wall. They couldn't find it, so they had to live with the smell for a week or two during a humid summer while they waited for it to dry out.

"We better try that wall-jumping thing you suggested," Dave said. "I don't think this tunnel leads anywhere good. If I had to guess, and I am, I'd say it leads to more tunnels."

"Like a maze?"

Dave nodded. "Yeah, like a maze with no exit. We'd wander around till whoever wants to find us finds us."

"OK. I'll pick you up again and jump up the—"

A rumbling filled the cavern, and Rocky leapt out of the way as the shaft of the chasm that brought them into the catacombs beneath Star-Mart caved inward, closing the way behind them, leaving them in pitch blackness.

Dave sneezed and wiped his nose on his sleeve. A low light filled the tunnel. The rocks glowed with it like they'd been infused with luminescent material. It reminded Dave of a glow-in-the-dark toy he'd gotten out of a cereal box as a kid.

"Guess we don't have much of a choice now," he said. "Looks like we have to see if there's an exit at the end of this thing."

"I can make one." Rocky balled his hand in a fist and slammed it into the wall. It shook, and dust and some pebbles fell from the ceiling. He put his hand back to do it again.

"Don't!" Dave exclaimed.

Rocky stopped with his fist inches from hitting the wall a second time. He turned to Dave and asked, "Why not?"

"You'll cause a cave-in, and I don't think either of us will be able to crawl out of it. I'm sorry, Rocky, but we can't punch our way out of here."

Rocky put his head down and shoved his hands into his pockets.

Dave sighed and put his hand on Rocky's shoulder. "Don't worry. If there are any monsters, you can punch them straight into the next century. You can go nuts like it's your birthday."

That put a smile on Rocky's face. "OK. Which way do we go?"

"We can't go back, so we'll have to go forward. Hopefully we'll come back out at the donut shop on the other side of the parking lot. I could sure use a coffee right about now."

They walked, using the luminescent green glow to see their way. Dave ran his hand against the wall, and he was surprised to find it rough against his fingertips. He thought it would be smooth from the glowing cracks, but it felt like they had fallen into a sandpaper mine.

It all felt too real, and Dave kept reminding himself that they might be in the Star-Mart still, lying on the floor having a seizure or a fit of some kind while the employees watched and panicked about how to deal with them. It made more sense than discovering an underground cave by falling through a sinkhole, and it wouldn't surprise him in the slightest.

"Maybe we fell into another dimension," Rocky suggested. "That's why everyone disappeared. The lights never went out, either. It just happened that the dimension we've been transported to doesn't have electricity."

"That makes about as much sense as anything I was thinking," Dave admitted. "It figures that the multiverse turns out to be real, and it's trying to kill us."

"How would we know for sure?"

"I'll let you know if I see a sign."

They came to a fork in the road. The way to the right led to a stone bridge over a chasm in the ground. The way on the left led downward, deeper into the maze.

"I think the bridge is a trap," Dave said, touching his chin with his finger. "It's made to look like the way out, and the other way was made to make us think we were going deeper underground. So, by that logic, we go left."

"Left," Rocky repeated. "Like toward the way that looks like certain doom?"

Dave nodded. "Yes, that's right."

"No, the bridge is on the right."

"I meant to say you're correct. We're taking the way to the left because the bridge looks so safe and inviting, so it has to be a trap. Do you understand what I'm saying?"

"OK."

"Is there any input you want to throw out there?"

Rocky shrugged.

"Alright," Dave said with a sigh. "Left is it."

***

Dave and Rocky ventured on the leftward path that led them deeper into the cavernous maze of glowing rock. The hallway ended at a domed chamber held up by several pillars arranged in a random sequence. They had to zig and zag to navigate.

"This reminds me of the Mines of Moria scene from Lord of the Rings," Dave remarked. "They got trapped and had to find the way out or get devoured by goblins and orcs."

"How did they get out?"

"They took the…" Dave paused, let out a long breath, and shook his head. "They took the underground bridge that led them outside."

Rocky looked at Dave with a cocked eyebrow.

"But this isn't Lord of the Rings, and we aren't in Moria. We should be cognizant about getting lost. This place is huge, and it would take forever to backtrack. I think they designed this room to confuse anyone unlucky enough to venture through it."

"I'm not worried about the room itself." Rocky pointed upward to the domed ceiling.

Dave had thought the chamber was illuminated by more of the glowing rock like the hallways, but that wasn't the case. Pale green specters floated above them, swirling as if locked in an eternal display of aerial acrobatics.

"They're beautiful," Dave said.

One of the specters floated toward them. Dave saw at once that he'd been wrong aside from its aura. Its face was a twisted nest of flesh and misshapen features, and it trailed a mess of knotted and nappy hair. It might've been a ghost of a goblin, but it shrieked like a banshee as it descended toward them, its claws ready to rip the flesh and muscles from their skeletons.

"Duck!" Dave exclaimed, lowering his body so the wraith-like being missed him by a foot. Rocky didn't heed Dave's warning. He leapt when he should have ducked and met the specter in midair. They collided, but Rocky's punch didn't faze it at all. It simply passed through him, letting his body fall to the ground with a thud.

"Rocky!" Dave shouted, kneeling next to him. "What happened? Are you OK?"

"It's so cold." Rocky curled himself into the fetal position and shook with his sobs and whimpers. "I don't want to die at the bottom of the harbor. Not again."

"You're not at the bottom of the harbor. That was a long time ago, and I promise you're not going back there."

Dave felt coldness spread throughout his body as something dragged him backward. He lost sight of Rocky as his back slammed into one of the stone pillars. When he fell to the ground, he was stunned to find carpet under him. It felt odd, yet familiar.

The surroundings had changed as well. He looked around himself and saw the living room of the house in which he'd grown up. It had been torn down years after he moved out, but it still stood in this dimension, though the colors were all off. They weren't as bright, but the Bryant home on Edgewood Avenue had always had a certain dimness to it.

"Nothing good will happen here," Dave said to himself as he got back to his feet. His voice had changed as well. It no longer had the timbre of a man. He'd reverted into boyhood—or at least some bogus illusion of it.

Rocky's reliving his death in the steel drum. What the fuck am I about to relive?

"David?" a voice called.

"Oh shit."

"David! There you are!"

Dave's mother entered the living room wearing a black coat over her pajamas. Dave remembered this moment well—as much as he didn't want to. She hadn't bothered to change her clothes when she got the call about her husband's suicide. She'd gone in what she wore and left her only child home alone.

"Come here, David. Sit with me for a moment."

She'd cry before she could start talking. She'd sob her eyes out without saying a single word for at least ten minutes. It'll feel a lot longer. It's going to feel like an eternity like it felt when she first had to tell her son that his father had jumped in front of the train. She'll talk eventually, and she'll tell the most graphic version of events, sparing no bloody detail about how Dave's father died or why he did it.

Mom didn't have a subtle bone in her body.

The memory of that day had ingrained itself in Dave's mind. He never forgave his father for what he did, and he might not ever, but the day he learned about the extremes a human can put themselves through to hurt someone they once claimed to love would be something that framed his life for a long time.

It'll be that way till Heather comes along.

"Come sit with me, David," his mother said, patting the couch with her meaty hand. "We need to talk about what happened."

Dave shook his head. "No. I don't want to. Not again."

The floor tremored, but Dave's mother ignored it if she even felt it at all.

"Be a good boy and sit with me, David. We need to talk about what's happened to…to…"

The tears spilled from her eyes. Even if Dave didn't sit with her as he had in his real past, she'd still act out her part in this macabre play.

"Fuck you!" Dave spat, meaning it for the specters putting on the show and not his mother. "I'm leaving!"

Dave ran for the front door as his mother hollered and wailed for him to come back. She was suffering, and she needed him to console her.

"YOU'RE GREEDY, DAVID! I NEED YOU, AND YOU'RE RUNNING AWAY. YOU'RE A COWARD JUST LIKE YOUR FATHER! EVERYONE YOU TOUCH SUFFERS FOR YOU, AND YOU'LL TURN YOUR BACK ON ALL OF THEM!"

The tremors had become a full-blown earthquake by the time Dave got to the front door. He kicked it, knowing it wouldn't open on its own. His body bounced back from the blow, but he did it again, repeating the action till it finally broke at the hinges. Dave jumped through the opening as the house crumbled and turned to debris behind him.

This brought him back to the cavern beneath the Star-Mart.

"Rocky."

Dave scrambled to get his feet moving under him. The wraiths were in a frenzy now, swooping downward like a flock of seagulls going after some airborne fries. They shrieked, sending waves of sound that somehow made the air thicker.

"Get up!" Dave shouted, kneeling by Rocky's quivering form once more. "Come one, Rocky!"

"I can't," Rocky groaned in a weak voice. "I can't fight them." He sniffed a stream of snot back up his nose. "They'll put me back in the drum!"

He's not wrong. He's not going to be able to punch these wraith motherfuckers into oblivion like everything else.

Something sucked Dave away from Rocky again, this time dropping him on top of a set of railroad tracks on a warm evening. His arms and palms were scraped from the rocks on the ground between the two metal rails. A bridge stood above him, and a man stood on the edge facing the rising moon.

"Shit," Dave muttered, getting to his feet. "Dad?!"

"Your mother made me do this!" his father called in return. "You and her both!"

"This isn't fair!" Dave shouted toward the sky. "I wasn't here for this! This isn't my memory to relive!"

The sound of the train whistle filled the night, and Dave turned to see it rushing toward him. He ran off the tracks, tripping again, rolling on the hard, pointy rocks. He knew he'd started to bleed in multiple places, but he didn't care. For all he knew, the injuries were as fake as the illusion itself.

The whistle blared as the train passed, and Dave turned in time to see his father's body splatter against it like a bug on a windshield. The train kept moving toward its destination as if it hadn't just killed a man.

"That's not right," Dave said, shaking his head. "The train stopped in real life when they realized they'd hit someone. I might not have been there, but I know that much is true."

The truth didn't matter, not in this dimension of pain and death. He wasn't there when his father died, and he was grateful he'd never seen the body or what had happened to it. The gory depiction his mother had painted with her words had been more than enough, but now the image of his father plastering the front of the train with his blood and guts burned into Dave's memory, and he knew it wouldn't ever leave him.

"Interesting," Dr. Nielsen said. He sat in an easy chair, watching the whole thing unfold with his legs crossed. "Part of you *does* blame yourself for what happened that night. Let's get into that since we have some time on our hands."

Dave balled his hand into a fist. "You dirty motherfucker!" He rushed forward, aiming his best Rocky-like punch at Dr. Nielsen's smug face. He passed right through the phantom shrink, hitting the black pillar back in the domed chamber in the middle of the Mines of Moria.

"Fuck!" Dave spat as he clutched his aching hand. It didn't feel like he'd broken any bones, but it still hurt like a sonofabitch. Another wraith came through the pillar, leaving a wall of slime on it. Dave ducked, letting it pass over its head. It shrieked as if someone ran over its foot.

Dave stayed as low to the ground as he could as if it would keep the wraiths from augmenting his reality again. He got back to Rocky, who whimpered like an injured animal in the fetal position. This time he whined to see his mother again.

Dave tried to pull Rocky to his feet. "You have to get up, Rocky. I'm not strong enough to drag you out of here and find the exit. I need you to—"

Another wraith passed through Dave's body, and he was back home in his living room looking at his mother's face. Her eyes were swollen from crying, and streams of snot hung from her nostrils.

"You've abandoned me, David. Why did you abandon your family?"

"It wasn't much of a family in the first place." Dave grabbed a figurine off the table. It had been one of his mother's favorites: A little girl with a duck and an umbrella. In this reality, however, it looked more like a troll with a black dog covered in spikes. He hurled it through the huge window that overlooked their street, shattering it into thousands of sharp pieces.

"YOU'RE DESTROYING OUR HOME!"

Dave climbed on the couch closest to the window and made his way through the broken window. He counted himself lucky the illusion gave him the spryness of his youth that had long since left him in the real world.

"This wasn't much of a home either!" With that, Dave dropped down to the bushes, and his feet landed on the hard stone of the cavern a foot away from Rocky.

"This shit is getting—"

Dave was pulled back again, but this time it felt different. The wraiths tried a different tact. They'd sent him to his present home rather than the one in which he had grown up. Like everything else, it wasn't *right*. Blood splattered and stained the walls, and the carpets were soaked with it. Body parts had been strewn all over the place, making the whole thing look like a cannibal party that went a little too wild, even for cannibals. Dave didn't check, but he knew who the parts belonged to, and the last thing he wanted to see was the severed heads of his wife and daughter, though he knew he'd find them, completing the horrific vision, crippling him as it had been meant to do.

"Look who's finally home," a voice said. Dave turned to see the Unmade Men, Leo and Johnny, standing by the entrance to his kitchen. They each wore a white apron that had been stained in human blood.

"We couldn't find you," Leo said, "so we started dinner. We figured you'd be home eventually."

"We've warmed a plate for you in the oven," Johnny added. "Come and try a bite. You can guess if it's Heather or Kayla based on taste."

"You sick fucks!" Dave stepped back. The wraiths wanted him to panic. "You're not real. You two were a couple of wannabe mobster assholes, but you aren't the types to cook people."

Leo's smile widened. "Make yourself a plate and be the judge on whether or not I can cook people before you rush to judgment, you coward fuck."

"Yeah!" Johnny added. "You're the one who did this by running away and leaving your family to be slaughtered in your name."

Leo laughed. "This is all for you. We figured you'd want to have a big family dinner again. Where's Richie? He must be starving too!"

Dave didn't engage the phantom Unmade Men again. He turned and kicked at the door. He rebounded as pain shot up his leg. It elicited a stream of laughter from behind, but he ignored it, kicked the door again, and put all his anger in the one blow, sending it off its hinges.

"I hope the two of you fall off a fucking cliff," Dave said as he exited into the cavern of wraiths.

Another wraith hit him the moment he freed himself, and another reality started. Dave's mother sat on the couch again, but this time the sound of the train entered. It smashed through the far wall, creaming Dave's mother in a shitshow of blood and gore. Dave turned away from the sight, closed his eyes tight, and repeated a mantra he'd made up on the spot.

"This isn't real. This isn't real. This isn't FUCKING REAL!"

When he opened his eyes, he was back in the cavern. "THIS ISN'T REAL EITHER!"

As it turned out, shouting at the wraiths and the cavern itself wouldn't be enough to dispel it.

Alright, maybe this part is real after all.

And that would have to act as the truth of his situation since he couldn't pull up a Google search and ask the infinite knowledge of the internet to tell him how to get out of his situation. Dave and Rocky had been trapped in a prison deep within a pocket dimension of sorts. Whoever or whatever wanted Dave planned on torturing him until they arrived to pick him up and subject him to whatever arcane tortures they had in store for him next. Rocky would be there too, but they'd leave him behind to be tortured and scared by the wraiths till he died or time itself came to an end.

"Get up, Rocky!" Dave exclaimed, getting back on the ground. He shoved the fallen superhero with both of his hands. "Get the fuck up already and save my ass!"

That got Rocky's attention. His whimpering stopped, and he wiped at the tears and snot on his face with his arm. He turned to look at Dave, ignoring the wraiths as they came toward him once more.

"Did you forget your promise?" Dave hated himself for the tact he needed to use to save both of their asses from their supernatural predicament, but he couldn't see any other option. "You said you'd protect me no matter what. Well, how can a superhero do anything curled in a ball on the fucking ground?"

Rocky gave a single nod and got back to his feet. A wraith came toward him, and he lashed out in vain. He wavered on his feet as another morbid illusion took over his mind, but he didn't fall again. He steadied himself despite whatever visions erupted inside his tortured mind. Dave could see his skin growing paler while frost grew around his eyes and nose. Another wraith passed through Rocky's body, and another did the same from the other end. The hero kept on his feet, throwing punch after punch at the coming wraiths to no avail.

Dave imagined how he could do it. He'd fought the illusions in his head the same way, though he'd fallen each time and had to regroup and refocus his resolve. Rocky had to have been doing the same to force the illusions out of his mind through nothing more than desperate determination and unadulterated grit. Even with him fighting and keeping himself upright, would it be enough to get them out of the cavern and back to safety?

Dave held the aching hand with which he'd punched the cavern's pillar while he watched Rocky fight an impossible battle on his behalf. Then, the solution came to him like a tsunami of inspiration.

"Don't punch the wraiths!" Dave shouted. "Punch the pillars!"

Rocky turned toward Dave for a moment and nodded. He took another swing, this time hitting the hard, black stone of the pillar closest to him. It shuddered with the weight of the blow, and the sound echoed through the cavern.

"Don't stop! Keep hitting it!"

Rocky punched the stone over and over again with indestructible hands and super strength flowing through his muscles. A crater formed as he worked, and the ground shook from his wrath. The wraiths attacked, but he ignored them as they passed through his body. They couldn't break his stride, and stone from above them fell to the ground and crumbled.

Dave looked up and saw light. He knew from the brightness it wasn't the same as what the wraiths or luminescent stones emitted. "There's our exit!" he exclaimed, pointing upward. He didn't know where it led, but it couldn't be any worse than where they were. "Can you get us up there?"

Rocky left the pillar and hoisted Dave onto his shoulders in a firefighter lift. He leapt into the air, kicking off the ground and through the cloud of wraiths, once again ignoring the coldness and the morbid memories they caused. He found footholds in the pillars and continued his flight upward with his wild kicks and boosts.

Dave fought as well, repeating his mantra every time they tried to make him relive false memories of his parents. He saw his mother again, dying in her hospital bed from cancer this time, thanking God she could finally die and see her husband.

"Everything that's happened since his death was a disappointment," she said before falling into the coma that would end her life hours later.

When Dave freed himself of the hospital illusion, he sat on the ground holding a dying Heather in his arms. They were in some parking lot on a cold, dreary morning. Only the tiniest bits of sunlight snuck through the gray clouds in the sky.

"You did this to me," she told him. Half her face had been sheared off, and her remaining eye scanned his face. "Why did you leave me behind to deal with your killers? You let me die and left your daughter motherless. They'll come for her next. You should be the one dying, but you're too scared to face that end. You'd rather let everyone around you die instead."

"That's not true," Dave said. "I didn't run because I was scared. I ran to keep them chasing me and away from you. Can't you see that?"

The only answer that came was a torrent of blood from Heather's mouth as she died. Dave let her corpse fall to the ground and stood. He looked up at the single ray of sunshine that broke through the clouds to warm his body.

"Let's go, Rocky. I'm through with this bullshit."

Then, before another illusion could start, the sunlight encompassed him, and the drab morning in the unknown parking lot of the wraith's dimension dissipated.

WHO THE FUCK IS ROCKY PHANTASMIC?!

***

"Dave? Wake up. People are staring."

Dave opened his eyes and sat up on the cool tile floor of the Star-Mart grocery aisle. People stared at him while keeping their distance. They would've assumed he collapsed unless they saw him come out of the floor after he and his superhero partner escaped a hellish dimension of darkness and illusions. None of them moved to help or offer to call an ambulance, though. At least they weren't taking pictures or videos with their cellphones.

"Are you OK?" Rocky asked. He knelt on the floor next to him with a smile on his face.

"We should've gone over that stupid bridge after all." Dave rubbed his eyes and tried to ward off the headache that had settled into his head. Jumping through dimensions and augmented realities had taken its toll on his supple gray matter. "Tell me I didn't dream all that shit with the hole that led to Moria."

Rocky shook his head. "It wasn't a dream, but it's over now. You got us out of there."

"No. I didn't do anything but suck and almost die. You're the one who got us out. You're the superhero, Rocky. I'm the shithead you're stuck with."

"You figured out what it was. You got me back on my feet and told me how to free us. If you hadn't done that, we'd be stuck down there forever."

You'd be stuck down there forever. I'd be retrieved and brought elsewhere to be tortured by your cousins.

"It's all over now, Dave," Rocky added.

Dave let out a long, shaking breath. "It's not over, Rocky. They're going to keep coming for me, and I don't know what else they have in their repertoire. I know what those wraiths did to you, even if I didn't see what you saw. They did the same to me, showing me the most horrid visions from my bitterest memories and their twisted imaginations. I can't take you through something like that again. It's not fair."

If there were any lesson to be learned, it's that this is my burden. It shouldn't be Rocky's too. I've done enough damage by leaving Heather and Kayla without so much as a note about where I've gone or how to keep themselves safe from this bullshit.

Rocky got to his feet and offered his hand to help Dave off the floor. "I chose the life of the superhero. I never assumed it would be an easy path to take, but it is the right one. Until this is over for good, you're stuck with me, not the other way around. It doesn't matter what happens. A hero's life is full of challenges, and death lurks around every corner. If I abandoned you now, I'd be no better than the villains pursuing you."

Dave couldn't stop himself from smiling at the sentiment. "Alright, then. I guess it's not going to be easy to shake you off. If you're going to continue being my superhero savior, we're going to have to get you that new cape we left back in the fabric department."

Rocky's smile widened, and they went back to fetch their carriage and finish their shopping despite people glaring at him. All the while, Dave made sure to step carefully enough to not fall through the floor again.

WHO THE FUCK IS ROCKY PHANTASMIC?!

12. THE PURSUIT OF THE UNMADE MEN

"I'm not arguing that violence isn't the answer to all our problems," Leo said as he sat in the passenger seat while Johnny sped down the highway. "It's our friggin' career choice, right? All I'm suggesting is that maybe killin' a bunch of people in a diner isn't the best way to go about bein' all inconspicuous and shit."

Johnny nodded, keeping his eyes on the darkening road ahead of him. "I got no problem with beatin' a man who doesn't know when to stop his mouth from flappin', but I ain't arguin' that we should be leavin' bodies lyin' around for John Q. Lawmaker to find."

"Good." Leo nodded. "We're in agreement." He moved the rearview mirror so he could get a better look at Duro's face. "Do you understand what I'm sayin' back there? We ain't a travelin' band of serial killers. We're to find this writer mook, deliver him alive, and kill his superhero compatriot. Capeesh?"

Duro didn't respond. He smiled his sick smile, showing off his bright teeth. He hadn't put his shirt back on since the violence he doled out in the diner.

"I don't know why I'm even botherin'." Leo turned his attention back to the dirt and trees as they whipped past his window. "I don't want to fuck this all up because our solution to our superhero problem thinks it's necessary to smash people to bits over what should've been a minor dispute."

Johnny fixed the mirror. He didn't feel much like meeting Duro's gaze when checking behind them. Even a millisecond of looking into the killer's eyes sent chills up his spine. It's not like Johnny hadn't ever killed anyone, but what he did was different than what Duro had done in the diner. Killing for work isn't the same as killing for the fun of it. They weren't the same, and they never would be.

"Ah fongool," Johnny uttered.

"What?" Leo asked.

"The cops are gaining on us. I knew we should've ditched this car after the diner."

Leo turned to see what Johnny had already spotted in the rearview mirror. Three state trooper cruisers were behind them, lights flashing. As they approached, the sound of their sirens increased.

Johnny smashed the gas pedal to the floor. "No point in obeyin' the speed limit now."

"Figlio di puttana!" Leo spat. "Can you lose 'em, Johnny?"

"I can try, but this is a backwoods road. This ain't like the city where I can make a dozen turns and spin them around."

"Fuck! This is what I was talkin' about with that diner massacre! We don't need all this fuckin' heat on our asses right now! Vincenzo's going to kill us when he finds out about this shit!"

The trio of cruisers closed the distance. One of the troopers shouted at them to pull over from a bullhorn, but Johnny wasn't dumb enough to listen.

Johnny took a hard right turn, eliciting a squeal of protest from the tires as they skidded against the road. The cruisers took the turn as well. It hadn't been enough to shake their tail. The road thinned, and the only option for them would be to get down a driveway and hide, but the cruisers were still too close to pull off a maneuver like that. The road had too many turns in it as well, and Johnny couldn't keep up the speed he needed to lose their tail.

"Fuck!" Johnny took a left and then another, heading back toward the main road. The cruisers followed, shouting the same orders at them to stop and pull over.

"I can't keep this up forever." Johnny turned onto the main road again and opened the engine as hard as he could. "They got us, Leo. We can't give these assholes the slip."

"Shut the fuck up and drive!" Leo snapped. "Let me think for a minute over here."

Johnny focused on the road and took a quick look in the mirror at their pursuers. They'd gained on his ass again, and they had no intention of letting up. The only thing that would stop them was a miracle of sorts. Maybe a moose or something would jump into the road between them and the troopers.

Fantasies aren't going to help, Johnny thought. As his eyes shifted to watch the road again, he caught Duro's face. Their supervillain companion beamed the widest grin Johnny had ever seen on a man. It reminded him of the look on the Grinch's face when he devised his master plan to steal Christmas from that pussy village at the base of his mountain. If Johnny could see Duro's crotch, he knew he'd be sporting a massive hard-on for whatever plans had been born inside his dark and silent mind.

This ain't gonna end good.

Duro reached forward and grabbed the wheel in a swift motion, pulling it hard to the right. Johnny's instinct took over and his foot slammed on the brake pedal at the same time. The car screeched as the tires burned against the road, sending gray smoke behind them. They came to a stop as the car hit a log off the side of the road and tilted into some thick mud.

***

"What the fuck was that?!" Leo snapped.

"It was Duro!" Johnny replied. "He grabbed the wheel and pulled us off the road!"

"This sonofabitch is gonna get us friggin' killed!" Leo turned to scold Duro, even if it meant his neck wound up twisted in some ungodly fashion. To his surprise, their resident supervillain had already left the car. He strode toward the troopers, who had stopped, blocking the entire road in a triangle formation.

"PUT YOUR HANDS ON YOUR HEAD!" the trooper with the bullhorn shouted. "NOW!"

Leo watched, shielding himself behind his seat. He couldn't see Duro's face, but he knew he'd be grinning like a bloodthirsty goblin now that killing was back on the silent psychopath's mind.

"THIS IS YOUR LAST WARNING! IF YOU DO NOT COMPLY, WE WILL OPEN FIRE!"

"They aren't fuckin' around," Johnny remarked.

"You ain't bullshittin'," Leo added.

Six troopers exited their cruisers with pistols or rifles aimed at Duro. They no doubt knew what had happened at the diner, and they weren't treating it as highway folklore. Whatever they expected from their target, they knew he'd kill them all if they gave him the chance.

It was almost a damn shame they didn't know Duro and what he could do to them for fun.

Duro raised his arms to shoulder level like a man enjoying the rain, inviting them to try to kill him. He continued to walk toward them without breaking his slow gait. The first bullet pinged off his chest, burying itself in a tree off the road. He continued his walk as if nothing happened, and the rest of the troopers opened fire.

Bullets bounced off Duro's skin like rain against a smooth stone. The troopers fired everything they had, but it did nothing. They could've unloaded every clip and spent every shell, but it wouldn't stop their doomsday from walking right up to them to do its worst.

"They don't have anything big enough for him," Johnny muttered while hiding behind his seat as Leo did the same next to him. A bullet hit the car, and they both flinched at the sound. They weren't bulletproof like their newest pal.

"Maybe we should've pulled over from the start," Leo remarked. "It would've saved us some wear and tear on the car."

Duro had made it to the troopers, who were either shooting at him or reloading. Some of them backed off as they fired, and one ran into the woods in a blind panic. As far as Leo could tell, he was the smartest of the bunch.

Duro flipped the nearest cruiser into the air in a smooth motion with his left arm, sending it spinning before it came crashing back down. It crushed two of the troopers and damaged the cruiser to its left. Duro grabbed another cop by the face and tossed them over his shoulder like a ragdoll. The body landed with the crack of bone against the road next to Leo's door.

"Fuck, that's a sickening noise," Leo muttered.

"Like you've never broken someone's bones," Johnny retorted.

"Not like that I haven't!"

Duro punched a cop right through his chest, splattering himself with blood and gore. The last cop fired a single shot from his pistol against Duro's temple at point-blank range, but it ricocheted into the air like every other shot they'd taken at him. With another swift motion, Duro hit him with the back of his hand, breaking the trooper's neck. When the trooper stopped spinning like a top, he fell to the ground and didn't move again.

With the work done, Duro ran into the woods.

"What the fuck?!" Leo exclaimed, getting out of the car and gingerly stepping past the trooper's body. "Duro! Where the fuck are you going?!"

"He's getting the cop that ran away," Johnny replied as he exited the car as well. "He's a thorough killer."

Leo gritted his teeth as he looked at the pile of broken cruisers and bodies Duro had left. Part of him urged his body to get in the car and drive as far away from their supervillain companion as possible. He couldn't, though. His rational side won the inner argument. Vincenzo wouldn't care about the carnage and destruction, but he'd sure give the biggest of shits about them leaving Duro behind.

Besides, he was the only one monstrous and obscenely strong enough to kill a superhero, and Rocky Phantasmic would be waiting with the writer.

"What are we doing, Leo?" Johnny asked. Maybe his mind had debated whether or not to leave Duro as well, though he'd work through it a lot slower than Leo had.

"We're waiting," Leo replied as he leaned against the side of the car with his arms crossed. "Once he's back, we'll get back on the road and switch cars like we should've done after the mess at the diner." Something within him snapped, and he started laughing.

"What's so funny?" Johnny asked.

"We're in for the shitshow of all shitshows when Duro meets little Richie Pimento. I don't care if he's Rocky Phantasmic, superhero extraordinaire. He's going to wind up as dead as those troopers or those tough guy mooks back at the diner. This story ain't gonna have a happy ending for him."

"Are you sure? Richie…Rocky, I mean, seemed pretty strong when we met him in New Haven. You saw what he did, and it didn't even look like he'd tried that hard."

Leo scoffed and spat on the ground. "Yeah? Well, he ain't never fought a sonofabitch like Duro, has he? We'll find out how strong of a little shit he is."

Duro returned from the woods dragging the body of the trooper who had run off. He tossed it to let it lie in the road with the others as proof he'd killed them all. He turned toward Leo and Johnny with his raging erection pointing the way.

"Oh, it's gonna be good," Leo replied with a shit-eating grin plastered on his face. "I don't care who the fuck Rocky Phantasmic is or thinks he is, but he doesn't have the swingin' balls to do what Duro does, and that's the edge that's going to make the difference between them. Duro's a killer, plain and simple, and Rocky's a wuss who got a taste of superpowers. That damn kid's going to be a red smear on the pavement when this is all said and done."

Duro went to them with his sickening smile showing the right side of his teeth. Even with the killing done, he still sported a throbbing erection that refused to go away.

"Come on, you friggin' psychopath," Leo said as his grin faltered. "We need to find a new set of wheels and get back to work."

***

Johnny stood on a ridge facing a lake somewhere past the state line between New Hampshire and Maine. They hadn't driven too far from where the bodies of six state troopers lay dead in the road, but far enough off the main drag where they wouldn't be easily found or even spotted. The car they had taken from New Haven couldn't be traced back to them. If the troopers ran the plates—which they would have most definitely done already—they'd come up with a dummy name of a man named Benjamin Pitt, who had long since died of mysterious causes. It was a good car, and it saddened Johnny a little to leave it behind.

"It's a beautiful night," Johnny said as he gazed at the sky through the break in the dark clouds. Duro stood on the other side of the car, silent as always, watching the stars through the same hole. If the frigid chill in the air bothered him, he didn't show it. If bullets didn't pierce his skin, maybe the cold didn't either. His erection had gone away, which was a good sign. As much of a killer as he was, he didn't seem to want to kill Johnny or Leo, not yet anyway.

"I don't know what happened in your life to make you the way you are," Johnny continued. "I know you can't talk, so I'm not expecting an answer or the story about how you came to have so much strength and power. All I know is that Rocky—the man you're here to kill—got his powers after Leo and I tried to kill him. So, maybe your powers came to you in the same way if I'm right about how Richie Pimento became

Rocky Phantasmic. You might've gone through hell to be rewarded with so much in return."

As always, Duro didn't answer. He stared upward as if he were counting the stars in the sky before the clouds obscured them.

"Shit. I don't even know if you understand English or not."

To his shock, Duro spoke. "Do you know why I get hard every time I kill?" he asked in a thick Italian accent.

Johnny turned toward him and shook his head.

Duro laughed. "It's because killing gives me an orgasmic rush nothing else has ever given me."

Johnny stared since he didn't know how to respond.

"You do not understand me at all." Duro walked toward him as the smirk on his face spread. "I didn't come into my power because I went through hell like what you did to that boy I'm here to kill. I was blessed with these gifts because I was meant to kill and do to others what they'd do to me if they had the gifts I possess. If you do not understand the evil of this world, then you'll never understand why I've been blessed by the demons who watch from their black dimension."

"I think I liked it better when you didn't speak," Johnny admitted. Although, Duro's mastery of the English language impressed him.

Duro laughed again. "I am not one for words, but I thought I'd spare a bit to put your mind at ease. You see, killing a man who boasts power and strength like mine will be the ultimate orgasmic pleasure. When this man is dead at my feet, I'll cum so hard I'll need a bucket."

With that, Duro looked back toward the sky. Johnny wished he'd never heard him speak. Even with all the bodies he'd buried or drowned over the years, he'd never taken pleasure in it, let alone become orgasmic or even aroused over the prospect of committing murder.

A car pulled up behind them, and Johnny spotted Leo in the driver's seat. He had chosen a plain-looking sedan with Maine plates. With luck, it would be hard to spot as they followed Vincenzo's compass.

Leo got out and slammed the door. "Sorry for the wait. I swapped the plates out in a Star-Mart parking lot to give us a little bit of extra camouflage. We don't need to be wastin' any more time with the cops if we can help it."

Johnny nodded. "Good idea."

Leo looked at him for a moment. "What's wrong with you? You look like you've seen a friggin' ghost or some shit."

"I'm alright." Johnny grabbed their bags and put them in the trunk of the new car. When he finished, he walked back to the front where Leo waited. "Did you get the boss's compass?"

"Oh shit," Leo said, jogging over to the passenger door of the car they were about to ditch. "I almost forgot. Don't need to lose that magical gizmo and face Vincenzo's wrath." He grabbed the compass from the glove compartment and stepped back to his compatriots. "Would you like to do the honors and get rid of this car?" he asked Duro.

Duro nodded, heaved the entire car off the ground, and hurled it through the air and into the lake, far away from the adjacent highway. The trio stayed for a minute to watch it sink into the frigid water.

"That's that," Leo said. "Let's see which way we're headed next." He opened the black box, and the compass needle pointed to his left. "What the hell?"

"What is it?" Johnny asked, getting closer. "It didn't break when we drove off the road into the mud pit, did it?"

"No, but it's shaking like a sonofabitch."

Johnny looked over Leo's shoulder and watched as the needle trembled like it was in an earthquake. It moved ever so slightly from the left to the right.

"Hold on," Leo said, noticing this as well. He held the compass out, stretching his arm as if it would somehow increase its signal. "It's moving. See?"

"I see it."

The needle moved, and Johnny heard the car before it emerged from under the canopy of the trees along the main road. The needle followed the car's trajectory, and it surprised him to find he recognized it as it sped past them.

"Holy shit," Leo said. "Those are Connecticut plates."

"That's the friggin' writer's car!" Johnny exclaimed. "He went back for it!"

"I'll drive." Leo snapped the compass shut and ran to get back into their stolen car along with Johnny and Leo. "We found the mook by accident after all that bullshit!" He backed up and made a U-turn to head down the sloping road toward the highway. "I can't believe we've finally got a little bit of good luck. Can you believe it, Johnny?"

Johnny nodded as he watched the dark road as Leo drove. He looked up in the mirror to see Duro's face again. He wasn't surprised to see the supervillain's devilish grin had returned. Johnny couldn't see below

WHO THE FUCK IS ROCKY PHANTASMIC?!

Duro's bare torso, but he knew he'd find him hard as a rock as images of death and bloodshed danced in his head.

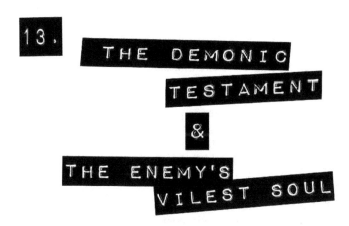

13. THE DEMONIC TESTAMENT & THE ENEMY'S VILEST SOUL

Heather stared across the table at Father Stephen's stoic face. She hated that she had to deal with him to save Dave and get back to their daughter. Kayla had to be scared out of her mind. She was smart for her age, and she'd be sure to pick up on Heather's parents' panic and overhear their conversations with the police regarding her and Dave's sudden disappearance. It was the thought of little Kayla being raised without her parents that spurned Heather onward as she forced herself to endure whatever would come while shadowing Father Stephen in his bloody quest to murder her husband.

"Are you going to make good on your promise to tell me what the fuck's going on," she asked, "or was that a lie to shut me up? The quiet act is getting old."

Father Stephen looked downward. "I said I'd tell you what I feel is safest to tell. Some of what I know is too dangerous, so I need to be careful how I continue."

Heather sighed. "All I hear are excuses. If you don't plan on telling me, then say so. Don't use it as a carrot to keep me complacent while you use me for my scent or whatever the hell you need me alive for."

"Perhaps you'll understand my plight once you've learned more, and you'll come to know why I can't tell you certain things. I didn't fully understand it myself at first, and now I wish I knew much less than what I've come to learn about our world and the other worlds surrounding it through the dark veil."

"See, saying shit like that without any other context is what's making me question your sanity."

They sat in a broken-down church, which suited Father Stephen, though Heather now questioned his priesthood as well as his sanity. Time had not been kind to the church deemed Almighty Father's Undying Light by the wooden sign half-covered in brown moss and fading spray paint.

The chill in the air seemed to grow worse after they'd entered the sanctuary of the church, and Heather kept her jacket around her body. The chain around her waist refused to warm up. The electricity in the old church didn't work either, which didn't surprise her, so the only light came from the red and white candles Father Stephen had brought with him among his stash of weapons and other odds and ends in four different duffle bags. He seemed to know the contents of each one without consulting a list or having to think about it first. Even if the man had been broken by happenstance or his twisted fantasies of macabre grandeur, he still had a sharp instinct about him.

"And the Enemy shall send the vilest soul in his collection back to Earth to do his bidding," Father Stephen said.

"What's that supposed to mean?" Heather asked.

Father Stephen shrugged. "It's a line from the Bible. It follows the description of the fiendish hounds we've already faced. If the words ring true, then the Enemy may send a phantom that once walked this Earth to come after us next."

"I went to catholic school for five years of my life, and I've never heard anything remotely like what you just said from our Bible classes. I think you're making this shit up as you go along to suit your narrative."

"I'm not talking about the Bible as you know it. There is another testament, one few living men have read. Only one copy exists that the Vatican knows of, and I have it in my possession."

"Where is it?"

"Safe."

Heather rolled her eyes. "I'm sure it is. What's this new Bible say that no one else alive has read?"

"It's called the Demonic Testament, and it's not a *new Bible*. It's more like a sequel to the one you know. It was written in the blood of virgins by the burning hands of demonic entities that have long since been removed from our world."

"That sounds like horror movie bullshit."

"Is it? You've seen firsthand what these creatures can send our way. Those demonic hounds we faced weren't overgrown puppies. They come from another dimension, one that resides in a chaotic sequence with our own. There are more than hounds, and their energy has been leaking into our world to create hellish scenarios, one after another, all stemming from the Enemy's want to return."

"You keep mentioning this Enemy character. Who is it, and how evil are they on a scale of a hungry shoplifter to Adolf Hitler?"

"Your mockery is not making this any easier."

Heather sat back. "Fine. Tell me some more about this Enemy. Do they have a name, or do they go by 'Enemy'?"

"I dare not speak their true name, especially not in a house of God, even one as decrepit as this one. The name he's known by in this world, however, is He Who Walks Above."

Heather felt as if the blood in her veins had turned to ice water when she heard the name, corny as it sounded. "Why do they call him that?"

"He stands thousands of feet tall and towers over entire cities."

"Is he the same as Satan or the Devil?"

Father Stephen shook his head. "No. Satan was a fallen archangel who turned his back on God due to his jealousy. He's quite content now, and he gets a kick out of being portrayed as the ultimate evil in so many books and media. The imagery of a devil has always been useful to deter men and women from sinning, though it's wearing off if you ask me."

The priest looked over Heather, and she knew he had an insult ready for her since he'd caught her in the act of sinning when they first met. The term 'adulteress' had to be waiting on the tip of his tongue.

"All that aside," Heather said, "does the Demonic Testament have any information on who He Who Walks Above is and what he's doing right now?"

"Yes and no," Father Stephen replied. "The Enemy was once a patriarchal demon of our world, keeping humanity under his thumb in bloody conflict and slavery. Our world, however, is one of science as well as demonic magic. The scientific principle of which I speak can be best summed up as 'for every action, there is an equal and opposite reaction'."

Heather nodded. "That's one of Newton's laws. I remember that from high school physics class."

"It's not the same but the principle behind it is apt. You see, for every ounce of energy the Enemy or any demonic presence uses in our world, there are two actions. The first is what the demon meant to do—its intentions fulfilled. The second is the rebounding opposite reaction—the consequence of its intention and actions. Not even the caster of the magic knows what'll happen when they cast their spell. There's a flip side to it, a cost associated with using such forceful magic on our earthly plane that was deemed by the science which governs us that God put into motion upon creation of the universe in our dimension, starting with what's come to be known as the Big Bang. Do you follow the logic?"

"I think so. Demonic magic from another dimension has to follow scientific theory from ours."

"Good."

"But what does this have to do with my husband? Why is he involved with this magic and science balancing act in the first place?"

"It's part of what's written in the Demonic Testament. To know why the Enemy needs to return, you'll need to know why he's no longer here. You see, he was banished not by God and his archangels but by an army of men. There was an ancient man of God and science who discovered the rebounding effect of the Enemy's magic. This man—whose name has been lost to unwritten history—used his hypothesis against the Enemy to shunt him back into its dimension, sealing it from returning.

"Now, however, that seal has been broken, allowing the Enemy's magic to seep back into our world. There is a spell along with a prophecy regarding this moment in the Demonic Testament. The blood of a man is the blood of his ancestors, passed down from father to son throughout the passage of time. David Bryant—your husband—holds the blood of his ancestors, and that blood holds a potent vileness that the Enemy needs to complete his resurgence into our dimension."

"But Dave isn't vile at all! He didn't even like his parents, and they died years ago!"

Father Stephen shook his head as he let out a long sigh. "It goes back further than that. My colleagues and I weren't able to trace it back far enough to know, but one or more of your husband's ancestors took part in some genocidal actions that went unrecorded by history. The taint of that culling still resides in the memory of David's blood, and the Enemy needs it in order to return. That's why he's sending men after your husband."

"He can't do it himself." Heather tapped her chin with a nail. "That means the men after Dave are sent by the demon."

Father Stephen nodded. "Correct. I don't know all the details of what the Enemy has done, but David is being led to fulfill the Enemy's prophecy, even if he thinks he is fleeing from it."

Heather let out a huff. "That is so messed up. Dave doesn't know what's coming for him, but he's heading toward it at the same time. Do I have that right?"

"Yes, though there is one other thing, something that's worth noting as we move toward the conclusion of my mission."

Heather looked into Father Stephen's face. "What's that?"

"It's another law of this dimension, summed up best as 'nature abhors a vacuum'. Did you learn of that in high school as well?"

Heather shook her head. "I haven't, but it sounds familiar. I may have heard it in a movie or something."

"It's attributed to the philosopher Aristotle, though some argue the statement's true meaning. It fits here to say that humans banished evil from their dimension and left a vacuum that needed to be filled. Humans themselves took on the mantle of evilness, somewhat unknowing that they were doing it. Nature does abhor a vacuum, and our species was more than able to fill the role of the adversary of good."

"And this is what the whole Demonic Testament is about?"

"It's more or less about the Demonic Apocalypse, which is what the Enemy's true goal will be if he completes his magic and returns to this dimension. That's why your husband has to die. He has yet to sire a son, and his death will put an end to all of this. I'm sorry it has to be this way, but as long as David Bryant lives, this world is in danger."

Heather crossed her arms and leaned back. "No. I don't accept that. I can't. Let me read this Demonic Testament, and maybe I can find another way to stop all this without killing the father of my daughter."

Father Stephen shook his head. "I cannot allow that. Trust me, there is no other way."

"You can't know that! Let me read it, and I might—"

"I said no!"

Father Stephen's booming voice echoed in the empty church. Outside, rain began pelting the roof with huge droplets of water. The rumble of distant thunder heralded a violent storm.

"I'm sorry," Father Stephen said in a voice that sounded as if he meant it. "Reading the Demonic Testament is demonic magic in itself. The rebounding effect will put an invisible demon of one's own making in the head of the reader and doom their soul to forever rot in the pits of

Hell after they die. I read the Testament, using its demonic magic to prevent the Demonic Apocalypse, but it will eventually become too much for me to bear, and the demon in my head will take over completely. I'll become my own version of the Enemy on Earth. Before that happens, I will have to be put down. I can't with a clear conscience allow you or anyone to befall that same fate. This is my burden, and I will not cause anyone else to carry it, regardless of their reasoning."

"Alright," Heather relented with a sigh. "Forget I asked. All I want to know is what kind of rebound are we talking about if the Enemy completes his magic? If he returns to our dimension, assuming this is all true, what happens to him then?"

Father Stephen shrugged. "I have a theory, but that's all it is."

"Tell me. I'm operating on faith and theories here, so throw me a bone, and we can go from there."

"If the Enemy crosses over to this realm once more, an equal entity will be forced into theirs."

"An equal entity?" Heather tapped her chin again. "You're talking about…"

"God," Father Stephen finished. "Our God will be ripped from us and sent to a dimension made from hate and not love. It will be done as a cosmic equalizer, but it will compound our suffering in our dimension. It will be an action that cannot be reversed."

"Jesus."

"Please do not use the Son's name in vain in the Father's house."

"Sorry. All this has me floored. It all makes me wonder what part you held back that was too dangerous to tell me."

Father Stephen looked away. He thought for a moment, but he didn't elaborate on what he'd left unsaid. Instead, he stood and said, "Come with me. We can take refuge here and rest for a bit. As I said before, you may not find much of it now that you know the truth of the world. We're close, I can feel it. If the storm coming is any indicator of what's happening, then the Enemy is close to his goals as well."

Heather felt there was more to say, but she didn't want to push Father Stephen too far. He had been good to his word thus far. Even if she was owed more information, it would have to wait. Now that he'd communicated what he'd supposedly read in the Demonic Testament, maybe he'd divulge more as they made their way to Dave and whoever wanted him for their rituals.

"Alright," Heather said. "I mean, I'm locked to the end of your chain, so I can only go where you allow me to, right?"

Father Stephen groaned. "This again? I'm not unlocking it. It's still too dangerous for you to have free will. Too much is at stake, and you should understand that now."

I understand plenty, Heather thought. *Even if you did read all that in a Demonic Testament sequel to the Bible, it doesn't mean you're not an unhinged psychopath posing as a priest. I can still save Dave. I know it, and you know it as well. That's why you're not allowing me free reign. You're as afraid of me being right as you are of me spoiling your hunt.*

Aloud, Heather said, "Fine. Just chain me to a radiator near a bed or something. I'll attempt to sleep and mull over all that information."

Father Stephen offered a single, solemn nod. "Good. Over time, perhaps you'll see the truth as I've come to know it."

"God, I hope not."

***

Father Stephen sat on a cot in the rectory. He had washed up as best he could in the kitchen sink using rainwater. Heather had a bucket if she needed to wash up, and he had brought her a cot near the restroom, giving her the amenities of their stay.

The storm worsened outside, and the hard rain that pelted the roof turned into a mixture of sleet and hail as the temperature dropped. There were no coincidences—as Father Stephen knew well—and this storm was a result of the Enemy's energy seeping into their world from wherever he'd cracked the veil between their respective dimensions. The closer they'd get to where he'd ruptured the veil between dimensions, the worse the storm would grow.

The adulteress had been right to question him. Father Stephen withheld information. She'd neglected to ask about evil energies that exist in the world already, but that should have been apparent by the context of their conversation.

This most recent crack in the veil wasn't the first, and it wouldn't be the last. The demon inside Father Stephen's head had given her more information than the priest wanted, but it wanted her to read the Demonic Testament for herself. It wanted to fester in the mind of another human, perverting the adulteress to its will, making her into a walking abomination of a human as he'd become.

This was the reason Father Stephen had waited to be under the roof of God's house before he spoke of it. Even a church as rundown and decrepit as the Almighty Father's Undying Light should be enough to ward off the demon's influence well enough to stop him from encouraging more than the passing of information, though it waned in its dying state. One day, in the near future, the church's title will be nothing more than an ironic eulogy of what once stood proud and tall.

But nothing built by man would last forever.

Thunder boomed above, and the walls of the rectory shook. Father Stephen remembered the prophecy he'd made earlier that night based on the words he'd read in the Demonic Testament.

And the Enemy shall send the vilest soul in his collection back to Earth to do his bidding.

Father Stephen held his shotgun. He'd loaded it with more sulfur rounds, which would aid him in ridding the world of any being that didn't belong. It wasn't a foolproof method, but it would be a deterrent at least. They should have been heading toward their destination, but they both needed to rest, and Father Stephen especially needed a night of prayer.

The storm that had only started to rage was full of demonic energy. He felt it deep within his soul. The Enemy had bided his time, and its final move would come soon like a thief in the night. It drew its soldiers and followers toward it, and things would get far worse long before they got better.

But not for me, Father Stephen thought, settling on the cot for a long night of watching and waiting. *When this is over, I'll be laid to rest on this plane and forced into an eternity of damnation on the next. I am grateful to serve my God and aid his creation of man. One day they'll put aside their evil ways, and my sacrifice will not be in vain.*

It felt foolish to be that optimistic, but that shred of optimism kept him moving despite how humanity had written its destruction in both their actions and inactions. Maybe they'd already grown beyond saving, but that wasn't a determination a single man like Father Stephen could make. It was up to God himself, assuming He'd remain in his place in Heaven after the Enemy made his final move.

"The Enemy will not win this battle," Father Stephen said as he fought against his body's weariness. "As long as my body and faith are intact, the Demonic Apocalypse will not come to pass."

***

As Father Stephen lost the battle to stay awake and keep watch, Heather lay on her cot while her mind refused to let go of what she'd learned. It was all a riddle, a puzzle, but pieces were missing. She had no doubt the priest left out vital pieces of information, but what hadn't he told her?

Was it all bullshit, or just some of it? What the hell am I supposed to make of all this?

Well, now she knew the dark secrets of this world and the next. Grateful as she was for no longer being in the dark about the plot against her husband, part of her wished she'd never asked in the first place. Father Stephen had been right from the start. Some things were better kept as secrets in the shadows, and ignorance truly is bliss.

I still don't know if I can trust him, but there's no other explanation. If I hadn't seen the demonic hounds for myself, I'd still believe Father Stephen to be a complete and utter psychopath. At least I can rest knowing he's a psychopath with some knowledge of why shit's going down like a bowling ball in the ocean.

A creaking noise followed by a bang echoed through the church, and Heather sat up in a sudden motion. The chain kept her tied to a pipe that had been exposed thanks to the wall crumbling, making investigating the noise an impossibility.

"It's the storm," Heather said aloud in a vain attempt to convince herself. "The wind blew some piece of this shithole inward."

The wind picked up its howling as if to remind her of its awesome force. The windows had all been boarded up, but she still felt as if they'd come crashing down at any moment. The hail returned as well, hitting the side and roof of the church. It sounded as if Heaven had declared war on the abandoned house of God.

Not God. The Enemy.

What was the name Father Stephen didn't like using?

"He Who Walks Above."

A clap of thunder split the night.

Heather shook her head to dispel her dark thoughts. Father Stephen might've been happy to discover he'd been right about that too. Now that she knew at least a partial truth of how the world worked, she'd be hard-pressed to find any kind of rest in it. She'd always assumed the world was a fucked-up place, but she also believed it was worth saving. Now, however, she wondered what one could do in the face of it all. Humans had become the evil in the world if Father Stephen's assessment of the Demonic Testament could be believed, yet something much worse worked tirelessly to come back into existence to take the throne of blood and bone from the human race and reclaim it for themself. Was everything really worth saving?

"Yes," Heather said, answering her own question. "It's worth saving for Kayla."

There has to be a way to stop this evil from spreading and returning while saving Dave. If I can keep Father Stephen talking, he'll let something slip I can use to end all of this. I just have to survive long enough to do it.

A crack of lightning illuminated the church through the cracks in the walls, and thunder boomed a millisecond later. Heather jumped, and her heart pounded in her chest. Nothing could be done at that moment. All she could do was lie there and pray, not that it would do any good.

Even if praying brought her some small comfort, it wouldn't do much to soothe her deteriorated nerves. She knew with every fiber of her being that the priest had told her the truth. Heather's intuition had never steered her the wrong way before, and she hated being right all the damn time.

The only question she had on her mind now was what she would do now that she knew the truth.

***

The Almighty Father's Undying Light church had been home to plenty of rats, raccoons, possums, mice, and other vermin-like denizens since it closed its doors to the public for good. When it was in its prime, the church filled its pews with worshippers from the small New England town. Times changed, however, and the church found itself without enough worshippers to keep itself open. The land had been sold, but the planned demolitions and construction had been halted when the company that planned on developing the land went bankrupt before they could get started.

The townspeople no longer believed that the Almighty's light shined on them. No, they were led to believe that the church had always been on tainted ground, and it led to all the disarray that had befallen the land once the services had ended and the church locked out its loyal worshippers. They left it to succumb to the ravages of nature and the vermin who had taken up residence inside its crumbling walls and leaky ceiling. Those who believed the land to be cursed were only partially correct. It hadn't been cursed by any force aside from the curse of man at the time, but darkness would eventually creep into the old church in search of blood and vengeance, for the vilest soul in the Enemy's icy grasp had come to The Almighty Father's Undying Light.

A hand of rotted grayish meat that had once been flesh in another life pushed open the door. The lock had been broken earlier that day before the storm, so entry was an easy task. A tainted soul in an undead body is something that could never cross the threshold of a church, but the light inside this particular church had long since faded enough to allow the tarnished entity to pass through it unhindered. Perhaps what was about to happen to those inside would snuff out the light in this place for good.

The shadows moved along the floor, concealing the figure as it walked. The wind blew through the open door, sending freezing rain through the aisles with gales of dark energy and magic that had remained alien to this world for uncounted centuries.

The thing that walked through the church could not claim to be man or beast. Those who've seen them in the past debated what they'd encountered. Some called them zombies, and others thought them to be ghosts. They were neither. They had no name in any tongue of man, and the closest translation from the demonic language named it One Who Walks Again.

It was once a living man with a name and a life. Death may take us all, but it doesn't keep everyone. Some souls slip through the cracks, and some souls are too slick with sin and all the wrong they've done. Even the strongest herders can't keep them. It makes them perfect candidates to return to the world of the living in the former flesh regrown.

He Who Walks Above has an expansive collection of souls he's collected throughout his long existence. Those souls who were too wily to remain in Hell find their way to his dimension, and he uses them well. They cannot return as living beings, but with the veil between dimensions weakening, they can assist their demonic deity by slipping back to their former worlds to do their master's bidding—if only for a short time.

The One Who Walks Again had its mission, and the will of He Who Walks Above urged it toward its goal. Two humans stood in its master's way, and for that, they had to die.

WHO THE FUCK IS ROCKY PHANTASMIC?!

When He Who Walks Above marks someone, he never lets them out of his sight.

***

The wind abused the church, and Heather heard the front door open and the elements enter. She remembered what Father Stephen had said about the vilest soul, and she couldn't get the image that story had implanted into her mind out of it. If the doors had been opened, anyone or anything could enter unbidden. Nothing could stop the Enemy from sending another unholy assassin after them. If someone came upon her with ill intentions, she'd be unable to run or defend herself. Father Stephen had made sure, above everything else, that she'd remain helpless without his intervention. Most men did that, even if unintentional. They wanted the damsel in distress instead of the strong, independent woman who could kick ass and save themselves. They wanted to be the heroes of the stories they told themselves.

Heather refused to call out to Father Stephen for help, and there was no way in this dimension or any other that she'd sit and wait for some demonic entity to kill her while she cowered in fear.

"Fuck this captive prisoner bullshit." She grasped the chain that bound her to the exposed pipe with both hands and brought all the slack toward her. When she'd gotten it good and taut, she pulled, straining the muscles in her arms. She planted her feet on the warped floor when the cot began to move toward the wall and put every ounce of muscle in her body to work on the tug-of-war game.

The pipe broke before Heather did. She fell backward when it came loose from the wall, clattering to the ground in a three-foot-long section along with an elbow joint at the end of it. The sound echoed throughout the hall and the church, and she looked over her shoulder as if some creature lying in wait would hear and come running toward her. With luck—if something had been listening—it would assume something had fallen due to the storm breaking its way into the church. Then again, would a vile soul dismiss something like that at all?

Stop thinking that way. You're going to drive yourself crazy long before anything else can do it for you.

The chain around Heather's waist wouldn't come loose, so she'd have to carry it with her. She gathered into the crook of her left arm and carried the pipe she'd pulled out of the wall in her right. If something came for her, she'd at least have the chance to bludgeon it into ground meat—assuming she'd get the chance.

Heather tried to be as quiet as possible. The storm covered up the sounds of her movements, but she couldn't be sure that whatever might've been sent wouldn't pick up on her footfalls. It seemed silly since she'd already made so much noise pulling the pipe from the wall and gathering up her chains, but moving with quiet intention somehow soothed her frayed nerves. She swore under her breath at how paranoid Father Stephen's story had made her, but maybe that was the point of it.

She climbed down the short set of stairs that led to the church's altar and main area. It had gotten colder, and the icy weather had taken over in earnest now. The wind whipped through the church, making it feel like a freezer full of pews.

Heather suppressed another urge to call out to Father Stephen for help to get the door closed. If he found out she'd gotten loose, he'd only find something sturdier than a pipe to chain her to next time. It would be the second time, and it stood to reason that he'd get more drastic with his punishments. She couldn't leave without the keys to his station wagon, and she wouldn't get far in the icy storm, even if she stole it.

She leaned her pipe against the wall and closed the doors. With her shoulder against it to keep it from blowing open, she wrapped the chain around the handles to keep them closed. But the damage had been done. What little warmth the church had was gone, and the frigidness of the weather bit harder in the darkness. The floors were slick with sleet and rainwater, but at least Heather's fear of some unknown phantom stalking her eased a bit now that she'd stop the storm from assaulting the inside of the church.

But, as it turned out, the Almighty Father's Undying Light had a nighttime wanderer. She assumed Father Stephen had woken to check the doors as well, but she could tell it wasn't him. She picked up and grasped her pipe as best she could and wished she didn't have to keep her left hand occupied with her chain.

"Who's there?!" Heather called. She hoped she'd be answered by a homeless person who'd be as scared of her as she was of them. "I'm not going to hurt you. I'm only here to get out of the storm."

The figure of a man turned toward her. He was broad-shouldered and at least six feet tall. He walked with a smooth gait, groaning as if annoyed by the woman shouting at him. The oddest part of the whole ordeal was the suit of navy blue he wore with the scarlet tie. Lighting flashed, and Heather got a full look at the figure and his face.

"Oh my God," she uttered, stepping back. "No!"

Heather dropped her chain and held the pipe with both hands. The Enemy of whom Father Stephen spoke had indeed sent a vile soul to hunt them down, and it came in the form of former American president Ronald Reagan.

Reagan opened his mouth and let out a screech that drowned out the noise of the storm. Heather felt her skin grow colder, even through the layers of clothes she wore since she hadn't been given a blanket. She held her pipe like a baseball bat, knowing she wouldn't be able to outrun her attacker.

To her surprise, however, Reagan didn't lunge at her after he ended his battle cry and closed his mouth with a dull snap. He strode between the pews in her direction. "Where is the holy man?" he asked. "I was sent to kill you both, and I'd rather get him first if it's all the same. You have a little extra weight to carry, so I'm not too concerned about you running away." He chuckled as his deadened gaze lingered on the chain on the floor by her feet.

"I don't know where he is," Heather replied. "Maybe you scared him off when you screamed like a fucking banshee."

"Pardon my excitement. It's been a long while since I've been in this dimension. I hope it's not too rude of me to admit that I find you quite beautiful. That's the other reason I want to kill the holy man first. I'd like to get to know you a bit better since my time here is limited."

Reagan chuckled again as he entered the range of Heather's pipe. She swung with all her mustered might behind it, slamming the metal elbow joint into the side of Reagan's smug face. He flinched from the blow, but his smile widened as he grabbed the pipe from Heather and tossed it behind him in a single, fluid motion.

"Sorry, young lady," Reagan said. He'd gotten so close Heather could smell the rotten stench of decay on his breath. "It's going to take a lot more than a pipe to the side of my head to stop me from getting what I want. Just ask Congress."

A blast came from behind, and Heather assumed it to be more lighting to accentuate Reagan's point, but the reek of sulfur and the look of pain on Reagan's face told another story.

"Step away from the whore!" Father Stephen ordered with his shotgun aimed at Reagan. It hadn't been an ultimatum, as he immediately fired a second shot into the fortieth president's back.

Reagan bent and picked up Heather's chain, dragging her as he turned and walked toward Father Stephen. She tried to pull back, but he was too strong, and her boots slid on the ice and water that covered the floor while she struggled in vain to get away.

Father Stephen held up his crucifix as a barrier as he had in the face of the demonic hounds, but Reagan only laughed at the sight of it.

"Your faith is waning, Father, and there is nothing of your God's light left in this place. I've come to kill you and bring your corpse back to He Who Walks Above as his prize."

"Oh?" Father Stephen didn't break his gaze with Reagan. "It sounds like he's grown frightened of me."

Regan chuckled again. "He's not frightened by you, but I'll admit you've gotten him miffed. It's too close to the end for him to be bothered by a simple man who's read his Demonic Testament and killed his hounds."

"I know those shots hurt you, and I know this crucifix weakens your resolve as well as your tenacity. If you know I've read the Demonic Testament, then you know I've read about what you are."

"I'm Ronald Reagan, President of these United States."

"You were! That was when you walked under God's sun, but it's rejected you, and so has He! Your body can remain here as all bodies do, but your wretched, blackened soul is no longer welcome on this plane. Go now and rid the living of your vile presence!"

Reagan scoffed. "You sound like the angel who judged me after I died." He stepped over Heather's pipe. "If you have any last words, priest, now's the time to say them."

Heather reached down to grab the pipe Reagan had ignored. His back was to her still, which she hoped would prove to be his undoing. There were two holes in his suit from each of Father Stephen's shotgun blasts. Reagan pretended they didn't damage him, but Heather saw the look of surprise and pain on his face as he took each of the blasts. The sulfur shots had hurt him. A lot.

Heather thrust the bare end of the pipe forward like a spear, aiming for the hole she thought would be closest to Reagan's heart.

Reagan turned toward her. "You little bitch!" he spat. He clutched her chain, pulling her closer toward him, readying a backhand that would surely snap her neck like a toothpick. Father Stephen didn't waver, and the priest wasn't finished fighting.

With a hard thump of wood against flesh, Father Stephen smashed Reagan in the side of the head with his crucifix. "The power of Christ compels you TO BURN!"

Reagan's skin blistered and smoldered under the power of Father Stephen's faith. The scream competed with the storm's winds, and Heather knew she had lost a few years' worth of hearing. She grabbed the pipe, tilting and twisting it to do as much damage to Reagan's internal organs as possible as he turned back toward the priest to exact revenge. The first thing he found was the end of Father Stephen's shotgun pressed to his chin.

"This is for the AIDs crisis, motherfucker," Father Stephen said, squeezing the trigger. The resounding blast turned Reagan's head into a cloud of gray and red. Heather fell back as blood and bits of the former president's brain rained down on her. The rest of Reagan fell to the floor with a thump, twitching as life left it once again.

Father Stephen glared at Heather. "You got yourself free again, I see. Also got yourself in trouble again."

Heather shrugged. "Yeah, I'll do that."

Father Stephen scowled at her, grabbed the chain, and pulled it taut while Heather got back to her feet. "Let's go, adulteress. They know where we are, so we can no longer stay in this place. We got lucky Reagan was easily distracted, but whatever they're going to send our way next, it'll be a hell of a lot harder to kill than some dogs and Ronald Reagan."

"So I take it asking to have this chain unlocked is out of the question?"

Father Stephen yanked on the chain, leading Heather back toward the rectory where most of their stuff was stored. "I still can't trust you, and I can trust you even less now that you know what's in the Demonic Testament. I can't have you running around unchecked and untethered."

"You…" Heather sighed, rolling her eyes even though Father Stephen's back was to her. "I saved your life. Again! The only reason I was able to do that is because I got free. I didn't run and abandon you either time, you vestment-wearing freak! I stayed and helped you finish the job. Isn't that worth something?!"

"Will you try to stop me from killing your husband?" Father Stephen turned to look her in the eyes, which seemed wilder than before. His mind had cracked even more from the pressure of everything and what he'd called the 'demon in his head'. He didn't have a single screw left that hadn't been loosened.

"You know I will," Heather said through gritted teeth. "I'll go through you to save him, chains or not. You might as well unchain me and let me help you find another way. Otherwise, I'm going to kill you the next chance I get."

Father Stephen laughed. "Thank you for your honesty." With that, he smacked Heather in the side of her head with the butt of his shotgun, and she fell to the floor while the world went into freefall and spun around her, fading into an unconscious bliss.

14. HEROES & VILLAINS: ROCKY PHANTASMIC VS DURO ASSASSINO

"I think we're going to have to get off the road soon," Dave said as sleet and hail assaulted his car. "I can't see shit, and I'm bound to crash into something."

"I can't see anything either," Rocky agreed, looking up from his new hoodie and cape. He had gone to work as soon as they left the Star-Mart parking lot, sewing his insignia over the Jets logo while Dave drove. The moment he had finished, he sewed the cape to the back. He now rode with it clutched in his lap like a talisman in case any trouble arose that required a superhero's intervention.

"We're going to have to wait this storm out. I hope it doesn't last all night." Dave pulled off the main road into a small, empty gravel lot. The tires crunched on the sleet and ice as the car came to a stop.

"What is this place?" Rocky asked.

Dave put the car into park. "I don't know. Looks like a nature hiking place or a hunting path. Or both. They have them all over the place up here off the main roads."

"Oh."

"This sucks." Dave looked up as the windshield was pelted with ice and hail. "I know the weather up here isn't always friendly, but this is ridiculous."

They waited in the dark car. Dave flipped through the radio stations hoping for some kind of news on when the storm would pass. He found one where a DJ admitted it hit them out of nowhere and the local power company had reported widespread outages already.

"If you can stay home," the DJ finished, "stay home! Here's Creedence Clearwater Revival by request."

Dave clicked the radio off and stared off into the woods as the wind howled through the trees. "That wasn't helpful. I can't go home."

"We'll be OK," Rocky assured him. "This isn't even snow. It's just frozen raindrops."

Dave nodded. "And we have all of our provisions from Star-Mart in the back. Even if we wind up trapped here all night, we'll be OK."

Rocky nodded and went silent again.

Rocky had been more stoic than usual following their trip into another dimension underneath the Star-Mart. At first, Dave assumed he had hyper-focused on making his new outfit, but something felt different about his super-powered compatriot. It didn't take a ghost psychiatrist made out of trash to figure out that Rocky Phantasmic had faced a foe that had his number, and he hadn't expected it. His armor had chinked, and now he had to live with the fact that he may face enemies on this mission that would prove too much for him to handle.

Even Superman gets his ass kicked from time to time.

A crash came from behind them, and Dave looked in the mirror. A sedan had pulled into the same lot, but they had taken the turn too hard and clipped a tree.

"Looks like we're not the only ones who had to get off the road," he remarked as the sedan's doors opened. "Maybe we should get out and help them get back... OH FUCK, THEY FOUND US!"

Rocky turned and saw the same thing Dave had spotted. It was them, the ones dubbed the Unmade Men, Leo and Johnny, Rocky's somewhat cousins. He pulled his hood over his head.

"They got someone else with them." Dave's eyes lingered on the man who had gotten out of the backseat. He was lean, full of muscles, and covered in a barbed wire tattoo that stretched across his arms and entire torso. Being a fan of men with ink, Dave stared a little too long despite the fear in his gut.

"We need to run," Rocky suggested. "You head down that path and into the woods. I'll deal with my cousins and their friend. Once I've finished with them, I'll find you."

"I'm not leaving you to—"

"There's no time!"

Dave saw no other option. "You better not take too long." He put on a thick pair of wool mittens he had purchased at the Star-Mart. "This storm will kill me if your cousins don't first."

"Go!" Rocky exited the car to face the Unmade Men and whoever they had brought with them. Dave exited the car next, trying his best to keep his footing on the icy ground as he ran toward the path's entrance. He wished he could take a picture of the map posted at the entrance, but he lacked a phone and the time to memorize it.

I forgot to check if Star-Mart had burner phones, dammit!

Dave's regretful inner monologue would have to wait. There would be plenty of time once Rocky finished off his enemies and came to retrieve him.

***

Rocky didn't look over his shoulder to track Dave. He kept his focus on the three men who had followed them from New Haven and walked toward him with purposeful strides. He knew Leo and Johnny well, but he didn't know the shirtless man with the fancy tattoo across his body at all, not that it mattered. The last time Rocky faced the Unmade Men, he'd beaten them plus two others.

"I'm a fair guy," Rocky told his opposition. "I'll give you this one chance to turn around and go home. If you don't, I won't hold back."

"That's the guy we told you about, Duro," Leo said. "Take him out while me and Johnny get the writer. Dig?"

The man named Duro gave a single nod and smiled. He cracked his neck as he walked toward Rocky, raising his fists for a fight.

He's confident in his strength, Rocky thought, *but I'm sure they didn't tell him what I can do. This won't go the way he thinks it will, but that's OK. I need to keep Dave—*

Duro nailed Rocky with an overhand that sent him flying into a tree. He bounced off the bark and landed on the ground as ice from the branches tinkled on the icy ground around him.

"That hurt," Rocky said, getting back to his feet. He hadn't felt pain like that since before his death, and Duro had moved so quickly he barely saw it coming. "What are you?"

Duro didn't answer with any words. He only smiled and attacked again, this time throwing a flurry of punches.

DANIEL AEGAN

***

"Come on out, Bryant!" Johnny called as he trudged down the sleet-ridden path. "No one wants you dead in the woods! Come out, and we'll make sure you're sippin' hot cocoa by a warm fireplace!"

"Yeah!" Leo added. "We don't want to hurt you! We never did! You shouldn't have run from us!"

Yeah, right, Dave thought as he hid behind some thick bushes. *That's just what someone who'd want to hurt me would say.*

The wind intensified, and the branches above Dave's head creaked. A branch broke from the strain, sending it falling to the ground a few feet away from him. He jumped out of the way to keep from being smashed, but it gave away his position.

"There he is!" Leo snapped, running toward him. "Get him!"

Johnny ran as well, lumbering through the brush and ice like the world's worst figure skater. The storm died down a bit, and Dave missed the sound of the wind and trees creaking to hide his steps.

Dave's mind went frantic. What happened to Rocky? He didn't think one man could detain a superhero that long, but Leo and Johnny hadn't come alone.

Was the third man too much for Rocky to handle? Who the fuck is that guy?!

***

Rocky had no idea who the man was who had pummeled him so hard his body made a trench in the Earth aside from hearing Leo call him 'Duro'. He got up, ignoring that his brand-new superhero outfit had gotten covered in freezing mud. There'd be time to wash it later after the fight ended.

"Maybe it was dumb of me to think I was the only one," Rocky said after spitting on the ground, "but I'm not that easy to beat either." He brought his fists up, striking a boxer's pose, glaring at Duro as he approached. "Bring it, you villainous bitch."

Duro moved with the wind, aiming another blow at Rocky's face. It missed as Rocky rocked to the side. He threw a punch of his own, but he opted for a body blow, nailing Duro's left kidney. Rocky swayed again to hit his opponent's other side with a superpowered punch that rang the villain's body like a bell.

Rocky stepped back with his fists up. "Did my cousins tell you I couldn't fight?" Hede risk a smile of his own. "They didn't know that Butch taught me some moves in case I found myself in trouble. He doesn't only cook pizzas, you know. He was a bare-knuckle boxer he was younger, and he's a damn good teacher."

Duro rushed in again, aiming a fist for Rock's head. He missed and hit a tree. It uprooted from the force of the blow, falling back into the woods with the sounds of snapping as it took out the limbs and branches from the tree next to it. The crashing of wood and ice when it hit the ground resounded in the night. Silence followed, broken only by the wind rushing around them.

Rocky threw a quick jab at Duro's chin. He followed up with another. He tried a third, but his wrist got caught in Duro's grip. Rocky tried to pull himself free but to no avail.

Duro's smile made him look like a confident and cocky predator. He swung his arm, bringing Rocky into the air and throwing him through the woods into another tree, breaking it in half. It fell with another crash, and Rocky's body joined it on the sleet-covered ground. It left him gasping for breath. The stars in his vision had almost gone when a swift boot connected with his side, sending him up into the air again. Duro leapt and spiked Rocky back down with both hands clenched together. He went through the soft soil and hit the ledge hidden below it.

Rocky crawled out of the hole and spat out a wad of dirt. He felt a tremor below him as if he'd disturbed something underground, but he ignored it. He had hit the ground hard, and something must have broken underneath the forest floor when his body smashed into it. A sinkhole in the forest didn't concern him, and his opponent wouldn't care much for it either.

He thought another strike would come the moment he showed himself, but it didn't. Duro stood with his arms at his side with the same grin on his face. Rocky also saw that Duro sported the biggest erection he'd ever seen outside a porno movie. That was something they never showed on villains in comic books. The bad guys never got horny in the middle of a fight.

"OK then." Rocky shook his head and put his fists back up. "I'm ready for another round if you are."

Duro smiled and obliged.

***

DANIEL AEGAN

Dave heard the trees crashing in the distance behind him, but he had no way of knowing whether the storm or Rocky's fighting had knocked them over. It took all his energy to run without faltering on the icy terrain while his pursuers did the same a dozen or so feet behind him.

"Give it up already!" Johnny called as he came over a log. "You can't run forever!"

"Neither can you!" Dave wished he didn't sound so exasperated. Quipping in the middle of the action came off better in the movies.

"Your friend won't save you neither!" Leo added, huffing as he chased after him. "We brought some muscle that matches his! He's going to wind up a red smear on the ground, and you're going to come with us. So, stop fucking running and give up already!"

Dave let out an audacious laugh. They sounded as desperate to catch him as he was to get away. They were fucked without him, and it showed. Since he didn't want to waste his precious breath with the taunt, Dave put his energy into escaping instead.

Well, he tried, anyway. He went over a ridge and tumbled through some brush and dead leaves, coming to a stop at the bottom in a puddle of dark water.

"Fuckin' shit." Dave attempting to assess the damage while he got back to his feet. A doe and fawn watched him, startled by his appearance.

"He went down that way!" Leo exclaimed from above. "Go down there and get him!"

"Aren't there any stairs?" Johnny asked.

"What the fuck?! Do you think we're at the friggin' mall?! Just get down there, you big-ass idiot!"

Dave turned back toward the doe, who leapt away with her fawn as Leo admonished Johnny from behind. The deer had only run a few feet when something came out of the ground and swallowed the frantic doe as it bleated. It looked as if the earth itself had come up as a gigantic brown mound to gobble up the doe whole, disappearing back underground afterward.

"OK," Dave said between labored breaths. "That's fucked up."

The fawn trotted off next, but the mound returned, taking it for dessert. This time, however, Dave caught a glimpse of the underground predator. It looked like a bulbous white and pale blue slug with a huge, gaping maw for devouring the creatures of the forest.

If it's big enough to eat a deer, Dave thought, *then it's big enough to eat a human*.

Dave heard the Unmade Men clamoring down the hill after him, making a ton of noise in their wake. The creature had gone back underground, and it would be sure to hear them coming.

Don't stand around and hope it'll eat them next. That dirt worm might be full after eating a deer and its fawn.

Dave swore aloud and got moving again. He didn't know how deep into the forest he'd need to go or what else lurked there. The soil surged behind him, and the moving mound returned, hot on his heels.

"Shit!" Dave scrambled to pull himself forward as the dirt gave out under his feet. "SHIT!"

He climbed atop a fallen tree. The creature leapt after him, clamping the bark in its massive jaws. Dave saw down its gaping mouth to the hundreds of teeth in the circular hole that led to the horrid creature's digestive system. It pulsated with the want to eat more like a gluttonous invertebrate.

"Come on!" Dave groaned. "Being chased through the woods by a couple of mobster assholes is bad enough. Why does this horror movie shit have to happen too?!"

The wormy creature gave up trying to get Dave off his tree trunk and dove back into the ground. The mound of dirt traveled toward the Unmade Men as it left.

"Good." Dave breathed a sigh of relief. "Maybe I'll finally get lucky, and those two walking douchebags will get eaten."

With that on his mind, Dave lowered himself back to the ground to put as much distance between himself and his pursuers as he could. He hadn't gotten far when danger burrowed underground again.

Dave swore under his breath as the ground swelled ahead of him. This one looked bigger if the size of the dirt mound was any indication of the creature below. As it closed the distance, it uprooted a tree and sent it down with a crash. Dave veered to the right, and the mound followed. He swerved to the left. His gambit paid off, as the wormy bastard couldn't turn as fast as it traveled under the earth.

A pile of rocks and boulders came into view over a small ridge like an island of hope and prosperity amid a sea of death and danger. He ran for it while forcing himself not to waste his focus on turning to see if the Unmade Men or the underground monsters still chased after him. He got to the rocks and climbed the outcropping, seconds before the underground creatures slammed into the shelf of ledge. A horrid shriek came from under the dirt as it turned and made an arc in the soil as it rounded a boulder.

"Go find the two assholes chasing me, you Dune extra sonofabitch!" Dave called after it. "I'm sure they're quite tasty!"

***

"Fuck this shit!" Leo snapped as he tumbled into the soft dirt. "Help me up, Johnny."

Johnny reached down and pulled his cousin out of the dirt with a heave. "You OK?"

Leo scoffed. "I'll live, but I may end up puttin' some holes in this prick for making me run all the way out here to get him."

"Vincenzo wants him alive."

"I'll put the holes where they won't kill him. Fuck! Let's just find him and get the fuck out of these fuckin' woods before we end up riddled with Lyme disease or some shit."

"You can't get Lyme disease in the winter," Johnny retorted. "All the ticks die when it gets cold."

"I somehow doubt you've based that on fact." Leo straightened himself out, brushing what he could off his clothes. "Besides, it's still fall despite the weather." He looked around the dark forest. "Where did that little titty-sucking writer go? I don't have the patience for this never-ending bullshit."

They both turned toward the sound of shouting and crashing.

"He's there," Leo said, a smile spreading across his face.

"What's he screamin' about, though?" Johnny asked.

"He probably saw a mean squirrel and dropped a load of shit in his pants. Snowflake fuck."

Johnny took his gun out of its hidden hip holster and turned the safety off. "I ain't messin' with any wolves or nothin' out here. Any animal comes near me, I'm blastin' it in the head."

Leo took out his pistol as well. "Good idea. I wasn't thinkin' about no wolves, but I heard they got bobcats and mountain lions up this way."

"What if the writer mook's dead? What if some animal got to him first and ate him?"

Leo shrugged. "We can't be blamed for that. Sure, the boss will be pissed, but what can we do? The friggin' moron ran into the woods on his own accord."

They listened for any more evidence of the writer or his screaming. The sounds of more crashing came from behind.

"Sounds like Duro's givin' Richie a decent fight," Leo remarked. "Serves him right to get his head knocked around a bit after gettin' in our way like he did."

Johnny would've responded, but the ground opened up ahead of them, and a huge, gaping mouth full of teeth emerged, sending dirt and other forest debris flying. It let out a guttural screeching and headed right for them.

"WHAT THE FUCK IS THAT THING?!" Leo exclaimed.

Johnny didn't waste his breath on profanities, though thousands of different swears in both English and Italian flooded his mind. He aimed his pistol and emptied the clip into the monstrous mouth. Leo did the same while Johnny reloaded, pumping every bullet in his nine-millimeter into the soft flesh. The mouth thing got the message and dove back into the dirt.

"What was that friggin' thing?" Johnny asked. "It looked like a giant asshole with teeth!"

"I don't know," Leo replied, "but I don't want to fuck with it again to find out. That's for goddam sure."

"At least we know what spooked the writer."

Leo reloaded his pistol. "This is my last clip unless we double back to the car. I didn't think we'd do much shootin' out here. Walk softly, Johnny. Maybe that thing will hear our footsteps if we're steppin' too heavy. Know what I'm sayin'?"

Johnny nodded. "Got it."

They did their best not to make much noise while they stalked the writer. They had no idea where he'd gone to hide or whether or not he'd been eaten by the mouth thing or some other forest predator.

Johnny turned and saw the dirt swelling like a growing tumor on fast forward. "Leo, run!" he exclaimed, surging forward.

Leo took one look over his shoulder, swore, and ran in the same direction.

The ground behind them fell inward as the underground mouth thing rushed toward their vulnerable feet. Leo aimed a shot into the dirt behind him as he ran, but all it did was knock a little of the soil into the air. The gaping jaws breached the ground in its hunger for living flesh.

Leo tripped after a tendril shot out from the ground and wrapped around his ankle. He clawed at the earth to find something more solid than the soil to pull himself out of the its tenacious grip.

"Johnny!" he shouted. "Help me for fuck's sake!"

Johnny turned, and his eyes widened when he saw Leo's peril. He didn't freeze, though. He never did. He walked toward Johnny, aiming with careful precision. He fired one shot, hitting the dirt next to the tendril. He fired a second, this time hitting the mark. The tendril loosened and went back into the ground, followed by the rest of the mouth thing.

"Fuck this whole thing," Johnny said, grabbing Leo's wrist and pulling him back to his feet. "We'll die out there, and the writer's probably already bit the big one. I say we wait by the cars to see if he comes back out. Or we send Duro to fetch him after he's done playin' with Rocky."

Leo nodded. "I know you're usually a man of few words, but when you're right, you're right. Let's get outta here. That writer prick's going to wish one of those things gobbled him up if we have to send Duro after his ass."

***

The tree rocked but didn't fall. Rocky's body wanted to collapse with the blow he'd taken that sent him reeling backward. The man named Duro stood. He'd taken as much of a beating, and he still smiled. Rocky didn't care. As far as he could tell, he still had a lot of fight left in him.

"This is it," Rocky told himself, getting his fists up again. He sweated hard under his hoodie, and he couldn't remember if he'd sweat at all since coming back to life as a superhero. "Every hero gets an archnemesis, right?"

Duro threw a left hook that rocked the side of Rocky's head. Rocky came back with a hook of his own to Duro's jaw, sending the villain's head snapping to the side. Duro might've been posturing like the fight meant nothing to him, but he'd grown tired after all.

Rocky slammed his forehead into Duro's nose. Duro hadn't expected the headbutt, and it showed on his face with a wince. If he was anything like Rocky, then he hadn't fought like this in a long time—maybe not ever.

"I'll give you credit," Rocky said as he sent a flurry of quick-paced body blows into Duro's abdomen, hitting him several times in the span of a second. "You've withstood everything I've thrown at you, but you forgot one thing. Evildoers never win against a force of good!"

Rocky threw the fight-ending punch with every iota of strength in his body powering his fist as it flew forward on a nonstop flight path toward Duro's face. Rocky's body cut the cold wind, and every muscle cried out in triumph as the punch to end all punches soared toward its mark to send the tattooed man called Duro into the stratosphere in an epic blast of superheroic fortitude and the power of all that is good and righteous in the world.

The sound of Rocky's fist slapping against Duro's waiting palm as he caught it filled the night air.

"Oh," Rocky said.

Duro aimed a punch similar to Rocky's in every way except completely the opposite. It was a supervillainous blow that sent Rocky flying through the air into the cold, icy darkness of the forest.

***

"This is so stupid," Dave muttered while his body shivered. He waited on the pile of rocks and ledge in the darkness. The storm had let up on its icy assault and had given way to a quiet calm that enveloped the forest. As it turned out, the weather was the least of his worries.

Dave hadn't seen the mounds of dirt moving since the last one that had chased him onto his monument of rock. He heard a lot of gunshots at once along with some shouts from the Unmade Men, but they had stopped aside from two more a couple of minutes after the first round of shooting. The only assumption Dave could make involved the gaping mouth-holes of the underground worm monsters and the deaths of the men pursuing him, but he couldn't count on his luck being that good.

Are those monsters still out there waiting for me to step back onto the soft dirt?

There was no way to tell. Dave couldn't even tell himself with any certainty that Leo and Johnny had met their ultimate fate via the worm things that had sprung to life from some B-movie plot written by some dumbass writer who saw Dune or Tremors one too many times. The woods were a clusterfuck, and there were no options to unfuck any of it.

DANIEL AEGAN

I need to make a run for it if I can. I'm going to be easy to find if I'm too afraid to leave this rock.

A sound came from behind Dave, and he turned to find a huge moose lumbering toward him. He scrambled up the rocks, unsure if he'd ever heard any stories of moose attacking people. Were they mean bastards, or were they sweethearts deep down? It wasn't something one should learn the hard way.

The moose walked around the pile of rocks, sniffing the air as it went. It lifted its head, observed Dave for a brief moment, huffed, and continued its slow gait through the forest.

That answers my question. Moose are indifferent to humans in peril. Good to know.

Then, the ground opened, and the moose got sucked down while bleating its heart out. It struggled against the suction of the hungry mouth, beating its front hooves against the wet, frigid earth as it struggled to remain on the topside of the ground. The worm creature rose, opened its monstrous maw and came down on the moose in a single, sickening swoop. The moose and the worm both disappeared underground as silence returned to the forest.

Looks like my previous question got answered, too.

Dave had zero options. He could sit and wait for Rocky to find him, but he didn't know how long that could take. He might freeze to death in his sopping clothes before that happened. Rocky had super strength and invulnerability, but he couldn't save Dave from the evil grasp of hypothermia.

Then, as Dave thought about how Rocky fared against his opponent, the young superhero flew through the air above him, snapping limbs and branches as he crashed through the canopy of trees. He hit a trunk, face first, and fell to the earth with a dull thud.

"Rocky!" Dave called, throwing caution and everything else he had left in him to the frigid wind. He climbed down from the rocks and ventured into the unknown darkness.

Rocky groaned and stirred, shaking his head as he rose to his feet. He looked to his side and saw Dave had come.

"You don't want to be here when Duro comes after me."

"Neither of us should be! Things are moving under—"

Duro dropped from the sky, slamming an elbow between Rocky's shoulder blades, driving him back to the ground. He picked his prey up by the back of his neck like a small animal and slammed him against the tree, holding him against it.

The worst part, by Dave's estimation, was Duro's erection.

"You were a good fighter, Rocky Phantasmic," Duro said in a thick Italian accent. He pulled his fist back, readying a final blow. "But you weren't good enough. If there is a Hell, I'd like to fight you again there."

"It's not over," Rocky said, grasping at the arm pinning him to the tree. "You haven't won yet."

Duro tilted his head, and his smile widened as he increased the pressure on Rocky's neck. "Arrivederci, hero." He was about to make his killing blow when a rock struck him on the side of the head. It didn't do any damage, but he turned toward the source anyway.

"Leave him alone!" Dave exclaimed. "It's me you want, right? You don't have to kill him."

"Dave," Rocky croaked. "Run."

Duro let go of Rocky's neck and let him fall to the ground. He focused on Dave. His gaze pierced through all Dave's mental defenses, chilling him to his core where the cold, wet breeze hadn't touched.

Dave stepped back, almost tripping when his feet met a shelf of ledge. He climbed onto the rock and met Duro's eyes, forcing himself to ignore his body's unyielding impulse to get the hell out there as fast as he could—not that he'd get away from a real-life supervillain with only his legs and whatever moxie he could muster to move them.

Duro's laughter chilled as much as his gaze. Then, like an act of a vengeful God, the ground swelled near his feet, and one of the worm creatures emerged, swallowing Duro in a single movement.

"Shit," Dave muttered. "I didn't think that would work after that worm gorged itself on moose meat." He looked to see Rocky getting back to his feet, looking at the space Duro had stood the moment before.

"Don't step on the dirt!" Dave called to him. "Get on the rocks with me or one of those things will get you next."

Rocky nodded and made a short jump to where Dave stood. He faltered when he landed, injured from his fight.

"Do you know which way to go to get back to the car?" Dave asked.

Rocky looked up for a moment and pointed in the distance. "I think I flew here from that way, so that should be our path to get back. We can get there quick if I carry you."

"Can you? No offense, but you look like hell right now."

"I'm not defeated yet, and it looks like we can't walk on the ground without calling whatever that thing was that ate Duro."

"OK. Then I guess that's the only way out."

Rocky nodded and picked up Dave like an injured child. Even after the beating he'd received, he still had enough strength left for the task at hand. Even after the fight of his life, he could still impress with his strength and tenacity.

They flew through the air a moment later. Dave knew Rocky didn't possess the gift of flight, but the long leaps through the air felt that way, especially for one who'd spent their entire life grounded. Rocky kicked off the trees of limbs when he could to keep them high above the wormy creature's feeding ground. His sense of direction proved correct as well, and he landed right where they'd parked.

"We should go now," Dave said, getting back into the car and bringing it to life. "I don't want to stick around here any longer."

Rocky got in the passenger's seat, but not before noticing the other car was still there. "What happened to my cousins?"

"I don't know." Dave backed up. The car's wheels crunched the ice in the small parking lot. "They chased me pretty far into the woods. With luck, one of those monsters ate them. They and their supervillain are going to end up as worm shit, and I'm OK with that turn of events."

Dave stepped on the gas and got back onto the main road to leave the whole ordeal in the woods behind him.

***

Leo and Johnny emerged from the trees forty-five minutes later after getting lost and wandering while trying not to intrude on any ground that would alert the creatures underground to their presence. They climbed down the small hill that led to the lot and saw the writer's car was gone.

"Fuck!" Leo snapped. "They got here before we did and got away!"

"That's it for Duro, then?" Johnny asked. "Did Rocky kill him?"

Leo spat on the ground. "No way he can kill Duro. That pussy-ass writer must have given us the slip and gotten away on his own, leavin' Rocky to get his ass handed to him."

A buzzing came from Leo's pocket, and he jumped. He pulled his phone out and looked at the screen.

"Shit. It's Vincenzo. His timing's perfect as usual."

"Are you going to answer it?" Johnny looked scared as if their Undead Boss got word through the unholy grapevine that they'd failed him again like a villain from a Saturday morning cartoon. With everything they'd witnessed, it wouldn't be surprising in the slightest if that's how it went down.

"I have to." Leo accepted the call and put it on the speaker so Johnny could hear. "Hey, boss. What's up?"

"Did you get the writer yet? Where are you?"

"We're in Maine. And to answer your first question…yes and no."

"Pretend I don't know what the fuck 'yes and no' means and elaborate a little bit for me."

"We were on their asses, but they ran off into the woods when we got close. There were some…complications, and they slipped past us. They can't be far, though."

"What kind of complications?"

"There were monsters, boss!" Johnny interjected. "I know it sounds weird… Well, maybe not as weird as people coming back from the dead, but they tried to eat us!"

Vincenzo let out a long groan. "Were these monsters too big for Duro? He's with you to take care of these types of things."

"That's a whole other thing," Leo said with a worried look for Johnny's benefit.

"Are you going to start giving me details, or do I have to have a follow-up session for every friggin' thing you tell me?"

"Duro went off to fight Rocky while me and Johnny went after the writer and almost got eaten by those monsters. We don't know what happened to him."

Vincenzo was silent while he digested that information. Finally, he said, "That is not what I wanted to hear, boys."

"Sorry, boss."

"I'm heading up your way now. Even though you fucked this up every which way from Sunday, the writer is still heading where he's supposed to go."

Leo blinked a few times to clear the cobwebs from his brain. "Wait, boss. Did you say you're coming to Maine?"

"Did you get some shit in your ears?! I need to finish this myself since you two bumbling snot-suckers can't handle picking up one guy."

"It's a little more complicated than—"

"I'm on my way. I'll be in touch." Vincenzo ended the call.

"What now?" Johnny asked, breaking the silence.

Leo shrugged. "We keep going. We got the boss's compass, and the writer couldn't have gotten far with the roads as shitty as they are. We should be able to catch up with him in no time assuming we don't hit any other snags."

As soon as Leo finished his bout of optimistic thinking, the ground swelled and opened, and one of the worm creatures burst from it, screeching as it broke through to the open air. Leo dropped his phone and aimed his gun at its asshole-like mouth, ready to pump it full of bullets like the last one. Johnny did the same.

The creature didn't attack, though. It slouched and hit the ground with a dull thud. The mouth burst open next, and Duro walked out covered in red, slimy guts and monster bile. The whole thing reeked like a pile of carcasses in the middle of a garbage dump.

"Holy shit, Duro!" Leo exclaimed, holstering his gun. "You scared the living shit out of us." He picked up his phone, checked to make sure he hadn't broken the screen before putting it back in his pocket. "We were wonderin' what happened to you. Did you kill the kid?"

Duro's eyes narrowed, and he let out a single huff from his nose. He walked passed Leo and Johnny toward the car.

"I guess that's a 'no'," Leo muttered to Johnny. "Let's get after them again. Duro's going to want some revenge, and I don't blame him." He walked back toward his car.

"Wait a second," Johnny said, jogging to catch up. "How the hell did Duro get that monster to come back here from inside it?!"

15.

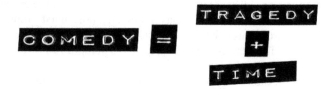

"FUCK!"

Cliff sat up in his hotel bed and gasped for breath. The sun beamed through the window. It hurt his eyes, but he didn't care. Nothing mattered except that whatever illusion had taken hold of him the night before had finally ended.

"I'm back. It was all a vivid fuckin'…"

'Nightmare' would've been the word Cliff used, had he not looked around himself before uttering it. Of course, that would've been an easy way to end the whole ordeal, but life didn't come easy—not to guys like Cliff Quentin.

His bedsheets were soaked, and it wasn't from him sweating or pissing the bed—which was something he'd have to be extremely drunk to do. The white sheets were brown and crimson, reeking of the human stew in the back of the demonic garbage truck. If Cliff didn't know any better, he would have guessed his bowels had dumped his liquified guts, but he knew that wasn't the case since he still breathed and didn't feel like an empty husk of a ghost.

"Oh no. It was all real?!"

Cliff swung his feet out of bed despite the tremors that had taken over his body. They squished in the carpet. There was a line of slime and more of the liquid leading to the door, and he knew there'd be a streak of it going right out to the street from where the garbagemen had dropped him off.

He ached in the raw places the bugs had bitten him as well. He had woken nude, and he could see the red spots and bumps all over his body. He wanted the hottest shower imaginable to wash away the stench. Maybe some scalding water could kill the germs that had to be swarming over every inch of his flesh.

Cliff jumped when he heard a buzzing, and he thought for sure the killer flies had returned. He stopped shaking when he realized it was his cellphone ringing from the pile of filthy clothes off to the side of the bed. He fished through his sopping clothes and found it in his soggy pants. He pulled it out with a shaking hand to see that it was Randy calling him. Cliff accepted the call.

"Hello, Randy," he said in a raspy voice. He coughed and swallowed the phlegm in his throat.

"You sound like shit," Randy greeted him. "Did you go on another bender last night?"

Cliff sighed. "Good morning to you, too."

"It's the middle of the afternoon."

Cliff looked at the bedside alarm clock and saw that the morning had come and gone. It was three in the afternoon already.

"So what?" Cliff tried to sound as nonchalant as possible. He didn't want to give away what he'd endured the night before. "I'm a night guy. It comes with the territory. I don't know why I'm explaining it to you. You know all this already."

Cliff kept his back to the bed while he spoke. He wanted to feel some semblance of normalcy in the conversation. What should he have told Randy? Would his road manager understand how he'd slipped through the cracks of reality into something excruciatingly alien and horrendously different? He'd think Cliff was high off his ass, insane, or both.

Then, Cliff realized how his night had ended, and he wondered why the garbagemen had kept him alive and brought him home instead of mashing and grinding up his body as they'd done with whatever had created all the blood, bones, and gore into which they'd tossed him.

"I got another gig for you," Randy said, "but you'll have to blow off tomorrow's open mic night in Easthampton."

"Oh? Can I still do the Boston show?"

"You should if you don't mind a lot of driving back and forth around New England."

Cliff thought about it. If he kept moving, maybe whatever dark entity hounding him wouldn't be able to keep up. If he slowed down again, they'd find him and give him another ride in the back of the garbage truck.

"Driving doesn't bother me," he replied. "It's all part of the 'back to my roots' thing. What do you have for me?"

"I have a show near Bangor."

"Bangor? As in Maine?"

"No, Bangor, California. Of course, Bangor, Maine, you ding dong!"

Cliff groaned as a headache roared to life in the center of his weary brain. "Sarcasm aside, I had no idea they had comedy clubs up that way."

"Well, now you know. It'll take five or six hours to get up there, so I suggest you start driving. The gig is tomorrow night. Oh, did I mention why I'm sending you up there?"

"Randy, you have as much tact as a flea that wants everyone to see its microscopic boner. Stop tickling my ass with a feather and tell me what you're dying to tell me."

"There's going to be a talent scout in the audience tomorrow night," Randy said with a ten-year-old's glee. "If you impress them, this could be your ticket back into the limelight. Specials, casinos, movie roles, and more of those sitcom writing gigs I know you love so much."

Cliff thought about it. Five or six hours on the road wasn't that long of a drive. He'd done worse before, and he'd still be in the area, give or take a hundred miles or so. By his math, he'd arrive in the Bangor area late, do the show on Wednesday, and probably drive to Boston on Thursday to get there in the late afternoon at the earliest. He had planned on spending Friday getting ready for the big show on Saturday night with his ritualistic preparations. He'd promised his Aunt Dorothea to spend some extra time at home with them, but he'd have to break that promise for Randy's opportunity. She'd have to understand.

Maybe the trip to Maine would also get the garbagemen off his back, and he wouldn't bring them to his family's doorstep.

"Hello?" Randy asked. "Are you still there, or did the call drop? Cliff?! Fuckin' cellphones! Goddam sonofa—"

"I'm still here," Cliff answered. "I'm just doing some math in my head."

"Don't. You'll hurt yourself. Besides, you got me to do the math for you, remember?"

Cliff forced a laugh. "Yeah. Go ahead and book the Bangor thing for me. Unbook this open mic bullshit down here. I don't want to stick around this town longer than I need to be here after last night."

Randy chuckled. "I'm sure there's a great story behind why you want to get the hell out of there. I'd love to hear it sometime."

Cliff looked over at the bed again and let out a long breath at the sight of the rotten juices soaking through the sheets and into the mattress. "I don't think this is one I'll tell any time soon."

"I'll make the calls and get you on the ticket. Do me a favor, though. Slow down with the drinking or drugs or whatever the hell you've been doing since Saturday night. I know this type of shit is like bread and butter to comedians on the road, but I don't want to see you get into some shit you can't get out of. What was it your grandfather used to say about ending up in the back of a garbage truck?"

"Don't." Cliff ended the call and placed the phone on top of the dresser.

The phone buzzed seconds later, and Cliff picked it back up. Randy had sent a text that read, "Rude! I still love you. You're going to tell me what happened in Easthampton if it kills me to get it out of you."

"Then rest in peace," Cliff texted back before putting his phone down again. He sighed, assessing the mess in his room. His credit card would suffer when they billed him to clean the whole thing and replace everything too soiled to be cleaned. Maybe they'd recognize his name and call some two-bit rag to drop some hot gossip about what a sick fuck Cliff Quentin is for dumping garbage juice, human slime, and God knew what else all over the hotel bed.

"Or maybe they'd call the police, thinking I murdered someone in here."

Cliff stood in the room as the dark thoughts and reek of garbage permeated his entire being a funky aura he could only hope to somehow shed.

"Someone promised me a scalding hot shower," he muttered, walking to the bathroom.

***

The hot shower did Cliff a world of good. He stayed under the water a long time to allow the images of what he remembered from the night before to wash away along with the grime and whatever else had been in the back of the garbage truck.

He thought about June and her husband and the threesome he'd left before he'd gotten the chance to climax along with his partners. Did he owe them an apology before he skipped town? It didn't matter if he did. He couldn't remember where they lived, and he hadn't gotten June's number. He could try to find them on their social media accounts like a stalker, but that felt like too much. In this case, it would be best for everyone if he left the swinging couple alone and let them forget about the time they brought some nutjob comedian into their bedroom.

How the hell would he tell them about why he'd left in the first place? Did he even know himself?

Cliff killed the water and stood in the cloud of steam. The insect bites still stung, but at least he'd gotten them as clean as he could with the skin-drying hotel soap. He'd have to see a doctor soon and get a blood test and a tetanus shot for good measure, but that would have to wait till next week at the earliest. Things had gotten a bit more complicated with his road schedule.

As Cliff dressed himself, he decided to leave his soiled clothes on the hotel room floor. They were already going to bill and admonish him for the mess, so chucking out his clothes along with the bedding would be the least of their worries. He left a fifty-dollar bill on the dresser as a tip for the poor maid who had to take care of it. He paused for a moment and added another fifty to it in hopes it would be enough to assuage both his guilt and the maid's disgust.

Cliff didn't bother checking out. The less interaction he had with human beings who'd wind up wrist-deep in his filth, the better. He didn't feel much like apologizing in advance for a room so messy the hotel chain might board up the door and pretend the room didn't exist.

At least I didn't leave them a dead hooker they'd have to toss into the dumpster for me.

The roads were busy, but Cliff hadn't gotten his ass in gear till after five. He figured he'd be checking into his hotel in Maine late and sleeping until midafternoon again. All of Tuesday felt like a waste, but that was part of the life he'd chosen. With luck, he could put all the negativity he'd experienced since New Haven behind him for good.

Then again, why would things be so simple?

The thoughts about how Aunt Dorothea would be upset with him leaving Massachusetts bothered him at first, but he did his best not to focus on those feelings too much. At this point, she probably expected him to ditch her, and she'd understand his reasoning to head to Maine. His career stood in the balance. Even if she couldn't understand the horrific nonsense that plagued his path, Aunt Dorothea and his cousin Missy would sleep well as long as Cliff stayed far, far away from them with his bullshit.

"There's a wild air in this part of the country. It's not about the chill in the air or anything about the weather. There's an energy up here in New England, and it's not always a good one."

Cliff turned to see the source of the voice as he stood at the rest stop urinal, and it surprised him to find a tall, blonde man standing there looking back at him. He wore a white jacket that looked like a cross between a trench coat and a bathrobe. Then again, fashion was a complete mystery to men like Cliff Quentin.

"Don't you know urinal etiquette?" he asked the stranger, keeping his eyes on his own work. "Look straight forward, do your business, and do not engage in conversation with another man while he's got his penis in his hand."

The restroom interloper chuckled. "That's funny, even if it's a bit too homophobic for my liking."

"It has nothing to do with being homophobic." Cliff thought about how he had kissed another man less than twenty-four hours ago, but he kept that detail to himself. There were some things one didn't discuss with a stranger in a rest stop men's room—not unless you were looking for something that exclusively happens in those places.

"Keep your mind on your business," Cliff finished, "and your business won't end up trickling all over the floor and onto my shoes."

The stranger laughed again. "You should be a comedian."

Cliff zipped up his fly and flushed the toilet. "Thanks. You should be in the audience for a shitty comedy show." He went to the sink to wash his hands, and it didn't surprise him in the slightest to find that the blonde stranger in the bright white coat followed to do the same in the sink next to him despite a whole row of sinks being open.

"I know what you're thinking," the stranger in white said. "You think I should back off. You feel like I'm sucking up your air and you'll choke without it."

"Something like that." Cliff finished his hand washing and left. He was ready for this freak to start some shit outside. He'd be sure to punctuate the point with a fist to his nose if it came down to it. He'd been through too much to let a restroom pervert get the better of him, and he didn't feel like putting up with any more of the back-and-forth the stranger started at the urinal.

"I think you and I should get some dinner, Cliff!" the stranger called as he left the restroom a few paces behind him.

Cliff stopped moving and let out an exhausted sigh. The asshole knew him after all. It figured. He turned toward the stranger with his hands balled into hard fists and looked him in the eye, ready to throw a punch or three if the situation warranted it.

"I don't know what you think is going to happen, pal, but I'm in no mood for this little dance routine. I've only been on the road for four or five days now, and it's been the screwiest time in my life. If you want to be an outlet for me to let out my anger and frustration, you can be it. I won't back down or hold back if you want to go that route. So tell me, brand new pal of mine, is this how you want to spend your night?"

As he'd done before, the stranger laughed and stepped closer without the slightest hint of fear or caution. "You're very dramatic for a comedian, but I guess it takes all sorts of personalities and energies mashed into a single being to do what you do. No man or woman is one-sided, and you've embodied that for yourself. I'm proud of you Cliff. We all are."

"Great. You're a fucking hippy, too. Does that mean you won't fight back if I punched your teeth down your throat?"

"You're mistaking hippies for pacifists. But yes, if you hit me, I will not strike you in return. I'm here to help you on your journey. That's all. Nothing more, nothing less."

Cliff scoffed. "And who the fuck are you to help me do anything?"

The stranger smiled. "My name is Sera, and I'm an angel."

Cliff had to force himself not to laugh. Instead, he simply said, "Bullshit."

***

Cliff had decided, among other things, that maybe Sera's claim of being an angel wasn't bullshit after all. He'd seen weirder shit than what the stranger claimed, and it had all happened in the last few days. Besides, the self-proclaimed angel had offered him a free meal and claimed to know the best spot in the area to eat.

"Alright, angel," Cliff said as the waitress left with their order. "I'll give you a bit of time while we eat. After that, I'm back on the road, and you're out of my life."

"Yes indeed." Sera had removed his coat at the door, and he wore a similar getup underneath it. It appeared to be a white sweater with a silver pattern on it. If Cliff didn't know any better—and he didn't—he'd swear it was meant to look like a breastplate. The kook had gone all-in on the whole 'angel' thing. "You've got a long way to go, still, Cliff."

"Not really. I'm around halfway there. Maybe three hours and change left to go. I'll be in bed by one in the morning if I'm lucky enough to get a quick check-in at my hotel."

Sera leaned forward to observe Cliff's face with his bright, blue eyes. There was something about him, angel or not. He exuded a feminine energy, even if his mannerisms and appearance were masculine in nature, aside from the long, white coat.

"We don't have long for this talk," the supposed angel said, "and you're a man whose patience is at its limit, so I'm going to cut to the chase, as they say. I know you'll balk at me for bringing this up, but I want to know about those who have been pursuing you over the last few days."

Cliff felt a good balking coming as Sera predicted, but he took a deep breath and let it go instead. "You mean like crazy fans at rest stops who claim to be angels?"

Sera laughed and shook his head. "Not at all, and you know it. I'm speaking about those who come in the dark to torment and deter your progress. The one who sent them is the one we call the Enemy, but he's also known as He Who Walks Above."

"I hate that stupid fuckin' name." Cliff looked away for a moment and took a sip of water. He turned back to Sera and added, "I haven't told anyone about that. Maybe I said something to that psychic back in New Haven, but that whole day is a blur to me now. If you really are an angel, tell me what it all means. Why am I marked, and why does this fucked up shit keep happening to me? None of this seems real."

"You've been marked by the Enemy as a potential threat to his plans. He doesn't want you to continue your journey, so he's sent some of his agents to get you to stop. You've proven to be tenacious, though, and you haven't backed down."

"You said that thing about my journey before. Are you talking about my standup tour? It's more of me just driving to random clubs and doing a bit of comedy. It's not much of anything but me trying to get my mojo back. Why the fuck does this demon asshole even care about it in the first place?"

Sera shook his head. "Oh, Cliff, you poor, misguided man."

"What did I say?"

"My pity for you is genuine, and I mean no insult by it. You've been drawn into a web of another's design by fate. You've become the plaything of an entity that rivals God Himself."

"It would be super neat if you could tell me why I'm his plaything and how I can get him to leave me the fuck alone."

Sera took a sip of water. "You can't. He wants to break you. To put a finer point on it, he wants you to break yourself."

Cliff huffed and shook his head. "It's like he's gaslighting me, but on a cosmically horrific scale."

"That's one way to put it."

"What do I do then? I feel like you're purposely not telling me. Am I supposed to live the rest of my life looking over my shoulder for crazed garbagemen? I can't live like that. No one can."

"That's the point, Cliff. The Enemy wants you to take that route. He wants you to believe there's only one way out of your walking psychosis, and that's death."

"Then why bother at all? Why not come and finish me off himself?"

The waiter returned to drop their plates between them. Cliff had ordered a sirloin and roasted potatoes, and the aroma was nothing short of heavenly. Sera had a salad, complete with raspberry vinaigrette.

"Is vegetarianism an angelic thing?" Cliff asked.

Sera laughed. "No, but they use the freshest ingredients for their salads here." He took a bite of lettuce with a slice of tomato. "It's so good."

"So, I was asking about why this demon guy who's after me hasn't finished me off himself. What's he waiting for? He could've killed me last night for sure and a hundred times before that."

"There are cosmic consequences for his actions on this plane. If he kills you, it may spoil his plans."

"But this colossal anal fissure tormenting me to the point of suicide doesn't count as killing me?"

"As far as demonic magic in your science-based realm goes, that is correct. To put it in simpler terms: If he kills you, then his prey may also die to balance the cosmic scales."

Cliff popped a piece of steak in his mouth. "Figures." He chewed and swallowed. "But why would his prey die? What's he after, anyway?"

"You've been linked to another by fate. You know him already. You came together for a brief period before this all started, though you've been dragged apart by evil intentions. If David Bryant is the one the Enemy needs to complete his plans, then you, Cliff, are the one who balances the Enemy's demonic magic."

"Is that what happened to Dave?"

Sera nodded.

"Shit, now I feel bad for being so pissy about him blowing me off Saturday night. If he's seen half of what I have, he's gotta be shitting his pants till he dies of dehydration."

Sera ate a piece of his salad, watching Cliff while he chewed.

"OK," Cliff continued. "I get it, I think, but why tell me all this now? What do you have to gain by telling me the universe's most major secrets?"

"I gain nothing from it. I've been lying in wait, unable to interfere in the Enemy's plans. We're ready to strike after he makes his move, but I fear it'll be too late by then."

"So, you're asking me to end this for you? You want me to unbalance a demon's magic by what exactly? Do I kill Dave? That doesn't sound too angel-like to me."

Sera shook his head. "No, Cliff." He sighed and put his fork down next to his plate. "I'd never ask you to take another's life, not even for this purpose. I wanted you to know why these things are happening to you. What's happening is not part of God's plan, and it's unfair for you to be in the position in which you've found yourself."

"Help me then, Sera! Next time those garbagemen come for me, swoop down and chop their demonic heads off!"

"Don't you see?! I can't interfere in a human's life like that! I risk a lot by even talking to you, but it's all I can do by angelic law. Even if an external tormentor is pulling your strings, an angel cannot stop it from happening. All we can do is warn you."

Cliff scoffed and cut into his steak. "That's convenient. And you said *I* should be a comedian."

"I'm sorry, Cliff, I am, but this is as much as I can do. Despite the Enemy's torments, you are still moving forward along with David Bryant. If you keep on the path fate has paved with coincidence and happenstance, you'll find yourself at his reckoning waiting to play your part in it. What you do from here is up to you."

Cliff sighed and swallowed the mouthful of steak and potatoes he'd been working on while Sera laid out the epilogue to his little speech. "Well, at least I got a free meal out of it. That's worth something, right?"

Sera smiled. "It sure is."

"Well, that can't be it. No words of wisdom? There's no secret to beating back hordes of evil garbagemen or whatever else comes after me? What am I supposed to do?"

"There is always solace in the word of the Lord." Sera placed a Bible on the table. The black cover had been inlaid with a gold crucifix on the front. Cliff wanted to ask if it was real gold, but he thought it might come off as rude in the least and blasphemous in the worst-case scenario.

"Here is where you'll find your answers," Sera continued. "Keep it with you, and you will be blessed."

"Thanks." Cliff reached across the table and took the Bible. "I hope it comes in handy."

Sera's smile widened. "Oh, I'm sure it will."

***

Cliff said goodnight after his off-putting dinner with Sera and got back on the road despite his misgivings about going to the show in Bangor. It wasn't that he didn't appreciate the angel's efforts. The problem with the whole thing was that it made things weirder than they had to be. When the evil nonsense was possibly the result of bad acid, dealing with it had been so much easier.

Now, however…

"If I go," Cliff said to the inanimate windshield in front of him, "I wind up this demon's shitlist. If I run away and hide…"

Rain pelted the windshield in big, obscene blobs.

What's hiding going to do? If this He Who Walks Above prick has a hard-on for me, then hiding isn't going to do a goddam thing. I have the show with the scout in Bangor, and I'll be fucked in my face and ass like a rotisserie chicken before I let some piece of shit with a four-word sentence for a name fuck my whole career up when I'm in the middle of unfucking it in the first place.

The unspeaking, mocking rain intensified as Cliff drove. He continued his contemplations of what Sera had told him, and he felt as if he'd reach enlightenment about his whole situation when a truck on a kamikaze mission almost knocked him out of his lane.

"MOTHERFUCKER!" Cliff snapped, somehow fitting the entire complex word into a single syllable. He swerved, using the breakdown lane to right himself, muttering a stream of obscenities that would get him canceled all over again if he said it on stage.

Cliff turned toward the truck that attempted an assassin-like assault on him, and his jaw dropped open. It wasn't the run-of-the-mill eighteen-wheeler or some construction vehicle with a vendetta against the road it had been created to upkeep. The truck driving parallel to Cliff's car was a garbage truck, and it looked all too familiar.

"Oh shit!"

Cliff slammed his foot to the floor, spraying rainwater behind him as he pressed his luck against the slick roads. His car lurched forward as he made his mad dash to get away from the garbage truck. He looked in his rearview mirror to see it gaining speed behind him. They turned on their high beams, flooding Cliff's car with orange-tinted light as they redoubled their pursuit.

"They're trying to run me off the road!" Cliff exclaimed. "That's their game, isn't it? I crash my car, die, and He Who Fucks Himself rests well knowing that the crash killed me and not him? Bullshit! You can't kill me that easily!"

The garbage truck continued its pursuit, changing lanes to match Cliff's trajectory. They were tenacious, and Cliff wondered if garbage trucks were meant to go that fast. He'd never seen one going faster than a snail's pace while they did their duty. Then again, he'd never seen one driven by demonic bastards in human costumes before.

What good was Sera's Bible or the words inside supposed to do if Cliff had to push ninety miles an hour on a wet Maine highway to get away from his demonic pursuers? He'd crash for sure if he tried to read the thing!

"Let me try this," Cliff said, licking his lips. "Our Father, who art in heaven… uh… Shit… Thy kingdom… Fuck!"

The whole car shook with the impact of the garbage truck ramming him from behind. He lost control as the wheels hydroplaned on the water.

"How the hell does this count as not killing me?!" Cliff exclaimed. He got out of the left lane and pulled to the shoulder, hoping to get the garbage truck, which was more back heavy than his rented sedan, to slip off the road, causing it to flip over and crash into the mud and trees off the highway. The garbage truck remained steady. Its demonic drivers knocked into Cliff's car again.

"This ain't fuckin' bumper cars, ya bastards!"

It took one last bump to force Cliff off the road, sending his right tires into the mud puddles. The car squealed, and the sound of metal against the ground filled the air. The whole thing spun on its tires three times, finally coming to a stop against a sign proclaiming the speed limit.

"You evil sons of bitches," Cliff groaned. He felt like he'd been through the merry-go-round from Hell, but at least he hadn't crashed hard enough to break his neck or back. His car faced the opposite way, and he found himself staring right into the orangish headlights of the possessed garbage truck. The doors opened, and the two garbagemen stepped out into the rain along with their clouds of flies.

Here's what's going to happen, Cliff thought as he felt his pulse quickening. *They're going to take you again and throw you in the back of the truck. You'll wake up somewhere else in a puddle of garbage water. Maybe they'll drag you back to Easthampton or New Haven if they're feeling evil enough. Either way, you're not making it your show in Maine.*

"The fuck I'm not."

Cliff reached over to the passenger's seat and grabbed Sera's Bible. "I sure hope you demonic motherfuckers like being read to because I got a bedtime story for... Wait... What's this?"

Cliff fumbled with the Bible, and a water pistol tumbled out of it, landing on the seat next to him. He peered inside to see that the pages had been hollowed out in the exact shape to fit the toy like it had to be hidden from the warden of Shawshank State Prison. The water pistol had a yellow water tank on the back, and Sera had put a sticker with a silver crucifix on it.

"Holy shit," Cliff said, holding the water pistol. "Holy water!" He pumped some air into the tank and looked toward the idling garbage truck. He didn't see the two garbagemen who were always with it, but they made their presence known by smashing the window next to his head.

A pair of grimy gloves pulled him out through the car window. Glass scratched at his jacket and poked the skin of his midriff. The garbageman got him out, but their grip faltered. Cliff spilled out of his shirt and jacket and did his best to keep his feet on the highway. The garbage tossed his clothes aside as he got colder and wetter.

Cliff bent and picked up the fallen water pistol. He aimed at the garbageman who had pulled him out of his car and said, "Walk away, get back into your truck, and fuck off forever. I know what you are and why you're here now, and I want no part of it. This is the only warning you'll get."

It sounded badass, and Cliff felt like a modern-day John McClane. Cliff's ultimatum and threat went ignored, and the garbagemen walked toward him, itching to get their hands on him and toss him in the back like rotting trash.

"Alright, fellas. You asked for this."

Cliff squeezed the plastic trigger, and a spray of holy water shot out through the air. He hadn't been sure if it would work how he had wanted with the rain coming down, but it seemed to do the job. The garbageman shrieked and put its hands on its melting face. Cliff smiled. For once, he could dish out the torment.

He aimed the water pistol at the second garbageman and drenched it in holy water. It shrieked as it crumpled to the ground as its body smoldered and smoked. The clouds of flies left the undead bodies for sanctuary in the trees that surrounded the highway.

"How do you like me now, you demonic fucks?"

The garbagemen didn't hear Cliff's quip. They were dead on the road. Well, as dead as something that couldn't be described as 'alive' in the first place could be.

Cliff looked over his handiwork, satisfied with the conclusion of their short standoff. His car had seen better days, and he felt fortunate to have sprung for the extra insurance when he rented it for his tour.

"I guess the tour's all over for now." He observed the damage to the car and two melting corpses on the road. He turned toward the garbage truck. Its engine rumbled, and Cliff felt like it was asking a question in vehicle language.

Cliff laughed. "Sure. What the fuck, right? I don't want to be late for the party."

So he climbed inside the truck ignoring the stench of death. The flies didn't return. Either way, Cliff felt better off without the little pests biting him as he tried to figure out how to get the monstrosity of the garbage truck rolling.

Cliff grabbed a map from the dashboard. "Huh. I'm surprised these fuckers could read, let alone need a map to get around." He saw they were headed in the same direction he planned on going, only they veered off the highway a little before Bangor to head a tad eastward.

"That's not where I planned on going," Cliff said, staring at the big, red circle on the map. "Wonder what these zombie motherfuckers planned on doing once they'd taken me out. Couldn't have been good."

Cliff shrugged, tossed the map on the passenger's seat, and put the truck into drive.

16.

MAINE

Migraines suck. What makes them worse is waking up with one that came on as a result of getting bashed in the side of the head with the butt of a sawed-off shotgun. As bad as that was, there was a step above that, and Heather experienced it as she awoke in the backseat of a broken priest's station wagon chained to the vehicle itself.

Heather touched the side of her head where the pain was at its worst and winced. She'd been bandaged, which meant Father Stephen had broken the skin when he knocked her into the void of her subconscious. Their little road trip couldn't be all sunshine and daisy-picking after all.

"Good morning," Father Stephen said as he drove down the highway, having spotted her stirring in the rearview mirror. "I hope you slept well."

Heather looked out the window as rain lashed against it. The sky had grown full of dark gray clouds, but the morning had already come and gone by Heather's best estimation. She had slept through an entire day.

"You're not supposed to let someone who's concussed sleep," Heather said. "I'll add knocking me out after saving your ass to the list of bullshit you've put me through."

"No less than you deserve, adulteress."

Heather groaned. "Can you let that shit go already? I already explained my open marriage, and you're not even close to being in the right place to judge other people. You're a priest who chains women to pipes and bashes their skulls after saving you."

"You've already brought that up."

"That's because it bears repeating."

Father Stephen nodded while he watched the wet road ahead of his station wagon.

"Can you pull over so I can pee at least," Heather asked, "or would you rather I go on your backseat? Is that the type of shit that gets you off, Father?"

"You have a foul mouth."

"Your whole existence is foul. Also, I haven't mentioned this before since we've been getting along *so* well, but you've smelled like shit the moment you shot your way into my hotel room. Is wiping properly a sin or something?"

Father Stephen whipped the car off the road so fast Heather thought she'd puke. Her chain bit into her side as she tried to brace herself. The station wagon's inertia slammed her into the door, pushing her migraine to its limits. She figured this had to be it. She'd pushed the priest too far, and he'd finally kill her and dump her body off the side of the highway.

All in all, it felt like a fitting end to her tale.

This can't be the end. Not when Dave's still in danger and the middle of all this supernatural bullshit.

Father Stephen pulled off the highway altogether and found a woodsy road leading nowhere but a clearing full of mud puddles and trees. The only logical use for a patch of real estate like this was to dump a body and let nature reclaim it through hungry scavengers and good old-fashioned decomposition.

Heather waited while Father Stephen got out. She got a handful of her chain wrapped around her hand, ready to use it like a brass knuckle. If he thought she'd accept her murder without a fight, then he was about to be proven wrong with a head wound that would make the one he'd given her look like a playground boo-boo.

Father Stephen jerked the door open in a swift motion and stood outside in the rain staring down at her. He didn't have a weapon with him unless one could count the glare in his eyes.

"Well?" he asked.

"Well what?" Heather asked in return.

"I thought you had to pee."

Heather remained a moment, realizing she must have looked silly with the chain wrapped around her hand. Then again, she could still clock him with it, steal his car, and leave him to soak on the ground while she went to the police to tell them everything—assuming they'd believe her.

It was one of the toughest things she'd ever done, but she dropped the chain so Father Stephen could unlock the part chained to his station wagon, allowing her to pee in the woods like an animal.

As much as she hated to admit it to herself, the time hadn't yet come to take out Father Stephen and continue without him. She needed to find out where they were headed first. Without knowing where Dave was or how to help him, she'd have to endure Father Stephen a little longer. All she could do was pee in the woods, thank him for letting her, and continue to plot against him until the opportunity to end her victimhood, save her husband, and return to her daughter presented itself.

"Thanks," Heather muttered without meeting the priest's gaze as she exited the car. The rain soaked her coat and clothes. It would make for an uncomfortable ride afterward, but it wasn't as if she'd had much comfort. She walked as far as the chain allowed her into a small clearing behind a copse of trees that looked like a popular spot for people to pull over and dump their trash out of their cars. Father Stephen held the other end of her chain like a patient dog owner, waiting for her to piddle and return for a head-pat, a '*good girl*', and a cookie.

And she felt like things had gotten better up to the point when Father Stephen asssaulted her on the side of the head with the butt of his shotgun. It's not like she'd warmed up to him and his stoic demeanor or anything, but she had gotten him to open up about his self-imposed mission. Heater had saved the priest's life after they'd been forced to fight together. Twice! It's not like they'd had a breakthrough, but she felt as if they'd made a little progress in their rocky relationship. Maybe the 'demon' inside Father Stephen's head—the one fueling his psychosis—didn't allow him to even come close to making nice.

Heather finished her careful pee behind the tree. She pulled her pants back up, kicking at some of the trash strewn around the place when something caught her eye. A glint of dull light bounced off some silverish item lying on the grass. She bent, remaining as cognizant as possible to not pull too much on the chain that bound her around the waist to alert Father Stephen to her movement. She picked up an eight-inch hunting knife someone had lost or tossed away with the other litter. It had a bit of rust along the blade, but it still looked sharp.

This was probably a murder weapon tossed off the highway. The thought almost made her laugh.

WHO THE FUCK IS ROCKY PHANTASMIC?!

"Hey!" Father Stephen called. "What's taking you so long?!"

It could be a murder weapon again.

Heather stashed the knife in her pants pocket, careful not to cut a hole in her thigh, and walked back to Father Stephen, who waited in the rain with the other end of her chain.

"I hope all went well," he said with a narrowing stare.

"What do you care how my pee went?" Heather asked with a scoff. "Am I getting in the back again, or would you rather I ride in the trunk now that I'm awake?"

"You can ride in the front with me if you'd like. Less conspicuous that way."

"Great. Thanks, Dad."

Heather sat in the passenger's seat in the front while Father Stephen snaked the chain through the station wagon and locked it to the back. He got back into the driver's seat and turned up the heat.

"Hopefully this dries us off while we drive," he said. "We should reach our ultimate destination soon. I can feel it."

I'm going to have to make my move soon then, Heather thought. The feel of the knife in her pocket made itself apparent as she conspired another escape attempt. Aloud, she asked, "Where exactly are we heading now?"

Father Stephen grunted. He pulled back onto the main road, heading northward based on the compass that he'd glued to the center of the dashboard.

"More of the silent treatment, then? What happened to the version of you that told me about the Demonic Testament and had a real conversation with me? You're the one who pulled me into this shit, not the other way around, and you've gone from shitty to halfway pleasant and back to shitty again. Why can't I get a straight answer from you about where we're going?"

"Maine."

"Maine? Maine's a big state. Where in Maine are we going?"

"I don't know. All I know is we're getting close. I'm on your husband's scent now, and it's been getting stronger."

Dave's gone to his uncle's cabin to keep away from all this bullshit. That's the only reason he'd come this way. I can find it on my own. I don't need Father Psychopath to drive me there.

"Things have gotten a bit more…complicated," Father Stephen said, breaking Heather from her thoughts.

"Complicated? How?"

"Something happened while you slept. Something...ominous and off-putting."

Heather sighed. "I'm not surprised. Since you brought it up, would you care to elaborate on what it is that happened?"

Father Stephen nodded. "Alright. So, it started soon after I subdued you."

"You mean when you knocked me out for no good reason."

"Can I tell the story?"

Heather nodded. "Go ahead. I won't correct you when you're wrong."

"OK. As I was saying, I was standing over..."

***

...the adulteress's unconscious form after *subduing* her in the side of the head with the butt of his shotgun. He let out a long breath and put the sawed-off shotgun back in its homemade holster on his back.

It would be easier to leave the adulteress behind. He could chain her to something steadier than an old pipe. She would live and die in the damned church, and the rats and other vermin to feast on her flesh unless something bigger came along. It would be no more than she deserved, the foul sinner.

"No," Father Stephen told the demon in his head. "Stop tainting my thoughts and urging my actions. This woman may be a sinner and deserving of being shunned, but I will not allow her to suffer and die!"

She's going to kill you. Her love for the husband she's scorned with her filthy actions will push her to do it. She'll leave you dead with your mission incomplete. If you allow her to live, then the world will die, and it will be YOUR FAULT.

"Shut up! Don't you think I know that already?!"

You don't need her anymore, You're close. You can find your prey's scent without his woman. Leave her here. Let this church be her prison and tomb. Maybe she'll pray and find the elusive light of the Almighty Father before she dies. There is no other option for her.

"I...can't. She's not innocent, but the punishment of death is not mine to give her. She'll live until it's her time to die. I won't kill her one moment before God determines her life is over."

God doesn't give a shit about this woman. Why would he?

"God loves all his children, especially the ones who have strayed from His path. He loves them most of all."

You're pathetic, and so is the image of God you've created in your mind. The real God has tired of your existence and can't be bothered to turn his head in the slightest to see this woman you're hellbent on rescuing. Leave her to die. It will be a mercy.

"No!"

Father Stephen left the rectory. He needed the adulteress out of his sight while he battled the thoughts in his head that had been put there by the demon that now resided inside him.

What's going to come of the woman after all this, assuming she'll live through any of it? After all she's seen and been through, where will she go? How can she live knowing what's creeping into her world from a much darker dimension? Living and dying by God's rules in this church is a mercy for her. Continuing her tutoring in the Demonic Testament is torture for her mind and soul. Give her God's mercy, and let her die in His house, decrepit as it has become.

"I will not leave her child parentless!"

Father Stephen's voice echoed. The wind howled again outside, but the assault from the sleet and hail had ended at least. He dropped to his knees, alone again. The argumentative voice in his head had stopped. Maybe it relented, knowing he'd continue to refuse to let a woman—a mother—die, or maybe being near the altar of the church had sedated it.

Not that it had worked for Reagan's undead form.

"This church was lovely when it was first built," a feminine voice said from behind Father Stephen. "It's a shame it's fallen into such disarray over the years."

"Good evening, Sera," Father Stephen said without turning around. "I've wondered if I'd see you again before the end. Are you here to help, or are you still standing on the sidelines as usual?"

Sera walked next to Father Stephen with his gaze on the altar that had been desecrated by the cruelty of time. "You know I can't help in any tangible sense, but I'm not *standing on the sidelines* as you put it."

"Why are you here then, angel?"

"I can hear the voice in your head screaming to be released. You've relied on a power that no human should have, and that power is eating away at your soul."

Father Stephen scoffed. "I knew the dangers when I read the Demonic Testament. Humans are on their own in God's grand scheme of things, so I needed to level the playing field. You know the Enemy's power here is growing, and I've almost found its source."

Sera nodded. "Indeed you are, Father. All the roads I've been watching lead to the same place, and the swelling of demonic magic pulses into the atmosphere. The Enemy's rage will not be sated until he's taken this dimension as his plaything."

"That's why David Bryant must die."

"No, Father." Sera shook his head. "More death is not the answer to your problem. David Bryant isn't the only one the Enemy can use to cross into your world."

"He's the one closest to aid in the Enemy's plot!" Father Stephen turned and looked Sera in his perfect, blue eyes. "Even if Bryant's death delays the Enemy, it'll be worth what I've done. Others will pick up my mantle, and they'll finish what's been started. Bryant's death stops the Enemy's plan before it comes to fruition. He'll have to start over, and that will buy us time to shut down the nexuses he's opened in our world before his dark aura leaks through them again. You know I'm right, so I don't see why you'd want to debate."

"I have not come to debate you. I've come to try to dissuade you from this mission your elders have appointed you."

"Right. A righteous angel." Father Stephen let out a short, mirthless laugh. "How much blood have you shed in your heavenly wars? I bet you could fill an ocean with it."

"The only blood I've shed came from demons or their undead spawns that can no longer be considered human. I've never killed any human for any reason."

"Only because your angelic code prevents you from doing it." Father Stephen stepped closer to the angel, locking eyes, knowing Sera could see what lived behind them. "I have no such code, and I'll finish what I've started. I'll do what you cannot and end the Demonic Apocalypse before it has the chance to start."

"You simply chose the easiest path to take, and you have the audacity to claim you're some kind of holy warrior."

"My path doomed my very soul, so don't assume I'm taking the easy way out of this battle. Do not insult my sacrifice because your kind aren't willing to do as I have. I walk the path set before me. If I have to become a martyr to this cause, then so be it. I see my path and where it leads. My elders in the Church see it, and God sees it as well. The only one blinded to what needs to be done is you and your ilk."

Sera stared into Father Stephen's eyes for a few more moments, then turned away and walked toward the exit. He turned back before opening it. "I know of the woman you've bound to your mission as well. You haven't done right by her, and you know it."

"What do you care if you won't interfere in what I'm doing with that adulterous whore?"

"You've stopped seeing the good in people, Father. Maybe it was the Demonic Testament's doing, or maybe it's the sickliness of this world in which you exist. Either way, it'll do you some good to pray for all you've done and all you hope to do. If all you choose to see is the obstacles the Enemy has thrown in front of you, you'll miss what he's been doing to others in this game of his. This isn't going to end well for you or them no matter what the outcome."

"I knew it wouldn't end well before I started. Fuck off back to your cloud, and let me know if you can do anything to help, angel. If you can't, don't stick your pretty little nose into shit you don't understand."

"That's the problem at hand, Father. I understand everything. It is you who lacks understanding." With that, Sera pushed open the door and went out into the windy night.

"Righteous prick," Father Stephen muttered. He turned to get back to his duty at hand. He had an unconscious adulteress who needed to be loaded into the back of his station wagon and a man who still needed to be killed. Morning would come soon, and time was running out.

There was no telling what the Enemy would throw at him next.

***

Father Stephen watched the road as he finished his short tale. Heather found it both ominous and off-putting. She'd slept through it all, and something much worse could've come for them.

"I could've met an angel," she said wistfully.

Father Stephen scoffed. "They're not as grandiose as you've been led to believe, and you can't trust the lot of them. Sera might be the worst of the bunch."

"How can you think that? It sounds to me like he wants you to stop before you make a grave mistake. I've tried having that same conversation with you. There has to be a way to end this without killing Dave or anyone else."

"There isn't! If there were, then I would've found it by now. I've read the Demonic Testament, and I know the magic the Enemy wants to utilize to return to our world. There are men with foul ancestry like your husband written about in blood on those pages, and they're the keys to opening the portal. If the Enemy gets your husband, it's the end of everything. Why can't you understand that?"

"I understand that you believe that. Sera was right. That's the easiest way out of this, and that's why you chose it. I appreciate your sacrifice, I really do, but there has to be another way!"

Father Stephen gritted his teeth and gripped the wheel. "You're missing a piece to the puzzle, woman. Angels aren't able to harm any human, not even the vilest of them, so they're powerless to stop the spread of evil in our world."

"What do you mean?"

"The angels were created by God to be his perfect, subservient warriors. He made them to fight off the forces of evil to give humans a fair shot at happiness. As time went on, God dictated a rule that an angel cannot harm a human for any reason, no matter how much evil resides in their heart. The Enemy has surrounded himself with human pawns, making it impossible for them to fight in his current state.

"I told you once before that a vacuum occurred when the Enemy was banished from our world, and humanity filled that vacuum by taking evil's mantle. That made us an enemy the angels cannot fight, and they've grown bored and restless over the centuries-long stalemate. So, in order to be useful again, they need the Enemy to return along with his demonic minions and undead soldiers. Without them, they will remain purposeless and grow duller as time marches onward."

Heather watched the stoic profile of Father Stephen. "You're saying the angels want you to fail. You think they want the Enemy to return so they have something tangible to fight."

Father Stephen nodded. "Yes, but I don't only *think* that. I *know* it. The angels aren't pure beings. Do not forget that Satan himself is a fallen angel, and the millennia haven't been kind to the rest of them. All they can do is push their subtle agenda to aid us, and it drives the warrior blood in their veins crazy to have to do it."

Heather thought for a moment, and the first half of Father Stephen's story popped back into her mind. She didn't speak it aloud, but she knew the priest listened to what he called the demon in his head rather than the advice of the angel. It had to be what pushed him to believe such wild conspiracies.

Or maybe everything he'd told her about the angels and Sera had some truth to it.

"Your thoughts are becoming impure again," Father Stephen said, pulling off the highway. "We can't have that."

"What are you talking about?" Heather asked, trying not to perspire or give away any of her anxieties over what the impure thoughts could be. "You told me your story, and I'm processing it. There's a lot of information to sort through. This trip of ours hasn't been a vacation for me, you know."

Father Stephen didn't reply. He drove down a woodsy road.

"Where are we anyway?" Heather asked. She realized she hadn't asked or been paying much attention to the signage on the road to figure it out. "Are we in Maine?"

Father Stephen nodded. "We've been here for quite some time. As I've said, we're nearing the end of our journey together."

What's the demon in his mind telling him about me? Is he having another inner debate to figure out whether or not to leave me chained in the woods to be consumed by bears or coyotes?

Heather's hand crept to her leg, where the old hunting knife waited in her pocket. Did Sera or another angel leave it there for her, or was it some grand coincidence that armed her against her captor? Either way, she had her secret weapon, and it may be the only thing she could use to save herself and escape.

Do it now while his eyes are on the road. Don't give him the opportunity to defend himself. Once this station wagon stops, you're helpless chained up like this, even with the knife. Stab him, take his keys, and find Dave.

"I can't read your thoughts," Father Stephen said. "I can *feel* them. I know what you're planning. It's not going to work, and I have no intention of killing you."

"No. You'll leave me chained to a tree and allow nature to kill me. There's no difference. You may not be pulling the trigger, but you're killing me nonetheless. All that demon in your head is doing is helping you bargain with your morals. That's what Sera tried to tell you. The ends don't always justify the means."

"Oh, but they do. We're not talking about adultery being OK because your husband is in on it. This is pure evil. It's as plain and simple as that.

DANIEL AEGAN

You think you understand evil from books and movies and other media you've consumed, but you know nothing of what's waiting in darker dimensions. You'd imagine death to be a sweet release, but it would only be the beginning of your torments. Imagine a life of toil and torture, only to die and be brought back to another dimension to start all over again, this time for eternity. That's what we're up against, and your failure to see that is why I have to leave you to finish my mission."

"You're insane."

"I am not. My mind is clear. It's the world that's gone insane, and I'm the only one willing enough to make the sacrifices needed to save it from both itself *and* the Enemy. That's always been my path, and I'll be damned if…"

Father Stephen took a sharp intake of breath as Heather's knife pierced his side. She had aimed high, hoping to make her stab count. As much as she knew it needed to be done, she didn't want the priest to suffer as he died.

"You bitch!" he exclaimed. He tried to hit her with the back of his hand, but Heather put her arms up to protect her face. The station wagon went off the road and came to a stop against an old wooden fence. The collision jarred him, causing him to gag and cough as his body jostled from the impact.

Heather took the opportunity and grabbed the knife again, wincing at her actions as she punctured the priest's skin through his wet clothes, stabbing over and over, doing as much damage as she could while Father Stephen remained immobile and unable to defend himself. If she didn't finish the job, she'd never find Dave and save him from whatever tormentors had him.

Father Stephen stopped fighting, and his breathing slowed. He gripped the wheel with both hands, staring at the rain as it pelted the windshield. He reached down, shut off the engine, and pulled the keys out, holding them out to Heather.

"I suppose this end is fair," he said in a raspy voice, dropping them into her hands. "The demon got the better of me in the end, and I do not blame you for what you've done. I'm sure the irony of it getting me killed won't escape it as it's sent back to the abyss from whence it came."

"Was there ever a demon, or was that evil in your mind the whole time?" Heather asked. To her surprise, the question made Father Stephen smile as blood poured from his stab wounds and soaked his clothes.

"I have an eternity in Hell to think on that one, adulteress." He turned to look at her with glassy eyes. "If you're taking on this mission in my stead, make sure you finish it. I know you don't want to kill your husband, but you'll come to see it's the only way. When that happens, make sure you end it as you've ended your captivity."

Heather shook her head. "No."

Father Stephen laughed and coughed. A small stream of blood fell from his mouth, soaking into his beard. "Defiant till the end." His voice had grown weaker, almost sounding like a whisper. "It's respectable, even if it's going to end up dooming the entire world to suffer under a demonic reign."

The priest bowed his head, taking one last rasping breath. He uttered, "No matter what you do, do not read the Demonic Testament." With his last words spoken and heard, he closed his eyes and died.

***

Heather worked as quickly as she could. She found the key to her chains and unlocked them. It felt as if a weight had been lifted off her soul as she tossed it behind her. She'd have the bruising and soreness as a reminder for a while, but she wouldn't miss her bonds.

She had to get rid of Father Stephen's body next. Luckily it was night, and the rain kept people indoors. No one had come when the car drove off the road. She pulled him out of the car and dragged him, leaving him in a mud puddle where he'd remain out of sight until someone happened to find him.

"I'm not good at eulogies," Heather said. "Even though you were a total asshole, I still feel a little bad about leaving you like this. For what it's worth, I hope you don't actually spend eternity in Hell. Maybe a century or two for chaining me up and bashing me in the head with your shotgun, but forever is a long time."

Heather searched her soul, but she couldn't come up with anything nicer than that. She jogged back to the station wagon soaked from the cold rain. She opened the back, looking for a map. She knew the town and street of Dave's uncle's cabin, but she didn't know where in Maine she was, and she didn't have a phone with a GPS in it to find it. Her only hope would be to navigate the old-fashioned way.

Father Stephen had filled the station wagon with weapons and all sorts of other goodies he needed for his self-imposed mission. Heather found the sawed-off shotgun he loved so much, a case of ammunition that had the aroma of sulfur, a loaded revolver, some throwing knives, and his big wooden crucifix. She also found a lockbox buried under some blankets.

"What's in here?" Heather asked, finding the right key on the priest's key chain. She popped it open and peered inside. She found something wrapped up in a cloth covered in some language she'd never seen. She reached inside and picked it up. It felt like a thick, hardcover book.

"No matter what you do, do not read the Demonic Testament."

Heather dropped the book into the lockbox. She closed it, locked it back up, and shoved it under the pile of blankets. As much as she disagreed with Father Stephen and how he went about his mission, she figured that last piece of advice would be a good one to take to heart. Even if the demon inside his head had been his own dark thoughts manifesting into violent actions, she refused to take the risk of reading it herself.

Besides, she felt like she'd learned more than enough about it already.

Heather finally found the map and closed up the back, keeping a mental list of all the various items stored there in case she needed them. The weapons would come in handy. Angels might not have been able to kill a man, but she sure as hell could. She'd already left one corpse in the rain. What were a few more in the name of self-defense?

If guilt came later for murdering a man and leaving him in the mud, she'd deal with it. For now, Heather had a mission of her own to finish.

"I'm coming for you, Dave," she said as she started the station wagon and pulled onto the road. "Stay safe a little while longer."

WHO THE FUCK IS ROCKY PHANTASMIC?!

"**Here's our safe house,**" **Dave said** as he pulled his car up the dirt and gravel driveway toward his Uncle Benji's cabin on the outskirts of Ellsworth, Maine. "I can't believe we've arrived after everything. Feels like we've been on the road for months."

Rocky leaned forward in the passenger's seat to look at the small, woodsy home. It had a big front porch with a set of wooden chairs and tables, which had been tied down since Dave's uncle had gone out of state. The whole place had been built from logs, and it looked like something out of a history book.

"Looks cozy," Rocky said. "Are you sure it'll be safe here?"

Dave sighed. He'd been so sure about the safety of this place, but that certainty had been lost the moment the Unmade Men and their supervillain buddy tracked them down and tried to kill them in the woods along with some uninvited monsters.

"It's as safe as anywhere else," Dave replied. "I didn't see any of the bodies after your cousin and your friends attacked us, so we have to err on the side of caution when it comes to assuming they died."

Rocky nodded. "We can make a stand here if need be. They won't catch us off guard this time, and we know their villain's capabilities. If I have to fight him again, I'll know what I'm getting into." He pounded his right fist into his other palm to accentuate his point.

Dave watched Rocky's serious face for a moment after he put the car into park. The young superhero had been through a lot in the last few days, and it had to be wearing on him. Sure, his body could take the abuse inflicted upon it, but his mind was a different story altogether. Punching monsters and stepping in front of bullets was one thing, but the shit they'd gone through had to have taken its toll on the young superhero's mind.

Rocky won't quit and go home, Dave thought. *He'll keep fighting till it's over, no matter which side wins. He's strong and steadfast, but every man—even superheroes—has their weaknesses and breaking points.*

"OK," Dave said, breaking the silence between them. "Let's get inside, get warmed up, and get a meal cooked up. Once we do that, we can figure out how we're going to defend ourselves from whatever else gets thrown at us."

Rocky nodded in agreement. "That's as good a plan as any I can come up with."

Dave smiled, got out of the car, and grabbed as much of their provisions as he could. He jogged through the cold rain to the porch to keep from getting soaked through his clothes. Rocky did the same and joined him as the sound of the raindrops clicked above the wooden eave over their heads.

The front door of the cabin had an electronic lock. "Good thing I remember the code," Dave said, punching in the six digits that unlocked it. They were inside a moment later, and he punched another code into the security panel on the wall near the door. "I remember this one, too. You can't use the cabin unless you know both codes. Part of my uncle's double security protocol."

"OK," Rocky said as he entered the cabin behind Dave.

"My Uncle Benji is my mom's brother," Dave explained, kicking off his wet and muddy boots on the rug by the front door. "He looked out for me a bunch growing up. He knew my mother was mentally ill, and he was there a lot more often after my father died. He never had a wife or kids of his own, which is probably why he could afford to have a cabin up here in the first place."

The cabin had a rustic decorum. Even the wooden beams on the ceiling were finished logs, and pictures that showed forest settings were all over the place. Lanterns hung from some of the walls, but they weren't functional.

"This place is nice," Rocky remarked. "I've only ever seen houses like this on TV or in movies."

"Yeah, Uncle Benji had me up here quite a bit. He made a ton of dough investing in the eighties and nineties. He tried to explain how to play the system to make your money make money without putting in much work, but I could never understand it."

"OK."

"Sorry. I went off on a tangent. Figured you might want some background content about my uncle and his place up here."

Rocky nodded as he absorbed his new surroundings. The cabin was a far cry from his basement apartment back in New Haven. He was still 'dead', so he'd be squatting or homeless before long unless he could find a job defending someone that paid well enough under the table and gave him a place to stay off the books.

"I'm going to try to call Heather again," Dave said, walking to the corded landline phone at the end of the kitchen counter. He still had no idea what she might've been thinking since his disappearance, but he knew he missed her and Kayla, and they deserved to know he was safe.

Dave picked up the phone and put it to his ear, but no dial tone came to it. He checked the wire and found it plugged into the wall jack. He knew Uncle Benji kept the landline since cell service sucked and he never trusted any of the cellphone companies, so he wouldn't have canceled the service.

"Shit," Dave muttered, putting the phone back on its base. "The storm must have knocked the phone lines down. We can't call anyone till they're back up."

"How long does that take?" Rocky asked.

Dave shrugged. "It's hard to tell out here. I do know that when the power goes out, it goes out for a long-ass time, so your guess about the phones is as good as mine. Could be days or weeks depending on the damage, and I don't know how long this storm is supposed to last."

Rocky fiddled with the lamp on an end table, clicking the button under the shade a few times. "Power is out, too."

"At least our luck is consistent. I'll see if I can find some candles before it gets too dark to find anything."

"Good. I'll get the rest of the stuff out of the car. I think the jugs of water are still in the back."

Dave went through the utility closet near the stairs and he found two cases of emergency candles. Uncle Benjy always liked being prepared, and he knew life out in the woods came with pitfalls like power outages and cold nights. He kept long wooden matches in there as well and Dave knew there'd be plenty of firewood stacked by the back door under the eave to keep it dry for the fireplace and wood-burning stove.

When Rocky returned with the jugs of water, Dave had some candles on the main table in the den. He went to work bringing in some wood for the fire and stacked it in the fireplace and the stove. He didn't plan on cooking anything more complicated than canned soup, but he could do that on the wood stove with no problem.

"What do we do now?" Rocky asked.

"I don't know," Dave replied. "We can get cozy for the time being and wait to see if the phones and power come back on since I don't know when they went out. Otherwise, we should stay vigilant in case your cousins find us again."

Rocky nodded. "Then you should probably move the car so they can't see it. Can you move it behind the house?"

Dave looked out the window. His red sedan would stick out, even though they were a few hundred feet from the road. "Sure. I can find a spot for it where it's not so visible. Get comfortable. I'll be back in a few minutes."

***

Dave returned once he parked his in the old barn his uncle used as a makeshift garage. It was filled with old tools and a snowblower that didn't work. It wasn't as if Uncle Benji needed it. He had groundskeepers who came to take care of the property.

By the time Dave got back inside, the rain had turned to snow, making the ground slushy and muddy. By morning, there would be a layer of snow on top of the ice, and the roads would be a nightmare to navigate. It looked as if they'd be held up in the cabin for at least a couple of days unless they were forced to leave.

Dave didn't want to think about what would force them to leave since he felt comfortable for the first time since being attacked on the streets of New Haven.

As the evening grew darker, Dave lit a couple of candles. He threw sheets on the beds upstairs, changed into some dry clothes, and came back down to cook some soup for dinner. Once they'd finished with their short meal and their bowls and spoons were washed and on the drying rack, they sat on the couch watching the fire crackle and hiss.

"We should get some rest," Rocky suggested. "I can keep an eye on things if you want to sleep."

"Are you not going to sleep then?" Dave asked. "You got beat up worse than me. If anything, you need some serious rest. You haven't even tended to your injuries."

"I'm sore is all. I'm not bleeding, so I guess I'm good. I haven't been beaten up like that since I got my superpowers, so I don't know if I have super healing. I feel like the soreness is going away."

"I can at least find you some aspirin or something. It might help with the pain."

Dave got up and raided the bathroom cabinet. His uncle kept some things in there out of habit, and he found a bottle of generic aspirin that didn't expire for another couple of months. He took two pills and brought them to Rocky with a glass of water.

"Found some," he said, handing over the water and the pills.

"Thanks." Rocky downed them along with the glass of water in one shot, handing the glass back to Dave after he'd finished.

"I think you should rest while you've got the chance." Dave returned to the couch after leaving the glass by the sink. "If something happens, you're going to need to be healed in case you have to fight your way through it. All good superheroes need to recuperate."

Rocky laughed. "OK. For now, anyway. The moment something goes down, I'll be back up and ready to fight."

"I can agree to that. I can't punch monsters and toss mobsters through the air myself, but I hope we don't get visited by either for a long while."

"Me too."

Dave continued to watch the fire alongside Rocky. They had some cards, and Uncle Benji had a pile of books in the cabin, but he felt content sitting in silence. Things had finally calmed. He needed an interlude in the insanity that had surrounded him for the last few days.

"What do you write?" Rocky asked, breaking the silence.

"What?" Dave asked in return. He had felt a thousand miles away for a moment, and he almost forgot he wasn't alone.

"You said you're a writer when we first met, and I was wondering what you wrote. Like books, right?"

Dave laughed. "Yeah, books. I try to, anyway. It's more of a part-time gig than anything else. There are a lot of obstacles I won't bore you with."

"OK."

"Sorry." Dave laughed again. "I didn't answer your question. I write long-form stories and novels. Lately I've been doing some more episodic shit, and I feel it would make for a great series. Do you know the comedian Cliff Quentin?"

"No."

"Well, I was going to meet him at a comedy club the night you saved me from your cousins. He and I were going to pitch this idea for a series based on some eighties and nineties bad horror and slasher movies, but we'd do it with a comedic twist. He's a writer too, but he mostly punched up comedy movies and sitcom scripts. Our show would be an homage to shows like Tales from the Crypt and Twilight Zone with a focus on cosmic horror, highlighting the audacity of it all. Actually, a lot of the stuff you and I went through since leaving New Haven feels like the kind of stuff we'd planned on parodying. Feels like the mother of all cosmic coincidences."

Dave thought for a moment about what they'd been through. Ghost psychiatrists, flesh-eating creatures, nightmare-inducing wraiths under a Star-Mart, and giant man-eating worms were all in the genre of chintzy horror movie bullshit he wanted to do for his show. When compounded with Rocky's story of reincarnation and his gaining superpowers to defend against all of it, it added up to something both spectacular and daunting at the same time.

"Shit."

"What?" Rocky asked, turning toward him.

Dave laughed. "It sounds stupid, but everything happening feels like it's something I would have written for this show I never got around to writing with Cliff. Even the stuff that happened to you would have been good fodder for it. Maybe I… No."

"What?" Rocky repeated.

Dave shook his head. "What if all this shit came out of my head? What if this is all from me somehow? Think about it. All this stuff's happening around me, and I can't imagine why. Dr. Nielsen said it had something to do with my ancestors, but what if that's causing all this shit to come from my mind and attack me and everyone around me?"

"That would be crazy."

"Crazier than someone getting tossed into the harbor and coming out a superhero?"

Rocky thought for a moment and nodded. "I see your point."

"That has to be it, right? I'm the creator of my torment. No matter what I do and how far I run from it, it'll chase me because it *is* me. It's been that way all along."

Dave felt Rocky's hand land on top of his, and he realized he was in the starting phase of an oncoming panic attack. He took a breath and let it out, getting his shaky body under control.

"Sorry."

"Don't be," Rocky said in a soft voice. "It's a lot, trust me. When I came out of the water and realized what had happened to me, I went through something similar. Who knows? Maybe you have a superpower where you can manifest these things. If you work at it, maybe you can direct it and be a superhero like me."

"Alright, Professor X. That's all well and good, but I don't know if the world works like that."

Rocky shrugged. "The world can work how we tell it to work sometimes. I wouldn't be here if that weren't true, and I'll be here to protect you if you summon more monsters or if someone else summons them. I'm still not going anywhere."

Dave looked into Rocky's bright eyes, leaned forward, and kissed him. It was an uncalculated action, and he was a bit surprised the young superhero let him do it. They stayed that way for a little while until Rocky backed away.

"Wait a second. What about your wife?"

"Don't worry about that. It's an open marriage, and she knows."

"Oh, OK."

They kissed again, this time quicker, and with some added passion. Dave's hands moved over Rocky's body, exploring his indestructible skin. His shirt was in the way, so Dave removed it, kissing Rocky's bare chest and neck, enjoying the aroma of his body.

If Rocky had ever done this with another man, he didn't say. He didn't protest the attention either. As a rule, Dave didn't date anyone under the age of thirty, but he liked the feel of the young, muscular body against his. The feeling seemed to be mutual.

"I've never done this before," Rocky whispered, breaking the kiss. "This isn't allowed in my family or their associates."

Dave backed away and bit and paused. He suddenly felt like a creep for initiating in the first place due to the fifteen-year age difference between them. Rocky might've also had some mental issues that hadn't been revealed or explored, and Dave realized he should have made sure of a thing or two before he kissed him.

"Are you sure you want to do this?" Dave asked. "If you don't, it's OK. I know this wasn't part of the deal when you agreed to become my protector."

Rocky nodded. "It's OK. I want to do this if you still do."

"As long as you're not doing this just because you think it's what I want. Well, I do, but… Shit. I just needed to be sure, I guess."

Rocky nodded and kissed Dave again, pushing him onto his back. The two of them stayed like that aside from a brief pause for Dave's shirt to come off. The fire blazed in front of them, adding to the heat between their bodies.

Dave felt Rocky's hardness against his own, and he moaned at the prospects of what was to come between them. He'd been thinking of it since Dr. Nielsen put the idea into his head, but he thought it would be too farfetched for them to hook up. Then again, Whitney Houston hooked up with her bodyguard in the movie with Kevin Costner, though he'd never seen it to know if it happened quite the same way.

A giggle escaped his lips as Rocky's mouth met his again, and Dave savored the moment, moving his legs so Rocky could get between them better. He reached down and caressed Rocky's stiff manhood, teasing it with his fingers, eliciting a moan from his young lover. Their kiss broke again, and Dave opened his eyes and looked toward the ceiling.

All the sudden prospects of making love by the fire died a quick and gruesome death.

A slug crawled on the ceiling. If it were a normal slug, Dave would have ignored it and gone about his business, hoping it wouldn't fall on his or Rocky's bare skin. This, however, was no ordinary slug. It had a bulbous backside of translucent pale skin and a face with dozens of eyes. Dave had never seen a bug so big, so he had no idea if garden-variety slugs had mouths with two sets of red and black pincers that opened and closed with the prospect of biting its victims as the one on the ceiling did.

"WHAT THE FUCK?!" Dave snapped, struggling to get off the couch.

Rocky moved back, a look of total embarrassment on his face. "What did I do?" he asked.

Dave shook his head and gasped. "It's not you, it's that!" He pointed upward, and Rocky's gaze followed, spotting the slimy interloper that had been watching them.

WHO THE FUCK IS ROCKY PHANTASMIC?!

Rocky launched off the floor. Once he was face-to-face with the slug, he threw a jab into its ugly face. The slug didn't acknowledge the blow. Its face jiggled like a living gelatin mold. It lashed out with black tendrils coming from its mouth, wrapping around Rocky's entire body, suspending him in the air.

Rocky's arms were pinned to his side, and the tendrils wrapped his mouth. His eyes widened, and he looked toward Dave as he fought to free himself.

"I need salt!" Dave tripped as he ran to the kitchen. He got back to his feet and dug through the cabinets, finding a container of salt. He opened the top and flung it upward on the back of the monstrous slug. It stuck to its back, but nothing else happened.

"Shit," Dave muttered. "I'm out of ideas."

Rocky fought against the tendrils, his muscles straining against them. They snapped, one by one, until he dropped to the floor, gasping for air. The slug opened its mouth, letting out a shriek that rattled the windows.

"Can you control them with your mind?" Rocky asked, looking toward Dave.

Dave shook his head. "That was just a theory. I don't think it's going to work!"

"I'll do my best to fight it. You try to send them back where they came from."

Dave wanted to argue more that he didn't know how to do that, but Rocky had already launched himself into the air, aiming a spinning kick at the slug's backend. His foot got stuck in its goo, and he hung upside-down while swinging in a vain attempt to get it loose.

This is bad, Dave thought. *What the hell am I supposed to do?*

Dave's flight-or-fight reflex hit him again, but there was no fighting to be had here. All his senses berated him for not running out of the door and driving until he hit the Canadian border. But what would that do in the long run? The monsters and Rocky's cousins would keep coming till they captured or killed him. Nowhere was safe.

"Grab my hands!" Dave exclaimed, reaching upward. Rocky grasped them, and Dave pulled, feeling his back screaming in protest. His feet left the ground for a moment, but it worked. Rocky's foot came free from the back of the slug with a pop, and they both fell to the floor with a crash.

"That thing has my sock!" Rocky looked up, watching it dangle from the slug's slimy back.

"We need to get out of here," Dave said. "I don't know how we're supposed to fight that thing."

"I can beat it. It's not like those ghost things in the caverns. It has a body, which means I can punch the hell out of it!"

"You can't! It's a blob of goo!"

"Even goo has feelings."

Dave wanted to ask what the hell that last statement meant, but Rocky went on the attack, flinging himself toward the ceiling again. He threw a flurry of punches at the slug's face, but it only jiggled and rippled. Once gravity won out, the slug opened its mouth, sending out a stream of flying insects right into Rocky's face.

Rocky punched and swatted at the bugs, splattering them a dozen at a time. Tiny globs of guts hit the couch and the walls as he fought them like a man having a standing seizure, but the whole thing had been a distraction. The back of the slug opened next, and another horrid insectile creature with the same pale, translucent pigmentation came out of it. This one had six legs and a stinger like a scorpion.

"Oh shit," Dave said, backing away as it looked toward him. "This one's after me!"

The bug crawled across the ceiling as Dave backed away. Rocky tried ignoring the swarm of bugs around him, but the slug had other plans. It dropped from the ceiling, opening its body as it fell, encompassing the young superhero in its bulbous body. Dave could see him floating in the back, fighting to get free like his body had been turned down to slow motion. As strong as Rocky was, he couldn't hold his breath and live inside slime forever.

"Rocky, no!" Dave exclaimed.

That, too, acted as a distraction, and Dave felt a puncture on the side of his neck. The newer bug's stinger had moved like a flash, and it had gotten him with a precise strike. Dave's hand went to his neck, and he felt it already swelling from the venom.

"Well, that's not fair at all," Dave said as his world went staticky. He wavered on his feet and fell backward into another time and place altogether.

***

WHO THE FUCK IS ROCKY PHANTASMIC?!

Dawn arrived with a red sun against an orange sky, lightening to a pinkish hue and finally a deep blue above. It rose over fields of dirt, rock, and grass that had been covered in blood and bodies. A murder of crows had come early to break their fast on what had been left for them. The other scavengers would come later but now was their time.

"What the fuck is this?" Dave asked, looking at the morbidity around him. He wanted to tell himself the setting wasn't real. He wanted to believe the insect's venom made him see this place as he had when the wraiths dumped him into visions of his past, but this felt different. It somehow felt more real. No amount of shouting or forcing himself back into reality would get him back where he needed to be.

This is the distant past, a voice inside Dave's head explained. *This is a time the writers of history refused to chronicle.*

"But where is this? *When* is this?"

If the voice had an answer, it refused to give it. It felt like Ireland or somewhere in that area of Europe, but Dave assumed that with no rhyme or reason. He walked with the field of bodies to his back in search of some village or signage that could clue him in on his current situation. The corpses had to come from somewhere, after all. Then again, so did their assailants.

Does this feel familiar to you? You never lived in his era, David, but your blood resides here. Perhaps it has a longing to relive its early days, back when it pumped through the body of a warlord.

A human figure emerged atop a crag with their back to the sunrise. A broad, stout man with a thick torso and reddish-brown beard that covered his face greeted the start of a new day. He wore animal pelts as clothing and held a wooden club in his right hand that had been adorned with sharpened bones to make the thicker end look like an early human's saw.

Yes, that's a tool you see, the voice confirmed, *but it is not one used for carpentry. No, he used this solely for killing. The men behind him are waiting for him to draw the first blood of the morning. Those in the village ahead of him are awaiting death, though they do not yet know it.*

Dave moved like he was in a dream. The voice had been right, of course. There were hundreds of men staying behind, all of them clothed in animal furs to ward off the bite of the early morning chill. Most of them held clubs or spears with pointed stones or bone, and others held chunks of wood for shields. None smiled. They all watched their leader, waiting for him to make his move.

DANIEL AEGAN

The village ahead was silent. Some people moved about carrying jugs of water or starting fires. They were either ignorant of the corpses so close by or uncaring of the battle that had caused so much death. Maybe it had been too far away for them to know what had happened at all, or perhaps they went about their lives knowing their end was coming, praying that it wouldn't.

Dave had no idea how far he'd walked since seeing the field of death and the feasting crows. Had it been minutes or hours? Were time and distance the same for him here, or was history being presented to him as a montage of events? The voice didn't seem to want to divulge that information.

The warrior held his club to the sky and let out a battle cry that echoed through the morning air. His soldiers did the same, adding their bloodthirsty screams to his.

The warlord led his troops to the village. The men emerged from their huts and homes to defend themselves, but they were outnumbered and outclassed by the barbaric army smashing into them. Their leader—Dave's supposed ancestor—cleaved and slashed at anyone who came at him with his club. He smashed a man's skull open with a two-handed chop, stepping over the corpse to saw at another's throat. Blood sprayed over him in a crimson cloud.

The warlord's club was covered in strips of flesh and gore, and his face turned into a mask of red. He looked over the village with wild eyes as his men finished the villagers. With his work done, he rejoined with his band of barbarian soldiers. They found the hiding women and children and ended their lives in the same brutal fashion as those who had already died defending them.

"What the fuck am I witnessing?" Dave asked the answerless sky. "Are these caveman wars or something?!"

The slaughtering warriors didn't bury the dead or burn them. They let them lie where they died, littering their village with corpses. The crows and other scavengers would have another feast in the afternoon that would surely last until nightfall. Bones and ghosts would be all that remained in this now-cursed place.

Before the scavengers could come, the warlord and his men set fire to the homes. Black smoke rose into the sky, merging with the rain clouds that blew over the village from the sea. The men celebrated. They cooked the dead over a fire and consumed their victims' flesh, laughing themselves into a frenzy over their defeated foes.

WHO THE FUCK IS ROCKY PHANTASMIC?!

As it turned out, they hadn't killed everyone. They had kept some of the women tied to posts, and they were raped and tortured as part of their celebrations. Their leader watched the aftermath from his place by the great bonfire, a satisfied smile on his face. They laughed and raped and consumed human flesh late into the night and left the smoldering homes and rotting corpses behind them as a new dawn rose.

You know this man, the leader of the war party, though you've never met him through the centuries that have passed since he walked this realm, killing and maiming as he saw fit to do. His blood is your blood, passed down from father to son throughout human history. You may feel a kinship toward his soldiers as well. Most of them are his brothers, half-brothers, nephews, and cousins. They all share blood with their leader, and your blood remembers its kinfolk well.

There were other villages and other people to kill and consume on the unnamed warlord's genocidal conquest. They left bloodied footprints wherever they traveled, never stopping until their blood soaked into the earth. By then, however, the sons had been sired, and the warlord's bloodline endured throughout told and untold history.

Dave knew this because the memory within the blood in his veins knew this. It had been diluted over the centuries, yet it retained the visions and splendor of death and destruction entrenched at its core.

Yes. Now you see what you've always been meant to see. Man evolved, and your line along with it. No longer does the want to kill and conquer rest in your mind, but the sins of your ancestors' history lie in wait deep within your heart and soul. It fuels you, adding its dark color to the stories you tell, but it wants to serve and shed blood for its true master instead of being fodder for your ridiculous tales.

Oh, David. You knew all along of whom I speak. His presence was felt then to all as you feel it now. He Who Walks Above's spirit has not been sated in its exile, and he comes now for you.

The ground shook, and Dave thought he stood on the fault line of an earthquake. Maybe he stood where Pangea separated. He had no way to tell how long before Christ this all happened, but his ancestors—if the memory in his blood spoke the truth—seemed as if they hadn't yet evolved much from Neanderthals.

Another quake occurred, and Dave saw what had caused it. He hoped for a dinosaur, but he spotted a leg instead, coming down from the clouds above. A humungous foot of pale, yellowish skin crashed into the ground. The whole of the being that stepped overhead could not be seen through the dark rainclouds. All that showed from the ground was its monstrous legs and an enormous penis parting the clouds.

"Look at that," Dave said, unable to look away as the towering demon passed over him. "He Who Walks Above isn't circumcised. I don't know why I'd think he would be."

The footsteps thundered, and the landscape changed along with it. Dave didn't know where He Who Walks Above needed to be or why he needed to be there, but he felt fortunate enough not to know. The last thing he wanted was to be privy to that information and witness what fueled an ancient demon's quest for himself.

Oh, but you'll be meeting him soon enough, David. Do not doubt He Who Walks Above, for he shall return to your dimension. When he does, you're the first person he wants to see.

Laughter followed, cold and dark, emanating from Dave's soul, spreading throughout his being in this millennium and all that came before it. It felt as if a portal to another dimension opened within his chest, and it only led to a vast, empty purgatory with nothing but a biting, frigid wind.

It took Dave a full minute to realize he felt that coldness because he'd walked out of the warm cabin and into the hellishness of the Maine snowstorm.

***

The world came into focus, and Dave had a private celebration in his mind that he'd returned to his own time without being bludgeoned to death by one of his ancestors or any of their genocidal, cannibalistic kinfolk. The bug's venom that had sent his consciousness and astral body back in time had worn off, and a wave of gratefulness washed over him.

Was that all it was, though? Dave thought, pleased to find that his thoughts were his own again and not some nagging memory stored deep within his blood. *How can I be sure it wasn't all a hallucination? For all I know, I'd been tripping balls on mutant bug venom for hours or days.*

"No," Dave said, replying to his thoughts. "That was different."

He knew it was true. Dave had done drugs, including a short stint where he'd dabbled with hallucinogens, and nothing had felt like what he'd been through after the bug bite to his neck. Then again, he didn't even know how to classify the thing that came out of the slug's asshole to sting him in the first place.

That thought process brought him fully back, and he realized he'd been standing in the snow a hundred or so feet in front of the cabin while thinking through the nightmare of his ancestry and the swinging cock of the demon walking over him. Everything in his mind pointed to something he'd forgotten and shouldn't have.

"Rocky!" Dave shouted, finally getting his feet moving back toward the cabin. He didn't know how he planned on getting his superhero bodyguard out of the slug's amoebalike body. Maybe he could jam a broomstick through its gelatinous girth and pull Rocky to safety assuming he hadn't been gone more than a few minutes. If his hallucinatory trip through time had lasted longer than that, poor Rocky might have drowned in mutant slug slime. Still, Dave had to try.

Dave's movement stopped, and he couldn't tell why. Not at first, anyway. He thought it had been another effect of the venom in his body, but he felt the vice-like grip on the back of his neck. He turned to fight against whoever had done it, but his captor grabbed his arm next, bringing it to the small of his back in a quick motion. The hand gripped him so hard he felt like his bones were going to snap at any moment.

"Don't hurt him too bad!" an unfortunately familiar voice shouted. "Boss wants him alive, remember?"

The voice belonged to Rocky's cousin, one-half of the Unmade Men. Dave's memory was still a bit hazy, but he was sure his name was Leo. His quieter partner, the muscles in contrast to Leo's mouth, was Johnny.

"Bring him to the car, Duro," Leo ordered. "Throw him in the trunk and tie his hands behind his back." He walked over and looked Dave in the face. "I knew I'd get you, you little prick. You counted us out after you ditched us with those friggin' underground monsters, but it takes a lot more than that to get rid of us."

"Yeah," Dave replied with a defiant smirk, "you and your friends are like the herpes."

Leo's fist connected with Dave's stomach. If he could've doubled over from the blow, he would have. Duro hadn't let him go, and struggling against the supervillain would prove to be an act of uselessness.

"What the hell are doing?!" Leo snapped. Dave gave a puzzling look through his pain, but he realized he hadn't spoken to him. He addressed the man holding him.

"Forget that friggin' kid!" Leo continued. "We got the writer, and that's what we've driven all this way for. Tell him, Johnny."

"The boss wants the writer," Johnny confirmed.

"Once the writer's with the boss," Leo added, "you can come back and kill that bratty superhero if you want."

"No!" Dave shouted, struggling to no avail. "I need to help him! He's in trouble!"

"Scratch that," Leo said with a chuckle. "We'll take this mook to Vincenzo, and then we'll come back to make sure the annoying brat's dead and piss on his corpse for good measure."

"Come on, Duro," Johnny urged. "Leo's right."

"Let's get the hell outta here either way." Leo hugged his body. "It's cold as a witch's tit out here, and I hate driving in the snow. Friggin' Maine can suck my left nut. The sooner this job is over, the better. Know what I'm sayin'?"

"I hear ya, Leo." Johnny walked to the car and opened the trunk, stepping back to allow Duro to drop Dave inside like a sack of groceries before one of the Unmade Men tied his wrists together behind his back.

Dave prayed with everything he had that Rocky had somehow gotten free of the slug and would come flying through the snow for a rematch against his nemesis, one he'd win, allowing them to live and fight another day.

That didn't happen though, and the severity of what that meant hit Dave full-on as the trunk slammed shut, leaving him in pitch blackness.

18. SAVE DAVE, SAVE THE DIMENSION

The tires of Father Stephen's station wagon crunched through snow and the ice underneath it, and Heather did her best to navigate through the veritable winter wonderland the storm had left in its wake. It was slow going everywhere around her, and municipalities that should've been more active in getting the roads plowed didn't care for Heather's urgency to save her husband from the hellscape that had formed around him like a vivid and contagious rash on the surface of reality.

All Heather could do was hope that Dave had gone to his uncle's cabin. Time had set itself against her, and her silent prayers focused on that clichéd race against the clock. If she couldn't get there in time, what kind of fate awaited him? She thought about the trials she'd faced, wondering how many tortures Dave was being forced to endure.

Shit, Heather thought. *I don't even know what day it is. Is it Wednesday or Thursday morning? How long has Dave been missing?*

It took Heather a minute to remember, but she'd been missing the same amount of time. She knew she should call her parents and let them know she was still alive and would see Kayla soon, but she'd have to stop to find a phone. It wouldn't be a quick conversation either, and the race against time wouldn't allow her a time-out. Maybe her parents also remembered Dave's uncle's cabin in Maine, and maybe they'd tell the police about it now that they'd both been off the radar for at least three days.

DANIEL AEGAN

I wonder if that forty-eight-hour thing is true. Will the police not look for us until we've been officially missing that long, or is that all bullshit for movies and TV shows?

She wondered if she'd have to tell the police about Father Stephen in her imagined scenario. Maybe she'd get away with killing him since it had been in self-defense—kind of. She pushed the thought out of her mind. Worrying about minor details like the priest's corpse she'd left barely hidden didn't feel prudent at the moment.

This whole thing is going to make a hell of a true crime documentary or podcast.

The station wagon acted as a mechanical beast despite Heather's misgivings of its outward appearance and age. It cut through the snow except for the places where it had piled over a couple of feet deep. If she kept to the main roads, she'd make it with little problems, but she'd have to take the backroads a while before she could make it to the cabin. She had to risk it. She'd come too far and through too much to let a blizzard stop her from finding Dave, solving his demon issues, and getting him back home with their daughter where he belonged.

Luck decided to be on Heather's side for once, and she made it up the long hill that led to Dave's uncle's cabin. It was plowed, even if it hadn't been done well. Up here, the residents sometimes had to take care of the backroads themselves to get around after a bad snowstorm or an old-fashioned nor'easter. When you lived in the Northeast, you had to be prepared.

The cabin's driveway, however, had not been plowed, and the station wagon only got twenty or thirty feet before the tires spun out, leaving Heather to trudge the rest of the way on foot. She left long trenches in the snow as she pushed her way upward, trying not to lose her footing and take a header into large mounds of frozen whiteness.

"I'm coming, Dave," she huffed, her words coming among the clouds of steam. "Wait one more minute for me, babe."

She couldn't see Dave's car, but that wasn't too disconcerting. She knew he had abandoned it back in New Haven when all the madness had started. If he'd gotten up here, he would have found another ride. That wasn't shocking either. As lazy as Dave could be, he'd proven himself resourceful several hundred times over when he needed it.

The thing that bothered Heather more than anything else was that the front door had been left open.

"Please be here," Heather whispered as she climbed the steps to the front porch, ignoring the numbness in her feet and calves from her short trek through the snow. She wasn't dressed for a post-blizzard hike. "Please be alive and well. We'll start a fire, warm up, and plan what to do next. Just please be here and OK."

She knew the door should've been locked good and tight. Dave's Uncle Benji had a keypad, so no one but him, Dave, or Benji's part-time caretakers should've been able to get inside unless they smashed their way through it. From the looks of the lock, whoever or whatever opened it didn't have to use force to gain entry, meaning someone had entered the code to unlock it. And since there wasn't a police presence around the house, someone had disabled the internal alarm system as well.

The weather hadn't been good to the inside of the cabin. Snow piled near the door, but it had melted as it swept inward. Dave's uncle would be sure to blow a gasket when he found out someone had been careless enough to leave the door open during a snowstorm.

On the mat by the door, stood Dave's black boots, and Heather's heart leapt in her chest. He had come here after all. Dave didn't come alone, either. A pair of sneakers sat next to them. A wave of relief emanated from Heather's core. Dave didn't have to go through whatever hell he went through on his own.

"Dave?!" Heather called, closing the door behind her. Maybe he'd slept through the storm that blew into the house in the middle of the night. He'd always been a heavy sleeper.

No answer came. She shouted his name again, and listened for some kind of movement in the house. The relief she felt that she'd found him died, and she pieced together what had happened.

Dave had come to the cabin as she assumed he would, but his stay turned out to be temporary. Someone or something came in the night during the storm and took him, dragging him through the snow and icy winds. He was lost again to her.

"No," she said, unable to help the tears from spilling from her eyes. "I'm too late. He's gone."

Then, a low groan came from the other side of the couch, and Heather's heart came back to life. She rushed over, hoping to see her husband sleeping on the floor, weird as it would be, but that wasn't the case. She found a younger man covered in what looked like drying soap and powder. Pieces of what could have been a weird animal or a huge bug lay around him in a circle, and the floor was covered in the same dried-up concoction that covered the young man's skin and clothes.

At least Heather now knew who owned the second pair of shoes by the door.

"Hey," Heather said, afraid to get any closer in case he hadn't been a friend to Dave after all. "Are you awake?"

"I can't fight it." The young man thrashed weakly. "Not from inside its slime sack."

Heather cringed at the phrase '*slime sack*', but the whole situation drove home the fact that Dave had been through his own personal hell after all, and the encrusted young man on the floor had been through it with him.

For a second I thought it might've been that comedian Dave was supposed to meet; Cliff or Clint or whatever his name is.

"You're not in the slime sack anymore," Heather said, kneeling on the floor next to him despite not knowing his identity or purpose for being there while Dave was still missing. "Open your eyes if you can."

The young man's eyes opened, and he recoiled at the sight of the woman kneeling next to him. He slipped on some of the unhardened slime on the floor and steadied himself against the back of the couch.

"Who are you?!" the young man asked, his eyes opened wide as if he'd just received an electric shock.

"I was going to ask you the same thing," Heather replied. "If it helps, I'll go first. My name is Heather Bryant, and I'm looking for my husband."

"Heather? You're Dave's wife?"

Heather nodded. "I am. Is he here?"

The young man got to his feet. His body shook a bit with the effort, but that may have been from the cold as well as his nerves. The fire had died sometime in the night, leaving nothing but black and gray ash.

"Dave was here with me before…before…"

"Don't say anymore right now if it's too much. I believe you. For what it's worth, I've been through some crazy and unbelievable shit the last couple of days. That's why I need to find Dave. I know this all revolves around him, and I need to make sure he's safe."

The young man nodded. "Me too. That's why I came up here with him."

Heather smiled. "OK. I'm glad he had a friend, but I still don't know who you are."

"I'm Rocky Phantasmic."

"Sure. That's a name, I guess. Why did you come all the way up here with Dave?"

"It's a long story."

"Shorten it for me. We don't have time to go through the whole thing right now, and any clue is as good as any if it helps us find Dave."

"OK. I died and came back to life as a superhero. A couple of cousins of mine tried to abduct your husband, and I saved him. Only we found out they're working for the forces of evil. Like, for real evil. So, we left New Haven to lure them away from you and your daughter. Dave is really worried about you both, by the way."

Heather nodded. "I've been worried about him too, but I can't blame him for running to keep us out of danger. What else happened?"

"Well, we had to fight some monsters and ghosts and stuff on the road, and last night some huge bugs got in here. I got eaten by the slug, and Dave...he... I couldn't protect him!" Rocky fell back to the ground, sitting against the back of the couch again, putting his head down. "I tried, but it wasn't enough! I couldn't get out of the slime sack in time, and some other bug got Dave, and he walked right out of the house. I could barely see it happening, but I fought as hard as I could. By the time I finally broke free and killed the giant slug, it was too late. Dave was gone, and I collapsed. I think I swallowed or breathed in too much of the slime, and it's probably poisonous."

Heather nodded. "That makes as much sense as anything else, I guess." She sat next to Rocky and put an arm around his shoulders. "Don't blame yourself for what happened to him. Even if you did die and return as a superhero, this stuff getting thrown at us is... I don't even know what to call it. Either way, there's no one alive who can fight it, and you did your best. What we need to do now is regroup and find Dave. Can you do that for me? Can you do it for him?"

Rocky looked up, snorted back the snot that had been dangling from his nose, and nodded. "Yeah. I can do that."

"Good. Get cleaned up and changed, and we'll figure out our next move. If we team up, maybe we can find Dave and save him before this shit gets even more out of control than it already is."

***

Heather waited while Rocky got changed and showered off the alien slime off his skin. She hadn't gotten much else in the way of information other than he called his cousins—who weren't his cousins by blood—the Unmade Men. She'd also discovered that their boss—who should've been dead like Rocky—was the one who wanted Dave taken alive. To compound everything, they had gotten themselves a supervillain for the sole purpose of fighting off Rocky so the others could get to Dave.

As it turned out, Heather hadn't been the only one having the most bizarre handful of days in their life. At least they'd have something to talk about when they reunited, assuming they…

No, Heather told herself. *Don't think like that, not when Dave's so close.*

She started a fire to warm up her half-frozen legs before she could get frostbite or worse. She thought about Dave out there somewhere without his boots, and he'd be lucky to keep both his feet if he wound up wandering through the woods to get to safety.

What made him leave like that? Heather thought, knowing she was asking for nothing. All signs pointed to him being taken by Rocky's Unmade Men or something else entirely. He might be in some cocoon somewhere as the bug Rocky had hastily described sucked his juices out of him.

Dave's OK. He has to be. These people or demons or whatever want him alive, and that's what matters. If he's still breathing, we can find him and save him.

The sound of scuttling came to Heather's ears, jarring her from her frantic thoughts. She looked around to find the source, but she couldn't pinpoint it. It came again, and she looked toward the ceiling of the pantry, but it was empty.

The door had been opened all night. Some mice probably got into the house, and they're looking for somewhere to make a little nest in the walls. Might even be a squirrel.

The sound returned, and whatever had entered the house scuttled between the ceiling and the second story. Heather walked, following the sound as it made its way across the house. It moved away from the upstairs bathroom, which meant Rocky would be safe if it happened to be anything deadlier than a rogue squirrel.

"Come on you, you little bastard," Heather whispered. She grabbed the poker by the fireplace and tapped the ceiling. "You hear me in there? Come out and play with me if you've got the balls."

The ceiling cracked, and the scurrying critter fell with bits of ceiling and lots of dust. It wasn't a squirrel after all, but a huge mutant insect. It looked like a cross between a scorpion and one of those disgusting translucent millipedes that lived in her basement. Dave had said they did more good than harm in the house, but they still skeeved her like nothing else.

This thing, however, had done no good. Rocky said it had stung Dave before he left into the snowstorm, but he had trouble seeing it all. Whatever the case may have been, the bug had returned, and it had a new target. It scuttled across the floor, heading straight for Heather with its stinger raised, looking to pump her full of venom. Heather didn't hesitate when it leapt into the air toward her, she swung the poker, using the bug's momentum to fling it far away from her to give her a chance to regroup.

There would be no need for it, though. Rocky had come downstairs in a green hoodie and yellow cape. He caught the bug by its head and ignored its stinger as it struck his face. He flexed his hand once, and its head exploded with a squish of brains and slime.

Rocky chucked the dead bug to the floor. "I wondered where that thing was hiding."

Heather breathed, holding the poker in case the bug hadn't died. "You weren't kidding about being a superhero, were you?"

Rocky shook his head. "Nope."

"Good. We're going to need all the help we can get if we're going to help Dave out of whatever trouble he's in, and those superpowers will come in handy."

Rocky nodded. "OK, but how are we going to find Dave? Do you know where he is now?"

Heather sighed. "I don't. I figured he may be coming here thanks to the trajectory Father Stephen took while following what he said was Dave's 'scent'. I didn't think of a backup plan if he wasn't here. I hoped you had a way of finding him since none of us seem to have our cellphones with us as a convenience for the plot."

Rocky squinted at her. "What?"

"I mean the bad guys' plot against the rest of us."

"Oh. Who is Father Stephen, though?"

"He's the crazy priest who chained me to his station wagon to help him hunt Dave. He thought the demon in his head could use me to catch Dave's scent."

"OK."

If Father Stephen could track Dave by scent, Heather thought, *So can you.*

No... I can't do it. Not that way.

What other choice is there? Dave's not going to come through the door with a gallon of milk and ask if you've saved him any cereal. He's gone, and you're no closer to finding him than you were before you came to this godforsaken cabin in the middle of nowhere.

"I have an idea," Rocky suggested, breaking the silence in the cabin. "We start driving and look for monsters or more weird stuff. If we can do that, we can find Dave."

"No. That'll take too long, and we don't even know what direction they took him. For all we know, he's halfway to Florida right now. Go in the back of the station wagon I've brought and bring me the lockbox in the back. Do not open it."

Rocky nodded and left through the front door, leaping off the porch to cover the ground so he wouldn't have to plow his way through the snow. His speed and agility were impressive. Dave had found himself a gem of a bodyguard when he came across this kid.

She watched as Rocky rummaged through the back of the station wagon for the box containing the Demonic Testament. It gave her time to reconsider what she planned on doing, but she couldn't see any other option. The longer they waited to come up with a better plan, the closer Dave came to being sacrificed to bring the Enemy from his dimension and cover the world in unending darkness.

Rocky found the lockbox, jumped over the snow again, and returned with it. "Got it. What's inside?"

"Trust me, Rocky." Heather took the box form Rocky and brought it to the kitchen table. "You do not want to know."

"Will it help us find Dave?"

Heather nodded. "It will. Head back out on the porch for a few minutes. I need to do this next part alone."

Rocky watched her for a moment, but he nodded in agreement before leaving and closing the front door behind him.

The box sat on the table. Still, Heather waited, despite the knowledge that she needed to keep moving or the doom of all mankind would come after Dave was killed for it. But she would never be able to unread the Demonic Testament once she read it.

Heather took Father Stephen's keys from her pocket and put the one into the lockbox that opened it. She turned it, listening to the click of its internal mechanism. Her hand rested on top of it, hesitating to do what she knew needed to be done.

Remember what happened to Father Stephen. Reading this doomed his soul for all eternity, and it put a demon into his head as well.

"There's no other way. Too much is at stake to turn back now."

With Dave on her mind, Heather opened the box and removed the cloth-wrapped tome inside. It felt warm to the touch even though it had been sitting in the back of the station wagon while she sorted through everything with Rocky. With a trembling hand, she unwrapped it, finding a crimson and brown cover.

The book had no title. Nothing proclaimed it as the Demonic Testament or gave any warning as to what would happen to those who read it. It was all scratched up by fingernails or claws. With a long, drawn-out breath, Heather opened the book to the first page and read the words that had been written in the blood of a virgin. They had been written in a language she didn't know, but she understood it, nevertheless.

***

Secrets get buried, but some don't get buried deep enough. If one does want to bury a secret, six feet is the minimum depth you should dig before deciding you've gone far enough. Some secrets, however, wind up buried under a pile of fresh snow. Those are the secrets that can come back to haunt you.

The figure of a man sat up in the woods, covered in snow. If anyone had been around to see it, they would have thought a snowman had been born from the earth in a magical winter miracle. Those kinds of things don't happen, not in this world or any adjacent realities in the multiverse. What can happen, however, is a man waking up after he believed himself to be dead.

Father Stephen swiped at the snow on his face, cursing under his breath. His whole body had gone numb from the cold, and he'd spent all night sleeping on the wet ground. He didn't know when the rain had turned to snow, but it had, covering his body like a shroud of white.

"You didn't bury me deep enough, adulteress. You didn't bury me at all!"

Then, it occurred to Father Stephen what had happened. He reached to his side to find the wounds inflicted by the adulteress when she stabbed him like an inmate in a bad prison movie. His coat and clothes had been torn, and he poked through them to the knife wounds. They were still there, frozen and bloodless. It was then he realized the numbness hadn't been from the cold. He could still feel it, but all that remained was the absence of pain.

His soul had left him, driven to Hell to reside for all eternity. If he focused hard enough, he could feel the burning, deep down in the forsaken pits where demons and devils reigned over all those who lost themselves to sins and the devilry of their own devices.

Father Stephen's body acted as a vessel—like all humans—and his vessel should no longer sustain life, but here he sat, conscious and connected to his tormented soul through some hellish channel he never knew existed.

"Oh shit. The demon has taken my body."

Father Stephen stood, unable to control the action. He knew he should find a shovel, dig a hole in the ground, and bury himself deep in the soil, never to be uncovered again. But that's not what he did. He took a long breath through his nose, taking in the scents and aromas of the woods around him, searching for the thread of a scent, one that would take him back to his prey.

A smile crept upon Father Stephen's blue face. Even though he'd died, it wasn't too late for him to finish his mission. David Bryant was still out there, and he still needed to be killed.

***

Heather left the cabin and found Rocky on the porch, staring off toward the horizon. He turned to look at her as she stood there, clutching the lockbox—once again locked—under her arm.

"Did it work?" he asked. "Do you know how to find Dave?"

"I do, and he's not far from us. If the roads are plowed, we might be able to get to him by nightfall."

Rocky nodded.

"I'm not sure what's going to happen when we find him," Heather continued. "I know you've fought some weird shit already, but we might be walking into a biblical debacle this world's never seen, and that's not even the worst-case scenario. Dave's not the only one in danger. Our entire dimension is ready to fall prey to an ancient demon who's been waiting to turn us all into jelly between his toes, and your superpowers might not be enough on their own. Are you ready for that?"

Rocky nodded again. "I promised Dave I'd protect him, and I'll do it no matter what happens. Whether it's the Unmade Men, an army of demons, or the devil himself, I'm going to save his life and keep on doing it! I've died once already, and I'll do it again if that's what it takes to save him and our dimension from whatever evil is out there."

Heather smiled. "Good. I'm glad you said that. I needed to know that you're all in. Also, I may need your help pushing the station wagon out of the snow."

19. PASTIME PLAZA: AMERICA'S CREATION DESTINATION

Once upon a time, there stood a retail store that stayed proud and true to being the six hundred and fifty-fifth of its kind in its chain, though it became devoid of any customers or employees since a fateful day in October. It wasn't a victim of too-low sales or being run out of business by online shopping or a new Star-Mart being built on the same strip. If only this store's fate could have been tied into something like that, then this short fairy tale might've had a happy ending.

This story ends at the beginning, where a demon called the Enemy by its foes and He Who Walks Above by those who fear it unleashed its magic into the world from its pitch-black dimension of death and darkness. A man named Hugh Buster broke the seal between dimensions, causing unbridled power to leak through the cracks in the veil, starting an unchecked chain reaction that led to anarchy, mayhem, violence, and a bunch of other weird-ass shit.

This story is of a Pastime Plaza store just outside of Bangor, Maine, one of over seven hundred American locations that had all been christened as 'America's Creation Destination' in its initial incarnation. It had once been a bustling beacon of tchotchkes, holiday décor, and hundreds of rainy-day activities for any mindset. The chain itself is run by proud Christian men who wanted a place to cater to proud Christian families, and in that, they succeeded.

That was until Pastime Plaza's CEO, a man named Jeffery Jennings but called Mr. Jennings by even his closest friends, used his various store locations to hide religious artifacts he had *liberated* from elsewhere in the world. If he hadn't, they could've wound up in some unchristian hands, and that wouldn't be part of God's plan for them, would it?

Mr. Jennings found himself pressed for time thanks to the sullied hands of the Federal Government knocking on every door he owned. His solution came to him in a not-unfamiliar pang of genius. He had plenty of storage space all over the country, so he sent what he couldn't keep hidden to every corner of America with a note to his loyal management soldiers to keep them safe for him and not tell a soul. It seemed like the perfect plan at the time, but now a portal was about to be opened to a dimension that makes Hell look like Candy Land, and an evil whose name should never have survived history wanted to come through to punish an entire dimension for its deserved imprisonment.

But the backstory doesn't matter. What's important is that the six-hundred-and-fifty-fifth Pastime Plaza to be built in America was no longer in operation, and almost no one knew why. Two men had died one morning before its doors opened, and they had not been opened to the public ever since.

If Mr. Jennings cared in the slightest about the fate of the store and the two men who died mysteriously on a chilly October morning, he hadn't breathed a single word about it.

***

"This friggin' place gives me the creeps," Leo remarked as he pulled up to the darkened red sign of Pastime Plaza. "I don't know why, but the empty store feels like a big-ass ghost to me."

"It's not that bad," Johnny said. "We've been in the Red Curtain Club when no one was in there, and it was OK."

"That's different. I know that place inside and out, and I've been workin' for Vincenzo with that as his base of operations since I dropped outta high school. Go into a store without any lights or people or nothin', and that's a whole 'nother story."

"We've been in plenty of empty stores, though."

"Yeah, and it's usually to *take care* of someone who needs takin' care of. That doesn't help this situation at all."

Leo drove to the back of the store. The car rocked as he revved it over some snow drifts. He pulled aside the dumpster near the loading dock. "Here we are," he said, putting the car into park. "Vincenzo's inside already. All we have to do is knock and bring him the writer. Easy-peasy."

They all got out of the car. Duro hadn't put on a shirt in days, but it seemed like his style demanded showing the skin. He walked to the trunk and waited with a scowl on his face that had been there since they stopped him from killing Rocky Phantasmic. He'd been hired to kill him, but too much had gone wrong to involve the little shit after they'd gotten the damn writer.

"We can finally put this whole thing behind us and go home!" Leo exclaimed, opening the trunk. "You awake in there, Sleepin' Beauty?"

"If I were Sleeping Beauty," Dave replied, "I wouldn't be able to reply, would I?"

"Listen to this mook, always with a joke! I bet your books are real funny. Get him outta there, Johnny."

Johnny reached into the trunk and pulled Dave out, getting him to his rubbery feet. "Don't you dare try and run. If I have to run after you in the snow, you're not going to like what happens when I catch you."

"I wouldn't dream of it." Dave looked at the three men surrounding him. By the look on his face, he didn't need to be threatened. He knew what would happen if he tried to fight or got out of line. He'd come to the end of his story, and going back a chapter or two wasn't an option.

"A writer should know this part," Leo said, chuckling to himself. "The end."

For once, the writer didn't have a smart-mouthed answer.

Leo knocked on the red door, rapping his knuckles against it three times. "Oh, Vincenzo, it's Leo and the boys! We got your package. Open up, it's cold out here!"

No answer came.

"Fuck this," Leo said, backing away. "Bring him around the front. Maybe the boss is waiting by the cash registers or something."

Johnny nodded and pushed Dave. "Come on. Let's go for a little walk." He stayed behind Dave, leading him with a hand on his shoulder toward the front of the store.

"Pastime Plaza?" Dave asked, reading the sign. "You guys and a bunch of monsters have been chasing me to get me inside America's motherfucking creation destination this whole time? You know this place is run by homophobic uber-Christians, right?"

"Shut up!" Johnny looked into the empty store, cupping his hands on the glass. "I see Vincenzo down one of the aisles. Looks like he's talkin' to someone."

"There ain't no one in there with him, Johnny, and I don't see a phone to his ear."

Johnny shrugged. "So? The boss is undead now, so he might not need a phone no more."

"Your boss is undead?" Dave asked. "That means he died and came back to life, right? Is he a zombie or a vampire or something else entirely?"

"Shut up!" Johnny snapped, slapping the back of Dave's head. "No one said nothing about that shit."

Leo groaned and knocked on the window. Vincenzo turned toward them, shook his head, and walked toward the door, holding a set of keys. When he got there, he unlocked it and let them inside the darkened store.

"What's the matter with you two?!" Vincenzo snapped. "I told you to bring him around the back!"

"We did, but you weren't there," Leo retorted. "No one's around this place anyway. What's it, haunted or something?"

"Stop askin' stupid questions and get inside!" Vincenzo waited by the door till all four of his guests entered. He closed the door and locked it behind them.

"How did you get the keys to this place anyway?" Leo asked.

"What did I just tell you about askin' stupid questions!" Vincenzo slapped Leo across his face. "It was a pain in the ass if you need to know. Now shut up and get that mook over here."

Vincenzo looked over Dave. "You've caused me and my boys here a shitload of trouble. You know that?"

Dave nodded. "Yeah. I suppose you want an apology."

"Another one with a mouth." Vincenzo rolled his eyes and stepped away. "You won't be jokin' when we cut open your belly and feed your entrails to whatever hungry demon wants it."

"No, I probably won't find that funny at all."

"Good. The last thing that's going to help you is a sense of humor. Then again, I don't think there's anything in this universe that can help you now." Vincenzo stared down Dave, who looked away. "That's what I thought." He sighed and looked at the others. "Did you smash the Pimento kid? He won't be coming 'round to bother us, will he?"

"He's toast," Leo replied. "He didn't come to save this mook when we took him, so whatever was in the cabin must have gotten him good."

Vincenzo let out a groan that echoed in the empty store. "You fuckin' idiots! Can't you do anything right?!"

"What?!" Leo retorted. "You wanted the writer, and you've got the writer. I didn't think it would be such a good idea to rile up Rocky in case he wasn't dead. Either way, he don't know where we are now."

"You better hope not. If he shows up, I'll make you fight him before Duro takes a crack at him. Capeesh?"

"Got it, boss." Leo looked away, let out a sigh, and thought, *If that little shit shows up here, I'm hightailing it till the fireworks are over.*

"Come on, Bryant," Vincenzo said, grabbing the back of Dave's neck, leading him through the store. "We have to get ready for the party, and you're the guest of honor."

***

Dave fought the feeling of panic that threatened to overtake his senses. What good would it do? He couldn't run, he couldn't hide, and his personal superhero bodyguard had drowned in slug slime for all he knew.

Even this new setting proved to be a bit too unsettling. Dave had worked in retail in his twenties, so being in an empty store wasn't anything new for him. Something about this particular Pastime Plaza seemed off, though. The shelves were still full, and some shopping carts had been left in some of the aisles with merchandise still in them. A store that's been closed for good should've been bare, and the fact that this one looked as if it had been frozen in time rather than shut down made it all the eerier.

The company wasn't helping the creepy vibes of the place either.

"Do you watch the news, Bryant?" the undead Vincenzo Scaletta asked as he led Dave through the store with a hand on the back of his neck like he was training a dog where to go to piddle.

Great, Dave thought. *I'm about to get a real-life villainous monologue.*

"I try not to watch it," he said aloud.

Vincenzo laughed. "Me neither. To be honest, I'm sick of hearing about the grown men and women running this country sniping at one another like a bunch of spoiled brats."

"Yeah, I don't like that much either."

"Good. At least we can see eye-to-eye on something. Anyway, the head honcho of this Pastime Plaza operation is this religious mook named Jeffery Jennings. This guy had way more money than he needed, as evident from his actions with it. He made a hobby out of collectin' religious artifacts from around the world and snuck them here to America where they don't belong. He planned to build a secret underground museum for him and his richest Christian buddies. You followin' what I'm sayin' to you so far?"

Dave nodded. "I think I heard something about that."

"To make a long story not so long, one of them ended up here, but it's not anything Christian or Catholic. No, this thing is from a time before all that. It's a key, you see; one that opens a portal to untold power in another universe. Someone cracked it open, and a certain someone took the opportunity to peek into our world. I think you know the guy waiting on the other side."

They walked up to a set of plastic double doors that led to the backroom of the store and its receiving area. It's where the artifact Jennings wanted hidden would be, waiting for the sacrifice that would bring He Who Walks Above back into the world. Dave remembered the long, devastating strides and the enormous swinging cock of the massive demon waiting to return from its dimension.

"I don't know what he's been feeding you," Dave said, "but nothing that he wants is going to benefit you in any way. There won't be any thrones for you, and you're not going to lord over a pile of riches like a storybook dragon. He Who Walks Above wants death and destruction in his name, and that includes you and your whole family. Hell, he'll probably wipe New Haven off the map altogether just to spite you for helping him."

Vincenzo scoffed. "You think you know something about it? I died and came back from the other side. I think I'd know a little more than you about what's waiting there."

"You know what it wants you to know. You're a businessman. Rocky told me a little about you and your family. You may be immoral, but nothing I've heard led me to believe that you're stupid enough to believe that a demon from another dimension will give you what you want."

Dave found himself on the ground a moment later with a pain in the side of his head. Vincenzo had shown his offense at the statement with his fist. Dave didn't find the polished tile when his senses returned to him. The receiving area floor was cold, filthy concrete. The light from outside didn't reach back there either, but a dull, purplish glow pulsed around them as if it had gotten aroused by Vincenzo's sudden burst of violence.

"What about what I said pissed you off?" Dave asked, turning toward Vincenzo's angry face as he got back to his feet. "Was it that you think I'm wrong or are you lashing out because you know I'm right and don't want to hear it?"

"You are in no position to talk down to me!" Vincenzo puffed out his chest as he spoke. He pointed a meaty finger toward Dave. "You put me through hell finding you, and I'm not going to get turned inside-out or have some other horror inflicted upon me because you don't want to fulfill your friggin' destiny!"

He's scared to death right now, but he's not going to crack. Not even a literal Armageddon is going to make him break character and admit how afraid he is.

"Listen to yourself!" Dave exclaimed. "You should be ordering guys to collect on their protection money or running illegal sports books, but you're shouting about destiny and trying to feed someone to a demon like you understand the scope of what's at stake. Open your eyes! You're being used by something so evil you can't even comprehend it."

Vincenzo's eyes narrowed. "Are you calling me stupid? Do you think I don't know what's waiting on the other side? I'm already dead, Bryant, and I don't care what happens to the rest of the world. If I can go somewhere quiet and not get pulled apart for all eternity, I'll consider that a win. So, you're going to get up, admit defeat, and do as I say. Otherwise, it'll be a slow and torturous death and afterlife for you. Capeesh?"

"If it's all the same," Dave said, taking a step forward, "I'd rather do this the hard way."

Vincenzo shrugged. "Fine by me. It's only the hard way from your point of view. For me, it's just another day at the fuckin' office." He reached and grabbed Dave by the back of his hair, pushing him deeper into the dark room. "You want to do this shit the hard way, sunshine. By all means, let's do this shit the hard way!"

Dave struggled to keep his feet from failing under him. His hair threatened to leave his scalp between Vincenzo's fingers. He saw that the ominous glow of the dark back room hadn't been from some neon light of a chintzy lava lamp the store sold. It came from the cracks between the stone of a four-foot-tall statue. Pieces of wood lay around it along with the blackened skeletons of two humans whose flesh had been scorched from their bones.

The statue itself had been covered with carvings of runes and strange writing, and its top was adorned with dark jewels of red and black. They sparkled in the dull purplish glow, twinkling like outer space as seen from some alien planet. It looked like something familiar, though, and it took Dave a minute to realize what it was.

Oh shit! That thing looks like a giant stone butt plug! Was it He Who Walks Above's?!

The Unmade Men and Duro had come to watch the show as Vincenzo shoved Dave to his knees in front of the glowing butt plug of doom. He pressed his weight onto the back of Dave's head, forcing his face inches from the artifact.

If I were writing this, this is where I would write in the superhero Rocky Phantasmic bursting through the wall to save the day along with my ass. Come on, Rocky. I know that butt-ugly slug isn't enough to kill you, and you're still a man of your word. You promised to protect me, and here I am, needing protection again along with the entire fucking world.

Dave looked up while Vincenzo held the back of his head with his unyielding grip. No crash came, and Rocky Phantasmic didn't burst through the wall. This was cold, hard reality's reminder that the real world didn't have death-defying climaxes and superheroic rescues. If some dickhead mobster villain like Vincenzo Scaletta and his patron demon called He Who Walks Above wants you dead, then you die. That's all there is to it.

"Welcome to the hard way," Vincenzo said through gritted teeth. "Don't worry. It'll all be over before you know it."

Come on, Rocky. This is the most perfect moment for a superhero entrance if I've ever seen one. Don't let it go to waste! Where the fuck are you?!

***

"Pastime Plaza?" Rocky asked, leaning forward in the station wagon to get a better look. "What is this place?"

"It's an arts and crafts store," Heather replied. "They sell a lot of holiday stuff, but they're heavy on the *Jesus* holidays."

"Oh. It looks closed."

"Or abandoned."

"Are you sure Dave's here?"

Heather stopped at the far end of the parking lot under the vestige of Pastime Plaza's big red sign. The area hadn't been slammed by the snowstorm like other parts of Maine in the area, but the sky looked as if it were about to punish the earth a little more before the day ended in earnest. Heather could also see the clouds weren't obeying the laws of nature over this particular patch of retail space. They turned in the air to create a funnel above the building. If anyone else saw, they'd be heading into their cellars and praying a super tornado didn't touch down over their home.

"That's the place," Heather said. "No doubt about it. Whatever the Enemy has planned, it's going to happen here, and Dave's already inside for it."

Heather felt Rocky's gaze. She hadn't divulged how she knew how to find Dave, and she'd insisted he not ask. Even though he'd seen some shit on his own, how could she explain to him what she had to forsake to save her husband and the entire world from some super demon?

She had to answer to herself as well. She had taken the same road as Father Stephen by reading the Demonic Testament to find Dave and put an end to all this demonic madness, but it was much too late for that inner debate. If the world existed and still spun tomorrow, then she'd be able to figure out if there was a way to undo what she'd done. Maybe a good exorcist could remove the demon from her head, but that would have to wait.

"So, what do we do now?" Rocky asked.

"That's the hard part. I figured out how to find Dave, but I didn't plan for what would happen after that. I read a little about the ritual, and it looked like they need Dave's blood to pry open the seams between dimensions and let enough of the Enemy's power out to allow him to break free from his imprisonment, return to our dimension, and cancel out God."

"A lot's at stake."

"That's putting it mildly."

"What are we waiting for? We need to get in there and save him!"

"It's not that simple!" Heather took a breath. She didn't want to snap at Rocky. The agitation grew inside her, and she didn't know if it had come from her worry for her husband's wellbeing, the impending Demonic Apocalypse that required his blood to begin, or the invisible demon that raged behind her eyes.

"Sorry," Heather continued. "I wasn't able to read enough about the ritual of the demonic prophecy behind it to know what's going to happen when we get in there, especially if we're too late to stop it. Father Stephen told me a little about it, but—"

"I'm not sitting around and waiting," Rocky said, opening his door. "You can read about it if you want, but I'm going to get Dave before they can bleed him dry and summon the demon."

"Wait!" Heather shouted as Rocky slammed the door. He leapt through the air toward the roof of the Pastime Plaza. She sighed, put the car into drive, and drove in the same direction, muttering as she went.

"Dammit, Rocky, you hot-headed little shit. I bet you didn't act this way when you were driving around with Dave."

***

Vincenzo held a knife in his left hand. He pointed the blade upward toward the metal girders that made up the ceiling. It looked like another rune-covered relic, a gift from a demonic benefactor or a third party. He lowered it to rest against Dave's neck, and its wielder bent to whisper in his ear.

"Do you have any last words before I open you up and call forth the awesome and unyielding power of He Who Walks Above, a demon who transcends time and space to return to us whole again?"

He's learned some big words for the benefit of his demon daddy, Dave thought. Aloud he said, "Just one: Don't."

Vincenzo chuckled. "A goofy little asshole till the end. Oh well. It suits you to die with a joke on your tongue."

The knife didn't slice through Dave's jugular like he thought it would. Vincenzo grabbed his wrist instead, cutting his palm down the middle. Dave winced, but Vincenzo's grip was too intense for him to pull it back.

"Thought I'd slit your throat?" Vincenzo asked with a wry chuckle. "Nah. I told you He Who Walks Above wanted to kill you himself. A handprint of blood should be enough to open this gateway."

"You can sever a tendon doing it that way," Dave muttered. "I don't know why they always do it like that in movies." His concern went ignored as Vincenzo forced him forward to slap the stony edge of the gigantic stone butt plug. Dave's blood smeared the glowing cracks and inscribed runes. It oozed from his palm. Vincenzo had cut deep, and the blood flowed onto the stone.

Dave's body petrified, locking him into place with his hand against the stone. He wanted to close his eyes tight to shut out the odd glowing that assaulted his retinas, but he couldn't. No part of his body remained under his control. All he could do was kneel and keep still while his hand bled between worlds.

This is it, Dave thought. *End of the world, and I've got a front-row seat.*

"Nothing's happenin'," Leo remarked from behind. "What's supposed to happen?"

"I dunno," Johnny replied. "Ain't some monster supposed to come out or something? We probably shouldn't be standin' here."

"Will you two shut the hell up?!" Vincenzo exclaimed. "Maybe it's not working because I got a couple of assholes in the peanut gallery who can't keep their mouths shut during a friggin' demonic ritual!"

Vincenzo looked at Dave, eying him as if the failure had somehow been his fault. "It's not enough blood maybe. I think I'm going to have to open a bigger vein after all." He brought the knife down, looking to cut Dave's wrist to get more blood out of him. Dave closed his eyes, knowing it was coming, powerless to stop it. As the tip of the blade touched his skin, the stone's glowing intensified.

"YES!" Vincenzo said, backing away. "His awakening has begun! Only one final step before he can fully materialize here."

Dave fell back, holding his sore hand closed. He wanted to find something he could use to stop the bleeding, but his eyes were transfixed on the opening portal between worlds. A crack like thunder sounded, and it was the end.

Or at least Dave thought it was.

Rocky burst through the wall, screaming in a rage. He had donned his green hoodie and yellow cape for the rescue. The Unmade Men pulled their guns, and Duro became erect.

"What are you waiting for?!" Vincenzo exclaimed. "KILL HIM!"

Leo and Johnny opened fire, but they should have known it wouldn't do anything against a superhero. Duro knew, and he walked through the crossfire without missing a step to get to his prey.

"I'm ready for round two, motherfucker," Rocky said, holding his fists in a boxer's stance. "There's more on the line this time, so I won't be holding back."

Duro smiled and rushed his opponent.

"Get the friggin' writer!" Vincenzo ordered.

Dave swore under his breath. He'd hoped that Rocky's sudden appearance would give him enough time to get away. He had no idea what else other than his blood Vincenzo needed to call He Who Walks Above into reality, but he didn't want to find out. He tried to crawl away to sneak outside while Rocky fought, but now Vincenzo's pair of lackluster cronies had him in their sights instead of the superpowered brawl.

They still need me alive for whatever comes next, Dave thought, getting to his feet. *That's got to count for something.*

Dave found himself out of options. The Unmade Men blocked the way back into the store, the hole Rocky had put in the wall was too high up for him to get through, and the only other exit was way in the back past Vincenzo and the glowing butt plug of doom.

Rocky took a hard hit from Duro, sending him flying into Leo and Johnny, knocking them both through the flapping doors to the main area of the store with a crash. Duro strode after them with a smile on his face and a boner in his pants. Dave took one look at Vincenzo and ran, following the rest of the crowd where he wouldn't be cornered.

"Get the fuck back here!" Vincenzo shouted.

"Not a chance!" Dave ran into the store, making a quick right down an aisle turn to avoid the Unmade Men, who were still tumbling over each other to get free. Rocky and Duro traded punches, knocking over everything around them in a clattering of metal shelving and merchandise. If it kept going, they'd eventually bring down the whole store. That suited Dave fine. Pastime Plaza never had been his creation destination for a myriad of reasons, and the fact a demonic ritual was taking place inside this one made him hate the franchise even more.

The only problem with the store coming down was that it would come down right on top of Dave's head.

The store had fallen into complete chaos. The energy that had surrounded the stone butt plug like an aura had leaked out, and it filled Pastime Plaza with its purple and black glow.

I liked it better when it was dark in here.

The lighting wasn't all that had changed. Something moved in the corners of the ceiling like liquid shadows. Dave saw them from the corners of his eyes. The shadows crawled like long, black insects coming downward on threads of silk webbing. One looked like a long millipede with a gaping mouth, and another looked like two spiders fused at their backs.

Dave backed away and tripped over some decorative brooms that reeked of a combination of cinnamon and dead leaves. The *insects* inflated like balloons as they descended. He Who Walks Above wasn't done with him yet, and he'd sent some of his more disgusting creatures to drag him back so Vincenzo could finish the ritual.

"Shit." Dave picked up one of the brooms. "Get back!" He waved it in vain like an old man trying to get a raccoon off his trashcans. The gigantic, black insect creatures weren't intimidated by the action whatsoever. Maybe they couldn't see, as they lacked the eyes to do so. They crept along, sensing his presence.

"Uh, I can use a little help here," Dave muttered, walking backward down one of the main aisles of the store. "Rocky, if you're not busy fighting a supervillain, can you come by and smash these bugs for me?"

No answer came from Rocky aside from the sounds of his fight with Duro. They were slamming one another to the floor, cracking and breaking the tiles along with the concrete underneath it. Most of the shelving had been busted, and Duro took a header to the ceiling after a huge uppercut from Rocky sent him skyward. He came back down unfazed by it, ready to start again.

They're going to be going at it all night.

Dave looked around for anything other than a fake broom to use as a weapon, but he had nothing unless he wanted to throw some paint-by-numbers books at them.

Why couldn't we have this epic battle in a guns and ammunition store?

"BACK AWAY FROM HIM, YOU UGLY MOTHERFUCKERS!"

Dave turned and found Heather walking toward him. She looked like a beacon of hope and madness, and he wondered if she was another illusion placed in his mind by wraith magic, hallucinogenic bug venom or some other fucked-up demonic method. Either way, she had arrived, and she had come to help him.

Heather held a crucifix in her left hand, and it wasn't a small one. It stood on the end of a pole over their heads and had a realistic Jesus on the top in all his suffering glory. In her right hand, she held a large open Bible. Maybe it was the light or maybe it was the power the word of God held, but Dave could swear an orangish glow emanated from the pages.

The most breathtaking thing about Heather's appearance—other than her being in a Pastime Plaza in Maine in the first place—was the look of fury and intensity in her eyes.

"This plane is not yours," she said, walking forward without flinching or breaking her stride. "Return to whence you came, foul bugs. Go back to the Enemy and reclaim your pitiful lives clinging to his demonic gonads for sustenance. This dimension and all that dwell reject you, bloodsuckers of the Enemy. RETURN TO HIM!"

Dave had no idea where the words came from, but he was sure they hadn't been in the Bible. He'd never been the most devout catholic growing up, but he'd never heard anything about any passages regarding interdimensional crabs that lived on a demon lord's ballsack.

The insects screeched from gaping holes in the middle of the abdomen where mouths should not be. They also backed away, frightened of Heather's appearance and words. It didn't seem to matter if they understood English or not. They knew a command when they heard it.

"I am a wielder of the Demonic Testament!" Heather proclaimed in a booming voice that drowned out everything except for Rocky's brawl with Duro. "You will leave this man and return through the cracks between dimensions. If you ignore my warning, I will smite you and send you back as fragments of what you once were."

The bugs leapt upward, reforming into the shadows in the corner. Dave watched them meld back into their dimension, and he turned to Heather.

"What?" Heather said, closing her large tome with a snap. "The words aren't that important. It's the intention of them that catches their attention. As a writer, I thought you'd appreciate that part of the process."

There were so many questions, but Dave pushed them aside. He rushed toward Heather and took her in a huge hug. "I can't believe you're here. You saved me!" They separated for a moment and shared a brief kiss.

"I haven't saved anything yet," Heather said. "Did your blood touch the relic?"

Dave nodded. "Yeah, but Vincenzo said there's another part. Whatever it is, they still need me alive."

"We need to get you out of here."

"What about Rocky?"

Heather looked toward the fight in time to see Rocky catch one of Duro's punches and send the supervillain flying toward the cash registers with a stiff kick to his stomach.

"Rocky Phantasmic's a motherfucking superhero," Heather replied. "I think he could handle the fight on his own."

***

Rocky held his chest, inhaling long, grateful gulps of air. The kick to Duro's hardened abs surprised the villain enough to send him clear across the store and crashing through the checkout counters, but it wouldn't be enough to finish him off for good.

"He's not invincible," Rocky told himself, urging his body forward. "If you're hurting, he's hurting. This ends now."

Duro got back to his feet, hurling a cash register. Rocky knocked it out of the air with the back of his hand, sending it into the wall where it smashed, showering the floor with pieces of plastic and metal. They stepped toward each other, each one determined to finish off the other in the most violent way possible.

"Can you keep this up?" Rocky asked, putting his fists up for another round. "Did you hear the bell ring yet, big boy? This fight ain't over till it's over."

Duro's smile remained as he threw a punch. Rocky tilted his head, letting it pass him. He felt the air rush past as it tried to keep up with the flying fist.

He's slowing down.

Rocky tossed a quick jab, connecting with Duro's jaw. He threw another, harder, and connected again, rocking Duro's head back with the action. He tried for a body shot, but Duro blocked it with his arm, sending a punch of his own into Rocky's gut, sending him into the air. His back hit the metal ceiling with a clang, and he fell back to the ground, breaking more of the floor.

I'm slowing down too.

WHO THE FUCK IS ROCKY PHANTASMIC?!

A boot to the back of the head slammed Rocky's face into the floor. It came down again, repeating the action. Stars flooded his vision, and the taste of copper flooded his mouth as it happened a third time. Duro picked him up by the back of his neck and brought his mouth to his ear.

"If you get up again," Duro whispered, "I'm going rip your fucking heart out of your chest and eat it while your boyfriend watches."

With that, Duro threw Rocky through the wall with what felt like the force of a supercollider. He landed outside in the parking lot, leaving a long trench in asphalt. When his body came to a rest, it didn't move again.

Duro stepped out of the hole Rocky's body made, taking slow steps toward the fallen superhero. The smile on his face—as well as his raging erection—remained as he looked over his fallen foe.

Looks like you won't be eating my heart now, asshole, Rocky thought as his body finally gave out, sending him into the deep, darkness of an unconscious void.

Sorry, Dave, but you'll have to wait a minute or two for me to come back from this.

***

"Well," Dave said, "Rocky went through the fucking wall. I think that's our cue to get the hell out of here."

"Agreed," Heather added. "Without ending the ritual, though, this place will remain a beacon of evil, a nexus between our dimension and the one housing the Enemy."

"Why are you talking like that? Are you a dark sage or something now?"

"We'll talk about it later. Right now, we need to get you out of here before the Enemy can complete his prophecy."

Dave rolled his eyes. "A prophecy? That's so lazy!"

"I know, but we can't end it till we find your opposite to balance out the demonic magic."

"My opposite? Demonic magic? After everything I've seen, I'm still lost. What does any of this even mean?"

"We'll talk about it later. We really need to—"

"Not so fast!" Vincenzo interrupted, emerging the double doors with his gun in his hand before Dave and Heather could escape the Pastime Plaza. Leo and Johnny flanked him, holding pistols of their own. "No one said we were done here."

"You can't be serious!" Heather exclaimed. "You see what's happening here, and you still want to go forward with this ritual?!"

"You don't know this guy," Dave said. "There's no reasoning with him. He's undead as hell."

"Undead?" Heather asked. "Then he's not going to like this." She walked forward, holding her crucifix ahead of her.

"Not so fast," Leo said, stepping forward. "I was an altar boy as a kid, but I ain't afraid of no cross, and sure as hell ain't afraid of no women carrying one."

Heather froze. It was a standoff, and she and Dave had no weapons other than a crucifix and a book. Vincenzo and his Unmade Men wouldn't shoot or kill Dave, but that didn't mean they wouldn't blow out his kneecaps to get him to stay still. They'd threatened it before, and that was before a portal to an evil dimension had been partway opened.

Dave put his hands up, showing them his palms, bloody slit and all. "We're unarmed, but you have to know that what you're trying to do is global suicide, even if you've been brought back from the dead already."

"I already heard that noise from you." Vincenzo walked around them in an arc, aiming his gun at his prey. "I'm going to step over here, you two are going to walk into that back room, and you're going to complete the ritual by calling He Who Walks Above into our world."

"Wait a second," Dave said. "The last part of this ritual involves me requesting for this demonic asshole to come devour all life on this planet?"

"Yes, and don't you think you can refuse. We have creative ways of asking, and if you don't answer when we *ask* you, we'll ask your women while you watch. We can get as creative as we need to be."

Leo and Johnny both chuckled at the prospect of torturing two human beings.

Vincenzo stopped moving, looking over Dave and Heather. "Well? What's it going to be? Are you going to come willingly, or do my nephews get to play a bit?"

"I don't know." Dave looked from Heather to Vincenzo to the smiling Unmade Men. "Can I have an hour or two to think about it? I'll need a day at the most, I swear."

"Don't antagonize the men with guns, Dave," Heather whispered.

Vincenzo laughed. "I should've known you'd want to do things the hard way again." He shrugged. "It's your party. Go get 'em, boys."

WHO THE FUCK IS ROCKY PHANTASMIC?!

Leo and Johnny stepped forward, but several things happened at once the moment they did. A loud rumbling came from outside the moment before the glass from the front door flew inward as a greenish metal behemoth crashed into the store, unhindered by the glass and debris in its way. Vincenzo turned toward the source of the commotion, screaming as the garbage truck sped through the store, coming right for him. The Unmade Men opened fire, shooting at it as it plowed over their boss, giving him a twisted facelift with its steaming grill. Brakes squealed and smoke came from the tires as the driver hit the brakes. The back fishtailed and rammed into a row of shelves, knocking the ones next to it over like a stack of dominoes, sending an entire display of picture frames crashing downward over Leo and Johnny with the sound of their screams mingled with the breaking glass.

The truck lurched toward Dave and Heather next, and they braced for the impact. A green and yellow blur flew inside from a hole in the store's wall, leaping between the truck and the endangered couple. Rocky held it at bay, his feet digging a pair of trenches into the floor. It came to a stop, and the young superhero collapsed.

"I'm not done yet," Rocky gasped, falling to one knee. "I promised to protect you, Dave."

"You did great," Dave said, kneeling next to Rocky and offering him a smile for support. "If you need to take a rest, now's the time."

"I don't…" Rocky faltered, leaning against the garbage truck's grill. "OK, I'm going to take a short breather. Let me know when that supervillain comes back."

"Alright. I'll let you know." Dave stood and looked at the windshield of the garbage truck, but it had been too cracked to see the driver—if it even had one. "What the hell is this?" he asked, turning toward Heather. "Did you bring backup?"

"No," Heather replied. "This isn't from me."

The door opened, and someone stepped out. Dave recognized the man he should've met days ago in a club back in New Haven called Deuce's Wild.

"Cliff?" Dave asked, stepping closer to him. "Cliff Quentin?! What the hell are you doing here?"

Cliff looked around the store like he was as surprised to be there as Dave was to see him. A small patch of blood oozed from a wound on his forehead. His gaze shifted and he looked at Dave, reality finally washing over him.

"Yeah? Who the hell are you?"

"I'm Dave. Dave Bryant. We were supposed to meet the other night, remember?"

"Dave Bryant?" Cliff walked forward, scanning Dave's face. He reached forward and grabbed his shoulders, squeezing them hard. "WHERE THE FUCK HAVE YOU BEEN?!"

"I got held up," Dave replied. "What about you? How are you even here right now, and why did you save our lives with a garbage truck ex-machina?"

The quizzical look on Cliff's face died as he laughed at the audacity of Dave's question. "Well, it's a funny story…"

20. WHERE THE FUCK WAS CLIFF QUENTIN?

Cliff never knew garbage trucks were meant for highway driving, but he'd been wrong before. It took some time to get used to the way it hugged the road and took its time picking up speed, but he'd gotten the hang of it after a dozen miles or so. He pushed his foot on the gas, edging the needle past sixty. He would have loved to drive faster but the road had grown slick, and he didn't want to go tumbling over a guardrail.

He'd left his rental car miles behind him. Sure, the company he rented it from would be pissed he abandoned it on the side of the road, but that wasn't anything a wad of cold, hard, American currency couldn't remedy. If he did well enough at the show in Bangor, he'd have enough dough to not worry about things like abandoned rental cars. Celebrities could ditch them wherever they wanted. The world was molded for them that way.

Hopefully those zombie corpses melt some more so people don't think I murdered a couple of garbagemen and stole their truck like I'm playing a real-life version of Grand Theft Auto.

"I know what this road trip needs," Cliff said, clicking on the radio. "Some music."

He turned the knob on the old radio dial, looking for some Maine station that played some classic rock or anything to make the monotony of the long drive not so monotonous. He found one in the middle of the dial, but the sounds of screaming and shrieking filled the truck's cab, and he turned the dial, finding some more screaming in a higher pitch.

"Fuck this," Cliff muttered as he shut off the radio. "Zombie garbagemen have shit taste in music."

Cliff drove in the quiet. The only sound piercing the cloudy afternoon was the rumble of the engine and the rolling of the tires against the wet highway. The water pistol that still had a little over half its store of holy water inside sat on the passenger's seat, waiting for a reason to be used. If all went well, there wouldn't be a need for it at all.

The silence reminded him to focus on his secondary mission as well if that's what it was. First and foremost, he needed to get to Bangor in time for his show, which he'd do with time to spare if the weather didn't deter him. He remembered what Sera the supposed angel had told him about his fate and how it was all tied to David Bryant in some way, though the fancy bastard had remained vague.

My path leads to his path. Was it something like that?

"Shit. I should've had him write it all down for me."

Cliff looked out the passenger window when something caught his eye in the side mirror. He thought he'd see a car driving from his blind spot, but he saw a stag running alongside his truck.

"Slow down, guy," Cliff said, watching the buck in the mirror. "You're going to get hurt."

It took a few seconds for him to realize something he should've thought right away.

"Wait… Can deer run at sixty miles per hour?"

Cliff looked again, and the deer tilted its head to look right back at him. Its eyes glowed orange, and its snout was covered with ticks and flies that crawled out of its mouth and nostrils. Its breath streamed behind it in a line of gray, and its fur was matted, covered with blood.

"Shit!" Cliff exclaimed, cutting the wheel to stay on the road after the sight of the pursuing stag had taken too much of his attention from driving, but that might've been the point. He reached for his holy water pistol while doing his best to keep the garbage truck in the right lane and watch the deer in his side mirror in his periphery.

"Come a little closer, you reanimated roadkill!"

Cliff unrolled the window and did his best to aim while keeping the truck in the lane. The stag backed off, putting itself out of range of getting squirted. A car behind blared its horn at it as it tried to pass on the left side. It failed, skidding to a halt against the guard rail.

"You better run away!" Cliff shouted at the deer. "I'll turn you into a highway patty if you come at me again, you zombie Bambi motherfucker!"

Cliff turned back toward the road, slamming on the brakes when he saw a roadblock ahead of him. The garbage truck lurched, and he thought for sure he'd flip it over this time. The back proved to be too heavy for a flip, and the whole thing came to a screeching halt before he could break through the roadblock and nail the downed tree blocking the right and middle lanes.

"Watch it, asshole!" a passing driver shouted before maneuvering around the fallen tree.

"Prick," Cliff muttered. "You don't have zombie wildlife chasing you down."

With a long sigh, he checked his mirrors and put the truck in reverse to get around the tree. He didn't see anything coming behind him, but he felt a thump once he reversed twenty feet or so.

"What the fuck is it now?!"

Cliff put it into park and got out, holding the holy water pistol at his side in case the stag returned to start a fight, but it had gone away. Maybe it felt different about starting shit once it saw that its prey wouldn't be a pushover.

Cliff made his way to the back of the truck, and he saw what had made the sound. People emerged from the tailgate, crawling from the dark well of putridness. Well, they were remnants of people. They were more zombie types, like the two men who drove the truck until he killed them and took it. They'd been stripped of their humanity, and the skin barely clung to their bones. They groaned and hissed, falling to the roads in puddles of bone, blood, and liquified guts.

"Jesus," Cliff muttered. "People are going to see this and think I'm a goddam serial killer with an undead garbage truck."

The back had been left open, either on purpose or accident by the truck's former drivers. Maybe the demonic stag had slipped out as well. Cliff had no way to tell how many living beings the undead garbagemen had collected.

"I long for a world of normalcy." Cliff pulled the yellow and black lever near the back of the garbage truck, and the back closed, crushing those who hadn't crawled out into jelly. He gave the rest of the crawling zombies a quick mercy squirting with the nozzle of his holy water gun, killing them on the right lane of the highway.

Snow fell from the sky, and Cliff looked upward at it. With luck, it would cover the bodies enough for no one to be any wiser to their appearance while they withered and melted from the holy water.

Cliff had no desire to deal with any more undead or demonic shit. He climbed back into the garbage truck's cab and put it back into drive.

That could've been worse, he thought. *Much worse.*

Cliff drove around the tree, checking his mirrors as he picked up speed once more. The zombie stag ran behind him, keeping pace with the truck but far enough away not to be struck or squirted again.

"You're going to be a dick about all this, aren't you?" Cliff asked, watching the creature in the mirror. "Why can't I be left alone for once in my damn life?!"

***

The snowfall intensified, and so did the traffic despite the late hour. Cliff wished he'd made it to a Bangor hotel safe and sound to ditch the garbage truck in the woods somewhere, walk out, and get another rental car. Maybe he'd get a gas can and torch the fuckin' behemoth out of spite. If anything in the world deserved to burn, it was the garbage truck from Hell.

But that future felt far away, and the snow showed no signs of letting up. A frigid wind cut through the air in a fury. The windshield wipers worked without rest, clearing the winter storm from the glass to allow Cliff to see four feet in front of him.

"I'm going to die before I get to Bangor." Cliff laughed despite the audacity of his life over the last few days. "Is this what I deserve? Is this what I get for wanting to do one fucking thing for myself instead of getting involved in Dave Bryant's fight against the forces of evil or whatever the fuck that fucking angel was blabbing about?! I didn't ask for this shit! Fuck the snow, and fuck He Who Walks Above right in his enormous, gaping asshole!"

A crack of lightning split the sky, giving Cliff a brief glimpse of what waited around him in the snow. The ground was so covered it didn't even look recognizable. The oddest thing about it was that the other cars seemed to have disappeared like the ground had swallowed them up and closed. Either that, or he'd gone somewhere else completely.

"Well, this is new."

WHO THE FUCK IS ROCKY PHANTASMIC?!

The garbage truck shuddered the moment the sentence left Cliff's lips as if it had had enough of his sarcastic blubbering. The engine rumbled and shook, sending vibrations through the entire truck. Cliff gripped the wheel as he tried to ensure he didn't chip a tooth while his whole body entered the same frequency. It only lasted a few seconds, ending with a sputter as the engine quit on him.

"Come on, you big motherfucker," Cliff muttered, turning the key. It clicked and something whirred from the other side of the dashboard, but the engine refused to turn over. After a few minutes, he gave up and sat back with a sigh as the coldness from the storm outside crept into the cab to surround him like an invisible shroud of wintry agony.

"Alright, Cliff," he said to himself. "You've gone and pissed off the patron demon of fucking shit up."

The feeling sunk into his soul that he would come to wish he'd tangled with the zombie stag instead of whatever came next. Then it hit him that the damn zombie stag was likely waiting outside for him to emerge from the garbage truck.

Cliff looked out the window, squinting in a vain attempt to see through the layers of icy white whipping all around him. If the stag was out there, he wouldn't see it when it came to hunt him.

The radio clicked, and the light behind the dial blinked into existence. The sounds of the damned screeching returned, but it faded as the dial turned on its own. A dark and slow voice spoke next with an almost gleeful tone.

"Does it bother you, comedian, that your path is tied to one who was marked for death? Do you know why you and the writer are both marked?"

"I don't particularly care at this point," Cliff replied to the radio voice. "Do what you want with the guy. It's none of my business. Leave me alone, let me go and get to my gig, and you can strip his skin from his bones for all I care."

"Oh, if I could only believe that you'd veer away from your destined path, comedian. Let me show you the memories in your blood, and you can decide for yourself whether or not this man's life is worth putting your own on the line to save."

"I already told you I don't care!"

Cliff hit the ground. The garbage truck was gone, and he landed in a pit of mud. He got back to his feet, realizing the snowstorm had dissipated or disappeared altogether. He stood in the middle of what he assumed was an ancient village. The people wore animal pelts and had dirt all over their faces like cartoon cavemen.

"Hello?" he asked, walking toward a dying campfire. "Does anyone here speak English? What is this place?"

No one answered. They couldn't see or hear him.

"I get it." Cliff laughed. "I'm like Scrooge, right? Where the fuck is the Ghost of Christmas Past?"

No ghost appeared. The distinct shouts of crazed men filled the scene instead, and the small village was overtaken in a matter of seconds by murderers and rapists, killing all in their path in an orgy of blood and blunt force trauma.

One man stood above it all, watching with a club of wood and bone, smiling as his men killed for him.

"*That is the one who shall sire a line of sons who will eventually sire one named David Bryant,*" the voice from the radio said within Cliff's head. "*The writer's blood still has the memories of this day and hundreds more like it. He covered the land in blood and semen to satisfy his primal need for genocide against those he believed were beneath him.*"

"Yeah, sounds like human nature alright, but what's that got to do with me?"

"*Watch.*"

Cliff saw what he'd been meant to see, and he knew it. A boy hid in a cave after finding refuge behind some stones. The boy sat with his eyes closed tight and his hands over his ears as his family and their kin were slaughtered outside. He wept silently so he wouldn't be found and killed like the rest of his kin.

"*Your blood holds the memory of this cowardly child, who hid here two whole days even after the men who murdered everyone he loved had gone to the next village. He grew into adulthood with the memories of that slaughter, but never spoke a word of it, lest he be killed for the crime of survival. He came to sire a son late in life who'd come to sire a line of his own, eventually creating you, comedian.*"

Cliff turned away from the crying child toward the cave's opening. "And what? Am I supposed to be pissed at Dave for something his ancestors did to mine? It's ancient history, dude! Let it go!"

"*You can ignore these atrocities, but your blood will remember. The writer is not your friend. Deep in your cores, you're the bitterest of enemies. It is your destiny.*"

Cliff scoffed. "I'm not buyin' it, asshole, so let me out of this shitshow and let me get to a hotel. Keep me out of your fucked up plans, and I'll stay away from the writer. Deal?"

The only sound in reply was a huff from whoever spoke from within Cliff's head. The next thing he knew, the ground had opened up, and he fell for miles in darkness.

***

Cliff awoke with a start to the sounds of horns blaring around him. He felt half-frozen in the cab of the garbage truck. He looked in his mirrors and saw snowplows clearing the highway around him as the sun rose.

"Shit. That damn nightmare put me out all night. I'm never going to make it to Bangor at this rate!"

Cliff turned the key with a silent prayer that it would start after resting for the entire night. It whirred as it did earlier, but it eventually turned over this time, roaring to life.

"That's my boy!" Cliff exclaimed, slapping the wheel.

He turned up the heat next, ignoring the smell of burning flesh that came with it. If he had eaten since his meal with the angel, he might've gagged and vomited from it, but he had to endure the reek or freeze to death.

"Idiot. Your demonic ass should have dropped me in a nice warm bed in a Bangor hotel. The sooner I'm off the road, the sooner I can get this shit over with. Not that I'm going to fulfill that fucked up destiny anyway, but you'd catch a lot more flies with honey than with vinegar, you ignorant fuck. Next time offer me a million dollars instead of torturing my ass."

With a polite wave to the plow driver staring at him to make sure he wasn't a frozen corpse of a garbageman, Cliff drove. More cars passed him while honking or shouting at him to speed up, but he ignored most of them. If they knew what he'd been through, they'd give him a pass for his shitty driving.

Then, Cliff spotted something else odd to put on top of his ever-growing pile of odd shit. A man stood by the side of the road looking both ways as if he were about to cross. Cliff hit the horn, startling him. He hit the brakes next, coming to a stop with the man by his passenger's side door.

Cliff moved over and cranked the window open, longing to drive something with automatic windows the next time he drove anything at all. "Hey," he said. "You trying to get killed out here or something?"

The man laughed. His face had turned blue from the cold, and his beard was covered in frost. His jacket was unzipped a bit, and Cliff could see the collar of a priest.

"I should be asking you the same thing, friend," the priest said with a smile.

Hell, after all this unholiness happening around me I could probably use a priest to keep the demons away.

"Hop in, Father," Cliff said, moving his holy water pistol. "I'm heading to Bangor if you need a lift. It's better than freezing to death on the side of the highway. Trust me, I know. It almost happened to me last night."

"Thank you," the priest said as he climbed inside and settling into the passenger's seat. "I appreciate the ride, and I was heading that way when I lost my mode of transportation."

Cliff got the truck moving again. "Yeah, this storm took out my rental car too, and I got saddled driving this thing down the highway."

"Oh. It is an odd vehicle, and you're not dressed like a garbageman."

Cliff laughed. "That's part of the joke, I guess. I'm a comedian. Cliff Quentin. You might've heard of me."

"No, I haven't, but that's OK. I'm a priest, so I don't watch too much comedy. Nowadays it's too…edgy for my tastes."

"I get that. Do you have a name, or should I just call you 'Father'?"

The priest laughed. "You can if it suits you. Otherwise, my full name is Father Stephen MacDougal."

"Please to meet you, Father Stephen MacDougal. Welcome to the nonstop garbage truck express to Bangor, Maine."

***

Cliff tried not to stare as he drove, but he couldn't help it. The heat blasted, but the blueness of Father Stephen's skin didn't fade. "Hey, Father, are you alright? How long were you in the cold?"

"I lost track of time," Father Stephen replied, "but I guess I slept on the ground for the whole snowstorm last night."

"What? Do you need to get to a hospital? I don't want you to die once your insides thaw and your body realizes it's dead."

Father Stephen laughed off the morbid joke. "No, no. I'm fine. I think this color is going to be my look from now on. I know it's weird, but not everything that happens in God's plans is pretty."

"That's the mild take on it, Padre."

Father Stephen turned toward Cliff. "Is something bothering you other than my outward appearance, my child?"

Cliff chuckled. "Are we in confession right now?"

"That depends. It doesn't have to be a confession, but we can talk if something is the matter. Part of being a man of the cloth is helping others with their problems, no matter what they are or where you find them. Besides, it's the least I can do to return the favor of the drive."

"OK. It's about the blue skin, but I'm not judging. I've seen some really weird stuff lately, and I don't know how much stock I should put into it."

"What kind of weird stuff have you seen?"

"This stays here, right? Didn't you take a priest's version of the hypocritic oath?"

Father Stephen laughed. "Yes. It was something like that."

Cliff inhaled deeply through his nose and in a quick tempo said, "OK, so I'm being targeted by demons. One mean bastard in particular. Oh, pardon my French. Anyway, that's how I ended up driving this garbage truck. The previous owners were zombies sent to stop me from stopping some shit I don't even know how to stop. The long and short of it is that I'm on this quest I have no business being on, and all I want to do is get to Bangor, do this comedy show, impress this talent scout in the audience, and get back into the business."

"I see." Father Stephen nodded as he watched the road ahead of them. His face remained passive as if he had no opinion either way about what he'd heard.

It could be worse, Cliff thought. *He could've jumped out of the truck after hearing that cockamamie story.*

"Is that all?" Father Stephen asked.

"There's more, but you'll really think I'm crazy if I told you."

"Tell me. I won't think you're crazy. I've heard a lot of confessions in my day."

"I met an angel at a rest stop, and he told me some stuff about how this is my destiny or something."

Father Stephen laughed again and shook his head. "Get off this next exit. We're going to head east for a bit."

"East?"

"East."

Cliff put on his blinker and pulled off the exit ramp, not questioning the directions. "You're not having me drive myself to a nut house, are you?"

"Oh, no, my child. I was thinking about the angel is all. That Sera is a meddlesome seagull."

"Sera? I didn't tell you his name."

"No, you did not." Father Stephen's left arm twisted so that his fingers clutched Cliff's throat. His hand had moved so fast that Cliff hadn't seen it coming till it was too late.

"You're going to take me to the place you're meant to go," Father Stephen instructed. "Your weird quest isn't over, though we have the same goal."

"I don't have a goal! I just want to do my show in Bangor and see my family in Boston!"

"You'll do what I tell you! Drive east and don't you dare stop. We're close, and we can finish him off together."

"Who?"

"David Bryant. That is where your quest ends."

"No it isn't! I'm actively trying to avoid it! Weren't you listening to anything I told you?!"

"It's no coincidence you picked me up," Father Stephen continued, ignoring Cliff's pleas. "You're the balance to the Enemy's magic he put into this world to collect and kill David Bryant to break through to our dimension. I was put in front of your path to ensure you're where you're supposed to be when you're supposed to be there. Turn left ahead at the rotary."

Cliff slowed to make the turn. Father Stephen's grip never faltered on his neck. Every time he shifted he felt the icy fingernails ready to tear out his throat.

"What are you, Father, since I know you're not a real priest? Are you an ice zombie or some kind of frozen demon?"

Father Stephen turned toward Cliff, watching him like a predator. "I am a priest. Well, I was one till I got killed by Bryant's adulterous wife. But the demon in my head wasn't ready for me to die. It brought me back, connecting my undead body to my immortal soul. As cold as it was outside, I could still feel the fires of Hell. Despite it all, I'm taking the opportunity to finish my mission, kill David Bryant, and save this dimension from the Enemy."

"You know, heroes don't usually threaten people with death to get them to help."

"I suppose not, but this isn't a movie, and I'm no hero. I'm going to do what needs doing. I apologize for your part in this, but I need your aid to finish my task. It's your destiny, after all."

Cliff scoffed. "More about my destiny. You're as bad as He Who Walks Above with that destiny shit, you know that?"

Father Stephen studied Cliff's profile. "Do not be so cavalier about using the Enemy's name."

"Why not? I want no part in this, and yet he's dragged me through hell to make me part of it. If he left me alone from the start, I wouldn't be driving this stupid garbage truck with an ice zombie priest threatening to rip my throat out! He has to be some kind of super moron to think for a second that everything happening isn't his own fucking fault!"

"Turn right ahead, and go down that road. We're almost there."

"No."

"What?"

"I said, 'fuck you'! I ain't turning anywhere. Fuck destiny, and fuck He Who Walks Above and any other demon who walks anywhere else. Fuck 'em all till their giant, uncircumcised dicks fall off and rot!"

"Let your anger fuel your revenge, and help me stop him from coming into this reality!"

Father Stephen let go of Cliff's throat and grasped the steering wheel, pulling it toward him. The truck veered, riding on its right two wheels for a moment before righting itself again with a thud against the road.

"What the fuck are you doing?!" Cliff exclaimed.

"Taking your destiny in my hands!" Father Stephen retorted, throwing an elbow into Cliff's face, hitting him right between his eyes, flooding his vision with stars. Cliff lost control of his feet, and he hit the gas instead of the break, sending them flying down the wet, snowy road at a breakneck speed.

"Yes, he's so close! I can almost taste him!"

Father Stephen cut the wheel again, pulling them into a parking lot under the mother of all funnel clouds. They smashed through a red and white sign for a Pastime Plaza store. If the parking lot hadn't been empty, they would have plowed into rows of parked cars.

Cliff grabbed the only thing he could, the holy water pistol, and fired a stream of water into Father Stephen's face, eliciting an unholy scream. The blue skin of his face turned red and melted, and the screams turned to burbles in his throat as smoke pooled on the cab's ceiling. Cliff kicked out at him hard enough to send him out of the door to splatter on the pavement as the back wheels of the truck ran over the priest's hips and waist. The door whacked the side of a bollard and closed again with a thud.

The momentum was too much for Cliff to stop, and the garbage truck slammed right through the front window of the store with a resounding crash.

WHO THE FUCK IS ROCKY PHANTASMIC?!

WITHOUT ANY EXCEPTION, ALL PROPHECIES ARE BULLSHIT

"That's more or less how I ended up here," Cliff finished. "If Father Stephen hadn't interrupted my leisurely drive through Maine, I wouldn't have haphazardly driven a garbage truck into the center of an arts and crafts store.

"Looks like I didn't kill that damn priest hard enough," Heather muttered.

Dave turned toward her, his brow furrowing. "You killed a priest? Who are you?!"

"You'll understand when you hear the whole story," Heather assured him. "For now, however, we need to figure out how to end this shit once and for all."

Dave nodded. Killing Vincenzo and destroying half of Pastime Plaza did nothing to contain the power coming from He Who Walks Above's big stone butt plug. The smoke and purple power surged through the building. Dave could've asked Rocky for some assistance, but his superhero bodyguard hadn't finished his rest against the garbage truck's grill. Rocky's body needed the short reprieve for when the shitshow started back up.

"Oh shit," Cliff said, looking toward the back area of the store where the nexus between realities was in the process of tearing itself a brand-new asshole. "Is that why this place looks like a giant tornado is going to come down and swallow it?"

"The Enemy's prophecy hasn't yet reached fruition," Heather explained, "but that doesn't mean he's done with it. He's going to keep leaking power into this world until he can reach through."

"Then what happens?" Dave asked.

Heather turned toward him as a foul breeze whipped through the store from the nexus. "Then we're all fucked on a cosmic scale."

"What do we do?"

"We have to figure out a way to shut it down." Heather passed Dave her crucifix and opened the big book she held in her left hand, scanning the pages as she flipped through them.

"What is that book?" Dave asked, looking over her shoulder. "Is that some demonic bible?"

Heather shut the book with a snap. "It's called the Demonic Testament, and you can't read it. I'll explain later, but reading it kind of curses you."

"Jesus. And you've read it?!"

Heather shrugged. "I had to. I wouldn't have found you otherwise."

"Oh. Then thank you, I guess."

"Ugh," Cliff groaned. "Enough with the mushy shit. Can you figure out what we're supposed to do so I can get to my fucking show in Bangor?!"

"Right." Heather reopened the book. Dave backed off this time, making it a point to not let his curiosity allow him to sneak a peek at whatever was written in the Demonic Testament. If it was so forbidden and cursed to read, they shouldn't have made it sound so badass, but maybe that was the point.

"Hey," Dave said, turning toward Cliff instead of Heather as she speed-read through the Demonic Testament. "What happened to the deer?"

"The what?" Cliff asked in return.

"Your story had a demonic stag in it, remember? It never came back after you picked up the priest?"

"Oh, that thing. No, it kind of just went away, I guess."

"Wow. Then why bring it up at all if it had no impact on the end of your story?"

Cliff blinked a few times. "I don't know. That's just how it happened."

"Can you two cut the chit-chat?" Heather asked. "It's hard enough trying to translate this ancient text without the two of you blathering on about your bullshit."

"Right," Dave said with a nod. "Sorry."

"Thanks. I think I've almost got it. We may need to—"

"Not so fast!" Leo exclaimed, climbing out of the pile of broken picture frames and shelving. He'd been cut under his left eye. He ignored the blood as it oozed from the wound. "We're not done here!" He turned and kicked an unmoving pile of flesh under a pile of picture frames. "Get up, Johnny! We got shit to do. Johnny! Johnny?"

Leo pushed the lump once more. When he saw it no longer moved like a living being would, he turned toward the trio of would-be heroes standing in the middle of the wrecked store next to the demonic garbage truck and the resting superhero sitting in front of it.

"You!" Leo said, picking up his gun with a blood-covered hand, aiming it at Cliff. "You did this to him!"

"Me?" Cliff asked. "That damn zombie priest grabbed the wheel and made me do it! Go out to the parking lot and shoot his corpse if you want!"

"ENOUGH!"

The shout made everyone jump and look around, even Rocky, who'd gotten back to his feet. It belonged to Vincenzo, but everyone saw him get creamed by a garbage truck to the face. Despite said creaming, Vincenzo limped from the other side of the garbage truck. Half his face had been torn off by the truck's grill, showing his skull and the inside of his mouth through his cheek, but he still had the wherewithal to aim his gun at the quartet of offenders standing in front of him.

"We're going to finish what we started," he said, "or I'll be finishing it with a pile of corpses."

Rocky stepped between Vincenzo and the others. "You'll have to get through me first."

A section of the ceiling caved inward, and Duro fell from a hole. He landed on Rocky, pushing his body into the floor with a cloud of dust and dirt.

"That dramatic of an entrance felt unnecessary," Dave muttered, looking up toward the hole. "Who was that for?"

"Shut up!" Vincenzo snapped. "Leo, help our writer friend to the back so we can finish this shit."

"You sure, boss?" Leo asked. "You don't look so good."

"I said do it!"

Leo nodded and stepped forward with his gun trained on Heather. "Come on, ya mook," he said to Dave. "Come with me, or I'll put a bullet in your woman's stomach."

Dave put his palms up again. "Come on, dude. Do we have to go through this again? Your friend is dead, and you can see what that evil energy's done to your boss!"

"I don't care." Leo stepped forward. "The boss said you gotta go back there and finish this, so you're going to go back there and finish this. Capeesh?"

"Don't," Rocky groaned, pushing himself off the ground with his fists buried in the cracked floor. His groans turned into a deep scream as he fought against Duro's force. He fell flat again, but he didn't quit trying to get up.

"Are you starting with this superhero bullshit again?" Vincenzo muttered. "Duro, get this little shit outta my hair already. I'm getting sick of this."

Duro moved his boot and picked up Rocky with both hands and tossed him toward the wrecked front of the store like a sack of potatoes. Rocky rolled through the glass and metal, coming to a crouched pose to face Duro's shirtless torso and growing erection with a look of unyielding determination on his face.

"We aren't done yet, villain," Rocky said. The posturing seemed to amuse Duro, whose grin widened as he stepped forward.

Vincenzo rolled his eyes as Rocky and Duro approached each other. "I've had enough of this whole ordeal. We're ending this! He Who Walks Above's prophecy will be completed here and now!"

A bolt of power burst from the huge bay doors, turned a corner, and pierced Leo's body. He shook and dropped his gun. Blood fired from his eyes and ears as his skin turned inside-out. His eyeless head turned toward Vincenzo. He tried to speak, but he couldn't, seeing as his vocal cords were now outside his body with the rest of everything else that shouldn't have been. Leo dropped to the ground with a moist splat.

"Fuck," Vincenzo groaned. "He ain't happy."

"Who?!" Cliff asked as he beheld horrors brand-new to him.

"The Enemy," Heather replied in a low voice. "He's here."

"He is?" Dave asked. He never got an answer. The energy formed a huge black and purple hand that darted toward him. It lifted him off the ground, and dragged him to the back to finish what had already began.

WHO THE FUCK IS ROCKY PHANTASMIC?!

Vincenzo smirked and followed through the forming clouds of dark energy.

Heather, gathering her will, guts, and Bible, chased after them.

"Well," Cliff said to himself with a sigh, "I don't think I'm making it my show in Bangor after all."

***

Rocky charged forward. He saw what had happened to Dave, and he knew he'd have to rush through the clouds of energy to save him. Firstly, however, he'd have to barrel through his superpowered nemesis to get the chance.

There were no more words to say. Duro wasn't a foe that would be swayed or distracted by witty banter. The only thing he understood was force, and Rocky had plenty of it to dish out.

Duro dodged the first punch Rocky threw his way, but it had been a feint. The real blow came from his left, aimed at Duro's lower abdomen. It hit, and the villain swayed on his feet from the unexpected body shot. Rocky followed it with a headbutt, smashing his forehead into his enemy's nose with another unexpected attack.

Blood poured from Duro's broken nose, and he shook his head in a daze. The look on his face told Rocky he hadn't been used to getting hurt like this. Duro snarled, moving forward to continue the vicious fight.

"Is that right?" Rocky asked, throwing another jab into Duro's broken nose. "You're not used to bleeding, are you?" A second jab hit Duro in the chin.

It would take more than a couple of punches to put down Duro. The supervillain followed up with a hit of his own. His fist smashed the side of Rocky's face so hard his head slammed into the ground. When Rocky came back up, he realized he'd been bloodied as well, and specks and pieces of broken glass stuck to the blood on the side of his face. Despite it all, he smiled.

"Joke's on you. I'm used to bleeding."

Rocky charged Duro, grappling him around the midsection, bringing him to the ground. He straddled the supervillain, pummeling his face and body with a barrage of hard punches. Duro brought his arms up over his bloodied face, but Rocky didn't stop. He expelled every shred of energy he had in his slender body. Duro's arms both surged forward, smashing Rocky's face, sending him back down.

Duro got to his feet and spat a wad of bloody salvia onto the busted floor. He cracked his neck, smiled, and looked at the beaten form of the young superhero. Despite Rocky's best efforts, it hadn't been enough to stop the beast of a man called Duro Assassino.

Then, beyond all semblance of sense and decorum of the fight at hand, Duro finally reached orgasm and ejaculated into his pants with a loud groan of intense, unabashed ecstasy. The look on his face was one of a man who'd had an orgasmic release after days of violently edging himself to the brink.

"Oh my God!" Cliff exclaimed, turning toward the source of the Duro's moan. "Is that guy cumming?!"

Duro turned toward Cliff. The wet spot on his pants grew as his erection shrank. He closed his gaping mouth, and it twisted into a grin. He walked toward his new target.

"Wait a second here," Cliff said, backing away. "Don't you need to recharge an hour or so before you go again? Want to change your soggy shorts before you start round two? I'll wait."

Duro chuckled, but his jubilation would be short-lived. Rocky jumped from the floor and clung to his back, clutching Duro's around his neck in a sleeper hold, wrapping his legs around the villain's body. Duro fought for breath as Rocky's forearm pressed against his throat, cutting off airflow.

"Supervillain or not," Rocky said, "you still need to breathe!"

Duro moved his body to shake off Rocky, but he proved to be too tenacious. The pair bumped into the back of the garbage truck during the struggle. Rocky's foot snagged the lever, and the back opened, letting the stench of death into the Pastime Plaza.

"Careful!" Cliff called. "There are mutant zombies in there!"

Duro shifted his weight forward, pulling Rocky off his back like a soaking wet sweater, slamming him onto the ground. Rocky bolted back up half a second later, nailing Duro in the chin with a lightning-fast uppercut. He followed up by jumping to spike Duro with both hands, sending him flying into the back of the garbage truck with a thud of flesh and bone against metal.

Cliff rushed forward and pulled the lever again, activating the garbage truck's crushing mechanism. It came down on Duro's body, and his screams filled the store as it smooshed his body into a gelatinous paste.

"Don't worry," Cliff told Rocky. "This is a demonic garbage truck. It should be enough to kill that bastard."

Rocky nodded. "I hope you're right. That guy was annoying."

The light coming from the back room brightened, and Dave's screams could be heard over the chaotic power surging through the store from the ritual. The debris on the broken floor floated in the air, and the sky above Pastime Plaza darkened to black.

"We need to help Dave!" Rocky exclaimed.

"Go ahead and help him then," Cliff said as Rocky rushed toward the back room. "If you need me, I'll be somewhere far away from the evil vortex of doom."

***

Heather struggled against the cloud of energy coming from the artifact. It felt like moving through thickening gelatin. Even with Father Stephen's crucifix staff, she couldn't push through it and stop the half-faced undead mob boss from torturing Dave.

She could see her husband, dangling in the air above the crest of the relic. The energy circled it, creating a whirlpool of purple and black. Vincenzo stood to the side, shouting for Dave to admit defeat and call forth He Who Walks Above with his blood memories.

"NO!" Dave shouted. The look of anguish and pain told Heather the energy tore at him, inside and out. She read about the ritual to complete the Enemy's prophecy in the Demonic Testament. Once the Enemy breaks Dave, causing him to call to He Who Walks Above, the barrier would shatter, and the world would succumb to a demonic shadow that hadn't been seen since before recorded history.

"The pain won't stop, but it can get so much worse," Vincenzo said. "That I promise you."

"NO!"

Blood oozed from Dave's eyes and ran down his face like crimson tears. He screamed again, and his body seized as raw power surged through him.

"DAVE!" Heather shouted, pushing herself past her limits to get through to evil power. The staff in her left hand burned, and the crucifix on top of it shattered into ashes. With her talisman gone, she flew backward. Rocky caught her, cradling her before she could hit the ground.

"Thanks," she muttered, getting back to her feet. "Do you think you can get through this shit?"

Rocky nodded and put his palms against the wall of power. He pushed his body, groaning as he indented the energy. A bolt fired from the relic, hitting him in the chest and sent him to the floor.

"Here," Heather said, lending a hand to help him back to his feet. "If we can't get through this, there's no hope. Vincenzo and the Enemy will keep torturing Dave till he cracks. Doesn't matter if it takes hours or days. They'll keep him alive, tearing him apart and putting him back together again until he can't take it anymore."

"There's a way," Rocky added. "There has to be."

"This is demonic magic, so there has to be a balance to it."

Rocky turned toward her. "I don't get it."

"It's all in the Demonic Testament. For every spell the Enemy expels from his dimension, the scientific principle of ours creates a counter to it. So, if the Enemy is using his magic to torture Dave, then the counter would be..." Heather turned, looking over her shoulder.

"What?" Rocky asked. "I was lost from the start."

"Where did that fucking comedian go?" Heather asked. She rushed back into the main area of the store where she saw Cliff walking toward the destroyed front end. "Hey! Don't leave!"

Cliff turned toward her. He'd almost gotten outside past all the broken glass and destroyed merchandise.

"What?" he asked. "I'm evacuating before this building gets sucked into that black hole back there!"

"There is no escaping this!" Heather exclaimed, jogging to get to him. "If they win—which they're getting ready to—there will be no distance you can run from it."

"What can I do? I've been through literal Hell, and all I've got to show for it is a garbage truck I don't even want."

"You're Dave's balance! If he's what the Enemy needs to fulfill his prophecy, then you're what's needed to stop it!"

Cliff nodded. "Right. I think I heard something like that from the angel or the priest—maybe it was both of them. What am I supposed to do again?"

Heather shrugged. "I don't know. You can try getting to Dave. Rocky and I couldn't get through that forcefield, but you might be able to do it!"

Cliff turned and looked toward the flowing power coming from the double doors. "I don't know if I can."

"You have to! It's the only way."

Cliff sighed. "Sure. After I do this, I'm going right to Bangor, though."

Heather nodded. "Stop the demon from killing my husband and destroying the world and you can go wherever the hell you want. I'll even rent you a fucking limo to drive you there if that's what it takes."

***

OK, Cliff told himself. *This is it. Bottom of the ninth at the World Series, overtime at the Super Bowl, and whatever happens during ties at hockey games during the Stanly Cup.*

He strode toward the clusterfuck to end all clusterfucks. He could hear Dave's screams and the orders being shouted by the old Soprano-looking guy he'd smashed in the face with the front of the garbage truck.

Whatever happens, you're doing the right thing for the right reason for once in your pathetic life. Don't fuck this up.

"What the fuck am I supposed to do?"

Cliff's foot struck something on the ground, and he looked down. The gun the now inside-out mobster had dropped lay there for the taking. Cliff bent and picked it up, feeling the weight of it in his hand.

"Huh. Safety's off."

Dave screamed something incoherent, and the half-faced mobster boss taunted him and laughed like a maniacal villain from an old cartoon. The whole thing would be over soon. Dave didn't look like the type of guy who could withstand this much torture, not that many people could.

"That's why it's called 'torture' and not 'pleasure'."

"What?" Heather asked. "Are you doing a bit right now?"

Cliff looked toward her and saw the tears on her face. She had put all her trust in him. He didn't have the heart to tell her that any woman who did never wound up feeling good about it later. Still, he had a gun, and a decent-sized target stood on the other side of the impenetrable barrier of evil.

Cliff walked as close to the door as he dared and aimed the gun at Vincenzo's head, looking to end the whole thing with a headshot through his exposed skull.

No. He's just the puppet. You need to shoot that huge butt plug thing. Don't hit Dave instead.

Cliff's hand moved, and he gripped the gun with both hands, closing one eye. He took a deep breath, licked his lips, and squeezed the trigger. His arms bounced up with the recoil, and he blinked through the flash of the muzzle.

The bullet flew through the air. If Cliff could see the world in slow motion like a movie ripping off its special effects from the Matrix, he would have seen it cut through the barrier with a glowing aura. It came through the other side unnoticed at first until it hit the relic in the center, shattering the stone as if it were made of brown Play-Doh and left outside on a dry summer day.

A burst of energy shot out in a dome, and the barrier around the Pastime Plaza receiving area dispelled. Vincenzo was sent back, and Dave fell forward onto the ground. Heather rushed toward her fallen husband and knelt next to him.

"Well," Cliff said, lowering the gun. "That was pretty fuckin' intense."

***

Dave swam in blackness. The last thing he remembered was the pain entering every fiber of his being followed by a bang and then nothing. He thought for sure he'd called for He Who Walks Above without realizing the words came from his mouth and he'd been killed or dragged into some other dimension to suffer the torture his ancestor deserved.

Then, his wife's voice brought him back to the correct reality.

"Wake up, you lazy asshole."

"I'm awake. Jeez." Dave opened his eyes and sat up. He found himself still in the Pastime Plaza receiving area with sand and rocks all around him. The acrid stench of smoke filled the air.

"This sucks," he said. "I thought for sure I'd be in a comfy hotel bed waking up from a coma that lasted long enough for this whole, sordid ordeal to epilogue by itself while I slept."

Heather laughed. "No. You have to live through this part. Sorry, babe."

Dave sighed. "There's no helping it, I guess. Tell me we won at least."

"Yes. We won. We stopped the Enemy's prophecy."

Dave scoffed. "Prophecies are bullshit anyway."

"Yes, and it's lazy writing. I know."

"Well, that all depends on context, really."

Rocky ran into the room. He was covered in blood and sweat. He saw Dave was OK, and he smiled, knelt, and pulled him in for a huge hug.

"Watch the superpowered hugging!" Dave exclaimed. "I was tortured about thirty seconds ago in case you missed it."

Rocky backed off, nodding. "We did it! We saved your life!"

"Not so fast," Vincenzo said, getting to his feet, aiming his gun at Dave. "We're still not done. I can still hear his voice in my head, and he aches for you, Bryant. Prepare to—"

A shot rang out in the receiving area, and Dave felt like he'd be hard of hearing in his left ear once the ringing shut the fuck up. Heather held a sawed-off shotgun, pointed at Vincenzo's chest. The barrels smoked, and the stench of sulfur filled the air.

Vincenzo looked down at the huge hole in his chest. "Oh fuck," he said, falling over.

"Is he dead?" Dave asked. "Like, for good this time?"

"I used sulfur slugs. They were good enough to kill Reagan's zombified body, so I figured they'd work on discount Ray Liotta."

"You had that thing the whole time?" Cliff asked from his place by the doors. "Why the hell didn't you use that instead of making me use the force or whatever the fuck it was that I did?!"

"I would've used it sooner," Heather replied, tossing the shotgun to the floor, "but I only had the one shot left. I'm glad this is all over either way."

"But I have more questions," Dave said. "First of all, where were you even hiding that shotgun? Second, what was that shit you said about Reagan's zombie?"

Heather laughed, but it died the moment Rocky fell to the ground with a big, wet thump.

"Rocky!" Dave said, crawling over to him. "No, no, no!"

"What happened?" Cliff asked, kneeling next to the fallen hero as well. "I thought he was a superhero or something."

"He was tied to Vincenzo in death and resurrection," Dave explained in a frantic voice as he looked at Rocky's still body with glassy eyes. "*Life for life*. When Heather shot Vincenzo, it must have undone whatever force brought Rocky back from the dead."

"How did he die?" Heather asked.

"He drowned," Dave replied.

Heather groaned and pushed Dave out of the way, straddling Rocky's hips. "We took first aid classes, you dummy! Do the breaths, and I'll pump." She put her hands together and pushed down on Rocky's chest, counting in a soft voice as she pumped. When she got to thirty, she nodded to Dave, and he breathed two breaths to fill his lungs with fresh air.

"Will this work?" Cliff asked, backing away. "You said he drowned, but I saw him drop like nothing."

"Come on!" Heather said, pumping again.

"You're not done yet, superhero," Dave said, cupping the side of Rocky's face. "The world needs you, Rocky Phantasmic. We're short on heroes if you haven't noticed."

"Breathe, Dave!" Heather snapped.

Dave went to Rocky's mouth again, breathing two more breaths into his lungs. Heather pumped as soon as he was done, keeping her rhythm while counting to thirty again.

"He's not gonna make it," Cliff said in a low voice. "He's too far gone. He's…"

Rocky coughed, and a stream of seawater hit Dave in the face. He turned his head and coughed up more. It spread out on the floor in a dark puddle. He gasped for air, and his eyes opened.

"Holy shit," Heather said, falling back and sitting on the floor.

Dave nodded while he patted Rocky's back. "It's OK, superhero. Get it all out. That's good."

Rocky coughed again, letting out some more of the water from his lungs. He wiped his mouth with the sleeve of his green hoodie and sat up, looking at the others in the room with him.

"Did I die again?"

"Yeah," Dave said with a laugh, "but we saved you this time. Go figure."

Cliff rolled his eyes. "You people are too much! I can't believe all this shit." He turned to leave, but he walked into a wall of a man.

"What's goin' on in here?" Johnny asked. He looked dazed, and half his face was covered in a mask of blood.

Everyone looked at one another, searching for an answer to Johnny's question in someone else. When none came, Johnny nodded and sighed.

"Boss lost, I guess." He shrugged. "Probably shouldn't've meddled with demons and shit, huh?"

"Probably not," Dave agreed. "Since your boss is dead, do you still have to torture me?"

Johnny stared at Dave for a bit, blinking. "My friggin' head hurts. If you give me a ride home, we'll call the whole thing square."

"Is that right?" Rocky said, standing in front of him. "There's no trick or a double cross?"

Johnny shook his head. "I'm done. I didn't sign up for no demonic shit. All I wanna do is go home, have a shot or three, fuck my girlfriend, and forget all this ever happened."

"I can second that!" Cliff added.

"Me too," Heather said, smiling at Dave. "What do you and your superhero friend think?"

Dave smiled back and looked up at Rocky. "Well, I can't argue with the majority. What do you say, Rocky? Should we conclude this little adventure of ours?"

Rocky nodded and fired a fist into the air above his head. "Good has triumphed over evil once again!"

"What he said." Dave got to his feet with a pained groan. "Let's get the fuck home before the ground opens up and we all fall into the pits of Hell."

DANIEL AEGAN

22.
A SHORT INTERLUDE BEFORE THE EPILOGUE

That last joke would seem like a good place to end this tale of cosmic horror, superheroism, and demonic influences, but that isn't where this story ends. You can end it here, and this narrative structure may encourage you to do so if you're uncomfortable ditching the whole 'happily ever after' thing. No one would blame you for turning back now.

What follows this short, final chapter is what English scholars across the globe refer to as an 'epilogue', which is defined as a literary device used to end a story to conclude the action. This is the moment you get a brief look into the future of the characters and see how they're doing after their story ends. In most cases of modern literature, they're used to set up a string of sequels.

This isn't the case here.

To summarize this cruel teaser, one would have to consider their options. Yes, the epilogue is how the story ends, but it's not required for your reading pleasure. In fact, there will be many who venture forward who would wish they hadn't read it at all. One may argue, however, that books are expensive, so why not read every word the writer painstakingly put onto the page?

The choice rests with one turning the page or flicking the screen on their e-reader. They can end on Dave's joke about falling into the pits of Hell and assume everything went well for the characters who lived through their chaotic adventures, or they can read onward and find out how it all *really* ends.

It's not a bad ending by any stretch, but some may want to finish the book here and imagine their own happier version of how the events contained in this book conclude. Maybe Dave and Heather win half a million dollars in the Connecticut State Lottery and take a long vacation with Kayla to a tropical island paradise and decide to never return to the bustle of their old lives. Maybe Cliff gets a major gig in a superhero movie franchise and winds up starring in eleven cinematic universe sequels. Maybe Rocky beats the piss out of an invading alien dictator and saves the planet from enslavement before marrying a reformed and uncloseted Johnny and living happily ever after.

It's all possible in the realm of imagination, but none of those scenarios are how this story ends.

So, here is your final warning. Close the book here, and you'll end with that fluffy optimism that everything can and will be OK for everyone everywhere all the time. Turn the page—either literally or figuratively—and finish the story on what may be considered a sour note by readers of a certain mindset. No ill will shall befall you for backing out a few pages early to spare yourself.

Godspeed to those readers who are brave enough to finish this story.

You have been warned.

DANIEL AEGAN

THE EPILOGUE.

"**Look at me, Daddy!**" Kayla yelled as she jumped on her brand-new trampoline. "Look how high I can go!"

"I see!" Dave said from his plastic chair in his backyard. The sun dipped toward the horizon as spring ended, heralding the coming of summertime and all it entailed. Bugs buzzed in the air, and the puppy Kayla had gotten for Christmas, a bichon she'd named Daisy, ran around, yipping the bouncing girl.

The day ended on a perfect note. Well, an almost perfect note.

"Mommy!" Kayla called, spotting Heather walking from the house. "Want to jump with me?"

"Oh, I can't, honey," Heather replied, making a faux sad face. "That's meant for kids. Maybe you can have some friends over this weekend to jump around with you."

"Yay!" Kayla jumped, landing on her butt, giggling as she fell over onto her side.

Heather sat in the chair next to Dave. Daisy ran to her and jumped on her lap, crawling up her chest to lick her face.

"OK, Daisy," she said. "I know you love me, but your breath reeks like dog food."

Dave laughed. "Better than smelling like her own asshole."

"Stop." Heather looked back at Kayla. "Why don't you go wash up for dinner, honey? Daddy's going to make some burgers on the grill."

WHO THE FUCK IS ROCKY PHANTASMIC?!

"I want a cheeseburger with ketchup!" Kayla said, climbing down off the trampoline.

Heather smiled. "OK. Take your dog with you. I need to talk to your Daddy before he lights the grill."

"OK. Come on, Daisy. Let's go wash up."

Kayla grabbed her dog with a short struggle and went inside, carrying Daisy like a fussy baby.

Dave's phone buzzed, and he opened it, reading the text. "Looks like Cliff's deal went through. He officially sold the show to WebFlix. They took it even with him playing a ridiculous recurring character named Porkpie Clinton."

"That's great!" Heather's smile beamed. "And Cliff's still OK with your telecommuting as the head writer?"

"Yeah, that's all worked out. I may have to take a field trip or two with him, but that's OK. Kayla can stay with your family. I'm sure they'll take her, even after we disappeared for that week in November while they were watching her."

"I'm happy for you, Dave. I mean that."

Dave sighed. "I don't feel happy, though. Not with... Are you sure you have to leave tonight? Can't you stay the summer with us at least?"

Heather looked away. "You know I have to distance myself from you and Kayla. As much as I don't want to go, I can't stay here any longer—not with the demon that got into my head from reading the Demonic Testament. You didn't know Father Stephen yourself, but I told you what happened to him and what reading that book did to him. I can feel it inside me, even now, whispering and urging in its subtle voice. It'll get the best of me one day, and I don't want to be around you or Kayla when it does. That's what it wants, and I can't let it beat me."

Dave looked away, focusing on a spot on the green grass he'd need to cut in a few days. "I wish you never read that fucking book in the first place."

"Me neither, but I needed to. There was no other way."

"I get that. I guess I just don't want you to go."

"I don't want to either." Heather looked at him. "I have to, though. I have to find an exorcist or someone who can help me before I can return. I also need to pass the Demonic Testament to someone who can contain it. It can't stay here, and it can't be destroyed. Anyone who tries to destroy it will only destroy themselves."

"I know. You're cursed. The book's cursed. We're all fucking cursed, aren't we?"

"No." Heather shook her head. "You're not cursed. Not you and not Kayla. You guys will be OK without me for a while. You have Rocky to help you out after all."

Dave laughed. "Yeah. We have our own personal superhero living in our guestroom to protect us against the forces of evil."

"Did you tell him I'm leaving?"

"I haven't. You didn't want anyone to know. Kayla doesn't even know she's going to wake up tomorrow morning without you here to greet her."

Heather turned and looked toward the house. The upstairs bathroom light was on where Kayla washed up. A wan smile spread on her face as she watched the light.

"Make sure she knows I'm going to miss her."

"Tell her yourself."

Heather turned back toward Dave. "I can't, and you know it. If she asks me not to go, I won't, and she'll be in danger of me and the Demonic Testament. I have to go for her sake."

Dave looked down. "This is all my fault. If only that genocidal maniac caveman hadn't sired my whole fucking family tree."

"Hey." Heather reached forward and caressed the side of Dave's face. "It's not your fault. None of this was your fault. How were any of us supposed to know that a super demon would come and flip our lives inside out?"

Dave shrugged and looked back at Heather's face. "I'm going to miss you, is all. Not knowing where you're going or when you'll be back isn't going to be easy."

"You're right. Tomorrow will be hard, but it will get a little easier every day after that. I promise it will."

"When you come home to us, that'll be the best day of all."

"It will be." Heather leaned forward and kissed him. "You know I love you, right?"

"I know, babe. I love you, too."

Heather stood, pulling Dave up by his hands. "Let's go inside. You have to get dinner ready."

Dave laughed as he got to his feet. "Yeah. I guess that's my job from now on. We're going to be eating a lot of hotdogs and hamburgers until I figure out how to cook like you."

Heather smiled and walked into her home. Dave knew she held her tears back, but they were there, waiting to spill out. He knew what she had to do and why, but it didn't make her decision any easier.

"Promise me one thing while you're out there searching for answers," Dave said.

"What?" Heather asked.

"Don't get involved with any other demons or shit like that. I don't think I can deal with it."

Heather smiled. "OK. I'll do my best."

***

Heather ate dinner with her family like nothing was wrong. She did her best to keep the heaviness in her chest at bay. Dave had given her a dozen or so poignant looks. After dinner and some board game time, they put Kayla to bed. The sound of the door clicking shut meant the time for her to leave had come.

She packed light and carried only cash with her. Her bag was packed with clothes and what little toiletries she thought she'd need. The Demonic Testament was there as well, hidden under one of the back seats wrapped in its blessed cloth inside Father Stephen's lockbox. She left her cellphone on her nightstand. As painful as it would be with no communication whatsoever with her family or friends, she had to do it. The demon would cast doubt every chance it got, and any conversations she had with Dave or Kayla would be used to send her home and put her family at risk.

"Goodbye," Heather said, looking at her house through her windshield. She saw Dave on the front porch, watching her. He raised a hand, waving goodbye as she pulled out of the driveway. It might've been the last time. Heather didn't plan on returning if she couldn't find some way to rid herself of the subtle whisperer in her head.

The road ahead would be dark, but she'd navigate it as best she could. The loneliness would eat her up, but she wasn't alone. Not completely.

Heather reached toward the floor while she waited at a red light. Her father was an avid bowler. He had been forever. When she moved out, she used one of his ball bags to carry some of her stuff with her. She had tried to give it back, but he told her to keep it. He didn't give her a reason why. He just wanted her to have it as a keepsake of sorts, claiming it may come in handy one day. He might've felt she'd take up bowling at some point, and he'd never know the true use for his old, worn brown and off-white bag.

She placed it on the passenger's seat and unzipped the top, reaching into the darkness to remove the human skull she'd hidden inside it. The car behind her honked as the light turned green, but she still took a few more seconds to knock the bag back down and place the skull on the seat.

"Was it comfortable in there?"

The eyes of the skull glowed with a dull light. "I was having a decent enough nap," the voice of Father Stephen replied. "That's all I can do now that this is all that's left of me after that comedian doused me with holy water and ran me over with a garbage truck."

"We're going to get you out of there. I told you that. If we can find someone to help me, then they'll be able to help you get to the other side."

"In theory."

"Yes, in theory."

"I can still feel my soul. Even though I'm still connected to this last bit of my former body, I'm still burning with eternal torment in Hell. I have to admit, having a peephole to the realm of the living is a perk. Even if you can't find someone to help me, at least I don't have to see what I'm feeling *down there*."

"Hey, don't be so pessimistic," Heather chided. "You're the priest who worked in some clandestine role with the Vatican. You know the ins and outs of this stuff, and you're going to help me find a way for both of us to shed the weight of the Demonic Testament."

"Sure, Heather. I'll do whatever it takes."

Heather laughed. "You didn't call me 'adulteress' that time."

Father Stephen laughed. It sounded odd echoing from the inside of the hollow skull. "That part of me was left behind, along with my body, flesh, and the rest of my bones."

"And what about the demon? Is it still there?"

Father Stephen sighed, which also sounded odd. "It's still hiding in whatever binds my soul to this skull, lying in wait. It's been weakened, though. I can tell you that much. I still don't understand all of this."

"What's there to understand?"

"I don't know how and why this all ended the way it did, and I don't know how I could've been so wrong to want to kill your husband. My path led me to you, and that led to ending the Enemy's plan rather than the postponement I would have been satisfied with had I been successful in killing him."

Heather laughed.

"What? Is that funny?"

"No. With all that talk about demonic magic and everything, I'd think you would have understood. You used too much of it on your quest, and you being led to me was your own equation being balanced out. You never believed in coincidence, right? Cliff Quentin was Dave's opposite and canceled out the Enemy's plans. Well, I did the same for you."

"Sure, that makes sense. In theory."

Heather pulled onto the highway. "Yeah, everything is in theory. I know you can't keep your fingers crossed since you don't have any, but lend some hope to mine that we can exorcise our demons so I can get home to my family again someday."

"I can do that."

Heather smiled, thinking of Dave and Kayla and all the days they'd have without her. It wouldn't be easy for any of them, but life didn't always work out for the better. With her family on her mind, she put her foot on the gas and headed west.

Somehow that direction felt right.

***

The stars twinkled in the sky, so far away from Earth. Dave watched them from the chair in the backyard. Kayla had gone to bed, and Heather… Well, there was no telling where she had gone. Part of her quest involved secrecy. She couldn't be tempted to come home by an outside force.

"Come back to us soon," Dave said, staring at the sky. In his heart, he doubted she would. Then again, miracles sometimes happen in real life. He'd experienced one or two of them himself if they counted.

"Hey," Rocky said, walking toward him.

"Hey, Rocky. How was work?"

Rocky sat, taking Heather's seat from earlier. "You know. Same old stuff with Butch. Did Heather go out for the night?"

"More than that." Dave let out a long sigh. "She's not coming back, Rocky, not until she can get that damn demon out of her head."

Rocky nodded. "I figured she'd leave soon."

Dave turned to look at Rocky's face. He was so sure the young superhero would fall into despair to learn Heather had left. He expected them to have to comfort each other as the tears flowed, but he'd discovered more and more every day how resilient Rocky Phantasmic could be.

"She left a few hours ago. I don't know when she'll be back either, not until she finds a good enough exorcist, at least. All that stuff she's read in the Demonic Testament doesn't tell her how to exorcise what it put in her head, but why would it? All I know is we won't see or hear from her until it's gone."

"It's alright. I'm sure you'll see her again soon."

Yeah, Dave thought, continuing to watch the stars as the coming tears burned at his eyes. *Maybe a day, maybe a few years, or maybe in another lifetime.*

"I would've gone with her," Rocky continued. "You know, to protect her in case some more monsters came after her. She wanted me to stay here, though, and protect you."

Dave smiled. "Yeah, I think she'd want that. She's always finding ways to keep me safe. That woman is something else. I'm going to miss the hell out of her."

Rocky reached over and put his hand on top of Dave's. "I know you will, but I also know she'll be back."

"I hope you're right, Rocky. After everything that happened back in November, I'd never thought that I'd lose her like this."

Dave and Rocky watched the sky for a little longer. Neither one of them checked the time or picked up their phones. After a while, Dave got up and stretched.

"It's time to go back inside. I know you can't feel it, but the mosquitoes are eating me alive out here."

Rocky nodded and stood. He walked back toward the house, leaving their empty chairs in the yard to remain under the night sky.

About the Author

Daniel Aegan lives a semi-private life in New Haven, Connecticut with his family. He's authored several novels and short stories. He specializes in mashing comedy with other genres like sci-fi, horror, fantasy, and villainpunk. He also enjoys chatting and collaborating with other independent authors locally and through social media.

Other than writing, he practices reading tarot cards for himself and others. He's been training and learning to tell the stories the cards tell. Most nights you can find him with the cards spread in front of him on the living room floor.

When he's not poring over his written words or reading the tarot, Aegan enjoys blogging, interacting with his fans and readers, and embarrassing himself publicly. He also works hard at his graphic arts and reads as much as his brain can manage.

You can find anything from The Aegan Multiverse, including Stoned Tarot at DanielAegan.com. The best place on social media to reach him is on BlueSky where he posts as DanielAegan.bksy.social.

Milton Keynes UK
Ingram Content Group UK Ltd.
UKHW020400021124
450424UK00014B/1379